TWO
TRAINS
RUNNING

TWO TRAINS RUNNING

Andrew Vachss

PANTHEON BOOKS, NEW YORK

Pantheon Books and colophon are registered trademarks of
Random House, Inc.

Library of Congress Cataloging-in-Publication Data

Vachss, Andrew H.
Two trains running / Andrew Vachss.
p.   cm.
ISBN 1-4000-4381-6
1. American politics—fiction.   2. Organized crime—fiction.
3. Conspiracies—fiction.   4. Gangs—fiction.   5. Racism—
fiction.   6. Black power—fiction.   7. Illegal arms transfers—
fiction.   8. Mafia—fiction.   9. IRA—fiction.
PS3572.A33T96 2005
813' .54—dc22   2004060127

www.pantheonbooks.com

Printed in the United States of America

First Edition

2   4   6   8   9   7   5   3   1

*For my mother and my father
who are as one
always*

TWO
TRAINS
RUNNING

A candy-apple-red '55 Chevy glided down the rain-slicked asphalt, an iridescent raft shooting blacktopped rapids. Behind the wheel was a man in his mid-twenties, with a wiry build and a narrow, triangular face. His elaborately sculptured haircut was flat on top, long on the sides and back, ending in carefully cultivated ducktails.

The Chevy's headlights picked up an enormous black boulder, standing sentry in a grove of white birch. The driver pumped the brake pedal, then blipped the throttle as he flicked the gearshift into low. He gunned the engine, kicking out the rear end in a controlled slide through a tight S-curve. As soon as the road straightened, he eased off the gas and motored along sedately.

A quarter-mile later, the driver pulled up to what looked like a miniature cottage. A lantern-jawed man slowly rose from his seat on the one-man porch. He held a double-barreled shotgun in his right hand like an accountant holding a pencil.

"It's me, Seth," the driver said, out his side window.

"I knew that a few minutes ago, Harley," the man with the shotgun replied. "Heard those damn glasspacks of yours a mile away."

"Come on, Seth. I backed off as soon as I made the turn," the driver said.

"You're getting way too old for that kid stuff," the man said reproachfully. He stepped closer to the Chevy. The driver reached up and flicked on the overhead light. The man with the shotgun glanced into the back seat, then shifted his stance slightly to scan the floor.

"Let's have a look out back," he said.

The driver killed his engine, took the keys from the ignition, and reached for the door handle.

"I'll do it," the man with the shotgun said. "You just sit there, be comfortable, okay?"

"Are you serious?" the driver said.

"You been here enough times, Harley."

"Exactly," the driver said, with just a hint of resentment. "So what's with all the—?"

"Ain't my rules."

"Yeah, I know," the driver said, sourly. "Let's go, okay? The boss said nine-thirty, and it's getting close to—"

"Next time, come earlier," the man with the shotgun said, taking the keys.

He walked behind the Chevy and opened the trunk with his left hand, leveling the shotgun to cover the interior. He pulled a flashlight from his belt and directed its beam until he was satisfied. Finally, he closed the trunk gently, walked back to the driver's window, and handed over the keys.

"See you later, Harley," he said.

1959 September 28 Monday 21:29

The darkened house was a featureless stone monolith, the color of cigar ash. Harley ignored the horseshoe-shaped brick driveway that led to the front door; he drove carefully past the big house, his engine just past idle, until he came to a paved area clogged with cars. He slid the Chevy into a generous space between a refrigerator-white Ford pickup and a gleaming black '56 Cadillac Coupe de Ville, and climbed out, not bothering to lock his car.

A short walk brought him to a freestanding single-story building. Its wooden sides had been weathered down to colorlessness, but the roof and windows looked newly installed.

As he approached, Harley saw his reflection in the mirrored finish of a small window set at eye level. Before he could knock, the door was opened by a short, bull-necked man wearing a threadbare gray flannel suit. The man's perfectly rounded skull was covered by a thick mat of light-brown hair, roughly trimmed to a uniform length. His facial features were rubbery; his mouth was loose and slack.

"It's me, Luther," Harley said.

The short man nodded deliberately, as if agreeing with a complex proposition. His slightly protuberant eyes were as smooth and hard as brown marbles, reflecting the moonlight over Harley's shoulders. Wordlessly, he tilted his head to the left.

Harley stepped past the slack-mouthed man into what looked like a modern two-car garage. A charcoal-gray Lincoln sedan was poised on the concrete slab, its nose pointing toward a wide, accordion-pattern metal door. Conscious of the other man somewhere behind him, Harley opened a door in the back wall, and followed a passage-way to his left.

He paused at the threshold of a large, low-ceilinged, windowless room. One wall was lined with file cabinets, another with book-shelves. Various chairs and a pair of small couches were scattered about, all upholstered in the same dark-brown leather. Most of them were already taken. A few of the seated men glanced expression-lessly at the new arrival, the youngest man in the room.

The far end of the room was dominated by a lengthy slab of butcher block, laid across four sawhorses to form a desk. Behind it sat a massive man in a wheelchair, like a stone idol on a gleaming steel-and-chrome display stand. He had a large, squarish head, with wavy light-brown hair, combed straight back without a part, going white at the temples. His ears were small, flat against his skull, without lobes. Heavy cheekbones separated a pair of iron-colored eyes from thin lips; his nose was long and narrow; a dark mole dot-ted the right side of his jaw. The man was dressed in a banker's-gray suit, a starched white shirt, and a midnight-blue silk tie with faint flecks of gold that occasionally caught the light. On the ring finger of his right hand was a blue star sapphire, set in platinum.

The man glanced at his left wrist, where a large-faced watch on a white-gold band peeked out from under a French cuff, then looked up at the driver of the Chevy.

"I was held up at the gate," Harley said. "Seth took about half a day to . . ."

Nobody said anything.

Harley took a chair, and followed their example.

1959 September 28 Monday 21:39

"Procter!" a sandpaper voice blasted through the half-empty news-room.

All eyes turned toward a broad-shouldered man hunched over a typewriter. "What's up, Chief?" he shouted back, without breaking his hunt-and-peck rhythm, eyes never leaving the keyboard.

"Get the hell in here!"

The broad-shouldered man kept on typing.

A pair of night-shift reporters at adjoining desks exchanged looks. One scrawled "2" on a piece of paper and held it up; the other crossed his two forefingers to make a "plus" sign. Each man reached for his wallet without looking, eyes focused on four large clocks on the far wall, marked, from left to right: Los Angeles, Denver, Chi-cago, and New York.

In perfect rhythm honed by long practice, a dollar bill was si-multaneously slapped down on each man's desk.

The second hands of the clocks swept on. One full revolution, then another. Two minutes and seventeen seconds had elapsed when . . .

"Procter, goddamn it!" rattled the windows.

The reporter who had made the "plus" sign plucked the dollar from the other's desk as Procter slowly got to his feet. His hair was as black as printer's ink; raptor's eyes sat deeply on either side of a slightly hawked nose. Wearing a blue shirt with the cuffs rolled above thick wrists, and a dark-red tie loosened at the throat, he stalked through the newsroom holding several sheets of typescript in his right hand like a cop carrying a nightstick.

Procter ambled into a corner office formed from two pebbled-glassed walls. Behind a cigarette-scarred, paper-covered desk sat a doughy man wearing half-glasses on the bridge of a bulbous nose. His bald scalp was fringed with thick mouse-brown hair.

"Chief?" Procter said innocently.

"How many goddamn times have I told you not to call me that?" the doughy man snapped, his scalp reddening. "You've got a lot of choices in that department, Jimmy. 'Mr. Langley' will do. So will 'Augie,' you like that better. Save that 'Chief' stuff for your next editor."

"So I'm fired?" Procter said, his voice not so much empty as without inflection of any kind.

"I didn't say that!" the doughy man bellowed. "You know damn well what I meant. This isn't one of those big-city sheets you're used to working for. We do things differently around here."

"I've *been* around here all my life," Procter said, mildly. "Born and raised."

"You like playing word games, maybe you want to take over the crossword. You haven't been around *this* newspaper all your life. You came home, that's what happened."

"Came home after being fired, you mean."

"I *say* what I mean, Jimmy. You're a great newshound, but this is your fourth paper in, what, seven years? We both know you wouldn't be working for the *Compass* if there was still a place for you with one of the big-city tabs."

"I—"

"And we both know, soon as a job on a *real* paper opens up again, you'll be on the next bus out of here."

"I can do what I do anywhere."

"Is that right? For such a smart guy, you do some pretty stupid things. What happened up in Chi-Town, anyway?"

"The editor spiked too many of my stories," Procter said, in the bored tone of a man retelling a very old story.

"So you went behind his back and peddled your stuff to that Communist rag?"

"That exposé never saw a blue pencil, Chief. They printed it just like I wrote it."

"Yeah, I guess they did," the doughy man said, fingering his suspenders. "And I guess you know, that's never going to happen here."

"I've been here almost three years. You think I haven't learned that much?"

"From this last piece of copy you turned in, I'm not so sure. Your job is to cover crime, Jimmy. Crime, not politics."

"In Locke City—"

"Don't even say it," the editor warned, holding up one finger. "Just stick to robberies and rapes, okay? Shootings, stompings, and stabbings, that's your beat. Leave the corruption stories for reporters in the movies."

1959 September 28 Monday 21:52

"You sure he's the guy we need for this?" a thin man with a sharply receding hairline and long, yellowing teeth asked.

"Red Schoolfield says he is," replied the man in the wheelchair.

"Yeah, but that's Detroit. We're just a—"

"You ever *been* to Detroit, Udell?" the man in the wheelchair asked. He waited a three-second beat, then said: "Okay, then, how about Cleveland? You ever been there, either?"

"I was there one time," the thin man said, his voice wavering between resentful and defensive.

"Good. Now, that's a big city, too, am I right?"

"It *is,* Mr. Beaumont. They got buildings there you wouldn't—"

"We're not arguing," said the man in the wheelchair. "In fact, you're right—Cleveland *is* a big city." He shifted his position slightly, so that his glance took in the entire room. "But here's the thing, boys. Detroit and Cleveland, they've got one thing in common. You know what that is?"

"A lot of niggers?" a jug-eared man sitting in the far corner ventured, grinning.

"Yeah, Faron," Beaumont acknowledged. "But you know what

else they've got? They've got a whole ton of folks just like us. White people."

"That don't make them like us," Harley ventured. He twirled one of his ducktails, a nervous habit.

"*Now* you're using your brain, Harley," Beaumont said, approvingly. "Being white's just a color. Doesn't make us like them, or them like us. There's things *inside* color. Even the coloreds themselves see it that way. Look who they pick for their preachers and their politicians. It's always the light-skinned ones, with that processed hair. The ones that got white in them, you don't see them mixing much with the ones look like they just got off the boat from Africa.

"And it's the same with us. With white people. Inside that color, we got all these groups. Like . . . tribes, all right? You've got the Italians, you've got the Irish, you've got the Jews, you've got the—"

"Jews?" a man with long sideburns, wearing a leather aviator's jacket, piped up, somewhere between a question and a sneer.

"Sure, Jews," Beaumont said. "What did you think, Roland? They weren't in our business?"

"I thought they was all . . . I mean, maybe in the business, but not at our end. Not like the stuff we—"

"You should read a book once in a while," Beaumont said, "it wouldn't hurt you. Wouldn't hurt you to pay attention to what goes on in the world, either. You go back far enough—and, trust me, it's not *that* damn far—you find Jews started the same way we did. With *this,*" he said, knotting a fist and holding it up to the faint light from the desk lamp, like a jeweler checking a gem for flaws.

"I never heard of a kike with the balls for muscle work," Udell said.

"Udell," Beaumont sighed, "you never heard of a lot of things."

"What's this got to do with Detroit and Cleveland, Roy?" asked an older, broad-faced man with eyes so heavily flesh-pouched that it was impossible to tell their color.

"That's getting to it, Sammy!" Beaumont said, nodding his head for emphasis. "Look," he said, slowly turning his massive head like a gun turret to cover each man facing him, "there's neighborhoods in both those cities where there's *mostly* people like us, understand?"

"Hillbillies?" a tall redhead with long sideburns said, chuckling. He was wearing an Eisenhower jacket over a thick sweater, despite the warmth of the room.

"You know I don't like that word, Lymon," the boss said. He didn't raise his voice, but his words carried easily, seeming to echo off the walls. "We're not hillbillies, we're mountain men. And this town, it's *our* mountain, understand?"

There was a general hum of agreement from the assembled men, but no one spoke.

"People like us, we're clannish," Beaumont continued. "We want to live among our own kind, even when we're feuding amongst ourselves. You go to any city, even as big a one as Chicago, you'll find a section where our people live. That's no accident. Those pieces of the city, it's just like this town here. You understand what I'm telling you? Red Schoolfield, he's in a bigger city than this one, sure. But only a little piece of it belongs to him. What we got here, it's all ours. Not just some slice—the whole thing."

The man in the wheelchair paused, individually eye-contacting each man in the room before he went on:

"You all know how it works. Remember when we were kids? You got yourself a candy bar, what happened? Some guys, they'd want a little piece for themselves, right? And if they were your pals, well, you were supposed to cut them in. But there was always this one guy, what *he* wanted was the whole thing. Am I right?"

Nods from around the room. The broad-faced man added a grunt of assent.

"Now, if this guy is bigger than you, or tougher, what do you do then? Well, you got choices. You can stand and fight, make him *take* it, but all that gets you is a beating.

"So the thing you do, if you're like *us,* you give up the candy, and you wait for your chance. Then you ambush the guy, maybe bust up his head with a brick. And next time he sees you with candy, well, he keeps walking. Or, even better, you get a few of your pals— the same guys you *would* share with—and you mob the motherfucker, pound him so bad he don't want any more, ever.

"You can't change a bully. The best you can ever do is make him work, make it cost him something. They don't like that, so they go and pick on someone else. That's where all this started, boys, what we have now.

"And the first rule is, *always,* you make sure you control your own territory. Maybe it's only a tiny little piece, but it's yours. Now, once you got land, a piece of ground that's really yours, you can't just let it sit there, you got to do something with it, am I right?"

More nods.

"Sure, I'm right! And I'm not talking about naming it after yourself, the way Old Man Locke did back when he opened the first mill, before any of us were born. I'm talking about making your living from it. Land is money. You can farm it, or you can brew mash on it, or you can open a little roadhouse, or . . . well, it doesn't really matter. What matters is that you get something going."

Beaumont's iron eyes swept the room, a seismograph, searching for the slightest tremor of inattention. Satisfied, he went on:

"You can see it happening, everywhere you look. The Irish, the Italians, they can run a whole city, but not by themselves. When they want to do business with people outside their tribe—and you know, they *have* to do that—they need . . . branch managers, I guess you'd call them. And, sooner or later, those managers, they see how things work, how much money there is to be made, they want to go into the business for themselves.

"That's what we did. That's how we got started here. We built up a beautiful thing for ourselves. We got the gambling, we got the girls—not just the houses, the strip joints too—we got the juke-boxes, we got the punch cards, we got the liquor, we got money out on the street, working for us. . . . And when dope hits this area hard—the way it has up in the big cities—we'll have that, too.

"But, remember, every time you got that candy, here comes some big guy who wants it all for himself. You understand what I'm saying?"

"Those wop bastards don't have a chance," the broad-faced man said, with the calm assurance of a man stating a known fact.

"It depends on what they want to put into it, Sammy," the man in the wheelchair said. "They know we've got the cops and the judges, but they also know those people aren't *with* us—they're just whores, charging us for every trick. When this jumps off, they'll stand on the sidelines, and climb into bed with the winners."

Beaumont looked around the room, using his eyes to lock and hold each man individually before he continued:

"Now, you know, they've already been around, the Italians. Sat down with me. Very nice, polite. They just want a little taste, is what they say. But it would never stop there. When they come for us, they're going to come hard."

"You really think one guy's going to make that much of a difference?" Lymon asked.

"You mean, do I think we need him?" Beaumont said. "Hell, no. What Sammy said is the truth. The outcome's not in doubt. But being a good general isn't just about winning wars; it's about keeping your men safe, too. And if this guy's half as good as I've been told, he'll get it over with quick."

1959 September 28 Monday 22:09

A battleship-gray '56 Packard sedan purred down the interstate, past the exit marked LOCKE CITY. A few miles later, the driver pulled into a service area. He drove to the pumps, glanced at the dash, noted the gas gauge read just below the halfway mark, and shut off the ignition.

"Fill it up with high-test, and check the oil and water, please," he told the young man wearing a blue cap with a red flying-horse emblem who came to his rolled-down window.

As the pump jockey went to work, the driver walked over toward the restrooms, hands swinging free at his sides. As he turned the corner of the building, he encountered a pay phone. The man slotted a coin, dialed a number, and waited, his back to the wall.

"I was told you'd be expecting a call. About your garage," he said into the receiver. His voice was flat, using neither volume nor inflection to communicate.

He listened for a few seconds, then said, "I can find it. Inside of an hour, all right?"

The man listened again, then hung up.

"Took almost twenty gallons," the pump jockey said when he returned. "Man, you were *empty*. Oil's okay, though."

The man paid his bill, got behind the wheel. He noted approvingly that the pump jockey had cleaned his windshield.

1959 September 28 Monday 22:30

A t the next exit, the driver circled back and re-entered the highway, heading back the way he had come. As he turned off at the Locke City sign, he pushed a button set into the gauge cluster. The four-digit row of numbers reset itself to 0000. A trip odometer began to click off the miles, the rightmost numerals, in red, indicating tenths.

From an inside pocket, the driver took a hand-drawn map, which he taped to the padded dashboard. He followed County Road 44, keeping the big car at a subdued pace, watching the odometer. When the mileage reading hit 013.4, the driver slowed slightly, his eyes another pair of headlights.

The dirt road was unmarked, barely wide enough for two cars. The driver turned in cautiously, pulled as far over to the side as possible, and extinguished his headlights. He rolled down his window, plucked a nearly full pack of Lucky Strikes from the seat next to him, and turned it around in his right hand, over and over, breathing shallowly through his nose.

Several minutes later, the driver tossed the pack of cigarettes back onto the front seat. With his left hand, he thumbed the fender-mounted bullet spotlight into life.

The big car crawled forward cautiously as the dirt road narrowed, became rougher. The spotlight picked up the remnants of a tar-paper shack. It had no door, no glass in either of its two windows, half its roof, and only three of its walls.

The driver steered into the clearing behind the shack. He stopped the car and stepped out, leaving the door open and the engine running. He circled the car, opening each of the other doors in turn. The overhead interior light was intense, illuminating the seats and floor of the Packard as brightly as if it were in a showroom. He then un-locked the trunk, activating still another light.

The driver stepped away from his car and lit a cigarette, holding it in his left hand. His right dangled at his side, empty. He stood ut-terly still. Not tense, motionless.

The night-sounds merged with the barely discernible throb of the Packard's engine, its power muted by a set of highly restrictive mufflers.

The driver raised one foot, ground out his cigarette on the sole of his shoe, and deposited the butt in the pocket of his dark-blue sport coat.

"Whisper *said* you was one careful motherfucker." A voice came out of the darkness, seemingly pulling a man along in its wake. A barrel-shaped black man wearing denim overalls and an egg-yolk-yellow T-shirt emerged: He was holding a long-barreled revolver in his left hand, pointed at the driver's midsection.

"Careful for me; careful for you," the driver said, nothing in his voice but the words themselves.

"You right about that," the black man said, moving closer, "if Whisper was right about you."

The driver shrugged, to show that decision was out of his hands.

"You know how the garage works?" the black man asked.

"I leave my car with you. You give me another one to use. When I'm done, I call you, and we trade back."

"Uh-huh. And Whisper, he told you, it costs a grand, right?"

"Five hundred is what he said."

"Price of everything's going up," the black man said. "That's the way it is, everywhere you go."

"Whisper said that, too."

"Prices going up?"

"No. That you'd try and hold me up for more. He under-estimated you—he was guessing an extra C-note."

A flash of white scythed across the black man's face. It might have been a smile. "You know what I mean, I say I been listening to the drums?"

"Grapevine."

"Right. People know you coming, man. They don't know your name, don't know your face. And I guess you don't want them to know your car, either."

The driver shrugged again.

"Sure," the black man said. "So what that means is, I got extra expenses."

The driver watched, silently.

"You ain't holding up your end," the black man said, the thin slash of white back in his mouth.

"The money's—"

"Of the *conversation,* man. This is what men do, they got a dispute. They talk about it, right?"

"We don't have a dispute."

"Sure, we do. I don't mean we enemies or nothing like that. Just trying to get you . . . involved, see?"

"In what?"

"In my problem, man. What I been telling you."

"Your 'extra expenses.' "

"*Now* you paying attention. I don't know you. Don't *want* to know you. But I know what you here for. So I got to figure at least *some* possibility I may never get that phone call from you, understand where I'm going?"

"That you won't get your car back."

"*That's* right! Now you getting with the program. I got a real nice . . . rental for you. You can drive a stick, right?"

"Yes," the driver said. He took out his pack of cigarettes, held it toward the black man.

"No thanks, man. Appreciate it, though. Anyway, what I got for you is a sweet little '49 Ford. But it's not running no flathead—got a '54 Lincoln mill with a *lot* of work into it. All heavy-duty: brakes, shocks, clutch, everything. Floor shift, Zephyr gears. Some wild-ass kid built it for drag racing. It don't have a lot of top end, but it'll walk away from any cop car in this town. Get you *good* and gone, you need to."

"Sounds fine."

"She *is* fine, man. What I'm telling you, she don't come back, I'm out a lot of coin, see what I'm saying?"

"No. No, I don't. I see you coming out ahead. My car's worth a lot more than some kid's hotrod."

"Yours is newer, sure. But that don't—"

"Mine's running a punched-out Caribbean engine," the driver interrupted. "Dual quads, headers, triple-core radiator, cutouts for the pipes. The whole chassis has been redone, and it's got a belly pan, too. You could drive it through a cornfield at thirty and it wouldn't get stuck. Got a second gas tank in the trunk: extra twenty-five gallons. Steel plate behind the back seat—"

"Damn!"

"There's more. Go look for yourself, you don't believe me. Cost you seven, eight grand, minimum, to build anything like it."

The black man's eyes narrowed. The pistol in his hand moved slightly. "Must make you worried, then. Leaving a valuable ride like that with a stranger. I mean, what if you called and I never came?"

"I'm not worried," the driver said. "Whisper vouched for you."

"Man can always be wrong."

"Whisper told you about me," the driver said. It wasn't a question.

The black man nodded.

"Well, he wasn't wrong about that," the driver said.

1959 September 28 Monday 23:39

Only Sammy, Lymon, and Harley remained behind after the others had been dismissed, their chairs drawn up close to Beaumont's desk. The men spoke in low, but not guarded, tones.

"We already lost one man," Beaumont said. "Hacker never came back with the casino collection. It's been over three weeks, and nobody's heard from him."

"That was a lot of money," the broad-faced man said.

"Meaning what, Sammy?" Beaumont asked, swiveling his imposing head in the speaker's direction.

"Everybody knows Hacker's route," Sammy said, unruffled. "It's no secret. All our collectors work alone. We never have anyone riding shotgun. Everybody knows that, too."

"You're saying—what?—we don't have any proof that it was Dioguardi?"

"I'm saying, it could have been Dioguardi, sending a message, sure," Sammy said. "But it could have been a hijacker, too, Roy. A freelancer, I mean. We got no shortage of those coming through here. Most of them, they've got enough sense to come to our town to *spend* the money they made off their jobs, not to pull one . . . but every deck always has at least one joker in it."

"Can't say it wasn't," Beaumont mused. "But Hacker was always a ready man. He wouldn't go easy . . . not unless he went willingly. And, you know, if you're going to take down something big, like an armored car, say, the best way is to have an inside man."

"Hacker wouldn't steal from us," the redheaded man put in, sure-voiced.

"I don't think so, either, Lymon," Beaumont agreed. "It was a good piece of change, all right, but not enough to live on for the rest of your life, if you had to stay hidden. When the cops came out here, they said nothing in his house had been touched. There's things a man wouldn't leave behind if he had time to plan his run."

"Hacker would know that, too," Sammy said, cautiously.

"He would," Beaumont said, nodding his head. "But you know what else the cops found when they went to his place? They found that hound of his, Ranger. Dog didn't even have food laid out for him."

"That does it for me," Sammy said, in a tone of finality. "Hacker loved that old dog. He expected to come home that night. Yeah."

"So what's our first—?" Harley asked, as a woman entered the room from the door behind Beaumont. She was of medium height, but looked shorter because of her stocky frame—an impression enhanced by her low-heeled shoes and boxy beige jacket worn over a plain white blouse. Her hair was the color of tarnished brass, worn short, with moderate bangs over her high forehead. She had Beaumont's iron eyes, but long lashes and artfully arched eyebrows banked their fire.

At her entrance, the assembled men all rose to their feet and started for the exit.

"Lymon, you mind hanging around a few minutes?" Beaumont said.

By way of response, Lymon sat down.

1959 September 28 Monday 23:52

As if by prior assent, the two men walked across the clearing to the waiting Packard. The driver reached into the trunk, removed a pair of suitcases, stood them on the ground.

"Watch this," he said, quietly. He lifted the heavy pad of felt that lined the floor of the trunk, revealing a flush-mounted keyhole.

"Now watch me," the driver said, emphasizing the last word. He reached—slowly—toward his belt, carefully removed the tongue of the belt buckle, extracted a metal rod with a single notch at one end, and held it up for the other man's inspection. He inserted the rod into the keyhole and turned his wrist—a shallow compartment was revealed. Filling the compartment edge-to-edge was a black, hard-shelled attaché case.

The driver removed the case, added it to the luggage on the ground, closed the compartment, pulled the felt back into place, and closed the trunk.

"Why you showing me all this?" the black man asked, more curious than hostile.

"I didn't want anyone tearing up the car looking for . . . whatever they might find. So I thought I'd show you where the tricks were myself."

"Pretty slick. But what's the story with that key in your belt, man? Strange place to keep it."

"It doesn't just open the compartment in the trunk. It's a speed key . . . for handcuffs, understand?"

"Yeah," the black man said, shaking his head slowly. "But when they bring you down, first thing, they take away your belt and your shoelaces."

"That's *after* they get you to the jail," the driver said. "Sometimes, their plans don't work out."

The black man stepped back a pace, but kept his pistol leveled.

"Look, man. Like I said, it was on the drums. Killer on the road, coming to town. Everybody knows there's a gang war coming. That's ofay business, got nothing to do with me, one side wants to bring in some outside talent. But if you kill a cop, even one of those blue-coated thieves that works for *this* town, that's gonna bring heat like an oil-field fire. That happens, you call the number you got for me, nobody's gonna answer. This big car of yours, it's gonna get butchered like a hog, man. Cut up so small its own mother wouldn't know it."

The driver looked at the black man's chest, expressionless.

"Whisper didn't say nothing about dusting no po-leece," the black man said, his voice feathering around the edges.

"Whisper didn't say anything," the driver said. "All he did was make a deal. And here I am, holding up my end of it."

"I—"

"If you don't want to go through with it, now's the time to say so."

"I didn't say nothing about—"

"You take the deal, you take it the way it was laid out," the driver cut him off. "What I do, that's not your business. What *you* do, that's not mine. But if I call that number and there's no answer, there's another number I can call, understand?"

"Whisper ain't gonna side with no gray boy against his own—"

"You took this deal, and you don't know Whisper?"

"I know him," the black man said, capillaries of resentment bulging on the surface of his voice.

"You never met him," the driver said, confidently. "You know him the same way everyone else in the game does, by reputation. That's all he's got, his reputation. Whisper vouched for you. You come up wrong, nobody's going to want to deal with him anymore. Not until he fixes the problem. Sets an example."

"You saying Whisper would do something to *me*?"

"*Get* it done, yeah."

"That supposed to scare me?"

"What it's supposed to do, it's supposed to get you to make a phone call. Ask him yourself. I'll wait right here while you go and do it. You call Whisper. After you speak to him, you still think you can go back on our deal no matter *what* happens, I'll just take my car and go. No hard feelings."

The black man's face tightened. "You must think I'm a stone fucking chump, Wonder Bread," he said. "I tell Whisper I'm even *thinking* about not holding up my end, that's the last business I ever get from him."

"Up to you," the driver said, making an "It's all the same to me" gesture. "One of us is going to be driving my car out of here. Who that is, that's up to you."

1959 September 29 Tuesday 00:04

"Every time that sister of his comes into the room, the show's over, huh, Sammy?" Harley said to the broad-faced man as they were walking toward their cars in the lot.

"Roy knows what he's doing," the broad-faced man said, a faint thread of warning in the blend of his voice.

"Yeah? I don't see what Cynthia's got to do with anything, myself. The way she acts sometimes, it's like she's the boss, not him."

Sammy kept walking, silent.

"You don't think it's a little strange, Sammy?" Harley persisted.

"What I think is, nobody ever got themselves in trouble minding their own business."

"I was just saying—"

"Harley, you're a comer. Everybody knows that. The man himself has his eye on you."

"So?"

"So listen to an older hand for a minute, son. There's a lot more to Royal Beaumont than a big set of balls."

"You saying—what?—people don't think I got the brains to run my own—?"

"I'm not saying that, Harley . . . although, when you pull kid stuff like coming late to meetings, you make folks wonder. Look, I know you've got a head on your shoulders. But having something's not the same as using it, you follow me?"

"Sammy . . ."

"I came up with Roy," Sammy said. "We go back. All the way back. You know what the smartest thing you can say about his sister is?"

"Nothing?"

Sammy reached over and squeezed the younger man's shoulder. "See how smart you can be when you work at it?" he said.

1959 September 29 Tuesday 00:12

"There's three toggle switches right under the dash," the driver said, pointing with his forefinger. "Just slip your hand under there, you'll feel them."

The black man deliberately turned his back and reached under the dash, tacitly acknowledging that the pistol he had been holding hadn't been the protection he first thought it was.

"First one kills all the interior lights; in the trunk, too," the driver said. "You push it forward, they won't go on, no matter what's opened. The second one—the one in the middle—that's the ignition kill switch. Push it forward, and you can't start the car, even with the key. The last one is the muffler cutouts. Okay?"

"I got it," the black man said, stepping back out of the car.

"Then let's go get that Ford of yours."

"I don't think so, man. You just wait here, we'll bring it to you. An hour, no more. Man like you, I'll bet you an ace at killing time."

"You're a funny guy," the driver said.

1959 September 29 Tuesday 00:21

"You're really sure we need an outsider in on this?" the tall, red-haired man asked. He had moved his chair so that it was alongside Beaumont's desk, canting his lean body at an angle to create a zone of privacy.

"An outsider's exactly what we need, Lymon," the man in the wheelchair answered. "You know how men like Dioguardi work. Before they make a move, they always count the house. They think they know every card we're holding. This man, he's going to be our sleeve ace."

"Where do you find someone like him, anyway?" Lymon asked. "The mobbed-up guys, they've got a whole network. They want a job done in, I don't know, Chicago, the boss there, he makes a call, and the boss in . . . Miami, maybe, sends him someone to do it. But that's not us. I mean, we *know* people, sure. But they're independents, like we are. They're not *with* us."

"That's true."

"You trust Red Schoolfield enough to use one of his guys? I heard that he wasn't going to be able to hold out much longer himself. Maybe he already made his deal."

Cynthia walked over to the liquor cabinet, opened two small, unlabeled, brown glass bottles, and carefully shook a pill from each. She expertly tonged three ice cubes into a square-cut tumbler, added water from a carafe, and brought it over to Beaumont. He plucked the pills from her open palm, put them in his mouth, and emptied the tumbler.

"More?" she asked.

"Please."

Without another word, Cynthia fetched the carafe and refilled Beaumont's glass. She returned the carafe to the liquor cabinet unhurriedly, clearly intending to remain in the room.

A silver cigarette box sat on Beaumont's desk. He opened it, turned it in Lymon's direction. Lymon shook his head "no," completing the ritual. Beaumont took a cigarette from the case, fired it with a table lighter. He adjusted his position in his wheelchair, blew a perfect smoke ring at the ceiling.

"This guy—Dett is what he calls himself, Walker Dett—he didn't come from Red. I knew Red had used him on a job. All's I did, I gave Red a call, asked him how it had worked out. Like a reference."

"So where did you find him?" Lymon persisted.

"You know Nadine's roadhouse?"

"Everybody knows Nadine. She—"

"This isn't about her," Beaumont said, the "Pay attention!" implicit in his tone. "You go out there, to her joint, once in a while?"

"Not really. Only when—"

"When they've got certain bands playing, am I right?"

"Yep," Lymon said, enthusiasm rising in his voice. "They get some real corkers out there, sometimes."

"Like Junior Joe Clanton?"

"That's one for sure!"

"Absolutely," Beaumont agreed. "Now, Junior Joe, he's no Hank Williams. But who is? What I mean is, Junior Joe was never on the Opry. And you're never going to hear one of his songs on the radio. But when word gets out he's coming to town, you know there'll be a full house somewhere that night."

"Yeah. I don't understand why he never got . . . big. That boy's got a voice like . . . well, like nobody else."

"Maybe that's the way he wants it," Beaumont said. "All men pretty much want the same things—the same *kind* of things, anyway—but different men, they go after it different ways. I know what Nadine has to shell out to get him to work her place. If he does that good everywhere he plays, Junior Joe's making more money a year than some of the big stars."

"And he gets paid in cash, right?"

"That could be part of it," Beaumont conceded. "But I don't think it's the whole story. Maybe . . . You remember Debbie Jean Watson? Hiram Watson's daughter? That girl won every beauty contest in the whole damn state. Far as a lot of folks were concerned, she made Elizabeth Taylor look like a librarian. Remember what happened to her?"

"She went out to Hollywood. . . ."

"And never came back. You know why? Not because she couldn't act. Hell, there's all kinds of movies where the girls don't have to do anything but *look* good. You'd think she could at least get some of that kind of work. Face like hers, body that could wake the dead, she walks in a room, she owns every man in it. But the thing is, Lymon, the *camera* didn't see her the way men do in real life. The way I understand it, those movie cameras, they don't work the same as a man's eyes do. You need a special look to make them love you. And Debbie Jean, she didn't have it."

"So maybe that's Junior Joe, what you're saying? He's got the voice for honky-tonks, but not for records?"

"I don't know," Beaumont said. "All I'm saying, there's reasons for everything."

"What's this got to do with—?"

"This Walker Dett, he's kind of like Junior Joe. A honky-tonk man, moving from town to town. You want him, you call this number. They give you another number—that one's always changing—and you just leave a message. Somebody calls you back—*maybe* somebody calls you back—and you make a deal. Like booking an act, see?"

"So how do people even know about him?"

"Same way they do about Junior Joe. Word of mouth. Which is why I asked Red Schoolfield, was he as good as people say? And Red, he said he was."

"It seems like a lot of trouble just to hire a gun," Lymon said. "There's always been plenty of freelance firepower around. Even more, since Korea ended."

"Plenty of horses get foaled every year, too," Beaumont said. "But how many of them end up in the Kentucky Derby? This guy, he's in a different class from anyone we could find around here."

"But what if the outfit guys really aren't planning—?"

"Don't kid yourself," Beaumont said, scornfully. "You think they're just talk? They already made it clear—they're *going* to get a taste of what we got. And once they get that taste, you know what happens next.

"Look, Lymon, they're all businessmen. Just like us. They want our action. What we have to do is make it so costly for them that it's not worth it. And this guy I'm bringing in, he's just the man for that."

"Beau . . . ?" his sister said.

"All right, Cyn. I know." Turning to Lymon, he said, "Doc says,

I don't get some sleep after I take those damn pills, they're not going to do the job."

As he got up to leave, Lymon asked, "Whatever happened to her?"

"Who?"

"Debbie Jean Watson. Like you said, she never came home."

"Oh, yeah. Well, it seems there's all different kinds of cameras. Movie cameras, she couldn't do a thing with them. But she was good enough for the other kind."

1959 September 29 Tuesday 01:19

The big house was quiet. The man in the wheelchair rolled himself down the hall to a master-bedroom suite, where flames in a stone fireplace cuddled rough-hewn logs. A triple-sized tub in the attached bathroom was surrounded by handrails. He backed his chair against the wall, and sat in darkness until his sister lit a thick red candle in the opposite corner.

"I suppose you'd like one of your awful cigars," she said.

"Sure would."

"You don't have to always have one before—"

"There's a lot of things I *do* have to do, Cyn. Some of them, I wish I didn't. I get the chance, do something I *like* to do, doesn't matter that I don't *have* to do it, right?"

"You could just *try* something else, for once."

"Why?"

"Because you might like it better."

"I couldn't like it any more than I already do."

"You might, Beau. You used to. . . ."

"That was when I still could—"

"Try one of these, instead," she said, walking over to his wheelchair, a red-and-gold box in her hand. "Special cigarettes. From Turkey."

"I . . . ah, what the hell, Cyn. You know I always give you what you want."

He reached for the box of cigarettes. Cynthia took a step back. "After," she said, caressingly. Then she knelt before the wheelchair.

1959 September 29 Tuesday 02:04

"These *are* good," Beaumont said, exhaling a powerful jet of smoke.

"See?"

"Yeah. But they won't last as long as a good—"

"So you'll have another," the woman said. "If you want one."

"I just might," Beaumont said. "Now, tell me, what's your read on the meet we just had?"

"Red Schoolfield is a moron," his sister said.

"I *know* that, Cyn. You think I didn't get word from other places on this guy I'm bringing in? Red's the only name the boys need to hear, that's all."

"Lymon's shaky," she said. "But that's nothing new—he's been weak for years. Of all the men, he's the least likely to go the distance, should it ever come to that."

"Yeah," the man in the wheelchair agreed. "And I think we could be walking close to that line now. That's why I called him aside at the end. He's been talking to the Irishers."

"Roy! How could you know that?"

"I know," he assured her.

"So this stranger, you're really bringing him here for Lymon?"

"No. What I told the men he was for, that was the truth. We talked about this, Cyn. Dioguardi's already putting some of our accounts in a cross. Look at the jukeboxes. Every joint in the county knows they have to use the machines we send them. Now Dioguardi's outfit's coming around, telling them they have to use *theirs*. And if they don't want to do that, they have to pay a tax to use *ours*. The squeeze is too tight."

"It's our town," the man in the wheelchair said, "so it's our play. And that's when this guy I'm bringing in earns his money."

"What about Lymon?"

"I was thinking of Harley. That boy's sharp. And he's good with his accounts, too. But he's never shown his stuff, not that way."

"He's awfully young, Beau. I don't know. . . ."

"Everyone who started with us, they're my age now, Cyn. If we're going to keep this going . . . after, we need a younger man. I know I'm right about Harley, he just needs more seasoning."

"I can't see men like Faron and Sammy—"

"—following a kid like Harley? It's not them we have to worry about, honey. They're old pros. And they're not going to be working forever, either. It's the next wave, men like Udell and Roland, that Harley's got to win over. And all the smarts in the world won't be enough for that—you know what he has to do."

"Yes," Cynthia said. "But . . . Oh, never mind that for now, Beau. When are we expecting this man you sent for?"

"Tomorrow, the next day, sometime soon. He's on the road right now, heading this way. Soon as he checks into the Claremont, he's going to call."

1959 September 29 Tuesday 03:55

"Can't sleep, Beau?"

"I don't need much, Cyn. You know that."

"Yes, but you need *some*. It's very late. Do you want—?"

"No, thank you," the man in the wheelchair said, almost formally. "I just . . . wanted to think some things through, I guess. You know how people tell you, when you got a problem, you should 'sleep on it'? Well, that's the coward's way. The right way is, you grab on and wrestle with it."

"You always were a great wrestler, Beau."

"Used to be, honey. Used to be."

"I don't think there's a man in this town who could take you at the table, right this minute," Cynthia said, shaking her head as if to dispute any doubters.

"I guess I *should* be strong, all those exercises you used to make me do."

"You *had* to do them, Beau. The doctors said . . . this would happen, someday."

"You can say 'wheelchair,' Cyn. The word doesn't scare me. Not anymore, anyway. When I was a kid, I hated those braces I had to wear. Now I wish I had them back."

"Beau, we don't have to . . . do any of this. We could go somewhere else. Florida, maybe. We have enough money. . . ."

"How long you think all that money would last us, we did that? Most of what we have, it's not hard cash, Cyn. It's tied up, in all kinds of things. The money that keeps you safe is the money that keeps coming in. Like an electric fence—the minute you turn off the power, anyone can just walk right through it." Beaumont looked at the glowing tip of his cigarette. "Power," he said, quietly. "That's what keeps us safe. And money, money coming in, that's only a piece of it. The men, *my* men, the men who stand between me and everyone else, you think I could buy that with money?"

"Of course not. Even if you were down to your last penny, Luther would never—"

"Yeah, I know, honey. But Luther's our own, like Sammy and Faron are. You can buy a man's gun, but that doesn't mean you bought his heart. Bodyguards, they're nothing but bullet-catchers— and they know it. One day, you pay them to stand in front of you; another day, someone else could pay them to stand aside.

"You look at some of those countries in South America. Every time you turn around, they got a new guy in charge. You think, how could that happen when the boss, he's got a whole *army* on his side? Easy. Somebody in that same army decides *he* wants to be the boss. You read between the lines, you can see it clear. The difference between a bodyguard and a hit man, it's whose money he's taking, that's all."

"Is that why Lymon—?"

"Lymon? No. He doesn't have it in him to even *think* about taking over from me. He's the kind of man who's got to be with someone stronger. That's why he's always been with me. And that's why he's talking to the Irish guys, too. Hedging his bets."

"But why would *they* trust someone like him? If he'd sell us out, why wouldn't he—?"

"—do the same to them? He would. And they have to know it. Once a man betrays his own, no one else can ever trust him again. Lymon was a good man, once. But even back then, he never knew how to plan ahead."

"Nobody can plan like you, Beau," his sister said.

1959 September 29 Tuesday 11:53

"Welcome to the Claremont," the desk clerk said, glancing down at where the guest had signed the register. "We have you in 809, Mr. Dett. That's a corner room, deluxe, with shower and bath, for two weeks, is that correct?"

"Two weeks, that's right," the guest agreed.

"Let me get you some help with that luggage," the clerk said, hitting a bell and hollering "Front!" simultaneously.

"Appreciate it," Dett said.

"Would you like me to send a boy out to take care of your car, too, sir? We have parking around the back, complimentary for hotel guests."

"No thanks," Dett replied. "I didn't drive. Came in on the plane from Cincinnati, then I grabbed a cab. I figured I'd rent a car while I'm in town. That's the way I always do it."

The desk clerk prided himself on being a superb judge of humanity, able to size up any new guest in minutes. He often regaled his mother with his Sherlockian deductions at the end of his shift. As he filled out the registration card, he covertly took stock.

The man on the other side of the counter was clean-shaven, the facial skin stretched tightly over sharp cheekbones. His dark-chestnut hair was cut almost military-short. His hands were well cared for, but two knuckles of his right hand were flattened, marked with white keloid starbursts. A simple steel watch with an expansion bracelet constituted his only jewelry. His dark-blue suit, although clearly well fitted, was what the clerk's mother would have dismissed as "decent." A gray felt fedora, a plain white shirt with a spread collar and button cuffs, and a black tie—a little wider than was currently fashionable—didn't help with the diagnosis. Nor did the man's luggage, an unmatched set of two suitcases, a Pullman and a smaller job, plus a generic attaché case.

A traveling salesman working the circuit would have made conversation about the weather, like a boxer sparring to keep in shape. A confidence man would be either flashier or more richly conservative in dress. A gambler would carry cash in the buttoned breast pocket of his shirt. A gunman would be wearing a shoulder holster. An itinerant preacher would have a Bible somewhere in sight. The clerk glanced down at the register, saw that Mr. Walker Dett had listed his business as "real estate," whatever *that* meant.

Under other circumstances, the clerk would have asked a couple of questions—*friendly* questions, of course. But there was something about this man, some . . . stillness to him, that made the clerk nervously finger the single pearl anchored precisely in the center of his plum-colored necktie.

"Rufus will show you up to your room, sir," the clerk said, as a handsome mahogany-colored man in his early thirties approached the front desk, dressed in a resplendent red bellhop's uniform, with rows of gold braid across the chest and "Claremont" spelled in the same material on his round cap. "We hope you enjoy your stay with us. If there's anything you need, just let us know."

"Thanks," said the guest. He picked up his attaché case, and pointed with his chin to the two suitcases on the floor. The bellhop hefted the two suitcases, said, "This way, sir," and started toward the elevator.

In response to the bellhop's ring, the elevator cage slowly descended. It was opened by an elderly man whose teakwood complexion was set off by a skullcap of tight gray curls. He was wearing a red blazer with the "Claremont" name and crest on the breast pocket.

"We need eight, Moses," the bellhop told him. "The top floor," he added, unnecessarily.

"Sure thing," the elderly man said. "Welcome to the Claremont, suh," he told the guest.

"Thank you," Dett replied.

The cage came to a dead-level stop on the eighth floor, the operator working the lever so smoothly there was no sensation of movement.

"Very nice," the guest said, touching the brim of his hat.

"Yes suh!" the operator said, flustered. He had been driving that elevator car for more than twenty years, and this was the first time anyone had ever taken note of his dextrous touch, much less complimented him on it.

The bellhop led the way down the hall. When he came to the last door on his left, he put down one of the suitcases and withdrew a key from his pants pocket in one fluid motion. He unlocked the door, pushed it open, stood aside for the guest to precede him, then picked up both suitcases and followed.

The bellhop opened the door to the bathroom, turned on the taps, opened the medicine cabinet. Then he walked officiously to the windows and drew back the curtains, clearly on a tour of inspection.

"This here's one of our very best rooms," he told the guest. "Over to the front side, it can get real noisy, with all the traffic in the street. Back here, it stays nice and quiet."

"It'll be fine," the guest said, handing over a dollar.

The bellhop's smile broadened. Most professional travelers generally thought a quarter was generous. The action men, the gamblers and the hustlers, they always went for halves. Only Hoosiers and honeymooners tipped dollars. Rufus, who knew an omen when he saw one, resolved to play 809 when the numbers runner came by that afternoon.

"If there's anything you need, sir, anything at all, you just ask for Rufus. Whatever you might want, I get it for you."

"This a dry town?" the guest asked.

"No, sir. Truth is, folks comes *here,* they want to get themselves a taste."

"Appreciate your honesty," the guest said, handing over a ten-dollar bill. "This'll buy me a fifth of Four Roses, then?"

"With plenty to spare, sir," the bellhop confirmed. "I'll be right back."

On his way over to the liquor store a block away from the hotel, the bellhop congratulated himself on not lying about the easy availability of liquor in Locke City—the guest had asked the question as if he already knew the answer. *Whoever he is,* Rufus thought, *he ain't no Hoosier.*

The man who had signed the register as Walker Dett tossed his two suitcases onto the double bed, gave the room a thirty-second sweep with his eyes, then picked up his attaché case and walked out into the corridor. He rang for the elevator.

"Going out already, suh?" the operator said, as the guest stepped into his car.

The man held up his hand in an unmistakable "Wait a minute" gesture. "I don't want to go anywhere. Just want to talk to you for a couple of minutes, Moses."

"Me, suh?"

"Yes, if you don't mind."

The operator turned his head, looking squarely at the man standing behind him. Waiting.

"My name's Dett," the tall man said, extending his hand to the operator. "Walker Dett."

"It's my pleasure to know you, Mr. Dett," the operator said, palming the five-dollar bill as smoothly as he handled the elevator car. "Anything you need around here, you just—"

"You had time, size me up yet?"

"No, suh. It ain't my place to be—"

"You're a man who keeps his eyes open, I can tell."

"Now, I don't know nothing about that, suh. All I can see, you some kind of a businessman. A *serious* businessman," the operator said. He kept his hand on the lever, ears alert for the buzzer which would summon the car.

"That's right," Dett said. "I'm here on business. And in my line of work, you know what's really valuable?"

"No, suh."

"Information. Every workingman needs his tools. And information, that's a tool, isn't it?"

"Sure could be, suh."

"Some people, they think, in a hotel, it's the desk clerk that knows everything that goes on. Others, they think it's the bellhops. Some, they read too many paperback books, they think it's the house dick. But you know what I think?"

"No, suh," the elderly man said, evenly. "I don't know what you think."

"I think it's not the job you do, it's how long you've been doing it that makes you the man in the know. I think, a man gets to be a certain age, instead of people having respect, instead of them *listening* to him, they talk around him like he's not even in the room. Like he's wallpaper. A man like that, he gets to hear all kinds of things. You think I could be right?"

"Yes, suh. I believe you could be."

"And a man like that, he's not just worth something for what he knows; he's worth double, because people don't *know* he knows. Could I be right about that, too?"

"You surely could, suh."

"You know what a 'consultant' is, Moses?"

"No, suh. I never heard of one."

"Well, a consultant is a man you go to for advice. You ask him questions, he's got answers. You ask him how to solve certain problems, he's got the solutions. Man like that, he could make a good living, doing what he does."

"Is that what you do, suh?"

"I think," Dett said, tucking another five-dollar bill into the breast pocket of the operator's blazer, "that's what *you* do."

The buzzer sounded. The two men exchanged a quick look. Dett stepped out of the elevator car, and the operator slid the lever to the "down" position.

1959 September 29 Tuesday 12:25

The knock on the door of Room 809 was that of an experienced bellhop—firm and deferential at the same time.

"Come on in," Dett called from behind the partially opened bathroom door. He had positioned himself so that the medicine cabinet's mirror gave him a clear view of the doorway. As the bellhop closed the door behind him, Dett slipped the derringer he had been holding into the pocket of his slacks and came out, giving his hands a finishing touch with the washcloth he carried.

"Here's your liquor, sir. I don't know how you takes it, so I brought you some ice, just in case," the bellhop said, holding up a small chrome bucket.

At a nod from Dett, the bellhop placed the bottle and the ice bucket on top of a chest of drawers. Next to it, he ostentatiously deposited the change from the ten dollars he had been entrusted with.

"There's too much there," Dett said.

"Too much? But, sir, you *said* a fifth."

"Too much money, Rufus," Dett said. "You're about a dollar heavy, the way I see it."

"Thank *you,* sir," the bellhop said. "I could tell you was a gent from the minute you checked in. You want me to pour you one now?"

"Just about so much," Dett said, indicating a generous inch with his thumb and forefinger. "Over the rocks."

"There you go, sir."

"Thanks."

"Yes, sir. If you need anything else . . . ?"

"What hours do you work?"

"Me? Well, my regular shift is six to six. But I never mind putting in no extra time, if it's needed. Everybody got to do that, even Mister Carl—that's the deskman."

"I got it," Dett said, carrying his drink over to the room's only easy chair and sitting down. It was clearly a dismissal.

The bellhop started for the door, then turned slightly, his eyes on the carpet. "Sir, what I said about needing anything else? That don't have to be from the hotel, sir."

"I don't want any—"

"No, sir, I understand. Man like you, he don't want no colored girl. But I got kind of an . . . arrangement, like. Make one phone call, get you anything up here you might want."

"I'll remember," Dett said.

1959 September 29 Tuesday 12:36

As soon as the bellhop left, Dett closed the curtains. Then he opened the smaller of his two suitcases, took out a wooden wedge, and walked over to the door. He kicked the wedge under the door, then turned the knob and pulled it toward him. Even against strong pressure, the wedge held securely.

Turning his back on the door, Dett moved to the window, parted the curtains a slit, and peered outside. He glanced at his watch, then carried the untouched bourbon into the bathroom and emptied it into the sink, ran hot water over the ice cubes, and returned the unwashed glass to the top of the bureau. Moving methodically, he filled a second glass with fresh ice cubes and added tap water.

From the larger suitcase, Dett took a box of soda crackers. He drank a little of the water, then began eating, alternating the slow, thorough chewing of each bite with a sip of water.

Finished, he took a series of shallow breaths through his nose, pressing the first two fingers of each hand hard against his diaphragm as he exhaled.

Dett closed his eyes. A nerve jumped in his right cheek, so forcefully that it lifted the corner of his mouth. He continued the breathing, going deeper and deeper, until he fell asleep.

1959 September 29 Tuesday 17:09

When Dett opened his eyes, the room was dark, but it was the artificial darkness of closed curtains. The luminescent dial on his wristwatch told him it was just past five; his body told him that it was afternoon. Dett got up, used the bathroom, and drank another glass of water.

Crossing over to the far wall, Dett again parted the curtains. He tried both windows, found they opened easily but only went up less than halfway, held in place by metal stoppers in the channels. Behind the hotel was an alley, on the other side of which was the back side of an undistinguished brick building.

Dett took a street map from his suitcase, turning it in his hands until he was oriented to his own location. *Office building,* he said to himself, looking out the window. *Probably goes dark after they close for the day.*

Dett picked up the phone, dialed "0," and told the hotel operator he wanted the front desk.

Connected, he asked the foppish clerk if he could get a sandwich sent up to his room.

"Certainly, Mr. Dett," the desk clerk said, pridefully. "At the Claremont, our kitchen is always open until one in the morning, for anything from a snack to a full-course meal. And you can get a breakfast order anytime after six as well. Just tell me what you'd like, and I'll have it sent right up."

"I'd appreciate that," Dett said. He ordered a steak sandwich, a side of French fries, and two bottles of Coke. Then he undressed, took a quick shower, and put on fresh clothes.

When the knock came, twenty minutes later, Dett wasn't surprised to see Rufus on the other side of the threshold.

"You do all *kinds* of work around here, don't you?" he said to the bellhop.

"I tell you the truth, sir. They got a boy in the kitchen, supposed to deliver meals to guests. But I got this . . ."

"Arrangement?" Dett said, smiling thinly.

"Yes, sir. I see you know how things work in hotels."

"How much of a piece does that Nancy-boy take?"

"Mister Carl? The way he work it, end of my shift, every dollar I get, he supposed to get a dime."

"He must do all right for himself, then."

"You mean, he got the same deal with all the boys? Yes, sir. He sure do. Man like him, he in a powerful position around here."

"Knows what's going on, huh?"

"Knows it *all,* sir. I swear, sometimes I think he got secret passageways or something. We had this little game going in the basement," the bellhop said, miming shaking a pair of dice in his closed hand. "Just a few of the boys, on our break, you know? Well, one day, I come into work, Mister Carl, he tells me there's a toll due. You see how he is?"

"Not yet, I don't."

"I don't follow you, sir."

"How much of a toll was he charging?"

"Oh. Well, he said it would cost a dollar."

"For every game."

"Yes, sir."

"So you stopped playing down there."

"That's right. How you know—? I mean, I apologize, sir. I didn't mean no backtalk. Just surprised, is all."

"Remember you asked me, did I see how he was? The desk clerk? Well, now I see how he is. Dumb."

"Dumb? No, sir. Mister Carl, he a pretty slick—"

"If he charged you a quarter for every game, how much would he have made?"

"Well, we used to play every day, so . . ."

"Right. And how much is he getting from your games, now?"

"He ain't . . . Oh, I see where you coming from, sir. Mister Carl, maybe he not so smart after all."

"Let's see if you are," Dett said, handing the bellhop two one-dollar bills. "If Carl gets a piece of this, I'll be real disappointed in you, Rufus."

"You ain't gonna have no cause to *ever* be disappointed in me, sir. My momma only raised but one fool, and that was my brother."

1959 September 29 Tuesday 18:19

The guest in Room 809 opened the steak sandwich carefully. He removed the lettuce and tomato, examining each in turn. Dett rolled his right shoulder—a small knife slid out of his sleeve and into his hand. He thumbed the knife open, then meticulously trimmed the outer edges of the lettuce, cored the slice of tomato, and removed every visible trace of fat from the meat before he reassembled the sandwich.

Dett picked up all the discarded pieces, carried them to the bathroom, and dropped them into the toilet. He flushed, checked to see if everything had disappeared, then washed his hands.

It took him almost forty-five minutes to eat the sandwich and French fries. He spaced sips of Coke evenly throughout, taking the final one after he swallowed the last of the sandwich.

Dett poured approximately three shots of the Four Roses into a glass. He carried it to the bathroom, emptied the contents into the toilet, and flushed again.

Then he sat and waited for darkness to bloom.

1959 September 29 Tuesday 21:09

Walker Dett washed his hands again, put on a tie, pocketed his room key, and walked out into the corridor.

"Evening, suh," the elevator operator said, as he slid back the grillework for Dett to enter.

"Evening, Moses," the man said. "I think I'll take a little walk, help me digest my dinner."

"Yes, suh," said the operator, sliding the lever toward the "down" position.

Dett stepped close to the operator, holding out his palm and tilting his head in a "Wait a minute" gesture. The operator's hand stopped the lever a fraction short of engagement.

"This elevator, it goes all the way to the basement?" Dett said, quietly.

"No, suh. Only the service car goes there."

"But there's no operator for that one, right?"

"That's right," the elderly man said, not surprised this quiet-voiced stranger would know such things.

"Can anyone just get in and run it, or do you need a key?"

"Used to be, like you say, anyone could just use it. But when Mister Carl took over—that was a few years after the war, if I remember right—he said that wouldn't do. So now, you want to use the freight car, you got to ask Mister Carl, and he loans you the key."

"But he's not the only one who has one?"

"Oh no, suh. Nothing could run if things was like that. Plenty folks got keys. They has one in the kitchen, the maintenance man has one, the maids—they don't like them riding the same cars as the guests, you know—the house cop . . . lots of folks, I bet. Me, I got one myself."

"Thanks, Moses," Dett said, moving his head slightly. The operator moved the lever a notch, and the car began to descend.

1959 September 29 Tuesday 21:59

Dett left the elevator car and walked over to the front desk.
"Everything satisfactory, Mr. Dett?" the clerk asked.

"It's fine," Dett assured him. "I was just going to take a little walk, work off my dinner." He patted his stomach for emphasis. "A little fresh air never hurt anyone."

"I couldn't agree more," the desk clerk said. "In fact, I'm somewhat of a physical-culture enthusiast myself."

Dett nodded slightly, as if acknowledging the obvious. "This area," he asked, "it's safe at night?"

"*This* part of town? Absolutely! Now, there *are* some sections I certainly wouldn't go myself, even in broad daylight. I'm sure you know what I mean . . . ?"

"Sure."

"So long as you stay within, oh, a ten-block radius, I'd say, you'll find Locke City a wonderfully quiet town," Carl said, smoothly.

1959 September 29 Tuesday 22:28

Dett strolled the broad avenue at a leisurely pace, his eyes on the passing traffic. In the time it took him to cover a half-dozen blocks, he spotted two police cars—black '58 Ford sedans with white doors and roofs—blending unaggressively with the traffic flow. Guard dogs, big enough to send a message without barking.

A message *received*, Dett noted. The wide, clean sidewalk was devoid of loiterers. No hookers looking for trade, no teenage punks leaning against the buildings, no panhandlers. Nothing but respectably dressed citizens, mostly in couples, and very few of those.

Dett stayed in motion, all the while watching, clocking, measuring. He walked down a side street, then turned into an alley opening. When that dead-ended, he retraced his steps, noting how deserted the whole area had suddenly become. He glanced at his watch: ten-fifty-seven. Somewhere in this town, action was probably just getting started, he thought. But not around here . . .

Relying on his memory of the street map, Dett found his way to the office building he had observed from his hotel window. Positioning himself so that he could view the back of the hotel, he noted the absence of fire escapes. He turned a corner and checked again. Sure enough, each floor had a fire exit at the end of the corridor, on either side, leading to a series of metal staircases that formed a Z-pattern all the way down to the second floor. The final set of stairs would have to be released manually.

Dett turned slowly, scanning the area. His eyes picked up another alley opening, halfway down the block. *They can't* all *dead-end,* he thought to himself, moving deliberately through the darkness, eyes alert for trail markers.

As Dett entered the alley, blotchy shadows told him that a source of light was somewhere in the vicinity. Maybe a streetlight positioned close to the other end? As he neared what he sensed to be the exit, the red glow of a cigarette tip flashed a warning. Dett took a long, shallow breath through his nose, sending a neural message to his neck and shoulder muscles to relax, deliberately opening receptor channels he trusted to watch his back.

He slowed his pace imperceptibly, and casually slipped his right hand into his pants pocket.

Two of them, Dett registered. As he got closer, his sense-impression was confirmed. They were in their late teens or early twenties; one, the smoker, sitting on a wooden milk crate, the other leaning against the alley wall, arms folded across his chest. *Jack-rollers,* Dett said to himself. *Must be a bar just around the corner, and some of the drunks use this alley as a shortcut.*

Twenty yards. Ten. Dett kept coming, not altering his pace or his stance. His ears picked up the sound of speech, but he couldn't make out the words. The man on the milk crate got to his feet, and the two of them moved off in the opposite direction, just short of a run.

Either they only work cripples, or they're waiting for me just around the corner, one on each side of the alley, Dett thought. He spun on his heel and went back the way he had entered, still walking, but long-striding now, covering ground. At the alley entrance, Dett turned to his left, walked to the far corner, then squared the block, heading back toward where the alley would let out.

The sidewalk was dark except for a single streetlight only a few feet from the mouth of the alley—it seemed to know it was surrounded, and wasn't putting up much of a fight. Dett crossed the street and walked on past. Not a sign of the two men.

He was nearly at the end of the long block when he noticed a faded blue-and-white neon sign in a small rectangular window. Enough of the letters still burned so Dett guessed at "Tavern," but the rest was a mystery he wasn't interested in solving.

Dett spent the next hour walking the streets, noting how many of the buildings seemed empty and abandoned.

1959 September 30 Wednesday 07:06

"He came back in around one in the morning," Carl said. He was in the breakfast nook of a modest two-story house that occupied the mid-arc plot of a gently curving block, seated at a blue Formica kitchen table on a chair upholstered in tufted vinyl of the same shade.

"Your shift—your *extra* shift, I might add—was almost done," a woman said, over her shoulder, focusing on her breakfast-preparation tasks. She was tall, fair-skinned, with sharp features and alert eyes, her white-blond hair worn in a tight bun.

"Not really," Carl said, bitterly. "You know how Berwick is. Expecting *him* to come in on time . . ."

"Well, Carl, he may not last. They all seem to come and go."

"He's been there almost two years."

"Still . . ."

"Mother, you don't understand. It's not just that he's always late, it's that he's so . . . arrogant about it. As if he *knows* I'd never say anything to the manager about him."

"Well, that's not your way, Carl. You were not raised to be a tale-bearer."

"Well, still, there's plenty I could tell Mr. Hodges about Berwick, if I wanted to. It's not just his lack of . . . dignity; he's a filthy slob, Mother. You would not *believe* the state he leaves the desk in."

"I know," the woman said. "But that's the way the world is, son. Some people act correctly, some people don't. We are not responsible for anyone but ourselves."

"I know he says things about me. Some of the colored boys, I can tell, by the way they look at me."

"Are they disrespectful to you?"

"Well . . . no. I don't mean anything they *say*. It's just . . . I don't know."

"Carl," the woman said, sternly, "there are always going to be people with big mouths and small minds."

She brought a pale-blue plate to the table. On it were two perfectly poached eggs on gently browned toast, with the crusts removed.

"It isn't like that *everywhere*," Carl said.

"Oh, Carl, please. Not that again."

"Well, it *isn't*," the not-so-young-anymore man insisted. "In some of the big cities—"

"You have *roots* here," his mother interrupted. "You have a place, a place where you belong. A fine job, a lovely home . . ."

"I know, Mother. I know."

"Sometimes, I get so worried about you, Carl. Every time you go on one of your vacations, I can't even sleep, I'm so terrified."

"There's no reason to be frightened, Mother," Carl said, resentfully. "I know my way around places a lot bigger than Locke City will ever be."

"Oh, Carl," the woman said, "I know you can take care of yourself. I raised you to be a competent man, a man who knows how to deal with whatever situation may come up in life."

"Then why do you always get so—?"

"I worry . . . I just worry that, one day, you'll go on vacation and you won't come back."

"That's ridiculous."

"Why is it so ridiculous, son? With your experience, you could get a job in a place like Chicago very easily."

"Not Chicago," Carl muttered.

"What?"

"I said, 'Not Chicago,' Mother. If I was going to live someplace else, it would be *far* away. New York. Or maybe San Francisco."

"I couldn't bear that," she said, fidgeting with the waistband of her apron.

"Don't be so dramatic, Mother. You know I would never leave you here alone. We could sell this house, and find a perfectly fine place somewhere else."

"Carl, if I had to leave Locke City, I would just *die*. All my friends are here. My own mother, *your* Grandmother Tel, is an old woman now. How many years could she have left? Without me driving over to her place to do for her, why, she'd end up in one of those horrible old-age homes. And there's my church. *Our* church, if you still went with me. My bridge club. My gardening group. I was born and raised only a few miles from this very house. There's some flowers you just can't transplant; they wouldn't survive. And your father—"

"Yes, I miss him, too," Carl said, sullenly.

"There is no reason to be so spiteful, Carl. I know you and your father had your differences, but he's been gone a long time. And I always protected you, didn't I?"

"You did," Carl said, blinking his eyes rapidly. "Come on, Mother. Sit down with me. I want to tell you all about the mysterious Mr. Walker Dett."

1959 September 30 Wednesday 08:11

Sun slanted through the partially drawn curtains of Room 809. Dett opened his eyes, instantly awake. He was on the floor, the double bed between him and the wedged door. Before going to sleep, he had balanced a quarter on the doorknob, and positioned a large glass ashtray beneath it. Had anyone tried the door while he slept, the coin would have dropped into the glass, alerting Dett but not the intruder.

Between the carpeted floor and the blanket and pillows he had removed from the bed, Dett had been quite comfortable. He was positioned on his side, back against the wall beneath the window. The derringer in his right hand looked as natural as a child's teddy bear.

Dett got to his feet, pulled the tightly fitted sheet off the mattress, then deposited it at the foot of the bed, along with the blanket and the pillowcases he had removed to construct his sleeping quarters. He plucked the quarter from the doorknob, returned the ashtray to the writing desk, and lit a cigarette. While it was burning, he emptied some more of the Four Roses into the sink.

After a shower and shave, Dett telephoned room service and ordered breakfast and a newspaper, specifying the local. While he waited, he dressed—another plain dark suit, another carefully knotted tie, this time a sober shade of blue.

Three eggs, yolks broken and fried over hard, four strips of bacon, a side of hash-brown potatoes, two glasses of orange juice, and a basket of biscuits took him more than an hour to consume.

Dett carried the breakfast tray outside his room and left it on the floor, next to his door. He went back inside and sat down to read the paper, turning first to the personals column—in case Whisper had a message for him.

A few minutes later, the door opened and a cocoa-colored young woman in a white maid's smock walked in.

"Oh! I'm sorry, sir!" she said, her amber eyes alive with anxiety. "I saw the tray outside, and I figured you was out. I'll come back later and—"

"That's all right," Dett said, sliding the derringer back into his pocket, shielded by the newspaper. "Might as well get it done now; I won't be in your way."

"Yes, sir," the young woman said, pushing her service cart ahead of her. "If you want to . . . stay in late, any day, all you have to do is put the sign up, and I'll know—"

"I'll know better next time," Dett said, mildly, lowering his newspaper. "Thank you."

"Yes, sir," the young woman said, still nervous over having blundered into the room without knocking. It was just the kind of mistake that Mister Carl would report to the manager, if the guest complained. At the Claremont, maids had been fired for less. She entered the bathroom, skillfully removed and replaced the three tumblers she found there, exchanged the roll of toilet paper for a new one, replaced the towels, added a fresh bar of soap. Even moving mechanically, she noted how clean and neat the guest had left everything.

"All right if I do the bed now, sir?" she asked, stepping back into the main room.

"Sure," the guest replied. "And my name is Dett, Walker Dett."

"Yes, sir. I mean, yes, Mr. Dett, sir."

The young woman's large amber eyes met the guest's pale-gray ones. She felt her face flush.

"And your name is?" the guest asked.

"Rosa Mae, sir."

"Rosa Mae . . . ?"

"Rosa Mae Barlow, sir."

"Thank you, Miss Barlow."

"You welcome, sir," the woman said, not sure of anything except that the man was making her . . . well, not nervous, but . . .

The maid bustled about the room, a model of efficiency. "I come back and do the vacuuming later, sir," she said. "It's a big old noisy thing, and you—"

"I'd appreciate that, Miss Barlow," the man said. "Starting tomorrow, I'll remember about the sign, all right?"

"Yes, sir. Anything you say all right with me, sir. Thank you."

1959 September 30 Wednesday 09:51

Dett waited several minutes after the maid left his room, standing with his ear to the door. Satisfied, he quickly stepped outside and hung the "Do Not Disturb" sign over the doorknob. He locked the door behind him, kicked his wedge under it, and then closed the window curtains completely.

Taking a small key from his pocket, Dett unlocked his attaché case, removed some papers, pens, and a road map, then lifted the false bottom to reveal a pair of .45-caliber automatics, bedded in foam rubber. He carried the pistols over to the easy chair, turned on the floor lamp, and worked the slide on the first one. He looked down the barrel, using his thumbnail to reflect light. He unwrapped a soda straw and used it to blow out the barrel, then repeated the process with the other pistol.

Dett opened four small unmarked boxes, each containing thirty-six cartridges. He upended the boxes and examined each cartridge with great care, inspecting the primer, checking the fit between the casings and the slugs. Some were hardballs, others had been converted to dum-dums with a carefully carved "x" on each lead tip.

Dett dry-fired each weapon before he filled a magazine with seven cartridges and inserted it into the tape-wrapped butt of one of the pistols. He racked the slide, then ejected the magazine and replaced the chambered round. He did the same with the other pistol, flicking the custom-made extended safety off and on with his thumb.

From the larger suitcase, Dett removed an over-and-under 12-gauge shotgun. The stock had been replaced with a pistol grip, the barrels sawed off so deeply that the red tips of the double-0 buck shells were visible.

One of the pistols went into a shoulder holster, rigged to carry butt-down. The other went into the inside pocket of a long black overcoat. The coat looked like wool, but it was made of a lightweight synthetic fiber, with a network of leather loops sewn under the lining, accessed by long vertical slits. The shotgun slid perfectly into its custom-tailored pocket.

Dett filled the left outside pocket of the overcoat with six magazines for the .45s, and the right-hand pocket with shotgun shells. He knew from both practice and experience that he could walk around for hours in the heavily loaded coat without revealing a hint of its contents.

After carefully arranging the coat over a wooden hanger in the closet, Dett took off the shoulder rig and removed the pistol. Then he relocked the attaché case and returned to the easy chair. He turned off the floor lamp, poured some more of the Four Roses into a fresh tumbler, and let the drink sit there as he smoked a cigarette through.

When he was finished, he emptied the bourbon into the toilet, tossed in his cigarette, flushed, and returned to the easy chair.

After a few minutes, he reached for the telephone.

1959 September 30 Wednesday 11:22

"So he a big spender, what's that to me?" the cocoa-colored young woman in the maid's uniform said to Rufus. "He may put some money in *your* hand, but he ain't leaving no dollars on his pillow for Rosa Mae Barlow, that's for sure."

"Don't some of those traveling men leave you something, when they check out?" Rufus asked.

"I *heard* of that," the young woman said. "But I haven't seen it for myself. Everybody in this place got a hustle going except the maids. People work in the kitchen, you know they take home plenty of extras. A man with your job, he got *lots* of ways to make money. Guest wants some liquor, wants a woman, wants . . . anything, you always got your hand out. Mister Carl, too. When they have those big card games up in one of the suites, you know he's got to be getting something for himself."

"I heard the girls who clean up after those games, they get thrown some."

"Some *what*?" the young woman said, tartly. "I got to work that shift, once. All night long, picking up after all those men. You know what *I* got thrown? A few pats on my behind, that's what. One of the men, he said it brought him luck, do that. Didn't bring *me* no luck, I tell you that."

"It will, honeygirl. Swear to heaven. A woman put together like you, *got* to bring you luck, someday."

"You got me mixed up with those whores you bring up to the rooms, Rufus," she said, pridefully. "All I ever got out of looking the way I do is some fancy man with a ten-dollar conk and a flash suit and a big car he ain't paid for telling me what a 'star' I could be. Man I'm looking for, he's not going to want me for that kind of thing. That's why I go to church."

"Little girl, listen to someone who's telling you the truth. I don't care if he's a saint or a sinner, if he's a man, he's gonna want what *you* got, because, Lord knows, you got *all* of it."

"What do *you* want, Rufus?"

"Me?"

"You, boy," she said, tartly. "What do you want with me? Or are you just practicing your lines, in case some country girl comes to work here?"

"Right now, what I want is for you to be a little curious about that man in 809."

"What for?"

"I got a feeling about him, that's all."

"I got a feeling, too," Rosa Mae said, smiling. "I got a feeling that Rufus Hightower thinks there might be some green on the scene."

"Where you learn to talk like that, girl?" Rufus said, an under-current of anger in his voice.

"I been around men think they slick since I first grew these," she said, putting two fingers under her left breast and pushing up just enough to make it bounce sightly. "And I'm a real good listener."

"Rhyme ain't worth a dime," Rufus told her, winking. "But I got a pound I could put down, you want to look around."

"You so cute." Rosa Mae giggled. "But I can't buy new shoes with a promise."

She held out her hand, palm-up. Rufus handed over a five-dollar bill, watched it disappear into her bra.

"Either the man had some friends come and visit, or he's a big drinker," Rosa Mae said. "That bottle of whiskey he's got in his room's been hit plenty. But he don't keep himself like a drinking man."

"What do you mean?"

"A drinking man, specially one that drink in the morning, he don't keep himself nice. This one, all his clothes hanging up in the closet, neat as a pin. I got nothing to do in his bathroom, either. Most of the time, a man checks into a hotel, it's like he thinks he got a wife with him, mess he leave everyplace. Not this one. It's like he cleans up behind himself."

"Next thing, you gonna tell me he makes his own bed."

"He don't *make* the bed, but he sure do strip it down," Rosa Mae said. "Right down to the mattress. Takes the pillowcases off, too."

"Yeah? Well, what's in his suitcases?"

"I don't be opening nobody's suitcases, Rufus."

"No, no, girl. I meant, he *leave* them open, right?"

"He left one of them like that," the young woman acknowledged. "Nothing in there but clothes. I didn't look in the bureau, but he got all his shaving stuff and the like in the bathroom."

"The man say anything to you?"

"This morning, he did. There's no sign on his door, it's after eight, I figure he's out working so I let myself in. He's just sitting there, in the big chair, reading the paper. I tell him I can come back later, when he's out, but he tells me, just go ahead."

"I know you-all said something besides that, Rosa Mae."

"He just . . . polite, is all. A real gentleman. Some of the men that stay here, they *like* watching me clean up their rooms. I bend over to make the bed, I can feel their eyes. This man, he wasn't nothing like that."

"Maybe he'd like old Carl better than you," Rufus said, grinning.

"You believe that, you three kinds of fool, Rufus," she said, turning to go.

Rufus watched Rosa Mae walk down the hall. The exaggerated movement of her buttocks under the loose-fitting uniform was a lush promise, wrapped in a warning.

1959 September 30 Wednesday 11:45

"Yes?" Cynthia's voice on the phone was clear and clipped, just slightly north of polite.

"May I speak to Mr. Beaumont, please?"

"Who should I tell him is calling?"

"I'm the man he sent for. I believe he'll—"

"Call back in ten minutes," the woman's voice said. "This same number."

1959 September 30 Wednesday 11:50

R ufus ambled over to the pay phone in the basement, dropped a slug in the slot, and dialed a local number.

"What?" a male voice answered.

"This be Rufus, sir," Rufus said, thickening his long-since-outgrown Alabama accent and introducing a thread of servility into his voice. "I calling like you said."

"Yeah?"

"The man, he a drinker, sir. Big drinker."

"Can he hold it?"

"Seem so, sir. But ah cain't say fo' sure, 'cause he might be one of those, sleeps it off."

"What's he driving?"

"Got nothing out back in the lot, boss. And there ain't no plate number on the books from when he signed in."

"He didn't come in on the bus," the voice said, brawny with certainty. "I need to know what he's riding, understand?"

"Yes, *sir*. You know Rufus. I got peoples all over the place. I finds out for you."

"All right. He ask anyone to bring him anything?"

"Not no girl, if that what you mean, sir."

"Stop fucking around," the voice said, "and just tell me what I'm paying you for, understand?"

"Yes, sir. I wasn't . . . I mean, no, sir, the man don't ask me for nothing. Not none of the other boys, neither. 'Cept for a bottle of whiskey."

"Get me that car, understand?" the voice said.

"I—" Rufus started to reply, then realized the connection had been cut.

Yassuh, massah, Rufus said to himself, twisting his lips into something between a snarl and a sneer.

1959 September 30 Wednesday 11:56

"He wants to see you," Cynthia told Dett on the phone. "Do you have transportation?"

"Yes."

"What kind?"

"A car."

"Yes," the woman said, without a trace of impatience. "What kind of car? Year and model. And the license plate, too, please. The guard at the gate will need this to pass you through."

"A 1949 Ford, kind of a dull-blue color. The plate is: Ex, Oh, Bee, four, four, four."

"All right, let me give you the directions. Please be here by two."

1959 September 30 Wednesday 12:11

Dett slid the locked attaché case under the bed. From inside his Pullman, he removed a sculpture made of gnarled roots wrapped around a pair of doll's hands, clasped together in prayer by a single strand of rusty barbed wire. He placed this so it would greet anyone who opened the suitcase.

Dett shrugged into his overcoat, worked his shoulders in a slight circular motion until he was satisfied with the kinetic fit, then left the room.

He answered, "Good afternoon to you, too," to the elevator operator, deposited his key with the desk clerk, and walked out into the fall sunlight, eyes slitted against the glare.

Two blocks away, Dett hailed a passing cab. It deposited him in front of a seedy pawnshop just over a mile away.

Dett entered the pawnshop, pretended to examine a display of rings in a glass case while a man in a green eyeshade completed a transaction. As the customer moved off, clutching a few bills and a pawn ticket, Dett caught a nod from the proprietor and moved toward the end of the long counter. A buzzer sounded. Dett lifted the hinged portion of the counter and walked past a half-open bathroom door to a large storeroom, stocked floor-to-ceiling with goods: musical instruments, appliances, rifles, and hundreds of smaller items. The back door opened into a narrow paved lot, surrounded by a gated chain-link fence, topped with concertina wire.

Dett closed the door behind him, took a set of keys from his coat pocket, and walked over to a faded blue '49 Ford with a primered hood and chromed dual exhausts. The coupe had a slight forward rake, because the rear tires were larger than the fronts. Dett opened the door, climbed behind the wheel, and started it up, frowning at the engine noise.

He slipped the lever into first, let out the clutch, and pulled out of the lot.

1959 September 30 Wednesday 12:56

"He should be here pretty soon, Beau," Cynthia said.

"Good," Beaumont grunted, concentrating on shaving, using a pearl-handled straight razor against the grain.

"Beau . . . ?"

"What?" he said, carefully rinsing off his razor.

"This is the first time we ever did anything like this."

"You mean, use a contract man? You know we paid—"

"An outsider, is what I mean. We paid . . . different people to do different things, but they were always local men. If they didn't . . . do what they were supposed to, we would always know where to find them."

"Find their families, too, is what you're saying."

"That *is* what I'm saying. This man, he's not just a stranger, he's like a ghost. You make some calls, and he magically appears."

"So?" Beaumont asked, patting his face with a towel.

"I was just thinking. . . . If we're big enough to attract so much attention . . . from people who want to move in on us, I mean, maybe we're attracting attention from the law, too."

"The law? In Locke City? They're all on our—"

"Not the ones around here," Cynthia said, pacing nervously behind her brother. "I'm talking about the state police. Or even the FBI."

"That's what you're worried about? That this guy's some kind of secret agent?"

"I'm just trying to help," Cynthia said, hurt.

"You *always* help," Beaumont said, soothingly. "I wasn't making fun of you, honey." He spun his wheelchair so that he was facing his sister. "Remember, when we were kids, how you'd jump on anyone ever called me 'crip'? If I hadn't had you—"

"I had you, too, Beau," she said, a hand on his shoulder. "Do you remember Billy Yawls?"

"I do," Beaumont said, a broad grin breaking across his craggy face. "That was when I still had the braces."

"Yes! And when you challenged Billy, for . . . grabbing at me . . . he *had* to agree to make it wrestling. Otherwise, he would have looked like a—"

"Sure. And I was a couple of years younger than him, too. But once I took that skinny little weasel to the ground . . ."

"They never knew how strong you were, Beau. Not until that day."

"Yeah, I . . . Look, I'm sorry, honey. In fact, I already thought about what you're thinking right now. But the only way the law could ever stick a pin in *our* balloon is from the inside, and they could never pull that off.

"You think if the FBI could plant its own men inside the big mobs they wouldn't have done it a long time ago? But they can't. The Italians, the Irish, the Jews . . . they're all related, some kind of way. And can you even imagine the feds trying to get a man inside one of the colored gangs?" he said, chuckling. "What would they do, dye one of their guys black?"

"I don't know, Beau. If the Mafia is really as big as everyone says, how could they all be related to each other?"

"Well," Beaumont said slowly, "you're probably right. But we're not like them. Not like any of them. We may not all be related, but we know every single man, all the way back."

"We don't know this man you just hired, Beau. Not like that."

"That's true," Beaumont said, nodding to show his sister he had thought deeply about her concerns before making his decision. "But he's just a contract man. It's not like we're making him one of us. He's never going to get inside."

Beaumont wheeled himself back to the specially constructed sink, slapped an astringent on his face, then spun again to face his sister.

"One thing we know about the feds, Cyn: they got unlimited funds. Money, that's power. It can buy things. It can buy people. The way it's told, that's how they got someone to give up Dillinger—the reward. But, still, John was way ahead of them."

"Ahead of them?" Cynthia said, almost angrily. "Beau, they *killed* him. Gunned him down right on the sidewalk."

"That wasn't John Dillinger," Beaumont said, a true-believer, reciting an article of faith. "It was a fall guy. A patsy. The guy they killed, I heard he didn't even have the right color eyes. Didn't have any bullet scars on him, either. No, honey, Dillinger's somewhere south of the border. He's not dead," Beaumont repeated, devoutly.

"But if what you say is true, then they *know.*"

"The FBI? Sure, they know. What difference does it make to them? They got Public Enemy Number One. Big heroes. So long as Dillinger stays missing, everybody's happy."

"But what if he ever—?"

"John Dillinger, everybody admired him for his moxie. He's the stand-up guy of all time. Busting his boys out of jail, carving a gun out of a bar of soap—can you believe suckers actually bought that one?—he's like a legend. But what people didn't appreciate about him was how smart he was. He never worked for any of the outfits. He stayed independent, worked with guys he knew he could trust, not guys some boss *told* him he could trust.

"John was a genius," Beaumont said, lost in idolatry. "He knew it's not about the truth of anything; it's always about what people believe. The papers, they played him up like he was a god. Hoover doesn't get Dillinger, it makes it look like the outlaws are stronger than the cops. So they make a deal. Hoover's boys kill a patsy, and Dillinger walks away."

"You don't *know* any of that, Beau."

"The hell I don't, girl. Those guys who write the newspaper stories, they're just like the people who write ads, like for toothpaste, or beer, or cars. It's their job to *sell* you something, not to tell you the truth."

"Even if it *is* so, people *do* inform," Cynthia said, hotly. "They do it all the time. Look at all those Communists."

"Sure. But those guys, they were . . . members. Real insiders, I mean. With this guy we're bringing in, you're not talking about one of us. He's nothing but a hired gun."

"But couldn't an FBI agent *pretend* to be the same thing? Like a spy?"

"Not a chance, girl. There's a line no undercover cop can cross, and this guy, he *lives* over it, see?"

"No," she said, adamantly. "I don't under—"

"The feds, let's say you're right, and they actually get one of their men inside one of the big mobs. Naturally, they'd have to let their guy do stuff, so nobody would get suspicious. If he had to steal, or hand out a beating, okay. But how is the FBI going to let one of their men *kill* someone? And this guy we're bringing in, he's put more bodies in the ground than an undertaker."

"If *that's* enough reason to trust him, then Lymon—"

"Exactly!" Beaumont cut her off. "Lymon's pulled the trigger himself, more than once. So if he tried to hook up with another mob, he might tell some of our secrets—what he *thinks* are secrets—to grease the skids. But he can't ever go to the law about us, not with what's on his own plate."

"But if all we know about this Dett person is rumors . . ."

"We got better than that, girl. A lot better. An actual eyewitness. Red said this guy walked into a nightclub, shot the bouncer, tossed a grenade into the crowd, and walked out, like he was delivering the mail."

"Why would Red want him to—?"

"It was war," Beaumont told his sister. "And this guy, he's a soldier. Only not like for a country, for whoever pays him. But Red says that grenade thing, it was Dett's own idea."

"God."

"Yeah. And that squares with what else I heard. Walker Dett, he's not just a shooter. He plans strategy, like a general or something."

"What kind of a man would do that?"

"That's not our worry, Cyn. All we care about is what kind of man *wouldn't* do it, understand? We don't know what this 'Dett' guy is, but we know what he's not. Whatever he is, he's no lawman."

1959 September 30 Wednesday 13:27

Dett drove the back roads gingerly, experimenting with the Ford's reaction to various maneuvers. *Piece of crap,* he said to himself, as he muscled the coupe around an unbanked curve. The steering was rubbery, and the brakes were a joke—even with skillful pumping, the stopping distances were way too long, and the car always nosedived to the right.

He wasn't lying about how it scoots, though, Dett thought. He had to balloon-foot the gas pedal to avoid spinning the rear wheels aimlessly in first gear, and even the first-to-second shift caused the tires to bark against the asphalt.

And the car *had* been delivered clean, inside and out. The only indication of prior human presence was the registration slip in the glove compartment.

"This is the guy you borrowed the car from," the black man in the yellow shirt had told him. "Police call the number I gave you, somebody say, 'Sure, I loaned my car to Mr. Dett.' Describe you good, too."

"Very nice," Dett had said.

"I know my business, Chuck," the black man replied, choosing to resent the compliment.

Dett followed the directions he had been given, keeping the Ford in second gear in case he needed the extra braking power on unfamiliar roads. Every time he eased off the gas, the dual exhausts crackled, announcing his oncoming presence. *Makes no difference,* he thought to himself, noting a dozen spots where a sniper could roost along the way, *it's not like I'm sneaking up on them.*

He spotted the black boulder, proceeded as directed until he came to the guardhouse. Dett slowed the Ford to a near crawl as he approached, his window already rolled down.

Seth stepped out, shotgun in one hand, and gestured with the other for Dett to get out of his car. Dett turned off the engine and climbed out of the Ford, tossing the keys underhand at Seth, who caught them smoothly without shifting his eyes.

"Your spare's about bald," he said, glancing into the trunk.

"Thanks," Dett said.

Seth placed the car keys on the Ford's roof, then stepped back to let Dett reclaim them.

Dett started the Ford, and motored along slowly until he came to the horseshoe-shaped driveway. He parked just beyond the entrance to the house, leaving the key in the ignition.

The door was opened before he could knock. A bull-necked man held his gaze for several seconds before he said, "You can't come in here with guns."

Dett nodded, holding his hands away from his body.

"Put them on that table over there," the man told him, his marble eyes unblinking.

Dett took off his overcoat, held it by the collar to indicate it was heavy, and draped it carefully across the table.

"That's all," he said, not offering to remove any of the weapons within the coat.

The marble-eyed man nodded. "Go down that way, there," he said. "I'll be right behind you."

1959 September 30 Wednesday 13:59

If Dett was surprised to see the man who hired him sitting in a wheelchair, it didn't show on his face.

"My name is Royal Beaumont," the man in the wheelchair said. "Have a seat."

Dett took the indicated chair. The marble-eyed man positioned himself at a sharp angle, so that Dett would have to turn his head to see him.

"Sorry about all the precautions," Beaumont said. "The times we live in . . ."

Dett nodded silently, his face impassive.

"Red Schoolfield says you did a hell of a job for him."

"I don't recognize the name," Dett said.

"Hah!" said Beaumont, more of a bark than a laugh. "This one doesn't put his cards face-up, huh, Luther?"

"No, Roy," the marble-eyed man said, mechanically.

"You're wrong," Dett said, not a trace of aggression in his tone.

"How's that?" Beaumont asked—curious, not annoyed.

"Some other man's name, that's not my card to play. Not even to hold."

"Huh!" Beaumont grunted. "That's cute."

"That's true," Dett said, leaving the multiple interpretations of his response hanging in the air between them.

Silence like a fine mist dropped over the three men.

Beaumont studied the man seated across from him, making no secret of it. Dett never dropped his veiled eyes.

"There's a lot of work I need doing," Beaumont finally said.

"Okay."

"Just like that, 'okay'?"

"If you called a bricklayer out to your house, told him you needed some work done, that's what he'd say, right? I mean, you'd have to tell him what kind of brickwork you wanted done, but, if he was good at his trade, whatever kind you wanted, you asked him, he'd say 'okay.' "

"You're no bricklayer."

"You're the one who put word out that you wanted me; you know the kind of work I do."

"I don't actually *know* anything," Beaumont said. "I *heard* things. I've been *told* things. But I don't know anything for myself."

"I don't do auditions," Dett said, opening his antenna for tension from Luther, picking up none.

"What's that mean?"

"If you want to see a sample of a bricklayer's work, you go look at a wall he's built for someone else. If that's not enough to convince you to hire him for a big job, maybe you ask him to build you something first. But a small job. Like a barbecue pit, say."

"So?"

"So, the kind of work I do, I don't make samples. You ask me to build you a barbecue pit, just to see how good I am, it costs you the same as a brick wall."

"You always talk like this?" Beaumont said. "In big circles?"

"Talking's not what I do," Dett answered him.

Beaumont, no stranger to edged ambiguity, nodded without changing expression. He reached for his cigarette box, tapped out a single smoke, and lit it with a gunmetal Zippo.

Not like some, snap their fingers for a flunky to light their smokes for them, show you what a big shot they are, Dett thought, appraisingly. *And the other one, he calls him "Roy," not "boss" or "chief."*

"You don't smoke?" Beaumont asked him.

"I wanted to keep my hands where Luther could see them."

This time, Beaumont's laugh was genuine. "You know what, Mr. Dett? You know more about Luther in ten minutes than some of the boys I've had working with me ten years. All they ever hear out of Luther's mouth is 'Yes, Roy,' or 'No, Roy.' So they think he's . . ."

"Dumb."

"Right," Beaumont said. "But . . . ?"

"He's a professional," Dett answered promptly. "No, wait. He's more than that. More than *just* that, I mean. He's kin, isn't he?"

"Not by blood. You understand what that means?"

"By what he's done."

"Yeah. By what he's done. By what he'd *do*. And what *I'd* do, too."

"I understand."

"I believe you do," Beaumont said, exhaling a thick stream of cigarette smoke.

1959 September 30 Wednesday 15:03

"I could get myself killed, talking to a goddamned reporter," the man in the moss-colored coat said to Procter. His eyes were wary behind the thick lenses of his glasses; his hands gripped an aluminum clipboard.

The two men were in the front seat of Procter's '54 Hudson Hornet, a rust-wormed brown coupe that was on its ninth owner and last gasp.

"All I want to know is where the new interstate is coming through," Procter said. "That's not too much to ask."

"Not too much to ask! Information like that's worth a—"

"It's worth whatever Beaumont paid you for it," Procter cut him off.

"I never said—"

"You know what, Yancey? You're making me tired. You and me, we've had a deal. A working relationship. I've held up my end of the bargain, haven't I?"

"I'm not saying you haven't," Yancey said, sullenly. "But when am I done paying that off?"

"Ever borrow money from a loan shark?" Procter asked him, smiling without showing any teeth.

"No. Why should I—?"

"It's the *principle* I'm trying to make you understand, Yancey. That's a play on words, you get it? The principle of principal and interest. A six-for-five man makes his living from when you *don't* pay him off. He doesn't *want* his money back; he wants you to keep paying the juice."

"You're saying I'll *never* get those letters back?"

"Right, Yancey. That *is* what I'm saying."

"That's blackmail."

"It was blackmail the first time I did it," Procter said. "Now it's just a habit."

"Jesus, Jimmy; we went to school together!"

"Lots of guys went to school together. You, me, Carl Gustavson . . ."

"It's not what you think it is . . . *was*. Those letters, they don't mean what you—"

"I'm tired," Procter repeated. "You think I'm bluffing, go ahead and call my hand."

Yancey pulled up the top sheet from the clipboard, revealing a road map with a number of red lines hand-drawn across it. "Yeah, you're the great investigative reporter, Jimmy," he said bitterly. "Big crime-buster. You know what? You're no better than the people you're going after."

"That's what it takes," Procter said.

1959 September 30 Wednesday 15:40

"I'm not doing nothing like that, Rufus Hightower. Stealing is no different than whoring; you can't do no 'little bit' of it."

"Did I ask you to *take* anything, honeygirl? Did I? No, I sure didn't. And I wouldn't. I know what kind of woman you are. Kind of woman a man marries, he gets lucky enough."

"Kind of man wants a fool for a wife, you mean," Rosa Mae said, not mollified.

"You *supposed* to be in the man's room, Rosa Mac. That's your job. You said you had to come back, do the vacuuming, right?"

"I *supposed* to be cleaning his room—not searching it, like some thief."

"It's not thieving if you don't take nothing. There's no crime in looking."

"Why you so interested in this man, Rufus? I know he never did nothing to you."

"Now who's playing someone like a fool, girl? You know it ain't me that's interested in that man. What I'm interested in is—"

"—money. Pastor Roberts says—"

"Think I give a damn what some high-yellow, straight-hair pretty-boy says? Every man got to have a hustle of some kind. You know how the song goes: if you white, you all right; if you brown, stick around; but if you black, get back. That's me, Rosa Mae. I don't have that nice paper-bag complexion; I ain't got good hair;

and my nose is spread all over my face. So I don't apologize for none of what I do. I may be about money, but I got a good use for it."

"And what's that?"

"Someday, I'll tell you, girl. I've been wanting to do that for a long time. But, for now, I tell you what it's *not* for—it's not for no big white Cadillac, like your jackleg preacher got."

"You just jealous, Rufus."

"You want to say I'm jealous because that man get you all big-eyed, you be telling the truth, girl. When I see you sometimes, just standing there, I say to myself, 'Damn, I wish that woman was waiting for *me*.' But I don't care nothing about that nigger otherwise."

"Rufus!"

"What you think he is, to all the white people, Rosa Mae? You think a colored man ain't always a nigger to them? Doctor, lawyer, preacher—don't make no difference."

"That's all changing now. If you went to church sometimes, you might learn about it."

"If *you* went to . . . Never mind."

"Rufus, you are the most downright . . . confusing man I ever met."

"Rosa Mae, if I was to tell you taking a look around that man's room, it would be doing something for our people, would you believe me?"

"For our people? You mean, like for integration?"

"For *our* people, girl. Not for mixing. I ain't about that."

"You . . . what? Rufus, why shouldn't we have the same rights as any—?"

"That's not what I meant," Rufus said. "Someday . . . maybe, I'll talk to you about all this. But not now. This ain't the time. This is the time to make some money."

"Well, I'm not going to—"

"That's all right," Rufus said, shrugging his shoulders. "You only work six days."

"Of course. I wouldn't work on—"

"I know. But you think the man don't want his room cleaned,

just because it Sunday? Don't worry about it no more, girl. I'll get Big Annie to do what I need."

Rosa Mae stepped back a pace from Rufus, widening her lively amber eyes. "You'll get caught, Rufus," she said. "Annie's like a cow in those rooms. The man will know as soon as he—"

"Then I guess I lose my job, pretty Rose. Because I got no choice. I *got* to do this."

He looked Rosa Mae full in the face for a long moment. "I'm sorry I asked you," he finally said.

Rosa Mae closed her eyes and stepped close to him, her voice just above a whisper.

"You be here at five-thirty," she said.

1959 September 30 Wednesday 15:59

"I guess what I need is an outside bodyguard," Beaumont said.

"I don't understand what that means," Dett replied.

"I mean, not a bodyguard who stands right next to me. Only Luther does that. A bodyguard who works . . . at a distance. Let's say, just to be talking, there was this guy who, I don't know, threatened to kill me, all right? Now, the kind of bodyguard Luther is, a thing like that was happening, he would never leave my side. You couldn't *make* him go. But the other kind of bodyguard, the one I'm talking about here, he might go out and look for the guy who was making the threats."

"I get it."

"But what I need done, it's a lot more than any one single job. You were in the service, right?"

Dett didn't answer, his face as blank as a career criminal's in a police interrogation room.

"Never mind," Beaumont said. "I was never in the army"—he rapped his heavy ring against the steel of his wheelchair—"but I always liked reading about military tactics and strategy."

Beaumont shifted position in his chair, but his iron eyes never left Dett's face. "We've got a good-sized operation here," he said.

"Been here for a long time. But now there's some who want what my people have. We know they're already on the march. So what I need isn't any one single job. It's more like a . . . campaign."

He leaned forward to grind out his cigarette. When he looked up, his head was tilted at a slight angle, his tone almost professorial. "Now they've got more men than we do—not right here, but access to them, no more than a phone call away. A long-distance call. But it's our territory they're invading, so they have to come to us. And in a million years, they'll never know the terrain the way we do.

"Still, it's not that simple. Some of what we do, it's out in the open. Easy to find means easy to take. Which is what they think. You know what makes a big army just give up and go home?"

"When there's no end in sight. Like Korea. A war like that, all it does is drain you dry."

"Right! Winning a war's a lot easier than trying to occupy the territory you take. If we wanted, we could make it too expensive for them, cost them too much. But there's something else we have to consider, something even more important. Locke City is a wide-open town, everyone knows that. We're right on the border of two other states. This is where people come, they want to have a good time. But if we start drawing too much attention, that could all go away."

"Attention from who?"

"Well, the papers, that would be the biggest problem. We've got everything covered locally, but the statewide paper, or, worse, the wire services, that's another thing."

"They had gang wars in plenty of cities, and they still kept their operations going. Look at Detroit, Chicago, New York. . . ."

"Sure. Towns that size, there's plenty of legitimate businesses to keep them running. But Locke City's only got one way to make a buck. And if people don't feel safe anymore, coming here to have a good time, they'll stop coming, period. That happens, there'll be nothing to fight over."

"What do you want me to do?"

"Do? Well, like I said, you're the strategist. Maybe you can put up that barbecue pit we talked about?"

"Front!" Carl's waspish voice rang more sharply than the desk bell.

Rufus materialized. Despite his overwhelmingly intrusive curiosity about everything that went on within the borders of his domain, Carl had long since abandoned his efforts at discovering how Rufus never seemed to be around, yet was always present.

"Mr. Travis will be staying with us, Rufus," Carl said, indicating a chubby man in a madras sport jacket.

Good thing you told me, faggot, Rufus thought to himself. *I never would have figured out why a man comes into a fucking hotel carrying a suitcase.* He smiled at the guest, said, "I'll take that for you, sir."

"Mr. Travis will be in 412," Carl said to Rufus, thinking fat men shouldn't wear madras plaid, never mind with a tab-collar shirt. He had already sized up—*No pun intended,* he thought to himself, smugly—the guest as a salesman even before he had seen his business card. A cut above a traveler who carried samples in his suitcase, but a step below the "detail men" who hawked new pharmaceutical products to local doctors and druggists.

Rufus had done his own quick evaluation, and was later rewarded with a quarter for providing the directions to a "high-class" house of prostitution. *You that kind of big spender, good thing you don't be trying your luck picking up a woman on your own, Porky,* Rufus thought behind his dazzling smile and grateful bow.

"You seen Rosa Mae around?" he asked Moses, as he climbed into the elevator car for the return trip.

"She be working somewhere, one of the rooms," was the noncommittal response.

"What's up with you, man?"

"Don't know what you mean."

"With the *attitude,* man. I just asked you a simple question, you get all huffy with me."

"Rufus, you know Rosa Mae. Her shift starts, *she* starts. That's a hardworking young gal."

"Too good for the likes of me, huh? Just because she call you 'Daddy Moses' like the young girls here do, that don't make you her father for real."

"Might be lucky for your sorry ass that I'm not," Moses said, unperturbed.

Rufus burst out laughing. "Our people need more men like you, brother. Square business."

1959 September 30 Wednesday 17:28

"I just want to talk," Procter said into a telephone receiver.

"No, you don't," a man's voice answered. "What you want, you want to listen."

"That's my business, Chet. Listening."

"Mine, too. Only you, you get a paycheck for it."

"And you get cash. That's nicer. No taxes."

"Paycheck's better. Regular is always better. Something you can count on."

"There was a time when you counted on me," Procter said.

"You don't forget nothing, do you?"

"I don't tear up IOUs, either," Procter said. "I'll see you tonight. By the water tower."

1959 September 30 Wednesday 17:31

"Rosa Mae, what is *wrong* with you, girl? You look like you seen a ghost."

"Not a ghost, Rufus. A mojo. A powerful one."

"What you—?"

"In the gentleman's room."

"Eight oh nine?"

"*Yes!* I finished cleaning his room, just like I'm supposed to. And then, like the fool you made me be, I opened his big suitcase. It wasn't locked or anything. And the second I opened it, I could see why. You know what a mojo is, Rufus?"

"Yeah. Hoodoo nonsense is what it is."

"No, it's *not,*" the young woman said, vehemently, almost hissing the words. "It's like one of those conjure bags you wear around your neck, to keep evil spirits off you. Only this one, it was *real* powerful. I could tell."

"I thought you was a Christian woman, Rosa Mae," Rufus scoffed, trying to soften her fear.

"I am," she said, staunchly. "I have been baptized, and I have been saved. But that doesn't mean I don't know things. Things my granny told me when I was just a little girl, before I ever come up here. I never saw one myself, not before. But I know about the barbed wire around the hands. That's a protection mojo, Rufus."

"So you saw this thing and—"

"And? And I slammed down the lid so quick I scared myself! I got my cleaning things and I got out of there."

"You didn't put it back where you—?"

"Rufus, are you crazy? I never *touch* it."

"Probably just some souvenir the man picked up somewhere. He's a traveling man, could have been anywhere."

"I never heard of a white man having anything like that. You could only get them way down in the Delta, my granny said. Or over to Louisiana. Special places, where they know how to work roots. Places like that, they wouldn't be selling no *souvenirs,* Rufus."

"Maybe he stole it, then."

"You can't steal a mojo! You know what happens if you do that?"

"What?"

"I . . . I don't know, exactly. But I know you can't do it."

"Rosa Mae, did you find out *anything*?"

"I done told you what I found," Rosa Mae said. "And I promise you, Rufus Hightower, I'm never doing nothing like that again, not ever."

1959 September 30 Wednesday 18:29

Dett circled the block three times, marking the pattern of the streets, weighing the odds. He was in his shirtsleeves, suit jacket next to him on the front seat; his heavily armed coat was locked in the trunk. Full darkness was a couple of hours off, and Beaumont had told him the man he wanted only showed up much later in the evenings, in the seam between the dinner crowd and the night-hawks.

Dett turned onto Fourteenth Street, a black asphalt four-lane, divided by a double white line. As he pulled up to a light, a candy-apple '55 Chevy slid alongside. The driver revved his engine in neu-tral, a challenge. Dett nodded in satisfaction at the assumption that the Ford he was driving belonged to some kid. He pressed down the clutch, slipped the floor shift to the left and down, and accepted the offer.

The Chevy took off a split second before the light turned green, but Dett's Ford caught up before the first-to-second shift . . . which Dett deliberately missed, his engine roaring impotently as the Chevy went through the next light on the green.

To avoid having the Chevy's driver offer him a rematch, Dett quickly turned off the main drag and made his way back to the pawnshop.

Just like the man promised, Dett said to himself, absently pat-ting the dashboard of the Ford.

1959 September 30 Wednesday 19:31

"Good evening, Mr. Dett," Carl greeted him an hour later. "It's been amazingly warm for this time of year, don't you think?"

"Well, I couldn't say," Dett replied. "I'm not from around here. Were there any messages while I was out?"

"I'm not sure, sir," Carl said, lying. "Let me check." He retrieved the key to 809, said, "Were you expecting anything in particular, sir?"

Dett answered with a negative shake of his head.

"Well, if there's anything you want me to keep.an eye out for . . ."

"I don't think so," Dett said. "Thanks, anyway."

"Is there anything I can tell you about our town, Mr. Dett? I've often said that an establishment like the Claremont should have a proper concierge, but our manager always says he could never find anyone who knows Locke City the way I do," Carl said, permitting himself a self-deprecating little laugh. "Of course, we have a wonderful kitchen, quite first-class, but the menu isn't as . . . varied as some more sophisticated travelers seem to prefer. Especially if you're going to be with us for—"

"Do you have any Korean restaurants in town?"

"Korean? Well, I must say . . . that's the first time I've ever been asked that one. I'm sorry to say no, Mr. Dett. We have a number of decent Chinese restaurants, and one Japanese place that just opened, if you are partial to Oriental cuisine, but . . ."

"How about French?"

"French?" said Carl, ever alert for double-entendre. But an instinct honed over a thousand encounters convinced him there hadn't been a trace of it in Dett's question. "I should say so. Chez Bertrand is a *lovely* place: four stars, without a doubt. Would you like me to make a reservation for—?"

"That doesn't sound like the sort of place a man goes to alone," Dett said.

"Well, one never knows," Carl said, raising an eyebrow a millimeter.

"You're right about that," Dett said.

"Very good, sir. You just let me know."

1959 September 30 Wednesday 19:41

Dett ordered dinner from room service. The steak came medium-rare, as he had requested. The green beans were firm, with a little snap to them as he bit down. The baked potato was in its skin, slit down the center, slathered with butter.

It took Dett more than an hour to finish his meal, washing down each fully masticated mouthful with a measured sip from one of the three Cokes he had ordered.

Dett got to his feet and stood by the window, watching the night.

He smoked two cigarettes, spaced twelve minutes apart, cupping his hands each time he struck a match, shielding the red tip in his palm whenever he took a drag.

Glancing at his watch, he emptied what he estimated at about four more shots of the Four Roses into the sink, running hot water behind it. He opened his Pullman, carefully removed the mojo, and transferred it to his smaller suitcase.

Dett put his tray outside the door, hung the "Do Not Disturb" sign over the knob, and turned off all the lights in his room. In the darkness, he removed all the weapons from his overcoat and returned them to their custom housings. He slipped his derringer into the side pocket of a blue denim jacket, worn over a black-and-red lumberjack shirt and faded jeans. On his feet were heavy, rubber-soled electrician's boots.

Turning the radio dial until he found a station with a mature-sounding DJ, Dett adjusted the volume down to bedside level. He cracked the door, then stepped out into the empty corridor and headed for the staircase.

Dett stepped out the side door on the first floor and into the night. He walked to the pawnshop in under thirty minutes; there he stood in line behind a tired-looking woman and a young man with pronounced hand tremors.

"How late are you open?" he asked the man behind the counter, after the place had cleared.

"Midnights, except for Fridays and Saturdays."

"You close early then?"

"Don't close at all then," the man said, adjusting his eyeshade. "We do some of our best business in that slot. Always got at least one other man with me, sometimes two."

"If you're closed when I want to bring the car back . . ."

"Just park it right out front. Or as near as you can get to it. I live upstairs. And I don't sleep much."

"I'm not worried about somebody stealing it, I just—"

"—don't want it on the street," the pawnbroker said. "I got it. I'll take care of it."

"I only have the one set of keys."

"I can take care of that, too," the pawnbroker said.

1959 September 30 Wednesday 22:07

The diner was a chrome-and-glass rectangle, standing in its own glow like a frontier outpost. The parking lot was almost empty, randomly sprinkled with a few cars and a single pickup. Dett backed the Ford into a remote corner, outside the spray of light from the windows.

"He always covers the same route," Beaumont had told Dett. "But not always in the same order. Thursday nights, he's going to hit Armand's place; that's one we know they've cut in on for sure. He's also got—"

"When you say 'cut in,' you mean your people have been cut out?" Dett had interrupted.

"No," the man in the wheelchair said. "Everyone has to get their jukeboxes from us. That's the way it's been ever since . . . for a long time. Dioguardi's people, they've been collecting a 'maintenance fee,' or a 'service charge,' or whatever they think is cute. This particular punk, Nicky Perrini, he tells them it's 'rent.' Don't ask me why."

The interior of the diner was a reflection of the parking lot— very few people, no two together. The long counter had only three stools occupied. In the booths strung along the windows, two men were working on solitary meals; one was reading a newspaper, the other staring into some private abyss.

No one looked up at Dett's entrance. He quickly scanned the interior, noting a sign for the restrooms at the extreme left, and took a counter stool a little more than halfway down the right side. A hundred-record Wurlitzer jukebox sat by itself in the corner, a squat chunk of pulsating neon, waiting for an injection of coins to bring it to life.

Dett took a menu from between a pair of chrome napkin dispensers and laid it flat on the counter in front of him. He let his eyes go out of focus, tuning in to his surroundings.

"What'll it be?"

Dett looked up, saw a short blond woman in a pink waitress's uniform with a round white collar and matching white bands on the short sleeves. She had a pert face with plump cheeks, her jaw saved from squareness only by a little sheath of flesh. Her eyes were a startling ocean green; they seemed almost absurdly large on either side of her button nose. Below her right eye was a crescent-shaped scar, dull white against her creamy skin, trailing like a permanent tear. Her mouth was small and lightly lipsticked, her lower lip heavier than the upper.

I've got much better clothes than these, leaped unbidden into Dett's mind. Before he could chase the thought, the counter girl said, "What you want is the lemon pie, I bet." Her smile sunbursted over him. "It's what everybody comes here for. At least that's what I tell Booker—he's the cook, but I'm the one who makes the pies."

"The lemon pie sounds perfect," he said, looking down.

"Money back if not satisfied," the girl said, nodding her head for emphasis. Her tousled blond curls bounced. "A cup of coffee with that?"

"Yes, please."

Dett watched her as she walked away. *Her arms are so round,* he thought, *but not fat. They look strong. I'll bet her legs are—*

The sound of the door opening behind him broke his reverie. He shifted his position on the stool, covering the movement by reaching for his cigarettes. Dett immediately dismissed the new arrival—an elderly man in an engineer's cap—and put the pack of cigarettes back into his jacket pocket.

"See if I'm lying," the counter girl said, sliding a substantial wedge of pie on a heavy white china plate in front of him.

"I know you wouldn't lie," Dett said, before he could clamp his mouth down on the words.

"How could you know something like that?" the girl asked, cocking her head and putting one hand on her hip. "Are you one of those people who think they can look in your eyes and—?"

"No. I don't have any . . . powers, or anything," Dett said. "Not like that. I mean . . . I could just tell."

"You don't even know my name," the girl said, smiling. "We used to have these nameplates," she said, red-tipped fingers lightly fluttering over her left breast, "but the pins tore up the uniforms something terrible."

"My name's Walker," Dett said, holding out his hand.

The girl hesitated a second, then reached over and shook his hand, formally. "You have nice manners, Mr. Walker," she said.

"Way I was raised."

"Then you weren't raised around *here,*" she said, flashing her smile again.

"No . . ."

"What?"

"I was . . . stuck, I guess. I was going to say, 'No, ma'am,' but I couldn't call . . . I mean, you're way too young to be called 'ma'am,' but you're too old . . . I mean too *grown* for me to be calling you 'miss,' so I was just . . ."

"My name's Tussy," she said, flashing her smile.

"Tussy?"

"Well, that's not my *real* name, but people have been calling me that since I was a little girl."

Dett stared at her until he realized his mouth was slightly open. He tightened his lips, said, "Where did you get a name like that?"

"When I was little, I was a tomboy. My mother didn't know what to do with me. One day, she was telling my dad he'd have to spank me himself because *hers* weren't doing any good. But he just said, 'There's nothing wrong with our Carol. She just likes a good tussle, that's all.' From then on, that was my name, Tussy. Even my teachers at school said it. Tussy Chambers, that's me."

"It's a beautiful name."

"Well, *I* like it. But I never heard anyone call it 'beautiful' before."

They must have called you *beautiful,* Dett thought, then smothered his thoughts as firmly as he had tightened his lips. "It's . . . unusual," he finally said. "Different."

"Pick up!" came a good-natured bellow from the kitchen.

"Milk or cream?" she said, ignoring the noise.

"Black's fine."

"Be right back," the blonde said, over her shoulder.

1959 September 30 Wednesday 22:19

Dett stared at the slice of lemon pie, examining it minutely, as if it could explain what was disconcerting him.

The counter girl came into his field of vision and his thoughts at the same time. "You did say black, right?" she asked.

"Thank you, yes," said Dett. He drank coffee only occasionally, preferring Coke with every meal except for juice at breakfast. When he did take coffee, he always laced it heavily with sugar. He was about to explain . . . something, when he felt the air behind him compress.

"You got the rent?" a voice said. A man's voice, young and trying too hard.

"Just a minute," Tussy said. "I'm serving a customer."

"Yeah? I could use a cup of coffee myself."

"Then have a seat. I'll get to you."

Out of the corner of his left eye, Dett saw a man in his mid-twenties take a stool near the register. He was wearing a one-button gray sharkskin suit, cut too tight to conceal a weapon. Dett's eyes went to the man's camel's-hair overcoat, which he had carefully folded on the stool next to him. *Right-handed,* Dett thought.

"Here you go," Tussy said, expertly sliding a cup of coffee onto the countertop in front of Dett.

"Thanks. I—"

She was already in motion, moving toward the man in the sharkskin suit. He said something to her Dett couldn't make out. Whatever it was didn't earn him a response, much less one of her smiles. She punched two keys on the register simultaneously, took out a couple of bills, and handed them over. The man in the sharkskin suit pocketed the cash.

"You're not going to try my pie?" she said, as she walked back toward Dett.

"I was just . . . looking at it," he told her.

"What good is *looking* at a piece of pie?" she said, smiling to show she wasn't being critical.

"It's part of . . . I don't know, exactly. You've picked flowers, haven't you?"

"Well, sure I have."

"But first you looked them over, right?"

"That was to make up my *mind*," she said. "There's *lots* of flowers, but there's only that one piece of pie."

"I—"

"Oh!" she said, blushing. "I'm so dumb. You're making up your mind, aren't you? Deciding if it looks good enough to—"

"No!" Dett said, more sharply than he had intended. He mentally bit down on his tongue. "I'm not good at explaining things, sometimes. I was trying to say . . . I was trying to say that it looks so good, I wanted to have *that,* too. Not just the taste. The whole . . . thing."

"I think I—"

"Hey!" the man in the sharkskin suit called. "What about that coffee, doll? I got other places I need to be tonight."

Tussy turned and walked toward the man. But she strolled right past him and into the kitchen. As Dett saw the man's face darken, he felt his heartbeat accelerate. *It's not supposed to do that,* he thought. *Not when I'm—*

The waitress came back through the swinging doors hip-first. As she passed the man in the sharkskin suit, she quickly placed a cup and saucer on the counter and kept moving, until she was standing in front of Dett again.

"You're *never* going to eat that," she mock-pouted.

"I . . . can't."

"Well, why in the world not?"

"Because you can't talk to a lady with your mouth full."

The waitress stepped back, as if the changed perspective would give her greater insight into the man before her.

"You're some piece of work, Mr. Walker. One minute, you're all tongue-tied; the next, you've got a line as slick as that boy's hair oil," she said, tilting her head in the direction of the man in the sharkskin suit.

"It's not *Mister* Walker," Dett said. "Walker is my first name. My name is Walker Dett."

"Uh-huh . . ." she said, but her lips were beginning to turn into a smile.

"If I start eating, you're going to go away?"

"Well, I have to—"

"Oh, I know, you must have a lot to do, being the manager here and all."

"Manager? Me? Managers don't wear uniforms like this."

"I'm sorry. I just thought, with you paying the landlord, this must either be your place or you're running it for someone."

"Oh! That guy, he's not the landlord. He just collects rent for the jukebox."

"Rent? I thought you bought those things."

"Well, you *do*. But you have to pay for the space. It's . . . a little complicated."

"I'm sorry. I didn't mean to be nosy. I was just . . . interested, I guess."

"You better eat that pie!" she said, sternly, and went back to the kitchen.

1959 September 30 Wednesday 23:09

By the time Dett was done with his pie, the man in the sharkskin suit had been gone for over a half-hour. The waitress had removed his cup and saucer, plucking a single bill from underneath. As she walked back toward Dett, she held up the five-dollar bill for him to see.

"Big shot," she said.

"He always tips like that?"

"Meg—she works the same shift as me; we take turns behind the counter—Meg says he does, but it's always a dollar, not a five. This, this is ridiculous."

"It made you mad?"

"Mad? Why would you think . . . Oh, damn! I'm blushing, right?"

"You're a little pink."

"You mean I'm a lobster! I know what I look like when I get mad. You don't have to be nice."

"Why did it make you mad, what he did?"

"Some of the girls, if they know a guy's a big tipper, they'll give him a little . . . extra. You know what I mean. Meg knows you're a big spender, you get a real floor show!"

"And you think that's what he expected?"

"I don't know *what* he expected, but . . . whatever it is, he'd better come around when Meg's behind the counter."

"The pie was perfect. It was the best I ever had."

"You're very nice to say that."

"It's the truth. But now I don't know what to do."

"What do you mean?"

"I'm not like . . . him," Dett said, tilting his head in the direction of the register. "I wouldn't want you to think I'm trying to be a big shot. Or that I thought I could buy anything—from you, I mean."

"I already know that."

"Thank you."

"You're welcome. You're a man with manners. Nicky, he's a pig."

"Nicky, that's the guy who gave you the—?"

"Yes. He walks around like he's some kind of gangster. Did you see those clothes? Hah! He's nothing but an errand boy, and everybody knows it. If Armand ever stopped paying the rent, it wouldn't be *Nicky* they'd send around."

"I don't understand."

"Never mind. It's not important."

Dett looked down at the empty counter.

"Oh, I'm sorry," she said. "I didn't mean to . . . snap at you like that. It's just that I've been here since three this afternoon, and I kind of run out of gas. Let me get you another cup of coffee."

"Thank you," Dett said.

1959 September 30 Wednesday 23:54

Probably has it laid out so he can get it done the quickest, like a kid with a paper route, Dett thought, glancing down at the red-penciled marks on the street map Beaumont had given him. He drove slowly past a two-tone blue '58 Mercury hardtop splayed arrogantly across two parking spaces directly in front of Penny's Show Bar. Dett found a pocket of shadow between streetlights, positioned his side mirror so he could watch the door, and settled in.

As he waited, Dett added up what he had learned so far. As a collector, Nicky Perrini was an amateur. He spent too much time in each place, talked too much, drove a car easy to spot, called attention to himself. *Somebody's nephew,* Dett thought.

It was almost twenty-five minutes by Dett's watch before his target finally emerged from the bar. As Perrini opened his car door, the interior light went on. Unless he had someone lying across the back seat, or crouched down in the front passenger compartment, the collector was alone.

Perrini drove off, the Mercury's distinctive canted-V taillights marking his trail. Dett followed, varying the distance every few blocks, checking his mirrors to make certain he wasn't being boxed.

After a few minutes, the Mercury slowed, and Dett pulled closer behind. Perrini drove past a single-story building with CLUB MIDNIGHT on its marquee. The street was lined with cars on both sides, every spot taken except for a large space directly in front of the entrance.

The Mercury turned left at the next corner, and slowed to a crawl. Dett did the hunter's math: *He's not collecting from that joint—he's going there for fun. And he hasn't got enough clout to use that VIP spot, so he's looking for a parking place.*

Gambling, Dett brought his Ford to a halt, then backed it into a narrow alley. He quickly put a red felt cap with tied-at-the-top black earmuffs on his head, slipped on a pair of deerskin gloves, and left his car. He flattened his back against the alley wall, then cautiously peered in the direction Perrini had driven. He spotted the Merc's taillights as it reversed into a spot between two cars, parallel-parking. *Probably at a fire hydrant,* Dett thought, stepping out of the alley and walking briskly in that direction.

Dett watched as Perrini locked his car, adjusted the lapels of his camel's-hair coat, and ran a comb through his hair. Perrini crossed the street, heading back toward the nightclub, moving with over-cooked self-assurance.

Approaching his target, Dett began walking with a limp, his right hand held stiffly at his side for balance. He looked down at the sidewalk, as if ashamed of his condition.

The gap between the two men closed. Dett felt a familiar calmness radiate from his center. His heartbeat slowed, his blood pressure dropped, and his senses sharpened like a safecracker's sandpapered fingertips. He unclenched his right fist; a length of lead pipe dropped into his gloved hand.

As they were passing each other wordlessly, Dett pivoted on his left foot and slammed the lead pipe into the back of Perrini's head.

The motion of his strike carried Dett down to one knee. He quickly scanned the street, then smoothly rolled Perrini over onto his back. The man's nose was flattened, and his front teeth had penetrated his upper lip—he had been unconscious before he fell, meeting the sidewalk face-first.

A quick search produced an alligator wallet from Perrini's inside pocket. Dett shifted position so he could check the street in both directions. *Thirty seconds,* he told himself, as he removed a driver's license before replacing the wallet. Adjusting Perrini's left hand so that it rested on the sidewalk, palm-down, Dett used the butt of the lead pipe to shatter the collector's expensive wristwatch, and maybe his wrist.

Dett walked back across the street, got into his car, and drove out of the alley. A few blocks away, he pulled over and tossed the lead pipe into a vacant lot. It didn't make a sound.

1959 October 01 Thursday 01:02

The diner was too packed for Dett to see whether Tussy was still at work as he drove by. He moved on, through the darkened streets, learning the city. It took him almost two hours to return to the pawnshop. Dett left the Ford in the street, locked it, and opened the trunk, where he traded in the denim jacket for his armed overcoat.

The dull metal shim Dett had left in the side door of the hotel was still in place. He let himself in, made it to the stairs undetected, and was in bed before three-thirty.

1959 October 01 Thursday 07:07

"When do you think he might be able to tell us something, Doc?" Detective Sherman Layne asked the stoop-shouldered man in a white lab coat.

"Maybe in ten minutes," the doctor replied, looking down at the body of Nicholas Perrini, "maybe never. He's in a coma."

"Yeah, I can see that for myself," Layne said. He was a tall, heavyset man, a human mass of ever-encroaching bulk who gave the impression of standing very close to whoever he spoke to. His voice—patiently insistent—reflected his personality. "What I want to know is, what's the odds?"

"Medical science isn't a horse race," the doctor said, haughtily, favoring the detective with his patrician-nosed profile.

"Too bad it's not. I could handicap a race a lot better than what you're giving me now."

"Sorry," the doctor said, making it clear he wasn't—apology had deserted his language repertoire the moment he had finished his internship, more than thirty years ago.

"Doc, I'm not trying to bust your chops, okay? In a case like this, there's a dozen possibilities. If I thought it was even money this guy would wake up and tell us who slugged him, I could save myself a ton of work digging into his life."

"That's important, saving work?" the doctor asked, archly. He had a high-domed forehead and thinning dark hair, carefully combed to minimize that fact.

"You got any idea how overstretched we are for something like this? An assault investigation, most of the time, you don't have to look any further than home, if you understand what I'm saying."

The doctor nodded absently, as he made some notations on the injured man's medical chart.

"Only, in this case," the detective continued, "this guy's home isn't a place where we want to be asking a lot of questions. Not without more information."

"I don't understand," the doctor said, stifling a yawn.

"He had his wallet on him. And the car was registered to him, too. Plenty of ID. We know who he is."

"So ask his—"

"He's got no family around here. No blood family, anyway. But we knew his name. He works for Dioguardi."

"I don't know who that is," the doctor said, his tone maintaining the distance between his world and the cop's.

"He's a gangster, Doc. Set up shop here a while back. We've been watching him, but, so far, he hasn't tried to move in on any of the local people."

"What does any of this have to do with—?"

"Anytime we find a guy lying in the street with his head bashed in, first thing we do is check to see if he's still got his wallet. That neighborhood, you have to figure he was rolled for his money. There's a club a couple of blocks away. Guy staggers out of that joint, drunk, there's men in this town would be on him like vultures on a corpse."

"But he still had his wallet . . ." the doctor said, drawn in despite himself.

"An empty wallet," the detective said.

"So maybe he *was* robbed."

"Who's going to brain a guy, snatch his wallet, remove all the money, and then put the wallet back?"

"People do strange things," the doctor said, returning to the disengaged distance he preferred.

"Yeah. And one of those things is gamble. He wouldn't be the first man to walk out of a club Tap City."

"Tap City?"

"Broke."

"Yes. I understand there *are* a couple of places around here where it's possible to gamble."

"Yeah. Just the way you want it," the detective said, reacting to the doctor's snide tone.

"The way *I* want it?"

"That's right. You, the good citizens of Locke City. You want folks to be able to play cards, have a drink, have a good time with a girl who isn't going to tell anyone about it. And what you want from *us,* from the police, what you want is for us to keep the animals in their cages. You don't want them breaking into your houses, stealing your cars, raping your wives. And we do that. We do it good."

"Is that so?"

"You know it is. Locke City's a border town. If you were in my business, you'd know what that always means. There's things people want to do, they're going to do them. And they're going to come to wherever they *can* do them. The factories closed up a long time ago. And they're not coming back. But we've still got good roads to drive on. We've got nice schools for our kids. The crime rate—the *real* crime rate—is one of the lowest in the state."

"You sound like you should be running for office."

"People like you make me tired," the detective said. "You like to pretend you don't know what fuel this town runs on. But you're happy enough that your taxes are so low."

The doctor raised an eyebrow theatrically. "So, if the tax rates were increased, then the sort of . . . vice you're describing would all go away?"

"*Go* away? No. *Move* away, maybe, but never disappear. Every time the government tries something like that, they just make things worse."

"Enforcing the laws would make things worse?" the doctor baited the detective, enjoying himself. This would make a wonderful story for his wife's dinner party on Saturday.

"You think medical school's the only place they teach sarcasm?" the detective said, dropping the temperature of his voice. "It takes money to run a criminal organization. I don't mean Bonnie and Clyde stuff, I mean a business. A business that *owns* a lot of busi-

nesses. Did you watch the Kefauver hearings? A criminal organization can't go to a bank for financing. And they can't *rob* enough
of them, either. Prohibition, that was their financing. And that was
when they started to organize, branch out, take over things."

"We haven't had Prohibition in this country for—"

"Prohibition doesn't have to be booze, Doc. It just means something you're not allowed to do. See, there's two kinds of crimes.
There's the ones everyone agrees you shouldn't do: murder, rape,
arson. . . . And there's the ones everyone *says* you shouldn't do, but
they don't mean it. I'm talking about fun, Doc. And not everybody's
got the same idea of what fun is. One guy spends his money deer-
hunting, another spends it in whorehouses."

"And because of your limited resources . . ."

"We have to concentrate on the crimes the citizens *really* care
about, sure. But even if we had a force five times the size we've got
now—"

"A better-paid police force, I trust?"

"You have a point you're trying to make?" Sherman Layne said,
his voice hardening perceptibly. "I must be missing it."

The doctor suddenly remembered some of the things he'd heard
about Sherman Layne around the hospital. Buying time to craft his
retreat, he took off his glasses and fussily polished the lenses on a
monogrammed white handkerchief. "The only point that matters
here is that there is no way to predict the course of an insult to the
brain."

"Are you trying to—?"

"An 'insult,' Detective," the doctor said, twisting his upper lip.
"As in 'insult and injury.' We can't look inside this man's head and
determine the extent of damage to the brain, much less whether it
will be permanent. He experienced extreme blunt-force trauma to
the skull. This caused what is known as a contrecoup injury. The
blow caused the brain to move forward at high speed, and impact
the cranial wall. Some patients recover completely. Some recover
physically, but they experience short-term memory loss. If that's
the case here, this man would recall who he is, but would have no
memory for the period of time in which the attack occurred."

The doctor took a professional breath, then said, "Some never come out of a coma. They remain in a persistent vegetative state, dependent on medical personnel and machines to keep them alive. Some die. Their internal systems simply shut down. This man is breathing on his own, which augurs in his favor. Beyond that, there is nothing I can tell you. Now, if you'll excuse me, I have rounds to complete."

1959 October 01 Thursday 15:33

"What are we supposed to do with this?" Beaumont asked Dett, holding up the driver's license of Nicholas Carlo Perrini.

"Not 'we,' me. I'm going to mail it to the people who've been sending that punk around to collect from your accounts."

"Why just the license?" Beaumont asked, genuinely interested.

"A town like this one, the cops are going to say he was robbed anyway."

"Because his wallet—"

"—will be empty, once *they* get done with it, right? That's why I smashed his watch. If I hadn't done that, the cops might have taken that, too."

Beaumont shifted position in his wheelchair, reached for his cigarette case. "When Dioguardi gets the license, what's he going to think?"

"He won't know *what* to think," Dett answered, "but he'll know for sure it wasn't any mugging. Getting the license in the mail, he'll know it's a message, from someone who knows what this Nicky boy was doing last night. And who he was doing it for."

"What's the point of that? He already knows we're on to him; you can't keep collections a secret."

"Right. So, when he started edging in, that was sending *you* a message, wasn't it?" Dett said.

"You'd think so," said Beaumont, "but you know what he's tapping? Nickel-and-dime action. Armand's, that diner where you saw him? They're paying him twenty dollars a week. Some of the clubs, maybe a little more. Place like Fat Lucy's—that's a candy store, where the kids hang out—probably no more than a ten-spot. But then there's that business with Hacker, I told you about it. If all that adds up to some kind of message, I can't read it."

"Yeah, well, when he gets the license, he won't know how to read *that,* either. Not until it gets explained to him."

"Our operation, we can afford to send the collectors out with cover," Beaumont said. "But with Dioguardi's penny-ante action, he did that, it would cost him more than he's bringing in. So he's either got to step up or step back."

Dett opened his hands in a "Well?" gesture.

"Oh, he was coming anyway," Beaumont said, calmly. "He probably would have tried another sit-down first, see if there wasn't some way I'd let him have a slice, peaceable. Like he did before, when he came out for a visit. But even if I went along, it would never have stopped there, and he knows I know it."

"That's why, after he gets the license, he gets a phone call," Dett said, watching understanding slowly fill the other man's eyes.

1959 October 01 Thursday 20:21

"There has to be more than that," Procter said to the jowly plain clothes cop standing beside him at the base of the water tower.

"If there is, we don't know it," the cop said. His hair was snow white, worn in a stiff brush cut, its precision and neatness a stark contrast to his cratered face, which was the color of old mushrooms.

"One of Sally D.'s men takes a baseball bat to the head, and you're playing it like he was some stewbum who fell off a barstool?"

"If you're asking, did we get a lay-off order, the answer is no," the cop said. "Besides, it doesn't look in-house. If that punk was dipping into the till, he might have caught himself a beating, sure. Maybe even worse. And, yeah, they might have left his head on a stake, make sure the troops get the word. But this . . ."

"How could you tell?"

"Well, for one thing, it was too clean."

"Clean? The guy's in a goddamn coma."

"*Very* clean," the cop said, reluctant admiration clear in his voice. "You hit a guy with a bat in the face, it's instant mess. *Splat!* You got blood spurting everywhere—including all over the guy holding the bat. But whoever did this, he was like a doctor, operating. One shot to the back of the head. Perfect. Little Nicky never saw him coming, I bet. And he sure as fuck didn't know what hit him. *Still* doesn't, from what I hear." The jowly man snorted.

"Maybe he doesn't, but I do," Procter said.

"Yeah?"

"Perrini got his arm up in time to block at least one of the blows. So it had to be a couple of men, one in front, one behind."

"You get what you pay for," the cop said, chuckling snidely.

"What's that supposed to mean?"

"It means, one of your stooges down at the station house gave you a look at the report, Jimmy. You saw that his watch was busted, so you figure he threw up his arm, tried to block the bat coming at his head, right?"

"But . . . ?"

"But you weren't on the scene. I was. Me and the great Sherman Layne. Whoever busted that watch, he did it on purpose. *After* Nicky was laid out, face-down."

"Huh! I never heard of that one. What did Layne say he thought it meant?"

"Sherman? He don't share his observations with the rest of us," the jowly cop said. "Me, I think it was like saying time's running out, or something like that."

"You read too many detective magazines," Procter said.

1959 October 01 Thursday 22:16

"Who the fuck is this?" The voice was hoarse with what the speaker believed to be intimidating menace.

"It's the boogeyman, genius. Now, I'm going to ask you just one more time, so listen good. I got something I need to mail to your boss. It's something he wants. Something that could help him with his business. I need an address where I can be sure it'll get to him."

"Listen, pal, you think I'm stupid? How's Mr. D. gonna know you didn't mail him a fucking bomb or something?"

"Because he'll get a stooge like you to open it for him," Dett said.

1959 October 02 Friday 10:17

"My plans have changed," Dett said to Carl.
"I'm sorry to hear that, Mr. Dett. Does this mean you won't be staying with us as long as—?"

"Oh, I'm staying, all right," Dett said, shaking his head. "In fact, I may be stuck—well, that's not exactly the right word—I may be staying longer than I thought."

"Of course," Carl said, agreeably. "Does that mean you would prefer a smaller—?"

"I'll be fine where I am," Dett said, "but I can't keep getting around on foot. I think it's time to rent that car."

"Oh, we . . . I . . . can take care of that for you, sir. Is there any particular sort of car you would like?"

"Something . . . respectable," Dett said. "Good-quality, but not flashy. I'm sure you know what I mean."

"Absolutely," Carl assured him. "Would dinnertime be soon enough?"

1959 October 02 Friday 11:44

"I don't know what he driving right this second, but I know what he goan be driving tonight, boss."

"Well?"

"Be a brand-new Chevy Impala. Four-door sedan," he said, emphasizing the first syllable of the last word. "Nice dark-green one."

"Plate?"

"Ain't got that yet, boss. But that ride I jest tole you 'bout, that's the one the deskman ordered for him from the rental company. It goan be delivered tonight; I get you the plate number then, okay?"

"Don't call this number tonight. Tomorrow's soon enough."

"Yessir. I—"

Rufus stopped in mid-sentence when he heard the line go dead.

1959 October 02 Friday 20:13

"When you first came in, you looked so different, I almost didn't recognize you."

"I'd recognize you if all you did was just change clothes."

"You did more than that," Tussy said, tilting her chin up as she regarded Dett, her big green eyes luminous. "I just can't tell what it is yet."

"This is the real me," he said.

"I—"

"Pick up!" came from the kitchen.

"I've got to run. This is our busiest time. That's why there's no space at the booths."

She whirled and moved toward the opening in the kitchen wall. Dett admired the way she snatched a pair of trays, pirouetted smartly, and swivel-hipped her way around various obstacles to a booth where a young couple was sitting. She off-loaded the two trays, chattering to her customers as she worked. Then she strode back toward the delivery slot to exchange the empty trays for three loaded ones, which she stacked onto a little cart and wheeled off in the opposite direction.

It was twenty minutes before she returned to where Dett was sitting.

"What'll it be?" she said, her pad at the ready.

"The lemon pie."

"That's not dinner; that's dessert."

"Well, I'm not really hungry."

"Then you shouldn't go near my lemon pie," Tussy said, smiling.

"I don't always say things as good as I want. I meant to say, even though I'm not hungry, your lemon pie is so good I still want some."

"You know what," she said, leaning on the counter and dropping her voice, "all we have left is one piece, and it's really yesterday's—I didn't get a chance to bake today. You don't want that piece. You come back tomorrow, earlier, if you can, and I'll cut you the first slice. It's always the best."

"I *will* come back. But that's not why I came. I wanted to—"

"Tussy, damn it!" bellowed from the kitchen.

"I'm sorry. Can you . . . ?" she said, and trotted off.

Dett sat quietly for a few minutes, eyes on a menu. When Tussy didn't return, he got up, went over to the jukebox, and invested a few nickels in Jack Scott.

By the time he returned to the counter, the stool he had been using was occupied, along with the three closest to it. High-school kids, in blue-and-gold varsity jackets with "Locke City Eagles" in block letters across the backs. Dett tapped one on the shoulder, a deep-chested young man with a knife-edged crewcut and a practiced curl to his upper lip.

"You're in my seat," Dett said, mildly.

"*Your* seat? I don't see your name on it, man," the youth said. His buddies laughed on cue, a practiced bully-sound, pack-rehearsed since childhood.

Dett's right hand slipped into his pocket, fingers coiling through a set of brass knuckles. He stepped closer, angling his left shoulder to shield his right arm from the target's view.

The hinge of his jaw. While his mouth is open . . .

A flash of pink in the corner of his eye. Tussy. Standing by the register. She pantomimed smoking a cigarette, pointed at the big clock high on the wall, then held out her palm, fingers spread.

Dett stepped back. Nodded his head "yes." He watched as she pointed behind her, nodding again to show he understood.

"Hey, man," the youth said, mockingly. "Didn't you have something you wanted to say?"

"No," Dett told him, looking away.

He turned and walked out of the diner, their laughter behind him like wind in a sail.

The back door to the diner opened, and Tussy stepped out into the warm, starless night. She looked to her left and to her right, then put both hands on her hips and said, "Well!"

"I'm over here, Tussy," Dett said, separating himself from the shadows. "I'm sorry. I didn't mean for you to think—"

"Oh!" Tussy jumped slightly, then recovered her composure. "I was just *playing*," she assured him. "Having fun. I knew you had to be around someplace."

"You're really good at it."

"At . . . what?"

"At playing. You mean, like playing a role, right? Acting. You're terrific, the way you do it. When you told me you would be taking a break out here—in five minutes, to have a smoke—it was like you wrote me a note. It was so clear, and you never said a word."

The waitress regarded Dett appraisingly. "I never heard that one before," she said, smiling to take the edge off her words.

"Nobody ever noticed how good you— Ah, I get it. You mean, you never heard that *line* before, huh?"

"I was just teasing," she said, quickly. "I'm sorry. I didn't mean to hurt your feelings."

"You didn't—" Dett began, then stopped himself as he realized that his feelings *had* been hurt. The knowledge stunned him, like an amputee who first experiences phantom pain in a missing limb.

"It's a zoo in there tonight," she said, taking a pack of Kools from her apron. "Do you have a—?"

Dett already had a wooden match flaming, cupped in his hands. He held it out to her by extending his arms, not stepping any closer.

"Thanks," she said, leaning forward.

"You're welcome," Dett replied, lighting a Lucky for himself with the same flame.

"Did you just move in around here?" she asked.

"Me? No, I didn't move in at all. I'm just in town on business."

"What do you do?"

"I'm in real estate," he said, suddenly disgusted with the vagueness of the lie that sprang so naturally to his lips.

"You mean, like houses? Or bigger stuff?"

"Well, it's pretty much just land. I work for some people who buy up big parcels when they think the land will be worth a lot more someday."

"Like if the state builds a highway through it?"

"That's kind of what I mean," he said. "But not through it, exactly. *Next* to it, that would be best. If the government wants your property, they can just take it."

"Without paying you?" she said, horrified.

"Oh, they have to pay. But they only pay what *they* say it's worth."

"That's terrible."

"It's one of the risks. The bigger risk is when you assemble a parcel and then you try and package it, so you can sell it to a developer. One little zoning change and you could end up with a worthless vacant lot instead of a shopping center."

"Oh. So you're on the road all the time?"

"Pretty much. But, sometimes, I get to stay in one spot for a while. It depends on what's going on."

"Nothing's going on here," she said, dragging on her cigarette. "Well, actually, there's *plenty* that goes on here. I guess you already know about it, being a . . ."

"Being a . . . what?"

"A man. A traveling man. Locke City's not exactly a tourist attraction, but we get a lot of men just passing through. Usually it's just for a few hours, though."

"This is a gamblers' town?"

"You didn't know? Where are you staying?"

"At the Claremont."

"That real-estate business of yours must pay pretty well," she said. Dett couldn't tell if she was actually impressed, or making fun of him. Maybe some of both. "I'm surprised you could even check into a place like that without the bellhops touting you on one of the fancy joints we've got here."

"Like casinos?"

"I've never been to a real casino, but we've got places here that sure *look* like what I imagine they'd be," she said, her voice a parody of civic pride. "Roulette wheels, blackjack dealers, slot machines, dice, the whole works. If there's one thing Locke City's famous for, it's gambling. We've got all kinds, everywhere you look."

"The police . . . ?"

"Are you some kind of detective?" she suddenly asked, stepping back.

"Me?" said Dett, honestly shocked.

"Well, you . . . you're not from around here. One night, you're dressed like a working guy, but tonight, you're all fancy. And you were asking all those questions—"

"No, I wasn't," Dett protested. "I was just . . . I was just talking with you. I'm not very good at it."

"Talking? You seem to do just fine with it."

"Not that kind of talking. Talking to say what I mean."

"I don't understand."

Dett took a deep breath. Let it out. Said, "The question—the *only* question I wanted to ask you was, would you go out with me? I mean, to a movie or . . . or to a club, if you want. We could—"

"Dinner," she said, smiling.

"Dinner? I—"

"That's what I'd really like. Have somebody wait on *me* for a change, see what it feels like."

"I would be very . . . I would like that very much. Is there a nice place you know about?"

"Well, there's actually a lot of nice places in Locke City. You'd be surprised."

"I . . . I don't know. I don't go out to dinner much. I mean, I *always* go out, to eat, I mean, but not to—"

"There are some very nice restaurants," Tussy repeated. "And they don't really cost much more than—"

"No, no," Dett said, holding up his hand as if to pardon his interruption. "This is my fault. I'm not saying what I mean. I want to take you to the nicest place in town. Really. I just don't know if what I was told is right. Have you ever heard of Chez Bertrand?"

Tussy's green eyes flashed behind the smoke from her cigarette. "*Everybody's* heard of Chez Bertrand," she said. "But a place like that costs the earth. And you'd have to have reservations, and—"

"That's where I'd like to take you. Please."

Tussy paused a beat, then nodded her head. "All right, then," she said, holding out her hand to shake, as if sealing a deal, "it's a date. My nights off are Monday and Tuesday. Which would you like?"

"Monday," Dett said instantly.

Tussy snapped her cigarette into the darkness of the parking lot. "This is my address," she said, carefully printing something on her order pad. "And my phone number, in case you have to change your plans."

"I won't," Dett said, as she tore the page from her pad and handed it to him. "Would seven o'clock be okay?"

"Perfect. I have to get back to work now, before Booker blows a gasket. Bye!"

Dett stood in the same spot long enough to smoke another cigarette, never taking his eyes off the back door. Then he slipped into the shadows.

1959 October 02 Friday 22:50

The '51 Mercury was a custom job: black with red-and-yellow flames on its de-chromed hood, chopped top, spinner hubcaps on whitewall tires, rear wheels hidden behind bubble skirts. It was parked in a clearing off a narrow dirt road, surrounded by woods on all sides. A river ran somewhere nearby, close enough to be heard.

From the Mercury's partially open windows came the doomed voice of Johnny Ace, "Pledging My Love." In the front seat, brief flashes of color, signs of movement, sounds of sex.

"They never know you're here, do they, Holden?"

Holden Satterfield didn't jump at the whispered voice behind him. He didn't flinch at the hand on his shoulder. He knew his friend Sherman would never hurt him. *He sure could hurt me if he wanted to,* Holden thought. *Sherman's a big man. And he's a police officer, too. A detective. But Sherman knows I wouldn't ever do nothing to people. I just watch them.*

Wordlessly, the two men retreated from Holden's watching place, their soundless movements as choreographed as tango partners'. When they got within sight of Sherman's unmarked car, the big man said, "You got your logbook with you, Holden?"

"Sure," the watcher said. "I always carry it, just like you said, Sherman."

"You got anything in there about a different Merc? A newer one; a '58, two-tone blue?"

"No, sir," Holden said.

"You're sure?"

"Sure I am, Sherman," Holden said, in an injured tone. "You know I never forget a car once I see it."

"I know," Sherman said, reassuringly. "But even the best detectives, they write things down. To keep a record, like I explained to you."

"Sure, Sherman. I know. Here," he said, "look through it yourself."

"That's all right," the cop said, waving away the offer. He knew Holden's compulsive watching imprinted itself on the damaged man's brain—the notebook was just to make things "official."

"Most of them, I know them, right away," Holden said. "They come back, over and over. But you have to watch close. Some of them, they bring different people in them sometimes."

"Is that right?" Sherman said, absently. He understood that Holden believed the cars to be independent creatures, visiting the Lovers' Lane of their own volition, carrying random cargo.

"Tonight, we had a '56 Buick Century—you can tell by the extra porthole; '57 Olds 98—they're a little longer in the back than the 88; '54 Ford, '53 Studebaker, the Starliner; you can always . . ."

Sherman Layne stood in the night, oddly soothed by the sounds of Holden's litany. *Anyone who parks where Holden patrols, they might as well be signing a hotel register,* he thought, proudly.

". . . a beautiful '55 Chevy, a Bel Air hardtop," Holden went on. "I almost didn't recognize it at first. The Bel Airs are all two-tones, you know. This one, it had the chrome tooken off the sides, except for one little strip. And it was this special red, all over. It looked like those apples you get at the carnival. You know, all shiny and—"

Harley Grant, sounded in Sherman's mind. "You sure it was a '55?" he asked.

"Oh, it was a '55, Sherman," Holden said, with absolute conviction. "They can't fool me. I always know how to tell. Like, there's a '56 Ford that comes here all the time. Only, what it did, it swapped the taillights for a '56 Mercury's. Did you know they screw right in? You don't have to do nothing to make them fit. So, if you just get a quick look at it, from the back, you can make a mistake. Now, the '55 Chevy, the grille is different from a '56; it doesn't go all the way across. And it didn't have fins, like a '57."

"You ever see it before?"

"No, I never did. I would've remembered it. That paint job, it was so beautiful, like the moon shined down on it special."

"What did the girl look like?"

"You know I never—"

"Sure, Holden. I know," Sherman said, gently. "I meant, did you notice anything about her? I mean, she was in this special car, so you'd think . . ."

"She had a kerchief on her head," Holden said, stopping to think before each word. Usually, he tried to speak quickly, to make people forget that he had spent his whole life being called "slow." But Sherman wasn't like those other people. Sherman was his friend. Sherman called him "Holden," not . . . other names.

"A white kerchief," Holden went on. "But, underneath, her hair was dark. And she never once took it off. They just sat there. Together, I mean. He was smoking, but she wasn't. I didn't stay long."

What the hell was Harley Grant doing in Lovers' Lane? He's one of Beaumont's top men. He could afford a motel. And he's got his own place, too. "Thanks, Holden," Sherman said aloud. "You're the best agent I've got."

"He's a pimp," Rufus said, flatly.

"So?" one of the men seated around a makeshift wood table in the back room of a garage challenged. "Who here *don't* have some kind of a scuffle going for him? This is a white man's—"

"Everybody here sings that tune, K-man," a tall man with a cadaverous face interrupted. "Omar doesn't say things just to be talking." He turned his head toward Rufus, expectantly. "Come on with it, now."

Rufus nodded to the cadaverous man. "Thank you, brother. When I hear my true name—*any* of our true names—said out loud, it fills me with power. I don't know where my father's father's father came from," he began, "but I know, wherever it was, they didn't have no names like 'Rufus.' The slavemasters branded us *deep,* brothers. And not just with their names. So we have to be two people—the one Mister Charlie sees, and the one he don't. Here, with my own people, I'm not Rufus anymore. I'm Omar."

As the others nodded approval, Rufus got to his feet, taking command. His voice was muscular but modulated, a high-horsepower engine held against a firm brake pedal.

"A black pimp is the white man's living proof. They see a nigger with money, how did he get it? He stole it, they think. Or he sold some pussy. Or some dope. Doesn't matter—the thing they know for sure, he didn't *work* for it, right? And when the colored man scores some coin, what's the first thing he does with it? Come on, brothers, tell the truth. He plays right into Charlie's game. Gets him the biggest ride he can, drapes himself in the finest vines, and goes looking for a place to show it all off."

Rufus held his hands at waist height, palms-down, creating a podium from the empty air in front of him. His eyes took in each man in the room, individually, before he spoke again.

"Stupid, *ignorant* motherfucker thinks he's on top of the world, right? Got everything a big black ape could ever want, including a white woman. But does a pimp *own* anything? Does he have a legitimate business? Or even a damn house he can call his own? Where's his money in the bank? Where's his land? Where's his *power*?

"Whitey goes like *this*," Rufus said, snapping his fingers, "and it's all gone. One day, this pimp, he's king of the block. Next day, he's down to the prison farm, digging in the dirt, while a man stands over him holding a gun. In some places I've been, that's a *black* man, the one holding the gun."

"A bank robber could end up the same way," said a somber-looking man in a neat brown business suit two shades darker than his sepia complexion.

"Sure!" Rufus agreed, readily. "But . . . let me show you some pictures, okay?" he said, pointing at an imaginary photograph on the wall of the garage. "There's one of some nigger in a suit with sparkles sewn into it, diamonds on his fingers, driving a big Cadillac. Now, over *there*, you see a picture of a black man with a gun, aimed right at the face of some bank teller. You're a white man, which picture do *you* like? That one," he said, gesturing, "you turn up the heat, he's going to kiss your ass. But *this* one"—he pointed—"you get in *his* way, he might just take your life."

"We're not in this for the image," said a bespectacled young man in a putty-colored corduroy sport coat.

"Not *our* images, Brother Garfield," Rufus said, skillfully transforming dissent into ammunition, "images for our children. Who are their heroes now? Some baseball player? Or a singer, maybe? People like that, you can dream about them, but you never get to see them up close. They're not real. But the pimp, the numbers man, the hustler—they're right out there, every day.

"Our children need another path," Rufus said. That's what we're in this for, brothers. That's why the New Black Men came to be."

"And it's not just the children," the cadaverous man echoed. "Plenty of our people haven't come to consciousness yet. Maybe a pimp can't be one of us, but there's no law says a pimp must *stay* a pimp."

"That's the truth, Brother Darryl!" Rufus said, deftly accepting the passed baton. "We know two things: One, this 'Silk,' he came to *us*. Two, him being a pimp, that means he got eyes and ears out there, hearing things we never would. A pimp, he gets to see the truth. A trick does things with a whore he'd never do with his wife . . . and he also *tells* a whore things he'd never tell his wife.

"That's how we made our connection for the guns, remember? One of Silk's women has this regular customer who's in the business. He told her, she told him, he told us . . . and it all came together sweet. They may hate us, brothers, but no white man ever minded making money off us. Mister Green always going to be the boss."

"Maybe there's something in it for Silk," Garfield said. "We're paying a lot of money for every shipment. Maybe he's getting a little commission for himself."

"If he is, that's a betrayal," Rufus agreed. "Because Silk says he's one of us. *Wants* to be one of us, anyway."

"Every man here has been tested," Darryl said, his voice barely audible. "His turn will come."

Rufus held up a lecturer's forefinger. "Like I said before, brothers: he's a pimp. Nobody's ever going to suspect a man like that could be with us. So, if he's down for real, he could be worth a lot to our cause. And if it turns out he's not, nobody's going to miss him when he's gone."

1959 October 03 Saturday 01:01

Tussy clothespinned her just-washed stockings to a cord strung from the shower-curtain rod, then padded into the living room in her bare feet. She was wearing a man's red flannel pajama top as a nightshirt; it came down almost to her knees.

The furniture was all pre-war, except for the radio and a console TV. Substantial woodwork, heavy fabrics. A working-class living room, it had been designed to be used only for "best," with normal social activities relegated to the kitchen.

On the mantelpiece was a stiffly posed photograph of a young couple. A short, powerfully built man in his early thirties, with a face already going fleshy, dressed in a dark, awkward-fitting suit, stared straight ahead. The woman next to him came only to his shoulder, even in high heels. She was smiling shyly—for her husband, not for the camera.

Tussy turned on the radio. The sad-but-not-surrendering voice of Patsy Cline followed her as she went into the kitchen to make herself a cup of coffee.

1959 October 03 Saturday 01:20

"This job I'm on, you ever do business with that guy before?" Dett spoke into a pay phone.

"I'm just a messenger," Whisper said, in the broken-larynx voice that gave him his name. "I don't read the messages; I just deliver them."

"I wasn't trying to insult you."

"I know," the softly harsh voice said. "Just remember our deal: keep it clean, keep it green. Right?"

"Right," Dett answered.

1959 October 03 Saturday 01:51

The maroon-lacquered Eldorado Brougham glided away from the curb, its stainless-steel roof reflecting the cold-fire wash of neon from the darkened windows of a backstreet bar. The man behind the wheel was dressed in a powder-blue suit, custom-tailored to his slender, athletic frame. Diamonds glittered on both hands and circled the face of his wristwatch. He checked his image in the rearview mirror, patting his stiff, processed hairdo back into perfection: he smiled at the reflection of his exquisitely featured face, perfect white teeth gleaming against his dark-parchment skin.

The pimp drove slowly past a street corner and came to a stop. A skinny girl in a short, tight red dress and matching high heels trotted toward the Eldorado as its window slid down. She leaned into the car for a minute. Dett could see her head nod vigorously under a luxuriant auburn wig. Then she ran around behind the car and got into the passenger seat. In less than five minutes, she got out, and the Eldorado pulled away.

Checking his traps, Dett said to himself. *Just where the old man said he'd be.*

Dett shadowed the Eldorado as it meandered. Mostly, the driver contented himself with just cruising by certain corners. Occasionally, he would pull over and pose, deliberately putting his status on display. Twice, hookers came to the car and got in, but neither stayed for longer than it would take to transfer recently earned cash.

"Silk don't go out in daylight," Moses had told Dett. "Like one of those vampires you see in the movies. Behind what he do, that make sense to me. Darktown, it's not like around here, suh. Man wants to get a haircut, get his car fixed, stuff like that, he can get it done even when the sun's way down."

"So he pretty much stays in . . . ?"

"Can't stay over in Darktown all the time, suh. A pimp, he's got to hawkeye his women while they working the street. And, you want to make money, you got to put your merchandise out where white men don't be afraid to come. Got plenty of men around here like a taste of what Silk sells, but . . ."

"He doesn't run any white women?"

"I think that's *all* he runs, suh. Word is, he's even got girls in some of the high-class houses. 'Course, you listen to any pimp, he'll tell you he got nothing but racehorses in his stable."

"So maybe the 'word' is just him, bragging."

"You mean, to build himself up? That wouldn't be Silk's way, suh. A man in his job, he's got to show a lot of flash, sure. That's how he pulls girls. But the last thing he want to do is attract attention from the wrong boys."

"The cops?"

"The Klan."

"This seems pretty far north for the Klan, Moses."

"That's 'cause you ain't colored, suh."

I have to take him while he's still on this side of the border, Dett said to himself, watching as the Eldorado positioned itself near a corner, just past the dull spray of an anemic streetlight. Halfway down the block, a sign hung suspended from a building front, the words STAR HOTEL barely illuminated by a surrounding rectangle of pale blue bulbs.

The Brougham was a pillarless four-door hardtop, the rear doors set "suicide" fashion, so that they opened out from the center. The pimp had all the windows lowered, creating a vista of white-leather-covered luxury for all who passed. He was leaning back, left hand on the mink-wrapped steering wheel, his right idly caressing a custom-made white Stetson.

"I want a girl."

The pimp twitched his shoulders, startled. Despite his pose, he had been on full alert, consulting his side mirrors constantly, his eyes never at rest. Where had this white man come from?

"I don't know nothing about no girls, man. Why don't you—?"

Suddenly, the white man was in the front seat next to him, a .45 in his lap, aimed waist-high.

"Drive," Dett said.

"Look, man, you don't got to—"

Dett gestured with the .45. Moving with deliberate slowness, the pimp turned the ignition key. His left hand never left the wheel.

1959 October 03 Saturday 02:11

"He asked a lot of questions, Beau."

"He's supposed to ask questions, honey. That's his job."

"I thought his job was to fight."

"Strategy *is* fighting, Cyn. I told you that, a hundred times. That's why we got him, remember?"

"Why did he need all that information about the . . . houses?"

"Probably figures, all the people using them, some of them have to be people we might want to know where they are, sometimes."

"You told Ruth to tell him whatever he wants to know?"

"Sure."

"But, Beau . . ."

"Ruth knows what I meant by that, Cyn."

"Because she understands men so well?"

"What's the matter, honey?"

"Nothing."

"Nothing? I know you better than that."

"I guess I just don't understand men and whores. Why anyone would want to . . . do things with someone they didn't love. Didn't even *know*. It's . . . ugly."

"And you're beautiful."

"Beau."

"You are, Cyn. You know you are. If you hadn't been stuck with a cripple baby brother to take care of, you could have—"

"I love you," she said, fiercely. "I never wanted . . ."

"Me, either," Beaumont said, torquing his powerful wrists to move his wheelchair in her direction.

1959 October 03 Saturday 02:40

In the secrecy of his room, the desk clerk angrily tore up a sheet of notepaper covered with neat, precise script.

Weak! he thought, contemptuously. *Is that the handwriting of a warrior? No!*

He returned to his task, starting with a fresh sheet. Save for the cone of light cast by the desk lamp, the room was in darkness.

It took him an hour to finish his letter. He read and reread the closing line: "Pure Aryan love." Finally, the clerk nodded in satisfaction and signed his name at the bottom.

Karl

1959 October 03 Saturday 03:52

In three different parts of town, Procter, Sherman, and Rufus each watched a different house, shielded by darkness.

In another, a pimp drove slowly through a maze of streets toward the warehouse district.

"Look, mister," he said to the gunman seated next to him, "whatever this is, it can be squared."

"If I wanted to kill you, you'd be dead," Dett said, conversationally. "I've got a silencer for this piece. I could have just walked by your car, popped you, and kept going. You never saw me coming. I could have put one right here." The man tapped the pimp's temple lightly with the tip of his .45. "You wouldn't have felt a thing.

"I know where you live," the gunman continued. "I know what car you drive. I know where you've got to be to do business. If I wanted, I could have taken you out, anytime."

"Why you telling me all this, man?" the pimp said, plaintively. "I never did nothing to you."

"I'm telling you so that you calm down," Dett said. "We've got to go someplace where we can talk. I don't want you thinking I need to get you alone so I can blast you."

"What we got to talk about?"

"Soon as we get there," Dett promised.

1959 October 03 Saturday 04:11

"This is good," Dett told the pimp. "You can turn off the engine now. And the lights, too, please."

"You making a mistake, man. Let me talk to you. I got money. *Serious* money."

"I don't want your money," Dett told him. "I want to be your friend."

"My *friend*? You got some way of making friends, man."

"Have I talked badly to you?" Dett said. "Haven't I been respectful?"

"Oh, yeah, man. You the most polite killer I ever met."

"I already told you—"

"Yeah, I know. I got it."

"Please don't do something stupid," Dett said, just short of pleading.

"Stupid? What I going to do that—?"

"You probably have a gun somewhere. At least a knife."

"In my coat," the pimp said. "The mink, on the back seat. But I got a permit for that piece, man. I'm a—"

"—professional."

"Right! I—"

"You see what I mean? About respect? We're both profession-als. Businessmen. That's why we can be friends."

"How are we gonna be friends?" the pimp said, willing calm into his voice.

"Friends help each other."

"What kind of help you—?"

"A man with a lot of ladies working for him is a man with a dozen pairs of eyes and ears."

"My girls' job ain't to—"

"Whores gossip all the time," Dett said. "He-say, she-say, that's what they do, right?"

"You can't be the law," the pimp said. "Otherwise, I be down at the cop house, and some cocksucking faggot detective be ready to put a phone book on my head, he wanted to know something."

"They did that to you?"

"When I was young and stupid, yeah. When I was still learning my game. But now? Not hardly, man. I ain't no street-nigger trash. I got lawyers and everything. And I got a license to do what I do, same as the one for the gun. Bought it from the same people, too. That's how I know you ain't no cop, understand?"

"Sure," Dett said. "That just proves you're a real professional. A professional, he knows the value of information, and he knows how to use it, too. Like right now. You used information you have about this town to tell you I'm not a cop, see?"

"You playing with me, man?"

"No. I'm being honest with you, that's why it sounds so strange. You know I'm not a cop, like you said. Not a local cop, anyway. But you know I'm not federal, too, don't you?"

"Yeah. Those boys dress even worse than you. And they never work alone. Always two of them."

"Okay, then. We can talk now, can't we?"

"You holding the pistol, man."

"I'm sorry about that. But I had to get you to go someplace with me. Someplace where you could just be yourself, no image."

"I *always* be myself, wherever I am."

"All right," said Dett, agreeably, "whatever you say. Now, tell me. Do you ever bring your girls to private parties?"

"No, man. I got some girls, sure. But they out there, on the street. Where you found me."

"A car like this, the way you dress, you must be holding a whole stable of racehorses," Dett said, deliberately echoing Moses's words. "Some of them have to be doing better than five-and-two tricks. Especially white girls."

The pimp closed his eyes. *I get it now,* sounded inside his head. *This is how it ends.* "What you want, man?" he said, wearily, not opening his eyes.

"I asked you about parties."

"Where *you* from, man? Around here, man wants some private action sent to his house, he don't want a nigger along for the ride, unless he driving a cab."

"So the girls would drive themselves?" Dett asked.

"I got another ride besides this one. They need to go someplace, they take that."

"Your girls turn lump tricks?"

"No, man. I don't do my women like that. But, sometimes, you know how it can be, customer can't get it up, he blames the girl."

"You ever lose a girl that way?"

"Girls come and go all the time, man. Cop and blow, that's the game. My bottom woman, maybe, *maybe* a couple of her wives-in-law, that's all I can count on, go the distance with me."

"No. I mean *lose* one."

"Like a trick *kill* a girl? No way, man. Never happen. I mean, I know it *could* happen, not saying it couldn't. I had girls run off. Every mack has that happen. But I never had one go to the morgue."

"I was in a place, once," Dett said. "There was a man there. Real big shot. Rich, well connected. He liked to hurt working girls; paid heavy cash for his fun. One night, he went too far, and a girl died."

"Why you telling me all this?"

"Because it was a weakness, what the man had. It made him easy."

"Easy for what?"

"Easy for me. For what I do."

"You're a blackmailer?"

"Sure," said Dett, his tone making it clear that the two men were mutually agreeing to a lie more comfortable than the truth they shared.

"Who you looking at?"

"I'm not particular. He's got to be connected, that's all."

"Connected, like in . . . ?"

"Dioguardi. Shalare. Beaumont. That level."

"Men like that, they don't be visiting no whorehouses."

"I asked you about private parties, remember?"

"Yeah, I remember. But I never did business with any of those men. Maybe some of their boys get their tubes cleaned once in a while. Probably do, as a matter of fact. But that ain't the kind of thing any of the girls would talk about."

"Too scared?"

"Scared? Of what? It's no big thing, not to them. Most tricks pump themselves up, anyway. Working girls'll tell you: with them, every man's got to be a *big* man, you know?"

"Yes."

"Who you looking at, man? A judge, something like that?"

"I'm not particular."

"You really *not* going to kill me?" the pimp said, opening his eyes. "Right?"

"We're going to be friends," Dett said. Not predicting, stating a fact.

"There's one guy," the pimp said, thoughtfully. "I don't know who he is, but he's the fish you want to land."

"Why is that?"

"Because, the way it works, the madam, Ruth's her name, she taps a girl, says she's going to get a visitor in the blue room, the girl knows what that means."

"This guy?"

"This guy. Only nobody ever sees him. They put the girl in this room, put a black hood over her head, then they put her shoulders into this harness thing, like. So she can't turn around. The door opens. The man comes in. Does his business, Greek-style, and leaves. Never says a word."

"Does he hurt the girls?"

"You mean, because he goes up the chute? No, man. The girls know it's coming, so they can get ready for it. And he lubes up, too."

"What if one of the girls doesn't want to—"

"You want to work Miss Ruth's house, that's part of the deal. She tells every girl, right up front. This guy, you may never get picked, but if you do, you're going. And the man *pays*."

"Any of your girls ever get a hint who he is?"

"Not a clue, man. The blue room, it's in the basement. There's a back door, leads right down to it from the outside. Whoever he is, the man don't have to come through the house. And one thing's for sure—Miss Ruth is never going to talk. She knows a lot of things, but she never says. She's famous for that."

"If this story is true, we'll be friends," Dett told the pimp.

"Meaning, if it ain't, you gonna find me some night and kill me?"

"What does it matter?" the velvet-voiced gunman said. "I know you're telling the truth. I know we're friends now."

1959 October 03 Saturday 09:22

"Lymon's been talking," Beaumont said.

"Lymon!" Harley said, shocked. "Who would he—?"

"Shalare. He's been talking to Shalare."

"Nah."

"What?" Beaumont demanded.

"I just mean . . . some of the men we got, they're like women, you know? Always talking. Yap-yap. Gossip. Maybe he had a beer with Shalare. Shot a game of pool with him. That doesn't mean he said anything about our business. Besides, we're not at war with—"

"Harley," Beaumont said, heavily, "I want you to listen to me. Sometimes, you have to take a couple of steps back, look at things from a wider angle. You see more that way. Shalare's coming at us same as Dioguardi is, only from a different direction. Dioguardi, he's a muscle guy. But Shalare, he's been plowing another field."

"Where? I never heard of his boys doing—"

"He's been buying politicians like a kid collecting baseball cards. Not the locals. You know the city council; they'll take money from anyone, for anything. But that's look-away cash; they don't have the clout to *change* anything. Shalare, he's been working the top shelf. The Assembly, the Senate, maybe even the governor."

"All that for this little town?"

"Yeah," Beaumont replied. "All that for this little town. And everything that's in it."

"But what could Lymon even tell them?"

"Lymon carries the bag for us. He could tell Shalare every stop he makes. And how much he leaves at each one."

"He's too smart for that," Harley protested. "You know Lymon; he's not a man to take chances."

"A man who never takes chances is a man who hedges his bets," Beaumont said. "I think that's why Lymon started talking in the first place. But now he thinks he's betting on a winner."

"Shalare?"

"Yes."

"He's wrong."

"Dead wrong," Beaumont said, nodding his massive head for emphasis.

1959 October 03 Saturday 10:05

"He said he was probably going to be staying longer than he planned at first."

"It must be very lonely for him, traveling all the time. Remember when we used to go visit your Aunt Madeleine in Chesterfield over the summers? Your father could never get time away from the store, so it would be just the two of us."

"And Madeleine. And that big slob—"

"Your Uncle Max was nothing *resembling* a slob," Carl's mother said, grimly. "He was an educated, cultured man."

"An educated, cultured Jew," her son retorted, venomously.

"I'm disappointed in you, Carl," his mother said, stiffly. "I did not raise my son to be a bigot."

"It's not bigotry to understand people," Carl said, with icy assurance.

"You never took the time to understand—"

"Uncle Max? I understood him very well, even when I was just a boy. He's like all of them. He gives the impression of being intelligent, but he's really just . . . clever. There is a difference, Mother."

"Where in the world did you ever get such a—?"

"There *are* racial characteristics," Carl interrupted. "It's no accident that Jews are good businessmen. They have a plan, a world plan. That's why they keep to their own kind. They even have their own language. They may *look* white, but they're not."

"Carl!"

"Mother, I wish you would pay more attention to history. The Jews are a tribe, a separate and distinct race. Now they even have their own country."

"*Everybody* in America once had their own country. You know very well that your own great-grandfather came here from Sweden."

"Yes. We're pure Nordic stock, on both sides. But what you say isn't accurate, Mother," Carl said, his voice both academic and concerned—a tutor who wanted to make sure his student really understood the lesson. "The Indians were born here, and they lived like wild animals. The coloreds were *brought* here, right out of the jungle. But those who came voluntarily, like our people, came from civilized countries. They came here to *be* Americans. And today, if I were to travel to, oh, I don't know, Paris," he said, airily, "I would be seen as an American, not a Scandinavian."

"But you *are* an—"

"But wherever a Jew travels, he travels as a Jew," Carl said, in a tone of finality. "They came here as part of their plan."

"I don't under—"

"The plan, Mother. It's well documented. The Jews want to control . . . everything. Look closely. See who *owns* things here. Who runs the banks. The newspapers. Look at Hollywood, it's *dominated* by the Jews." Carl took a sip of his coffee, watching his mother's face over the rim of the cup. "If you look closely, if you read between the lines, you can see the pattern emerging. The whole so-called civil-rights movement is really run by the Jews. You can see

Jew money everywhere. Anytime a colored man is arrested in the South—well, not *every* time, but when it's a big case, the kind we read about even here—you'll see he has Jew lawyers. Who's paying for that? Some sharecroppers who took up a collection? I don't think so. The Communists who were exposed, how many of them turned out to be Jews? Look at the Rosenbergs. Who were *they* loyal to? Not America, Russia. And where do most Jews come from? Russia."

"Carl!"

"Calm yourself, Mother. Most of what has been reported in the popular press about the Nazis is nothing but Jew propaganda. You don't *really* believe six million people were gassed to death, do you? Research shows that was physically impossible."

"Carl, I never pry into your affairs, but—"

"Oh, I know you saw the flag, Mother. It's just a symbol. A symbol of racial purity."

Carl's mother began sobbing softly. "You can't . . ."

"Ssshhh," he said, reaching over to stroke her shoulder.

"Carl, people *were* killed over there. And it wasn't just Jews they put to death. They killed Gypsies and . . ."

"They never exterminated Aryans," Carl said, firmly.

"But . . ."

"I *know*," Carl told her quietly. "Mother, I truly know."

1959 October 03 Saturday 13:39

"You never write anything down?" Beaumont said.

"Would you want me to?" Dett asked.

"I'm not saying that. But all that information you asked for, it's a lot to remember."

"It's a skill you can teach yourself. Like driving a car, or shooting a gun. Takes practice, that's all."

"Makes sense to me," Beaumont said. "That's something I can understand. What I'm not so clear about is why you'd want to meet Dioguardi's people way out in the country."

"You ever see the way cops search a house?" Dett said. "They look into everything. They look under everything. But they never look *up*."

"That's why you want that old shack? Because it has that crawl space up top?"

"Yeah. Besides, I need them to think I'm local. An out-of-towner wouldn't even know how to find that place, right?"

"That's true. But how do you know they're planning to jap you?"

Dett's eyes were gray mesh, absorbing without reflecting.

Moments passed.

"Yeah, you're right," Beaumont finally said. "What else would they do?"

1959 October 03 Saturday 15:22

"He frightens me," Cynthia said. "Every time he comes here, he . . . he changes the air we breathe, somehow. I can't explain it."

"It's not like you to get spooked, honey."

"I know it's not," she said, crisply. "That's why I'm saying it now."

"You want me to cut him loose?" Beaumont asked.

"You'd do that, Beau? On nothing more than my . . . feeling?"

"Of course I would, Cyn. This . . . business we're in, it's probably like any other. There's people you can never trust, people you can trust sometimes, but how many do you ever meet you can trust all the way?"

"I don't know. You handle all the—"

"You," Beaumont said, lovingly. "From the minute I was born, you."

1959 October 03 Saturday 16:04

"You said one car," the pawnbroker said to Dett.

"I said one *space*," Dett rebutted, neutral-voiced. "There's never going to be two cars back there at the same time. Just different ones, alternating."

"That still should be more—"

"I came here as a courtesy, so you wouldn't be surprised when you saw another car in the space I rented. I've always been polite to you, haven't I? And I dealt fair, paid you what you wanted, didn't I?"

"Yes. But—"

"All right. I'll tell Mr. Beaumont you want to change the deal."

"Anyone can say a name," the pawnbroker said, in his professional bargainer's voice.

"They can," Dett agreed. "Sometimes, a man thinks he can make an investment with that. Spend a dime on a phone call, say a name, and get back a big reward. You seem like such a smart man. With your own business and all. I thought we were friends."

"I—"

"You're going to make *some* kind of call. If you make the right one, you'll see I'm a man who tells the truth about who his friends are. If you make the wrong one, you'll find out something else about me. When I come back, you tell me if you still want more money for that space, okay?"

1959 October 03 Saturday 16:22

"That was Nat," Beaumont said, hanging up the phone. "What could he want?"

"He said Dett used my name."

"Well, he *should,* shouldn't he? You were the one who sent him to Nat."

"I'm not saying he did anything wrong. I'm just a little surprised. Nat was trying to shake Dett down for a few extra bucks. You'd think Dett would just pay it; what's the big deal?"

"I don't know."

"Me, either. But what Nat *really* wanted was for me to be sure to tell Dett he called. Can you make any sense out of that?"

"I think he did something that scared the hell out of Nat," Cynthia said. "And that's not such an easy thing to do."

1959 October 03 Saturday 22:22

"You got a name?"

"I'm the man who sent your boss the letter."

"Oh. The cute guy. What d'you want now, pal?"

"I want to speak to your boss. Just like I said the last time I called."

"The boss isn't going to talk to some punk hustler. There's a hundred ways you could have gotten that license."

"You talking *for* your boss? Or are you just talking?"

"You'll never know, pal."

"Okay, messenger boy. Tell your boss I won't be using the mail to deliver the next package."

"Hey! If you—"

1959 October 03 Saturday 23:45

"What'd he look like?" Rufus asked Silk. The two men were in the back booth of a sawdust-floored juke joint, walled off from the other patrons by three men who stood in a fan around them, facing out.

"Like any of your regular hillbillies, man. Kind of tall, but not no giant. Slender, but not skinny. White skin, but not ex-con color. He just . . . average-looking, I guess. Not the kind of man leaves an impression. Except for his eyes."

"What color?"

"I couldn't even tell you, brother. Not in the light we was in. But it's not the color, it's the look."

"Like nobody's home?"

"That's it! Even when he smiled—"

"And he gave you those?" Rufus asked Silk, looking down at the pimp's open palm. "Just *gave* them to you?"

"You know what they are?"

"Looks like a pair of gold dice. With little diamonds where there's supposed to be dots."

"*Solid* gold, brother. *Real* diamonds. You never heard of these?"

"Supposed to be some kind of good-luck charm?" Rufus asked, his mind flashing to an image of the mojo Rosa Mae had described.

"You know how the greaseballs be moving in on our policy banks?"

"*Our* banks?"

"You know what I mean, man," Silk said, deliberately not taking offense. "The numbers game is a colored thing. Always been. We invented it. Got a whole big industry behind it: dream books, charms, stuff like that. Naturally, Whitey sees us making some money, he wants it for himself."

"You got me all the way over here so you could tell me that?"

"I know you don't feature me, man. Behind what I do."

"I don't care what you do," Rufus said. "I care about what you are. You're a black pimp, that's okay. What I got to find out is what comes first. Black, or pimp."

Silk leaned back in the booth. He lit a cigarette with a small gold lighter. Half-closed his eyes. "Young boys, they think being a pimp takes a steel cock. What it takes is a steel mind."

"Uh-huh."

"They think it's the perfect job, what I do," Silk went on, unruffled. "All the free pussy in the world. What they don't know is, there's no such thing as free pussy. You pay, one way or the other."

"Why you telling me all this?"

"Outsiders, they don't understand The Life," the pimp went on as if he had not been interrupted. "They think a whore's a cold-blooded cunt. Like a slot machine—you slide in the money, and they open up. You want to know the truth? To be a high-class working girl, like the kind I got, you have to believe in love. That's what they get from me. That's what I pay with. See, a real mack, he knows everything comes from here," Silk said, touching his temple in the same spot Dett had with his .45. "I talk for a living. I'm not going to do that with you. I came here to show you something. You don't want it, I'll just—"

"Something besides these trick dice?"

"Those dice are famous, man. Maybe not where you live, but every player this side of St. Louis knows them. Belong to Brutus

Farley, king of the Cleveland policy game. That's where I came up, Cleveland. Back then, the whole East Side belonged to Brutus. That policy money made him too rich for anyone to touch. He had all kinds of legit businesses. *Colored* businesses. Barbershops, liquor stores, gas stations. Owned him some apartment buildings, too. Word is, Brutus got his stake rolling bones; that's what he started his bank with. Those were his lucky dice, man. He always carried them with him, wherever he went."

"You're sure those are the same ones?"

"Brutus always had men around him," the pimp continued, ignoring the question. "Not collectors—you don't need muscle to collect for numbers—bodyguards, like. He had a pair of mother-fuckers so ugly make a gorilla run back into the jungle, he see them. *Huge* boys. Carried so much iron they clanked when they walked, too.

"A few years ago, Brutus disappears. Him and his two body-guards. For a while, some of the people under him was able to keep things together, run the bank. But they couldn't hold it. Now you still got a numbers game in Cleveland. And you still got our people working as runners. But the wops own it."

The pimp puffed lightly on his cigarette. "Nobody ever knew what happened to Brutus," he said. "Some people say he had enough money, he just went someplace else, live out the rest of his life in peace. Some say he's laying in the cut, waiting to make a comeback. But it was on the drums that he got done, and that's what most people believe."

"You think this guy, the one who snatched you, *he* did that?"

"Where else he get those dice, brother? You know him, right? You said he staying at your hotel. What do *you* think?"

"He's . . . he's kind of a nice guy. Real gent."

"He was nice to me, too. Polite and everything. Kept his voice soft. But I'll tell you this, Brother Omar. You don't like what I do, but you know what it take to do it. My game, it *is* game. *All* game. You got to play people like a violin. Know what strings to stroke. And you can't play them unless you can read them. This guy, what'd you say he called himself . . . ?"

"Walker Dett."

"Yeah. I know he go by a lot of different names, but I never heard that one for him before."

"What are you talking about, man?"

"You ain't going to catch me saying his name out loud, brother. Not his real name—that's the worst kind of bad luck there is," Silk said fervently. "I never thought I'd ever see him, not with my own eyes. But I always knew he'd be a white man."

1959 October 04 Sunday 00:06

B ack in his room, Dett extracted a small brass canister from a compartment inside his suitcase. He unscrewed the top and carefully tapped several tiny crimson flakes into the palm of his hand. He licked them delicately off his palm, and immediately drank a full glass of water, swallowing slowly.

Seating himself, he dialed a local number. When it was picked up at the other end, Dett said, "That property we talked about? The one with the crawl space up top? I don't believe I'm going to have an immediate use for it, as I had thought. I need to explore other options. When would be a convenient time for us to meet?"

Dett listened to the response, then hung up.

In the nightstand drawer, he found a local phone book. "Chambers" was a common name in the area. He found two "T. Chambers"es and three "C. Chambers"es. No Tussy, and no Carol. Working slowly through the addresses, Dett finally came to a match with the one Tussy had given him. The phone number was the same, too. Both listed under "Abner Chambers."

Dett dialed the number.

"Hello?" A woman's voice, sleepy-soft.

Dett hung up.

1959 October 04 Sunday 01:10

"There's no way I can get that," Lymon said, the mouthpiece of the telephone receiver cupped protectively in his hand. "I don't even know when he goes out there to see him, never mind what they talk about."

"You better get *something*," a whiskey-roughened voice said. "If you can't, you're not much good to us, are you, then?"

"I already got—"

"—paid, is what you got. Paid good."

"You know I'm not doing it for money. I'm with—"

"—us? You're with us, are you? That's fine, isn't it? But you're not a *soldier*, boyo, you're a spy. A spy for peace. Remember what you were promised?"

"Yeah. You said there'd be no—"

"—and there won't," the voice assured him. "We'd rather do it peaceful. But we *are* going to do it. Now, listen to me, my friend. Being with us, that's not like betting on a horse. It's not even like riding a horse. You've got to *be* the horse."

"I *am*, goddamn it. Haven't I proved—?"

"All you proved, so far, is that you're a smart man. Right now, we'd rather have a bloody dummy, if he had some good gen for us, understand?"

"Yeah. I'll try and—"

"Try *hard*," the voice said, its tone matching the last word.

1959 October 04 Sunday 01:15

"It's too risky, boss," Rufus said.

"Piece of cake," the man in the driver's seat of the Chrysler Imperial responded. He was slightly under average height, but his bodybuilder's physique gave him the presence of a much larger man. "The guy who'll be doing the search, he'll already be a guest in that hotel. Checked in, all nice and legal. So, even if someone sees him in the hall, so what?"

"I ain't worried about nobody seeing him in the *hall*, boss. Mr. Dett, he comes and goes. There ain't no regular pattern to him. If he was to walk in and find someone searching his room . . ."

"You let us worry about that," the man said, pursing his thick lips into a Cupid's bow.

"Nah, sir. I cain't do that. That little job is all I have, and I done had it a long time. The man finds out someone got into his room, he gonna know somebody used a passkey."

"Anyone could pick one of those hotel-room locks."

"Mebbe so. But how he gonna lock the door *behind* him when he go?"

"That's where you come in," the powerfully built man said. "All you have to do is—"

"I ain't doing that, boss," Rufus said, firmly. "Not for no kind of money."

"Big words," the man in the driver's seat said.

"I'm big *scared,* boss."

"Look, no job is such a—"

"It ain't the job, boss. It's that man I'm a-scared of. You ain't met him."

"I met plenty like him," the bodybuilder said, confidently. "Just a hired gun. They're the same as whores; they just do different things for their money."

"If you says so, boss. You knows about things like that. I know you not scared of nothing. But, me, I cain't do that. I just cain't. Swear to Jesus. Even if I didn't get caught doing it, that man would know."

"He's a fortune-teller, too?"

"Boss, please. I got another idea. Get you the same thing you want, I promise."

"I'm listening," the man said. He spread his hands before him, palms-down, admiring the manicure he'd gotten earlier that day.

"Your man, he just wants to search the room, right?"

"Right."

"So how about *I* does it for you, boss? You tells me what you wants me to look for, I tells you if it's there."

"Searching a place, that's no job for a—for an amateur. There's ways to do it, make sure nobody knows you've ever been looking. There's guys do that for a living, they're like ghosts. Float in, float out, never leave a trace."

"I could do it, boss," Rufus said, eagerly. "It's not like this the man's house; it's a hotel room. Guests, they be *expectin'* people goin' in and out, all the time. You got the maids, the maintenance men, the room-service people. You got—"

The man in the driver's seat leaned back against the thickly padded cushions, scratched a spot on his dimpled chin. "You're a good man, Rufus," he said. "We've been doing business a long time. You're reliable, I know that. You say you're going to do something, you do it. I can count on you."

"Thank you, boss."

"But this here job, no offense, it takes a lot of . . . You got to be able to think, not just do what you're told—make decisions on the spot."

"I don't understand, boss."

"Yeah. That's kind of what I'm afraid of. Look, Rufus. Let's say I ask you to find a little red box in his room, you could do that, right?"

"Sho'!"

"Uh-huh. Now, what if I ask you, just find out what you can about the man, what do you do then?"

Rufus nodded several times, as if pondering the problem before solidifying his thoughts.

"I looks for papers, boss. Papers and numbers."

"Tell me more," the man said, a slight posture-shift revealing his heightened alertness.

"Anything with names or numbers on it, that wouldn't mean nothing to me, I guess. But I figure *you* would know what stuff like that means."

The bodybuilder turned to look at Rufus's earnest face, again noticing that slight yellowish cast in the man's eyes that had always disconcerted him. *Probably got one of those nigger diseases,* he thought.

"You're smarter than you look," the bodybuilder said. "And that's a very good thing."

1959 October 04 Sunday 02:12

B*uick Roadmaster, four-door hardtop, coral body, with a white roof,* Dett thought to himself, watching the empty car. *This guy, he's making enough to afford an Imperial, like his boss, but he's smart, driving something a step down. Shows respect. They like that stuff.*

Dett had spotted the Roadmaster during one of his careful sweeps of what Beaumont had called a "fringe territory." The target's car was docked just off a decrepit street lined with storefronts—two liquor stores, a spot-labor joint, a deserted-looking greasy spoon, and a Chinese laundry. Most of the storefronts were empty. Some were boarded up; others forlornly displayed FOR RENT signs in their dirt-encrusted windows.

Before he had located the Roadmaster, Dett had eye-marked a half-dozen teenagers moving along the sidewalk. They were identically dressed in shiny black rayon jackets, with "Hawks" on the back, in gold lettering. The rest of their uniform consisted of gold chauffeur's caps with black bills, narrow-cuffed jeans, and engineer boots. *Garrison belts, with the buckles sharpened, probably some switchblades,* Dett thought, dismissing the idea of those kids carrying firearms. The gang moved in a wedge behind their leader, sweeping down the empty sidewalk. As they passed a storefront with black-painted windows, they all moved to the edge of the curb.

They don't want any part of that place, Dett thought. *Must be Dioguardi's joint. Which means that's where the target is now. So his car's got to be around here somewhere, too. Those kids, they probably keep an eye on it for him. . . .*

Dett gave the gang a two-block lead, then slowly followed in their wake. They descended a flight of stairs below street level, and disappeared.

Dioguardi owns that building, Dett calculated. *Lets them use the basement for a clubhouse; they watch the street for him. Same as it's done everywhere.*

After a quick glance at his watch, Dett shrugged his shoulders and kept driving, heading for Lambert Avenue. "That's the dividing line," Beaumont had told him. "You got white on one side, colored on the other. Only time they cross is to rumble. The white kids are the Golden Hawks; the coloreds call themselves the South Side Kings."

"You know how big they are?" Dett had asked him.

"The Hawks? Maybe twelve, fifteen of them are real members. But, for a fight, they might get some other white kids to pitch in, even if they weren't affiliated. The coloreds, it seems like there's more of them, but I couldn't tell you for sure."

I could tell you, Dett had said to himself, thinking of a recent job he'd done in Chicago. But he had only nodded.

A few blocks away, Dett brought his rented Impala to a stop on Lambert, a wide boulevard lined with what appeared to be thriving businesses on both sides. *The DMZ,* he thought to himself, noting the pair of black-and-white patrol cars down the block. The cars were pointed in opposite directions—one parked at the curb, the other blocking an oncoming lane of late-night traffic—as the drivers discussed something through their opened windows.

As Dett watched, another prowl car loomed in his rearview mirror. *Three in five minutes,* he thought. *A few blocks south of here, I didn't see one in over an hour.*

He started the Impala, pulled out of his parking space, and drove several blocks down Lambert. He was not surprised to see still another black-and-white before he turned back in the direction of the Hawks' basement.

The patch of broken ground between two short blocks had never been used for sandlot baseball games. Choked with rubble, it looked like the place where junkyards dumped what they couldn't sell.

Dett pulled alongside the vacant lot. Stepping out briskly, he opened the Impala's trunk, reached in carefully with both hands, and extracted a crosshatched weave of Scotch tape. He sprinkled dirt lightly on the sticky side of the weave, turning it cloudy. Using his back to block what he was doing, he reversed the weave so that it adhered to the license plate on the rear bumper. Then he stepped back to inspect his work, satisfying himself that the plate was un-readable, even at close range.

The Roadmaster was still in place, almost directly under a working streetlight. Dett parked ahead of it on the one-way street, climbed out, and walked slowly back. A wine bottle wrapped in a brown paper bag was in his left hand. His walk was determinedly steady—a drunk who knew he was loaded.

The drunk's walk got sloppier and sloppier as he neared the Buick. By the time he was ten feet past the car, the booze seemed to get the upper hand—he slumped against a deserted building for support.

A minute later, the drunk was sitting on the sidewalk, his back to the building, chin on his chest. Under the brim of his hat, his eyes swept the surrounding terrain like a prison searchlight after the es-cape siren sounds.

Less than twenty minutes had passed when two men turned the corner to the drunk's left.

Dett watched, *Two!* registering clinically in his technician's mind.

As the men came closer, Dett's eyes noted that they were both wearing black topcoats and pearl-gray snap-brims. His mind dis-missed the information, focusing on the vitals—they were approxi-mately the same height.

Anyone watching would have seen a drunk struggling to his feet, using one hand to brace himself against the building wall. The drunk stumbled toward the two men, weaving slightly.

One of the men parted his topcoat, revealing a white silk lining as he reached into the pocket of his slacks and pulled out a set of car keys.

Dett staggered down the sidewalk toward them, a wet-brain on autopilot, determined to walk home despite the ground rippling under his feet.

Slow down, Dett said inside his mind. The movie playing on the screen of his eyes began to crawl forward, frame by frame, as his world telescoped down to a narrow tunnel.

At five yards, Dett made a pre-vomiting sound. The man with the car keys involuntarily drew back, looking at Dett in disgust. Dett tossed the paper bag to his left. It seemed to hang in the air for seconds, pulling the eyes of both men into its arc before the bottle inside shattered on the sidewalk. The one with the car keys shook his head in contempt. The other, more experienced, was already reaching inside his coat as Dett drew his pistol from under his left armpit—*Exhale . . . slowly, slowly*—and gripped it in two hands, the left hand pulling back against the slight forward pressure of the right, wrists locked.

One man's hand was already under his lapel as Dett's .45 cracked. The shot caught him in the center of his chest, dropping him instantly. Without shifting his feet, Dett ratcheted his shoulders a few notches and cranked off another round, nailing the other man in the stomach.

Dett bent forward and carefully shot each man between the eyes. He turned and walked unhurriedly past the dead bodies toward his car, the .45 dangling at his side.

No lights went on. No sirens broke the night.

Dett slipped his pistol back into its holster and kept walking, moving quickly through the slow-motion movie reel unfurling all around him.

The ignition key was already slotted in the Impala, the protruding portion wrapped in black electrical tape so it wouldn't catch the eye of any casual passerby. The door was unlocked. It only took Dett a long heartbeat to get in, start the engine, and smoothly pull away.

Dett drove to the pawnshop. But instead of parking in front of the building, he pulled around to the side, and opened the padlock to the chain-linked lot, using a key the pawnbroker had insisted on giving him.

When he drove out a few minutes later, Dett was behind the wheel of the Ford, dressed in laborer's clothes. His hands reeked faintly of gasoline. He was unarmed.

1959 October 04 Sunday 03:09

"What did he say? *Exactly*," Dioguardi demanded.

"He said, 'Tell your boss, the next package I deliver, I won't use the mail.' Then he hung up. Fucking cocksucking—"

"He didn't ask for anyone, Vito? Like last time?"

"No, boss. It was just what I told you, word for word."

"Would you know the voice if you heard it again?"

"I . . . Maybe, I don't know, Mr. D. It was a white guy. Not a kid, but not too old, either."

"He didn't have any kind of an accent?"

"No. It was like . . . it was like talking to a machine. What do we do, Mr. D.?"

"When he calls again, you tell him I want to talk."

"Maybe he won't—"

"Yeah, he will," Dioguardi said, grimly confident.

1959 October 04 Sunday 03:23

Moonlight transformed the gleaming aluminum skin of the Airstream trailer into a shimmering, eye-tricking image, like a metallic mushroom growing in a dense forest. The trailer was mortally wounded—first ripped and torn beyond repair in a head-on collision with a hell-bound semi, later stripped of anything that could be turned into cash, and finally left to rot in a far corner of the junkyard. A red dot glowed from somewhere inside what was once its doorway.

"It's almost half past, Omar," Kendall said to Rufus.

"I know what time it is, brother."

"They was never so late before."

"You got someplace to be, K.?"

"Yeah, man. Always. Right here, with you, wherever you is. All I'm saying—"

"That's them," Darryl interrupted, as jaundiced headlight beams cut the night.

A dark-gray panel truck turned into the entrance to the junkyard. On its side were the words "Acme Transfer Company" in red, flowing above a painting of a deliveryman wheeling a file cabinet on a hand truck, the sleeves of his shirt rolled up to display bulging cartoon biceps.

The truck did a slow-speed slalom through the piled-up car

corpses until it came to a cleared area where the remains of the trailer sat.

"Why it always got to be two of them?" Kendall whispered to Rufus.

"There's more than two of *us*," Rufus answered. "They're the ones walking into the lions' den."

"Don't ever feel like that to me, brother. Those some spooky motherfuckers."

Rufus was already on his feet, moving toward the truck, which had come to a gentle stop.

A man emerged from the passenger seat, dropping lightly to the ground. He was dressed in a black leather jacket over a white turtle-neck jersey and blue jeans.

Like he bought that whole outfit an hour ago, Rufus thought to himself. *And look at those shoes—they're made for a suit.* "You're late," he said aloud. "I wasn't sure you'd be coming."

"We had to take a detour," the man said. He was a couple of inches shorter than Rufus, with a face older than his trim physique.

"I've got your money," Rufus said.

"And we've got your goods," the man replied, twitching his mouth.

As they spoke, the driver climbed out of the truck, walked around to the back, and opened the doors.

Mutt and Jeff, Rufus thought, noting the driver's height. *But they shop at the same store.*

The shorter man made a "Welcome to my establishment" gesture with one hand, indicating two rows of neatly stacked wooden crates.

"I don't see any—" Rufus said.

"Everything's there," the man cut him off. "You've got four to a crate, so that's twenty-four total. Behind, you've got extra thirty-round magazines, plus five thousand rounds."

"We said fifty."

"You said fifty M1s," the man corrected Rufus. "What you've got here, my friend, is two dozen M2s. They may be Winchesters, but they're not the kind you could walk into a gun shop and buy, not ordnance like this. It's all military, right out of the armory. Brand-new and perfect. An operation like we run, if you want to *keep* doing it, you take the opportunities as they're offered. Twenty-four is what we could take out *safely*. So we know we can always go back."

"The price—"

"The price is the same," the man said. "And it's cheap at that. The M2s have a selective fire switch. You know what that means?"

"Yeah, I know what it means. But two dozen machine guns still means only two dozen men can hold them. My buyer wanted fifty, like I said."

"This load is what we *have,* friend. You want it, or not?"

"I want it. But not for no—"

"We didn't drive out here to bargain, friend," the shorter man said. "If you don't want to take the package, we know other people who will. The only reason we even bothered to come all the way out here was because you've been such a good customer."

"I don't see why we can't . . . adjust the price," Rufus said, resentfully.

"We took the same risk for twenty-four as we would have for fifty," the man said, his tone indicating he considered his position very reasonable. "And we'd spend just as much time in prison if we were caught. We have expenses. People to pay, all along the route. Nobody *we* had to pay wanted to hear about any 'adjustment.' Look, like I said, you're a good customer. We'll make it up to you on the next shipment. What do you say?"

"I'll get the money," Rufus said.

"Good. We'll start unloading, then."

1959 October 04 Sunday 04:19

"I still think it was stupid, Fred," the driver of the panel truck said to the man next to him. They were back on the interstate, twenty miles from the drop-off point, heading west. "What if they had refused the load?"

"You don't understand those people, Milt," the man in the passenger seat said. "They *expect* us to try and change the deal, from time to time. If we didn't, they'd get suspicious."

"So what if they did? So long as they take the guns, what difference does it make?"

"The difference it makes is, maybe, the difference in our careers, partner."

"I don't get what you're saying, Fred. We were told to—"

"What I'm saying is, this whole thing started as an assignment. The Bureau needs to know who's buying guns, and the best way to know that is for us to be in the gunrunning business."

"Right. So?"

"So knowing who's buying guns isn't the same thing as knowing what they're going to do with them."

"You think they're going to just tell us?"

"Well, they *did* kind of tell us, Milt, if you think about it. That is, if you count that fairy story about some nigger in a junkyard who's an international arms trafficker," the shorter man said, scornfully. "Still, up to now, they haven't asked us for anything except what we're supposed to be selling. Guns. Now, we know something from the *kind* of guns they buy, don't we? Sure!" the shorter man said, answering his own question, as was his habit. "But think what we might learn if they got the idea we could get inside an armory somewhere. Who knows how far they might go?"

"That's why you told him—?"

"Exactly!" Fred said, clapping his hands in self-satisfaction. "I planted a seed. That's what the Bureau calls initiative, partner."

1959 October 04 Sunday 04:26

"I don't like those boys," the cadaverous man said.

"I don't like them, either," Rufus replied. "But I like what they deal in."

"Every time we make a buy, they get a real good look at you," the cadaverous man said. "And they know this place, too."

"Yeah. But K-man already made the calls. By daybreak, those guns are going to be on their way to ten different places."

"They only brought two dozen."

"So some units will get less than we planned on. But these are real machine guns. We never had any of those, before."

"I don't like dealing with whites, brother."

"For what we need, who else could we be going to?" Rufus said, not expecting an answer.

1959 October 04 Sunday 08:08

The North Side block was a solid chunk of attached, identical two-story buildings—retail establishments, with apartment units above.

Behind the block was an alley almost as wide as a two-lane road, with a row of garages facing the rear of the buildings. Exposed wooden stairways provided access to the rear doors of the second-floor apartments. The railings sported a fresh coat of cream paint. A couple of tenants had decorated their portions with flower boxes. A portable barbecue grill stood on one landing, an armchair covered with a canvas tarp on another.

The Shamrock Inn's façade was sun-faded brick, with a pair of narrow, vertical-slit windows standing like sentries on either side of a heavy black oak door. To its right stood a laundry; to its left, a dry cleaner.

Above the Shamrock, two men sat at a small table covered with red-and-white-checked oilcloth. The table was placed precisely in the center of a bare room, set well back from the thickly curtained front windows.

"That's a mighty big slice of honeycake you're feeding me here, Sean."

The whiskey-roughened voice belonged to a small, compact, ginger-haired man with a deeply cleft chin, dressed in a white corduroy shirt buttoned to the throat, neatly pressed chinos, and lace-up brown work boots. His features placed him somewhere between his late thirties and early fifties; his eyes were a deceptively soft blue. The lobe of his right ear was elongated, like a piece of pulled taffy; the left lobe was missing, leaving a ragged edge. His hands looked as if they had been grafted onto his body from a man twice his size.

"Not a word of it, Mickey Shalare," the ruddy-faced man across from him said. He was in his mid-sixties, wearing a double-breasted blue suit that emphasized his considerable bulk. "It's sweet, that I won't deny. But it's gospel-pure, on my mother's love."

"It's really going to happen, then? The coalition?"

"It's *already* happened, my son. By Thanksgiving, it'll be locked down tighter than a church secret."

"You really think this country's ready for one of us at the top?"

"One of *us*? Oh, I wouldn't think so," Sean replied, a grin flashing across his face and disappearing quickly, a subliminal message. "But a Catholic? That can be done, yes."

"People in this part of the country—"

"—vote the same way they do everyplace else, Mick. One at a bloody time. And not nearly so many of them as could. A lot of folks here, they don't even bother."

Sean paused, catching the expression on the younger man's face. Then, clearing his throat dramatically, he spoke again. "Sure, we understand there's some . . . bad elements in these parts. But you think those boys who like to dress up in hoods and robes are going to try burning a cross on the White House lawn?"

"Not them," Shalare said contemptuously. "They don't have the bottle for it. But—"

"You're going to tell me that there's plenty *think* like them, though, are you? Well, listen to me now: their votes don't count."

"How can they not count, Sean? The ballots are blind."

The bulky man took a slow, contemplative sip from a heavy brown mug. His posture shifted subtly; his voice took on an almost professorial tone. But his words were hard metal, without even a trace element of condescension. "In this country, the way they have it set up, there are only two parties. If you want to cast your vote for the idiot who promises you a worker's paradise, or for the moron who swears he's going to ship all the darkies back to Africa, well, you can do it. But your vote won't count, do you see? You'd be at a horse race, betting on a pig.

"Besides," the bulky man continued, running a hand through his thick, reddish gray hair, "it's the big cities where the real numbers are. And that's where we're the strongest. Strongest by *far,* I do promise you."

"And if this should happen, it will mean . . . what, for our people?" the ginger-haired man asked, a beveled edge to his flinty voice.

The bulky man changed position so that his elbows were on the table, his body language inviting the smaller man to do the same.

"This kind of talk . . . it's not meant for anyone to hear."

The smaller man's complexion darkened as quickly as a finger-snap. "Are you saying that I—"

"Ah, Mickey Shalare," the bulky man interrupted, holding up his palm for silence. "Do you think any of us forget how you held your own against all the King's men, even down in the pit of their dungeons? Right after the Gough Barracks it was when they came for you, and there's good and true men who wouldn't have breathed free air these past years, were it not for your devotion."

"Yes, and . . . ?" the ginger-haired man said, not softening.

"And I never forget what my mother taught me at her knee, son," the bulky man said, dropping his voice and glancing over his shoulder before returning his eyes to Shalare's. "Poverty's bad, but stupidity's worse. Green, that's the color of grass, too."

"I had a mother, myself, Sean," the smaller man said, his over-sized hands splayed on the tabletop. "Below us is my own place. The apartments on either side of this one, the only tenants are women whose husbands are never coming home, and they don't keep company, understand? There's a pigeon coop on the roof, and the boy who takes care of them is the youngest son of Michael McNamara himself. Here, where we're sitting, it might as well be a Bogside estate."

"Yes, 'here,' indeed," the bulky man said. "No Brit soldiers on patrol outside, sure. But America's not the Promised Land—we've got our enemies 'here,' do we not?"

"Aye."

"And they buy our people the same way they do at home—every chance they get."

"I've been in Locke City long enough to learn the way of things, Sean. Here, it's us who does the buying."

"The police—"

"Not the police. Everybody who wants to do business here pays them. It's like a bloody tax."

"The big men, the men who are putting this together, they don't rent the police, Mickey. They own them."

"Maybe in Boston or Chicago. Not here," Shalare said, emphatically.

"Is that so?"

"It is. But that doesn't mean they're free agents. Around here, it's Mr. Royal J. Beaumont who holds those cards."

"That's why I've come," the bulky man said. "Why I've been sent, I should say."

"You never did answer my question," Shalare told him, making it clear that bridge had to be crossed first.

"What it's going to mean for our people? Just *imagine* it, Mick."

"When I was down in that little cell, I used to imagine all kinds of things, Sean. They didn't keep me long, but they kept me cruel. I had to make up beautiful stories in my head, just to stop from going mad. Because that was all I *could* do, yes? That's not the way it is anymore. Now I'd want to see the road map. Hold it in my hands."

"Well, I'd be lying if I said I could give you that," the bulky man admitted. "It's not as if we'd really be running the show, is it? You know we'd only have a seat or two at the table."

"So we'd be a bloody minority again, you're saying?"

"It's not the numbers, Mickey, it's the strength. Look at Korea. The war's supposed to be over, but America's still standing between two raging forces, to keep them from each other's throats. Just like the Limeys *say* they're doing back home."

Ignoring the smaller man's puzzled look, the emissary opened another organ stop in his mesmeric voice. "Now listen close to me, Mickey Shalare. Because that's the key I gave you, right there. *That's* what has to change. Not just at home, all over the world. You have to know your enemy. And the Brits, all we ever need to know about them is that they're colonialists in their hearts. It's in their very souls. Right this minute, they've got far more troops in Africa than they'll ever have in Ireland. It's the bloody British *Empire,* isn't it?"

"It is," Shalare agreed. "But you make it out as if they're the only ones."

"Who? The Americans? They're done with all that."

"Are they, then? Wasn't it you just talking about Korea?"

"Ah, but the Yanks don't think Korea's *part* of America, do they?" The bulky man said, sweeping away the comparison. "They don't want to *stay* there. You know how many bloody Koreans there are? Occupying that country, why, it's just impossible. They'd have to slaughter everyone first, like they did the Indians, here, and *then* they'd have to persuade enough Americans to go over there and live. Or transport them, the way the Brits did the Aussies. No, the Yanks have a different scheme. They want to do as they did in Japan. Put their lackeys in power and get the hell out."

"Sure," Shalare said. "And that's what the Brits would like to do, too. But the very moment they leave . . ."

"And *that's* where the change has to come, Mick. We have to show them a different model."

"Speak plainly," Shalare said, his tone matching his words.

"All right, then," Sean said, squaring his shoulders. "Every time the Brits pull out of a place they once controlled, what happens? The country they leave behind celebrates with a civil war, doesn't it? Look, they're supposed to be leaving Nigeria soon. Now, that's a *big* country. I've been there. I swear to you, if you closed your eyes and couldn't see skin color, you'd think you were in England. They speak English like the Brits, they have a parliament like the Brits. Why, even their money is in pounds. Lagos, that's their capital city, it's got buildings as tall as London's. Very . . . cosmopolitan, I'd call it."

The bulky man paused a beat, then said, "All that, it didn't come from farming, Mickey. What they have there is oil. A *lot* of oil. Just like the Arabs, maybe more. British Petroleum probably pumps more out of Nigeria than anyplace else on earth. And the minute, the very minute the Brits take their troops out of there, there's going to be bloody chaos. You know why?"

"Because they're a pack of fucking savages," Shalare said, folding his oversized hands.

"No, my son," the bulky man said. "It's because the Brits picked one tribe out of all the different ones to be their pet. The same way they picked the Ulstermen to be their darlings in our country. So it was one tribe that got all the businessmen. And the lawyers and the doctors and the judges and the politicians and the . . . Well, you see, don't you?"

"I do," Shalare said. "And when we finally drive them out of—"

"No, no, no," the bulky man said, his ruddy face set in hard lines. "Not drive. *Induce.* How long now have we been trying to force them off? It's been twenty years since the S Plan, and what has changed? What good have the border wars done for us? Operation Harvest? It's been almost three years now, Mickey Shalare. And all we've gathered from it is blood and tears."

"The Jews managed it," Shalare said, stubbornly.

"In Israel, you mean? Sure, they got the Brits out. But you're not saying *that's* a country at peace, now are you? I mean, they're bloody *surrounded,* aren't they?"

"So what's the answer, then?"

"America," the bulky man said, his voice heavy with the weight of the word. "We can do from here what we could never do from home."

"So—we should all emigrate, then?" Shalare said.

"No," Sean said, ignoring the heavy sarcasm. "We should build a power base inside a country that can call the shots. This isn't about the righteousness of our cause; it's about the power we need to prevail. And that won't come from gunfire, not in the end."

The bulky man leaned back in his chair, as if to withdraw from the smaller man's level stare. "Am I wrong, Mickey Shalare? Am I wrong to say that, for all our sacrifices, for all the Irish mothers and wives and sisters who mourn our soldiers, we've nothing to show?"

"If it *wasn't* for those sacrifices, we'd all be living under the yoke of the—"

Sean filled his chest with air, injecting power into his voice without raising the volume. "Damn, man, won't you see? We've put all our strength into trying to drive them out. And come up short. But what if America were to side with us?"

"Against the Brits? You can't be *that* drunk this early in the day."

"The next president is going to owe a lot of debts, Mick. And we're going to be holding some of that paper. Our cause has taken . . . aid, shall we say, from other governments all along. But when we take it under the table, it's always much less by the time it reaches us, isn't it? On the black market, every hand that touches the goods, a little sticks to it. But if we could get it direct, think of the possibilities! That's a stake worth playing for, isn't it?"

"I don't see it," Shalare said. "The Yanks aren't going to arm us, no matter what we do in this damn election."

"Not *arm* us, Mick. *Support* us. Stand with us. Push the Brits out with political pressure, as we were never able to do with guns and bombs."

"Sean, it sounds sweet, like I said. But I can't see it, much less taste it."

"Ah," the bulky man sighed, "will you give me a listen, Mickey Shalare? Our cause, we say it's for a united Ireland, do we not? But we don't mean a word of it, no more than the tribes in Nigeria really want to live together. There's plenty that could call themselves 'Irish,' yes? But how many of *us* are there in that big stew?"

"Most of the—"

"Nah, Mickey. Don't fall into that trap, now. You think every Catholic in Ireland is with us?"

"No," the smaller man said, coldly.

"No," the man opposite him agreed. "And here? In America? There's those who send us support, sure. They're *with* us, but they're not *of* us. But in this election, we're playing a role all out of proportion to our numbers, if you follow me."

"Yes, but—"

"But damn nothing! I'm telling you, straight out, they cannot put their man in power without us doing our part. And when it's over, it's not those 'Irish-Americans' they'll owe, Mickey. It'll be *us*. Because, inside every local political machine that can bring the Irish vote, we've got those of our own."

"Sean . . ."

"Will you *listen*? I said our *own,* Mickey Shalare. Because they've got the talkers and the poets and the dreamers. They've got the precinct captains and the police chiefs. They've got the silver tongues and the greasy palms. But what they don't have is the *soldiers.* Men of commitment. One of us is worth a thousand of them, and the people trying to make this happen, well, they understand that."

"You really believe—?"

"It's not what *I* believe, Mickey . . . although I *do* believe. It's the decision of the leadership. But the only way it happens is if we keep the coalition in place. That's why I've been sent to you now."

"Yes?" Shalare said, a dozen questions in that single word.

"This whole territory has been Beaumont's for a long time. You and that wop Dioguardi, you've both been coming at him, but from different directions."

"Dioguardi's a stupid thug."

"Granted. And you're a soldier. A general, I should say. You've built up a fine collection of allies, all over the state."

"With the Organization's money," Shalare said. "I know."

"Ah, that's not where I'm going at all, Mickey. Haven't I *been* talking politics from the moment I came here today? And that's why Dioguardi is important."

"Dioguardi doesn't have one single—"

"If you're going to say 'judge,' or 'senator,' you're right. But what he *does* have is friends. Or bosses, more likely, the way those people work. And the people over *him,* they've reached out to *us.*

"You understand? We're all of us agreed, each for his own reasons, sure, but all as one for *this.* The last thing we need now, when we're so close, is some kind of raging gang war. The big cities have gone quiet. The way they're supposed to. Oh, there's crime. Always will be. And there's people making their living from it. Always will be that, too. But there's a deal in place, Mick. From New York to Chicago to Detroit to Los Angeles to Houston to New Orleans to . . . Well, if you took a map of America and stuck pins in it for all the places who've come under our control, you'd hardly be able to see what's underneath.

"I've been around a long time, my son. And if I've learnt one thing, it's this. A free press doesn't mean it's not a *tame* press. So this whole business of crime, it makes a headline once in a while, but it's not the daily fare. If you read the papers—I don't mean just here, I mean anywhere throughout this country—you'll see nothing but teenagers on the crime pages. That's what's got this country all in an uproar. Not the men at the top. Not who controls prostitution, or gambling, or booze. No, what scares Americans is crazy children who kill each other over who gets to hang out in what sweetshop."

Shalare calmly regarded the man across from him. "Still, the crime-fighters always get the vote, don't they?"

"Not if that's all they have to offer," the bulky man shot back. "A man named Dewey found that out a few years back, didn't he? Now, listen," he said, a quicker, deeper current entering the dark river of his voice, "Kefauver's done. He had his chance. He won't be on the national ticket ever again. The Democrats are going our way. All the way. The train has already left the station. But if the press starts up again, if bodies start dropping in the streets, the public could turn on us."

"Turn to where, Sean? Who*ever* runs for office in this country, they always say the same things. They all promise to clean up whatever mob's making the papers."

"Sure," the other man said, not rising to the implied challenge. "But this election, it's going to be paper-thin. We're going to need every last vote. That's a huge machine to keep oiled, Mick. The coalition has to come at it from both sides. We need the organized groups to work the vote. And we need the wild kids to keep the public's eye off us."

"What is it you want from me, then? Every single politician on my payroll is actually on yours, already."

"You've been brilliant at that," the other man said. "Stunning, really, considering how little time you've had. It's the other side of your work that's the problem."

"Sean . . ."

"Dioguardi. You and him, you've got to call a truce."

"We're not at war. He wants the—"

"You *both* want what Beaumont has. So it's just a matter of time before you step on each other. And it's Beaumont we've got to approach."

"What do we approach him *with,* then?"

"With whatever it takes, Mickey. But it's got to happen. Beaumont's been the ruler around here since before most of the other big dogs were puppies. Like I said, my son . . . every single vote."

"Spell it out."

"The killing has to stop. Dioguardi's lost two men. Three, really, if you count that boy in a coma."

"Wasn't any of our work," Shalare said flatly.

"Who, then? Beaumont?"

"Nobody knows. Some think it's just one of their vendettas. Among themselves, I mean. Those people are like that."

"I told you, that's *over.* If the Commission—that's what the Italians call their council—was going to sanction a killing, it would be Dioguardi himself who got done. And *that* would only be because he refused to go along with the plan I told you about."

"It wasn't any of us," Shalare repeated.

"Then it had to be Beaumont."

"I might be able to tell you something about that, in a short time."

"You have someone . . . ?"

"I do."

"When you talk with him, then, will you ask him a question? For us?"

"Aye," Shalare said.

"The question isn't what you think. Sure, we need to know if it's Beaumont hitting Dioguardi's men. If it is, we'll ask him to stop. A truce, we can call it. A freeze, more likely. Everybody keeps what they have, nobody goes after anything that belongs to another. That will work for Beaumont, because he's the one who's got what the others are coming after. It's in his best interests to work with us."

"So the question is . . . ?"

"The question is this: if Beaumont were to go, are any of his people in a position strong enough to take over and keep his enterprises going, like proper businessmen? Or are those hillbillies crazy enough to start a war?"

"I'll ask," Shalare said.

"That's all *we* ask," the man across from him said, smiling broadly as he extended his hand.

1959 October 04 Sunday 09:04

"Nobody saw anything?" Procter asked, notebook open in his lap. "In that neighborhood? The only people on the street that time of night are the kind who don't volunteer as witnesses," Chief George Jessup said, sitting behind his ornate desk, framed between an American flag to his right and the state flag to his left.

"So all I can go with is—"

"It was a murder," Jessup said, as if underscoring an indisputable fact. "Anything beyond that would be pure speculation at this point."

"My sources tell me it had all the earmarks of a gangland assassination. A professional hit."

"Or a jealous husband," the chief said, dismissively. "This is off the record, but we've got it on pretty good authority that the deceased—Tony LoPresti—was a class-A cockhound. The other one, Lorenzo Gagnatella, he was probably just in the wrong place, with the wrong guy."

"You think so? I heard whoever shot them gave each one the coup de grâce. That sounds pretty professional to me."

"Anyone's ever gut-shot a deer would know to do that much," the chief said.

1959 October 04 Sunday 09:12

"That's all he wanted for his meal last night?" Rufus asked Rosa Mae. "Nothing else?"

"Celery sticks, carrots, radishes, lettuce, and a red onion," the young woman recited, as if reading back an order.

"That's nothing but a salad."

"No, Rufus. He didn't want them mixed. Didn't want no dressing, either. Now I got to get going. I'm going to be late for church."

"That's no kind of meal for a man. Especially a drinking man."

"I don't know about that," Rosa Mae said, shrugging her shoulders. "Clara down in the kitchen said they didn't even know what to charge for all that. She had to call upstairs to ask."

"That is one strange white man."

"You didn't know that, behind what I told you was in his suitcase, you're not as smart as everyone says you are, Rufus Hightower."

1959 October 04 Sunday 10:10

"How long have we known each other, Lymon?"

"All our lives, I guess. I was in the same class as Cynthia, from the time we started school. I guess we could count up the years, but that'd just make us sound old," Lymon said, smiling. "How come you ask, Roy?"

"Oh, I don't know. I guess it's just natural. In times of crisis, you always look to the people you know you can count on. And talking about how far back you go with them, it's kind of a comfort, I suppose."

"Crisis? Come on, Roy. I know Dioguardi's been nibbling and all, but that's happened before. We always come out on top."

"It's the top that's the problem. The top over *us*."

"Us? We're not part of—"

"Everybody's part of something, Lymon. Look, who's the mayor of this town?"

"Bobby Wyeth. He's been the—"

"Uh-huh. And who's the *boss* of this town?"

"Well, you, Roy. Who else?"

"Yeah. But if you were an outsider, you wouldn't know that, would you? If you wanted something, I don't know, a permit to put up a building, or a license to open a club, you'd go on down to City Hall, right?"

"I guess. . . ."

"And Bobby—not that you could get to *see* Bobby yourself, right off—he could take care of that for you. Everyone knows how that works—you have to take care of the person who takes care of you. If the job is big enough, the pie gets cut up right in Bobby's office, and he passes out the little slices. Passes them *down,* okay? But if it's a small-potatoes job, the cut travels *up,* from the building inspector or whoever, until it finally gets to Bobby."

"Sure."

"Well, we don't get a taste of *that* pie, Lymon. We're not supposed to; that's not the deal. But all of what we *do* get, it comes from the same place, like a lot of wires plugged into the same socket."

"Well, sure, Roy. I mean, I guess so."

"You know what they call the vote, Lymon?"

"The . . . what?"

"The vote. The *right* to vote, actually. What they call it is the 'franchise.' "

"You mean, like a Howard Johnsons?"

"I don't think that's what they were thinking of when they named it, but that's what it comes down to. See, it costs money to be elected. Money and muscle. The money and muscle, that's what buys votes. And once you control enough of those, you get to *make* money. Like Bobby Wyeth does. Like we do."

"So in every town . . . ?"

"In every town, every village, every city, every state—hell, in every *country*—"

"—Whoever runs the show, he gets a franchise to make money," Lymon said, like a schoolboy reciting out loud, to reinforce the lesson.

"Right," Beaumont said. "But that's not what we're talking about here. Without us, Bobby Wyeth isn't the boss of anything. His whole operation, it's like a damn army tank. Once it gets rolling, it doesn't matter who the driver is, what's going to stand in its way? But a tank's still a machine. And machines, they don't run on air. They need gas. They need oil. They need maintenance."

Beaumont paused a beat, then went on: "And that's us, Lymon. We're the only place the machine can get what it needs."

"Maybe that was so, once," Lymon said, thoughtfully. "But now, any election day, Bobby Wyeth can put a hundred precinct captains out in the street."

"He can," Beaumont conceded. "And if they want to keep their city jobs, they'll be out there, bringing in the voters. That's the way Bobby pays: with jobs, mostly. And I don't mean just cleaning the streets, or driving a bus, either. Being a judge, that's a job, too."

"So you're saying Bobby doesn't need us anymore?"

"No. No, I'm not saying that at all. We need each other. That's the way it works. The way it works everywhere. Real power is never public. You can't rub folks' noses in it; they won't stand for it. We've got enough on Bobby Wyeth to put him *under* the jail, we wanted to do that. The first nickel he ever took, you handed it to him yourself, didn't you?"

"Yeah. And that was before he ever got elected, too."

"So we could put a lot of dirt on him, so what? There may be some rubes out there who actually think politicians *aren't* all crooks, but there aren't enough of them to elect the town dogcatcher. The newspapers make a big deal out of political corruption, but the average guy, he *expects* a man in office to make something for himself. Bobby's got a house that had to cost him ten, fifteen years' salary . . . and there's no mortgage on it. He drives a new Cadillac every year, dresses like a movie star. And nobody cares. Or, if they do, they don't make a lot of noise about it."

"I don't think that's true, Roy. There's plenty of legit ways for a man who's mayor to make money. People don't *know* Bobby's got his hand in the till. Not for sure, anyway. If the papers ever got hold of—"

"You know what people *actually* hate about political corruption?" Beaumont said, slicing the air with his right hand to silence the other man. "They hate that they don't have it going for *them*. Who doesn't wish he could get a parking ticket fixed? Or get his son a good job, just by making a phone call?

"See, the people everyone thinks are running the show, they're really not. None of them, Lymon. That's the way it is, everywhere.

There's always men like us. We're the power. Not because of what we know; because of what we do. What we're *willing* to do. Because, no matter how high the hill any of them stand on, it never takes anything more than a good rifle shot to bring them down."

"Christ, Roy! What did Bobby—?"

"Bobby didn't do anything," Beaumont said, sighing. "I'm just trying to explain some things to you, old friend."

"The . . . crisis?"

"Yeah. Exactly. Bobby was here yesterday. Asking for money."

"What does he need money for? The election's not for another year. And who's going to run against him, anyway?"

"He needs money to get out the vote," Beaumont said. "Not for him, for the ticket. The national ticket. The governor himself put out the word. Come 1960, this country's supposed to change hands, Lymon. And what Bobby was told is, he has to deliver *double* the vote from the last election. And it better all be going to the right place."

"Okay, but why is that such a big deal for us?"

"Because they didn't come to *us,* Lymon. If that greedy little bastard Bobby wasn't too cheap to spend his own money, like he was supposed to, like they *expected* him to, we never even would have known."

"But so what, Roy? What does it mean?"

"It means we're not sitting at the table," Beaumont said, his iron eyes darkening to the color of wet slate. "And in this game, if you're not sitting down at the table, sooner or later, you get to be the meal."

1959 October 04 Sunday 12:02

"Beau, I think—"

"Wait till Luther gets back, honey."

"Where did he go?"

"He's just making sure Lymon gets out okay, like he always does."

"I don't see how people can be so cruel."

"What do you mean?"

"Every time you have a meeting, Luther's in the room. He stands right over there," she said, pointing to an unlit corner of the office. "But, for all the notice anyone takes of him, he might as well be a stick of furniture."

"They don't mean anything by it, girl."

"Maybe they don't. But it's still a rotten thing to do. Remember how the kids always made fun of him when we were in school?"

"I stopped that soon enough, didn't I?"

"You did," Cynthia said, a smile suddenly transforming her into the pretty girl she had been in her youth. "You, Sammy, Faron, and . . ."

"That's right, honey. And Lymon. He was with us back then. With us all the way."

"Beau, are you really so sure he—?"

"Wait till Luther gets back," the man in the wheelchair said.

1959 October 04 Sunday 12:11

"We can't have this now," Salvatore Dioguardi said, an emperor issuing a command. The gangster's facial features were dominated by thick, fleshy lips and a wide forehead notched by a widow's peak of tight, raven-black curls, mismatching the chiseled hardness of his carefully cultivated body. His custom-cut suit was the color of ground fog, making his upper body appear even more imposing. He wore a white-on-white shirt with the top two buttons unfastened, and sported a matching silk handkerchief in his breast pocket. On his feet were buttery black slip-ons whose simplicity drew the eye to the craftsmanship of the shoemaker. A diamond pinky ring blazed on his right hand. At his elbow was a saucer covered with multicolored tablets and capsules. Each time he paused, he put some of the pills into his mouth, and swallowed them with a few gulps from a tall glass of tomato juice.

"We? Who's 'we,' Sal?" the man seated across from him asked, his voice a semi-challenge. He was a decade older than his boss, his dark complexion a stark contrast to the white scar tissue that covered most of the left side of his face. His suit would have been at home on a mortician.

"What're you saying, Gino?" the bodybuilder half-snarled, drumming his fingers on the snow-white linen that covered the table. The two men were seated in a shielded corner of Dioguardi's restaurant. The wall beside them housed a hundred-gallon aquarium overstocked with brightly colored fish. In the too-early-for-customers gloom, it looked like a miniature cave in a vast ocean.

"What I'm saying is, how're we supposed to do what they want?" the scar-faced man said. "It wasn't us who put Little Nicky in a fucking coma. It wasn't us who clipped Tony and Lorenzo. They call us all the way up to Chicago for this big meeting, give us the word, we have to keep things quiet. Everything goes on hold. Okay. Only, how're we supposed to *do* that, with that fucking cripple picking us off?"

"We don't know it was Beaumont."

"Who else? It wasn't Shalare. What would be in it for that Irish fuck to make trouble now? He's got nothing we want."

"Right, it's not Shalare," Dioguardi agreed. "Because, the way I was told, he got the same word we did. Through his own people."

"So who does that leave? When it was just Nicky, it could have been anyone. He's got a mouth on him, that kid. No finesse. But Tony and Lorenzo?"

"I'm not saying it *wasn't* Beaumont, okay?" Dioguardi said, clenching his fists.

"Let's say it *was*. What're we supposed to do about it?" the scar-faced man said, reasonably. "One, it's not like the guy's walking around, where we could maybe get to him. Two, even if we could, I don't know, drop a bomb on that fucking fortress he lives in, that's just what we was told *not* to do. We're supposed to make something stop, but the only way we could do that, we can't do. So?"

"Don't forget those phone calls," Dioguardi said.

"The guy who sent us Nicky's license?"

"Yeah. Him."

"What about him? It's probably just one of Beaumont's—"

"There's one way to find out."

"You're not going to meet with—?"

"I only wish I could," Dioguardi said, cracking his knuckles. "Nicky was an asshole. And Lorenzo wasn't any big loss. But Tony, he was a *man*. Anyway, whoever it is, I can't see him walking in here, could you?"

"So what's our move, Sal?"

"I want you to tell everybody to pull back. Let this burg go back to being Beaumont's town. For now."

"How are we going to—?"

"What? Feed our families? That's what a war chest is for, Gino. Like a union's strike fund. We've still got a good cash flow from back home."

"Pull out, then?"

"No. They said not to do that. *Not*. When this is over, the whole thing, this territory, it's ours. The Commission said so. But we have to wait our turn, like always. So, what we're going to do, we're going to do nothing. If it *was* Beaumont, and he doesn't see any of our people in his spots, if we stop all the collections, he'll think we got the message."

"And if it wasn't?"

"Then this guy, this guy that likes to send things in the mail, he's the one we got to fix."

"You think he's going to do more—"

"Nah, G. He's already made his point. Nicky, that was a message. If I'd talked to him then, Lorenzo and Tony would never have happened. Whatever he wants, he wants it from *us*. Otherwise, what's he calling for? So we'll hear from him again. And that's when we'll know."

1959 October 04 Sunday 12:20

"Wouldn't you like to get another suit, Luther?" Cynthia said. She was walking beside the marble-eyed man, her hand on his forearm.

"This is the one Roy bought for me," Luther said, tenaciously. "He bought it with his own money."

"He'd buy you another one, Luther. Or a whole bunch of them, if you wanted."

"This is a very good suit," Luther said, stubbornly. "Roy picked this out for me himself. Right in the store. When he was still . . . when he was still going out."

"I know, Luther. But that was a long time ago. Your suit's pretty old now. It doesn't fit as good as—"

"It fits good," the slack-mouthed man answered, his voice growing even more mulish.

"All right, Luther," Cynthia said, patting his forearm. "You know best. Come on, let's go talk to Royal."

They entered the office together. Beaumont was slumped back in his wheelchair, eyes closed. As they crossed the threshold, he sat up straighter, reached for his cigarette case.

"What do you think?" he asked Luther.

"Huh?"

"Remember when Lymon was here? Just now?"

"Sure, Roy. I remember."

"Good. And you remember that game we play? The special one we made up?"

"Oh! Okay, he had a gun, Roy. I didn't see it, but I—"

"Not that game, Luther," the man in the wheelchair said, the calming gentleness of his voice reaching out to his lifelong friend. "The other one."

"I think . . . I think I do."

"*Sure* you do," Beaumont said, encouragingly. "You've got a sharp mind, Luther. You just have to remember to . . . what?"

The marble-eyed man stood rigidly, his brow furrowed, the slackness of his mouth even more pronounced than usual.

"Concentrate!" he suddenly said.

"That's the ticket! Just let it come. . . ."

Luther went silent. Beaumont and his sister watched the slack-mouthed man's face writhe as he struggled with his task.

"He was, Roy," Luther said, suddenly. "But I can't say . . . I mean, you didn't ask him no questions, so I don't know . . . I don't know when, exactly. But he was lying about something. I know he was."

"You never miss, Luther," the man in the wheelchair said, nodding his head like a man accepting his fate.

"Which is better for you, the white rice, or the brown rice?"

"Rufus, what are you talking about? You call me back down here on my day off—"

"I'm talking about some truth, Rosa Mae. Truth a girl as smart as you ought to be knowing."

"I didn't know you were a race man, Rufus."

"You see a colored man that's *not* a race man today, I know his name."

"His name?"

"Tom. That would be his name. Uncle Tom."

"You know that's not . . . I mean, look at you, in this hotel. The way you talk to the guests, butter wouldn't melt in your mouth. Is it Tomming when *you* do that, Rufus?"

Rufus tilted his chin up, as if regarding the young woman before him from a new perspective. A smile no hotel guest had ever seen softened his eyes.

"No, baby," he said. "That's called putting the dogs to sleep."

"Rufus," the young woman said, as she stepped very close to him, "if you be so two-faced, why do you want to show me the secret one?"

"Because a woman like you, a fine, strong woman, an *African* woman, she doesn't want a clown for her man."

"You're not my—"

"Not now, I'm not," Rufus said. "But, one day, I'm going to be."

Rosa Mae's amber eyes widened in surprise. "Just like that, you say it."

"Just like that, I *mean* it."

"I know what you want, Rufus Hightower. Tom or no, a man's a man."

"A Tom's no man, honeygirl. Anyway, you can't be lumping us all together in your mind. That's the way Whitey thinks about us, right? Niggers, all they want to do is dance, eat watermelon, get drunk, and make babies."

"I don't like that kind of—"

"That's what they call us, girl. And *they* don't care if you like it."

Rosa Mae put her hands on her hips. "What does that have to do with—?"

"It's the same kind of being dumb, Rosa Mae, no matter what you call it. Just 'cause you know *some* men, that don't mean you know *all* men. You think what I want from you is under that skirt, you're wrong."

"You mean you're like Mister Carl?" she said, grinning, trying to move the conversation to a safer place.

"I mean what I say, girl. I want you to be my woman. And not for one night, or one week."

"We never even been—"

"What? On a date, like kids? I'm not a kid, I'm a man. A full-grown man. But I'll take you anyplace you want to go, little Rose. Do anything you like to do."

"You know what I *really* like to do?"

"Yeah," he said, holding her eyes. "You like to read."

"How did you—?"

"Because I know *you*," Rufus said. "I really know you, Rosa Mae. And all I want is for you to know me."

1959 October 04 Sunday 12:40

"How do you think he does it?" Cynthia asked.

"I don't know, honey. I think it has something to do with the wiring in his brain. One time, when we were kids, I was trying to help him with his homework. It was arithmetic, I remember. Long division. Luther would just *stare* at the paper for hours. Like he couldn't read numbers, or something. I told him Miss Bayliss—you never had her; she came in after you were past her grade—would never know who did the homework, just write down what I told him. And Luther, out of nowhere, he says to me that Miss Bayliss has a baby."

"What was so—?"

"Miss Bayliss wasn't married, Cyn. But she left, in the spring, before school was out. To have the baby, people said."

"You're saying Luther *knew* that?"

"He did. And right after that, he started to know when people were lying, too. He'd just blurt it out. One time, Victor came to the clubhouse with this whole stack of magazines. He said he stole them, right out of Mr. Titleman's store. He had candy, too. Enough for everyone. And a model-airplane kit. Now, Victor wasn't just bragging, Cyn. He *had* the loot, okay?

"Out of nowhere, Luther pipes up, 'No!' We asked him what he was talking about, and he said Victor never stole that stuff. Victor hauled off and punched him, right in the face. But Luther didn't cry. He never would, no matter what anybody did to him.

"I was . . . upset, I guess. I mean, I could stop outsiders from picking on Luther, but Vic, he was with us. In our club and everything. So I . . . I had to find out. I went down to Mr. Titleman's store myself. I could always get people to talk. Probably they felt sorry for me, being a cripple and all."

"Beau!"

"Come on, Cyn. We don't hide from the truth, you and me. Anyway, I said to Mr. Titleman, Gee, Victor sure had himself a lot of magazines, and a new model airplane, too. I was a little worried, saying that, because if Victor really *had* stolen the stuff it would be like ratting him out. I had a whole story ready, about how Victor had gotten it all from some big kid none of us knew. But Mr. Titleman just busts out laughing. He says, 'Yeah, that boy walked in here with a five-dollar bill, and walked out broke.'

"After that, I got Victor alone. He didn't want to tell me, but I got him in a lock and told him I'd break his arm if he didn't. That's when he admitted he'd gotten the money when his uncle came to visit the family for the first time ever. A big shot, from Chicago, the uncle. He gave Victor a fin, just like that."

"How come Victor lied about it?"

"All the kids were stealing stuff then. But Victor, he was too chicken to do it himself. When his uncle gave him that money, he saw his chance."

"That was horrible, hitting Luther like he did."

"Yeah. But I could see, right then, it could get even worse if I didn't do something. So I told Luther it had to be a secret, just between us. Luther, he could *keep* a secret. I told him, anytime he knew someone was lying, he could tell *me,* but nobody else. And ever since then, he never has."

"But, Beau, you already knew Lymon was—"

"What Luther's got is a gift, Cyn. I figure, a gift like that, it just shows up one day; it could just as easy go away, too. So, every once in a while, I like to check."

"You're not fooling anyone, Beau."

"What?"

"You didn't *want* Lymon to be lying. You wanted there to be some . . . explanation, for him talking to Shalare. If Luther had said he was telling the truth, you would have . . . I don't know."

"You always know," Beaumont said.

1959 October 04 Sunday 12:58

"Tomorrow's my night off," Tussy said.

She listened silently as the voice at the other end of the line droned on, occasionally nodding her head as if the speaker were in the room with her.

"I'm sorry, Armand. You know I'd do it if I could. Have you tried Wanda?"

She sipped her coffee from a daisy-patterned mug, the receiver held against her ear by an upraised shoulder. A cigarette smoldered in an ashtray on the yellow Formica counter.

"What about Ginny?" she asked.

As Armand continued to plead his case, Tussy put the cigarette to her lips and took a shallow drag.

"I have a date," she finally said. "No, it isn't anyone you know."

You never miss your water until the well runs dry, she thought to herself, remembering one of her mother's favorite sayings.

"No, I *can't* make it another night, Armand. We've got reservations."

Another shallow drag. Another sip. Then, "What difference does it make where, Armand?"

Tussy poured the dregs of her coffee into the sink, ran the tap to clean out the cup before she placed it on the rubberized drying rack.

"Oh, don't be ridiculous!" she said. "I'll see you Wednesday night, okay?"

1959 October 04 Sunday 14:01

"You work for Mr. Beaumont?" the willowy brunette asked. She was dressed in a tasteful dark-cranberry business suit over a pale-pink blouse, wearing a minimum of expertly applied makeup. Her heart-shaped face was fine-boned, dominated by deceptively vulnerable eyes the color of burnt cork, framed by a pair of cat's-eye glasses. "I've never seen you before," she said.

"You see everybody who works for him?"

"Probably everybody but that sister of his, sooner or later," the woman said, her face composed, not reacting to Dett's ignoring her question. "And the big man himself, of course. Most of them aren't regulars. After all, this is the highest-priced house in the county. Most of those boys, they can only come here when they're flush."

"It's a beautiful place," Dett said. "Must cost a lot to keep it up."

"It does, for a fact. I wish your boss understood that a little better. Between what I pay the law and the things some of these girls get themselves into . . ."

"Yeah. So you can't be making a living just taking care of one . . . group."

"You're not part of Mr. Beaumont's organization," she said, her suddenly icy eyes briefly drifting over Dett's face.

"You were expecting me," Dett said, without inflection. "Whoever you spoke to told you to cooperate with me."

"And what you want is information about my visitors."

"Yes."

"You're a camera guy?" she asked, an unmistakable hint of contempt in her modulated voice.

"No."

"What are you, then?"

"A strategist."

"That's a big word."

"If you say so."

"I have to make a phone call," the woman said. "You can wait right here, in my office, if you like. Or, if you want, I have a couple of girls who aren't busy right now."

1959 October 04 Sunday 14:19

"What's he doing?"

"That's Sherman Layne," the stubby, mostly bald man in the passenger seat of the plain-Jane sedan said to the much younger man behind the wheel. "He's a cop, local. And that's a whorehouse. Ritziest one in the county, according to our briefing. Maybe he's doing a surveillance on some guy they think's holed up there. Or maybe he's just taking down license-plate numbers."

"Same as we are," the younger man said, peevishly. His protruding Adam's apple bobbed with each word.

"You think we can always be out chasing the Ten Most Wanted, Dave?" the older man said, chuckling. "This is just like the army—everybody's got their job to do."

"Our job must be KP, then."

"No," the older man said, idly tapping his asymmetrical nose with a thick forefinger, "although it may seem like it. We're part of something, even if we don't always know what it is."

"I wish we did. I wish we could—"

"Observe and record," the older man said. "That's the job. That's *today's* job, anyway."

"That's a weird place to have a whorehouse."

"You're an expert, Davy?"

"Come on, Mack," the younger man said, reddening. "It's sitting down in that little clearing, all surrounded by woods. Anyone could just sneak up on it. That cop, where he's parked, nobody inside would ever spot him."

"Who's going to sneak up on it?"

"I . . . I don't know. Kids, maybe. To get a thrill."

"Only if they had binoculars that worked at night, and what kids have the money for equipment like that? Come on, Dave. Look closer. See all that open ground? There's no way anyone could move within fifty yards of that door without being spotted, day or night."

"You really think there might be a guy hiding out in there?"

"Who knows?" the older man said, shrugging his shoulders. "It's not our problem."

"What if he was a bank robber, Mack? You know, we have jurisdiction if there's been a—"

"We don't have any 'jurisdiction' to do anything but what our orders are," the older man said, firmly. "That's how agents get themselves in trouble, freelancing. And . . . Hey, there he goes. I guess the cop saw everything he had to see."

"You think maybe he's coming back? With reinforcements?"

"Jesus H. Christ, Dave. This isn't a goddamn gangster movie; this is real life."

1959 October 04 Sunday 14:30

"All right," the brunette said, re-entering the room where Dett waited, "what do you want to know?" Her voice was business-like, just short of brusque.

"Who comes here in secrecy?"

"Secrecy?" she said, coolly. "You mean 'privacy,' don't you?"

"No," Dett said, watching her eyes. "I mean the man nobody sees. You bring a girl into the room he uses, put a hood over her head, bend her over, and tie her up. The man comes into the room. He doesn't say anything, just does what he does. After he's gone, you go in there and untie the girl. Everyone who works here knows they could be picked for the job, but they never know when their turn is going to come."

"Who told you such a—?"

"Someone who doesn't work here anymore, so don't waste your time asking around."

"No, I mean, who told you a story like that?"

"It's not true, then?"

"Of course not. We cater to all kinds of . . . tastes here. And I'm not saying we *wouldn't* put a girl in the position you described. Or even that we *never* have. But the idea that this happens all the time, for the same man—"

"I told Beaumont this was a waste of time."

"Well, that's all right. Surely you understand the way these girls exaggerate their—"

"I told him it was a waste of time," Dett went on, level-voiced. "I told him you wouldn't cooperate."

"But I just *said* . . ."

"You're lying," Dett said, his voice as cold and flat as a glacier. "A woman as smart as you, you're not owned by anyone. You pay Beaumont because he's the powerhouse in this town. A business expense, like a lawyer, or an abortionist. But you couldn't stay in business if you didn't keep this place neutral. So this isn't Beaumont's house. Dioguardi's men come here, too, right? And Shalare's. And people who don't work for any of them. People with money of their own. You don't work for Beaumont, you pay him. That's a big difference. If Beaumont was to disappear tomorrow, you'd just pay someone else."

"You seem to have figured everything out," the woman said, lighting a cigarette in what Dett recognized as a time-buying gesture.

"Except the man's name."

"What good would that do you?" she said, her tone implying she was actually interested in the answer. "So he likes the girls, so what? I could see it if he was a priest, or a—"

"I told you, this isn't about blackmail."

"What, then?"

"That's not something you want to know," Dett said.

"What if I told you I don't know his name?"

"I'll tell you what I told Beaumont."

The brunette looked a question at Dett, not speaking.

"I told him that you were going to play your own game, for your own reasons. And I was right. So there's only one thing to do."

"Which is?"

"Put you out of business. Then the man I'm interested in will have to go someplace else for his fun. The next . . . manager will be glad to work with me."

"Putting me out of business wouldn't be such an easy thing to do," she said, clipping her words to keep the sudden fear out of her voice.

"No harder than this," Dett said, striking a wooden match on his thumbnail.

1959 October 04 Sunday 14:49

"I wish you didn't have to do this."

"Do what, honey?"

"*All* of this," Cynthia said.

"We had no choice, girl. If I hadn't started the—"

"Not at the beginning, I know. But now? What difference could it make, Beau?"

"You want to go back to the way we were before this all started? That can happen, Cyn. That can *always* happen, if I get weak."

"You were never weak, Beau."

"Neither were you. All we wanted was to live in peace, right? But would they let us?"

"Oh, Beau," she said, despairingly.

"What?"

"You never wanted to live in peace," she said, bringing her hands together in a prayerful gesture. "Never once. You and Sammy and Lymon and Faron and . . . all of you, you made enough during the war to start real businesses. But you—"

"We *did* start real businesses, damn it!"

"What, the bowling alley? That was just a place for you all to . . . meet, and everything."

"We weren't doing anything people didn't want done, girl. Otherwise, we couldn't have made a living at it."

"Beau, you don't have to take care of everyone, like you were their father."

"Who's going to do it, if I don't? Somebody's got to run the show. *Our* show, I mean. If we don't have our own people in charge, some other outfit will just come in, and . . ."

"Is that why you want Harley to . . . ?"

"He's the one I've been thinking of, yeah. I've been watching him for a long time, and he's got the cold mind you need to run a complicated operation like ours. Sammy says so, too. But if Harley ever wants to be in charge, he's got to show what he's made of, else-wise no one will follow him. You know that, Cyn. If I hadn't—"

"Don't, Beau."

"Don't what?" the man in the wheelchair said, defiantly. "Say the truth? I'll say it, Cyn. I'm not afraid of it. If I hadn't killed Lenny Maddox, he would have eaten us like a slice of apple pie, with vanilla ice cream on top. One bite—*poof!*—we're gone. Right down his pig's gullet."

"I don't like to talk about that."

"It was him or us," Beaumont said, reciting his lifelong mantra. "I . . ."

"Honey, you had your little salary from the dress shop, and I had what we were making from the bowling alley. When we were kids, remember where we lived? Remember *how* we lived? All of us would have fit into one room of this house."

"We never needed such a—"

"I didn't kill Lenny Maddox to buy us a house, honey. We had no choice. No choice I could live with, anyway."

"I thought you were going to die that day, Beau. I was so terri-fied, I was frozen. I just sat and stared at the telephone. I knew it was going to ring, and the . . . somebody was going to tell me you were dead."

"I remember when they searched me that last time," Beaumont said. The iron of his eyes began to lighten, like an abating storm. "They just sort of slapped at my clothes, before they let me into the back room. The cripple in his wheelchair, getting an audience with the pope. Maybe they thought Lenny was going to lay his hands on me, cure me like one of those faith healers."

"Beau . . ."

"Yeah, what did he have to worry about?" the man in the wheelchair went on, relentlessly. "It was broad daylight, not even ten in the morning, when we drove up to that roadhouse he owned. Me and Luther. The cripple and the retard."

"Beau!"

"No, that was *good,* Cyn. It's always good when they underestimate you. Lenny thought I was coming to beg. That's what cripples are, right? Beggars. He had a couple of men around, like he always did. But he'd been feeding at the trough so long, he forgot where he came from. He let them stand around outside his office, so I wouldn't be embarrassed, having to beg in front of them.

"I thought I might die that day, too, Cyn. And I was ready for it. I don't mean I was *looking* to die, but I could face it. The same way I made all the other guys face it. Before we took off, I told them, 'By tonight, we'll have us some ground. It's either going to belong to us, or we'll be under it.' "

Cynthia turned toward her brother. Her face was as blanched as it had been on that day so many years ago, when she had waited for the call. And, just as then, she never said a word.

"He never knew how I could move in this thing," Beaumont recalled, patting his wheelchair as if it were a prized racehorse. I kept talking, about the bowling alley and how I wanted to expand it, maybe even add a skating rink. That's what I was there for, to ask his permission. Before he knew what was going on, I had rolled right up to where he was sitting. I put everything I had into that one punch. Right here"—touching a spot just below the inverted V of his rib cage—"and all the breath just *whooshed* out of him. Then I got these"—holding up two clawed hands—"around his throat and clamped. He never made a sound.

"When I wheeled myself out of his office, I had Lenny's own pistol in my hand. Got both of his men"—snapping his fingers, twice—"before they even knew something was wrong. And then Luther opened up, just like I had told him.

"Our guys swooped in the minute they heard the first shots. All we had to do was hold our position: me inside the office, Luther out by the car.

"The minute I saw Lymon and Sammy coming through the trees, I knew we were going to make it. Lenny's boys never had a chance. It was over so fast, I think I must have held my breath all the way through it."

"I was so—"

"The paper said it was a gang war. Remember, honey? The Locke City Massacre, they called it. But the cops never even came around—there wasn't a single one of Maddox's men left to finger us. We lost Everett that day, but we didn't leave him there. Faron got hit, too, but he was just winged.

"The cops put it down to out-of-town talent. I *knew* Lenny Maddox had to be doing the same thing to other people he was doing to us. People a lot bigger than we were. Everybody figured he finally stepped on the wrong toes.

"Lenny Maddox, he was never really a big man. It's just that, around here, he was bigger than anyone else. He never bothered to *organize* things—we were the first ones to do that. And by the time outsiders started looking our way, we were dug in too deep."

"That's just what it feels like sometimes, Beau," Cynthia said, looking down at her hands clasped in her lap. "That we're dug in too deep."

1959 October 04 Sunday 15:05

"Walk with me, Brian O'Sullivan," Mickey Shalare said to a square-shouldered man whose flattened nose, cauliflower ears, and scar-tissue eyebrows marked his profession as clearly as would a doctor's bag in a never-callused hand.

The former prizefighter got to his feet with a feline grace that belied his time-thickened body. He tossed down what was left of his pint with one hand, and wiped his mouth with the back of the other.

The two men left via the rear of the Shamrock Inn without speaking. Shalare's pristine white '57 Chrysler 300C hardtop was parked parallel to the wall of the alley, only the driver's door accessible. He unlocked the car, climbed in, and slid over to the passenger side.

"Get in, then," he called to Brian.

Puzzled, the boxer got behind the wheel. The Chrysler was Shalare's pride and joy—no one else was ever permitted to drive it.

"Take us out to the Flats, Brian."

The boxer started the car, then crawled forward to where the alley opened onto a side street.

"Come on," Shalare told him. "This isn't some pram you're pushing here."

At Brian's glance, the smaller man said, "Not much good having a motor like this if you can't make it go, is there?"

"Sure. But how come I'm the one driving?" Brian asked, with characteristic bluntness.

"You're driving because you're the man I trust."

"With your car?"

"With my life," Shalare said, in that steel-in-honey tone all his men recognized instantly.

They rode in silence for about twenty minutes, through city streets, out past a subdivision that had been built on the town's hopes for a huge paper mill—a hope that had died an unnatural death years ago.

The houses, formerly individual monuments to working-class pride, had fallen to a depth below disrepair. Once-proud patches of greenery on the postage-stamp lawns had given way to arid dirt; neatly trimmed trees and hedges had been replaced with rusting car parts and salvaged junk.

The big Chrysler cleared its throat and leaped forward, as if fleeing the decay around it.

"This is some piece of machinery, yours, Mickey."

"It is. The Yanks know how to build things, I'll give them that. This one, it's not as posh as a Jag, maybe, but it'll run away from any of them on the highway. Won't be breaking down every other day, either."

"How fast will it go, you figure?"

"Well, I've near seen the end of that speedometer, Brian."

"A ton and a half? You didn't, Mickey!"

"I did. But I suspect the dial turns to blarney once it gets into those high numbers. A bit . . . optimistic, you know."

"Still."

"Oh, it's got a mighty engine, no doubt. She's a man's car."

"Yes she is!" Brian said, enthusiastically. "But she handles real nice. Some of the ones I've driven over here, they might as well be lorries."

"Turn toward the freight yard," Shalare said.

Brian took a series of alternating lefts and rights on unmarked streets of cracked concrete, past smokestacks as dead as cannons abandoned on a forgotten battlefield, until he finally wheeled the big car to a careful stop. Through the panoramic windshield, the two men looked out at an abandoned railroad spur, its tracks rust-frozen in their last-switched position from years ago. A trio of linked box-cars sat forlornly on the track, waiting for the locomotive that would never come again.

"That's not you, Brian," Shalare said, quietly.

"I wish I knew how you did that, Mickey. I remember Tommy Hardison saying, 'Mickey Shalare has the special sight, you know. He can see right into your mind.' I thought it was the booze doing his talking then. But I've seen you do it myself, time and again."

"You're still the Irish Express, Big Brian. And you'll always be."

"In the pubs, maybe," the flat-nosed man said sadly. "But not in the ring, not nevermore."

"You were managed by maggots, that's what happened."

"Wasn't no manager inside those ropes, Mickey. It was just me. Me and whoever they put in front of me."

"You had too much heart, Brian. Always willing to have a go, no matter what. And that's what those bloodsuckers wanted to see. Not a scientific contest between athletes, no. Blood, that's what they fed on. If they'd brought you along, the way they do some, you'd have been a champion for sure. Who doesn't know that?"

"Ah, Mickey, I was never no—"

"Don't you be saying that!" Shalare cut in, sharply. "Who had a better right hand than Big Brian O'Sullivan? You put a lot of good men to sleep with it. No matter how the bout might be going, you always had that puncher's chance. Any man that would stand in there and trade with you always ending up going inside the distance."

"Aye. It was the ones I couldn't catch that did me in, Mickey.

But, Jesus knows, there was no shortage of those kind, after a while."

"John Henry Jefferson."

"Yeah. He's the one who started it, that time in Detroit. You'd think, a name like that, he'd be one of those colored boys who'd come straight at you, hammer and tongs. Anyone who'd try that, I had something for them, didn't I, Mickey?"

"Swear you did, Brian. Swear it to God."

"John Henry Jefferson," O'Sullivan said, reverently. "He was as slick as a weasel in a river of oil. Must have hit me with a dozen jabs before I could get my gloves up. I never even felt them. Flick-flick-flick. Light as feathers. He was as quick as a scorpion, but I was sure he couldn't hurt me. I knew I could just walk through those pitty-pats of his, get to his ribs, slow him down. You remember?"

"I never will forget. I was saying to myself, this boy's not a fighter; he's a dancer. Fast and pretty, but he's got to slow down sooner or later."

"But it never happened," O'Sullivan said, regretfully. "Those feathers had razors in their tips. Cut me so clean I never even knew it until there was a red mist over my eyes. And he just got faster. Hands *and* feet. He'd pop up out of the mist, slash and dash, then come at me all over again. I was a bull, but he was the matador that night."

"If it had been anyone but Big Brian O'Sullivan in there with him, they would have stopped it."

"Ah, you know I'd never let them do that, Mickey. My corner kept telling me what to do, but I just couldn't do it. You want to know something? John Henry Jefferson was the cleanest fighter I was ever in the ring with. You think I didn't try to step on his foot, anchor him down? You think I didn't hit him behind the head whenever I could grab him? Or go to lace him, up close? Well, I did. I did all that, and more. But did he? No. No, he didn't. He just sliced pieces off me like I was a rare slab of roast beef, the kind that's got warm blood right in the center."

"You did us all proud that night, Brian. Won the whole crowd over to your side. Even the coloreds were screaming for you at the end."

"I couldn't hear a thing, Mickey. Just my heart pounding in my ears. I wanted to catch him so bad. But I didn't get one in. Not in the whole ten rounds, not one."

"Ah, if you had, it wouldn't have *gone* ten rounds."

"I always believed that—it's what kept me going. I could always take three to give one, but carrying the equalizer's no good if you can't land it."

"That Jefferson, they all took a lesson from him."

"They did. After that, everyone knew how to fight me. Stick and move, pile up the points. But not one of them could do it like John Henry Jefferson. I was sure he'd be the next champ."

"You saw when he fought Swede Hannsen? On the television?"

"Swede Hannsen. Aye, I saw it. Mickey, me, *I* was faster than Swede Hannsen. And I had twice his punch. Never would he get in there with me."

"That's why he was undefeated when he met Jefferson, Brian. He was brought along right."

"If you call ducking anyone who could bang being brought along right, I guess he was, then. When he knocked out John Henry Jefferson, it almost knocked *me* out, right in the pub where the fight was showing. I couldn't believe it."

"You know what the odds were on that fight, Brian?"

"The odds? If I was a bookmaker, I would have given pounds to pennies that—"

"Jefferson went in the tank, Brian."

"For money? Why? He was next in line for a title shot. Or close, anyway. The Swede was just a tune-up for him."

"The mob owned Swede Hannsen," Shalare said. "Lock, stock, and barrel. Whatever they paid Jefferson, they made it back a thousand times betting on their man. Maybe they promised Jefferson he'd get a rematch, with Swede guaranteed to lay down next time. Or maybe even that title shot. With a loss to Hannsen on his record, he'd be the underdog against the champ, for sure."

"I *fought* the man, Mickey. You never get as close to a man as when you do that. I don't believe you could pay John Henry Jefferson enough to make him take a dive."

"So they told him what would happen if he didn't," Shalare said, shrugging. "There's always ways, if you're not with people who can protect you."

"I heard he turned into a boozer after he lost to Swede."

"I don't know about that, Brian. But it *was* a liquor store he was coming out of when he got gunned down."

"You mean, you think it was because—?"

"We'll never know," Shalare said, his voice thick with implication. "They never caught the shooter. It could have been anyone . . . a jealous girlfriend, some people he owed money to. . . . Or maybe he started making noise about spilling his guts. That would do it, in a heartbeat."

"He could have been champ," O'Sullivan said, his voice heavy with true Irish sorrow at the hand Fate sometimes deals. "He really could have."

"He might have made a pact with the Devil, or maybe he just wasn't strong enough to keep them off. But it all comes down to the same thing, Brian. He didn't have people."

"I had people, didn't I, Mickey? So why wasn't I—?"

"You had people," Shalare agreed. "But your people, they didn't have the power. Oh, we had enough for some things, sure. No one ever approached *you* to throw a fight, did they, Brian? And if they had, you know they would have come soft, not hard. Money they would have offered you to go along, not a beating or a killing if you didn't. If they had threatened you, they'd have threatened us all, that they knew.

"They had the boxing game all locked up, the Italians. We could keep them from leaning on you, but we couldn't get you a title fight, no matter how many you knocked out.

"It's not like liquor once was. That they never controlled, try as they might. There was always room for an outsider to come in and start a business for himself. And it's the same today. Gambling, girls, money-lending, all of that's an open market.

"But the fight racket, it's like this giant pyramid. The higher you climb, the less room there is for others to compete. So any man with the skills and the heart, he can be a boxer. But the top, well, that's not for the best fighters, it's for the fighters with the best connections."

"So you're saying, if I had caught up with John Henry Jefferson that night . . ."

"It'd be you they would have come to for the tank job with Swede Hannsen, that's all."

"And that will never change?"

"It's changing right now, Brian. And we can all see it coming. Instead of fighting wars over bookmaking or booze, we've been after other prizes. Bigger and better ones. The unions, they're the real future. You know why?"

"I . . . I guess I don't, Mickey."

"Because the unions, they're the lifeblood of the politicians. A union's a vote-making *machine,* Brian. Every member is going to vote the way their leaders tell them. And their wives and children and brothers and sisters and fathers and mothers, as well. They're going to raise money for the candidate. They're going to go out in the streets and drum up support. Carry people to the polls, and make sure they do things right when they're inside the booth, too.

"The Italians are coming from one direction. So, instead of meeting them head-on, we're moving in at an angle. Look at Boston. Or Chicago. The Italians are paying the cops, but we're paying the politicians. Who do you think is going to be stronger, in the long run?"

"Yeah, Mickey!"

"But that game has changed. We've got to share now."

"Share what?"

"Share what we've got. Combine forces. Because the next president of the United States, he's going to be ours, Brian."

"Mickey, come on."

"I don't mean in our pocket, like some little alderman we can make or break in an hour, Brian. But ours, for true. A man we can count on to protect our interests."

"The next president, well, that's going to be Mr. Nixon, isn't it? How could we hope to—?"

"It won't be that shifty-eyed, pope-hating little rodent, Brian.

No it won't. It'll be a Democrat, if we all pull together. A Democrat who's going to give us territory no one will ever take back from us, nevermore."

"What shall I be doing?"

"Ah, that's you, Brian, isn't it?" Shalare said, admiringly. "Irish to the marrow of your thick bones. The Italians, you'd think they'd be just like us, wouldn't you? Come to this country in rags, treated like bloody slaves, scratch and claw for everything they ever get. Only the Italians, they're a bunch of little tribes. Not villagers, like we have, where a man from Armagh might think he knows a thing or two that a man from Londonderry might not, and true enough. No, I mean . . . well, the ones from Sicily, they're not the brothers of the ones from Rome. They don't stand together. And they never trust one another."

"The Prods are Irish," O'Sullivan said, mildly.

Shalare regarded his old friend intently. "They are," he said, speaking slowly and carefully. "But they come farther down the road, Big Brian. In good time. For now, they're not our concern, any more than the Italians are."

"Who is, then?"

"Royal Beaumont," Shalare said. "They named him right, too. Royalty he is, Brian. Where we're sitting right now, all around us, this is all his."

"All this pile of junk?"

"All the *land,* Brian. When the mills closed down, when the factories went bust, the whole town had to find another way to live. That was a long time ago. If you looked at a census, you would be thinking Locke City is a quarter the size it once was, so many people have left. But it's a sweet cherry tart of a town now. It's known for a half-dozen states around: the place you can come to for whatever you need. Or whatever you want.

"Beaumont's been the power here since way before we came. Through one front or another, he probably owns half the property on the tax rolls in this whole county."

"If this is the kind of property—"

"He owns the land under the Claremont Hotel, too, Brian. And the whole block the First National sits on. He owns office buildings downtown, apartment units all over the city, that little shopping center over in—"

"Mickey, I must be slow. I can't see where any of this matters to us."

"It matters because Beaumont's going to come along, Brian. He's a way clever man. All this property, it's . . . Well, land doesn't have a value, the way a silver coin does. It's worth whatever someone will pay for it. This desolate plot we're looking at now, it would all turn to gold overnight if the government decided it was needed. For a munitions plant, say. Or maybe a federal prison."

"Ah."

"Yeah. And who makes *those* decisions? While Beaumont's been buying land, we've been buying the people who decide what that land is worth, see? I got it from the leadership itself. We're to stop our squabbling with the Italians—yes, and they with us—and put all our strength into the one objective. Beaumont's going to be approached. And he'll come right along, I know."

"Well, that's all we need, isn't it?"

"Maybe it's not, Brian. You know we have one of his men."

"That Lymon fellow?"

"Him indeed. And what he tells us is, Beaumont's brought in an outsider."

"For what?"

"For murder. That's his game, this man. A hired killer."

"Aimed at us?"

"No, that's the . . . twist. Lymon thinks he's being aimed at Dioguardi."

"Well, good luck to him, then."

"It's not that simple, Brian. There's two men dead already, another so deep asleep he probably won't ever wake up. But from what we hear, Dioguardi himself doesn't think that was Beaumont's doing."

"Wasn't he told same as us? That we're all to be under the flag of truce?"

"The thing about a liar is, he thinks everybody else is one, too. Dioguardi's a treacherous devil; so he thinks we must be treacherous devils ourselves. The way his mind works, he probably believes it's *us* trying to reduce his ranks, shooting from behind the cover of the white flag."

"Three men?" Brian said.

"Yeah, that isn't much, I know. But if he hits back at us, it could torpedo the whole big plan."

"The election? How could a man like Dioguardi stop something so powerful?"

"Because it's going to be paper-thin," Shalare said, quoting his recent visitor. "If Beaumont gets us all back to fighting, we're not going to be able to pull this off. And even if he's *not* playing games, moving us around like chess pieces, unless he plays *with* us, it's going to hurt. The entire political machine in this county is his. And we need it to be ours."

"So what do we do?"

"We bring Dioguardi the head of whoever's picking off his men. Because that *has* to be the man Beaumont brought in, even if Dioguardi himself can't see it."

"Where's he staying?"

"Not now. It's too soon. We have to wait for Lymon to give us more. Otherwise, Dioguardi won't appreciate the gift, see? We need proof that he's Beaumont's man, not ours."

"And it's *our* man, Lymon, that'll do that."

"It is. He's a treasure to us."

"If Beaumont knew, he'd be buried treasure."

"He doesn't," Mickey Shalare said. "It took me the best part of two years to get this going. I was slow. I was careful. And now I'm almost ready."

1959 October 04 Sunday 15:30

"Two white males. Fifty-seven Chrysler two-door hardtop. Alpha, X-ray, Bravo, four, zero, two, local," a man sitting behind a pair of binoculars mounted on a tripod said, his clipped voice etching every syllable. "Copy?"

"Two white males. Fifty-seven Chrysler. Alpha, X-ray, Bravo, four, zero, two, local," a man with a notebook open on his lap repeated.

"That's Shalare's car, his personal car," the spotter said. "But I can't make out the faces at this angle."

"That's not our job," the other man answered.

The two men, identically dressed in smog-gray jumpsuits, were stationed on the top floor of an abandoned factory that had once mass-produced steam boilers. They had been dropped off at midnight, offloaded from an unmarked delivery van, together with canteens of water, freeze-dried rations, a chemical toilet, two sleeping bags, and a variety of distance-viewing devices, including night-vision binoculars.

"It probably *is* Shalare," the spotter said. "This is where he brings anyone he wants to talk to alone. I wish we could get a listening device on that car of his. It would be a gold mine."

"That's not our job," the other man repeated. He lifted his eyes from his notebook to the corner of the room, to where a long padded case lay on the floor.

1959 October 04 Sunday 15:39

"When I said 'dug in too deep' before, I didn't mean like in a bunker or anything," Beaumont said. "I meant dug in the way roots do."

"That means a lot to you, Beau? Those roots?"

"Well . . . yeah. Yeah, it does, Cyn. That's been the difference for us, all these years, right? I mean, the Italians, remember when they were holding those hearings, about the Mafia, on TV? They'd talk about this 'family' or that 'family,' but all they meant was some gang called by the boss's name. That's not real family. Not a band of brothers. Not like we are."

"It's still *your* . . . organization, Beau. Without you, they couldn't—"

"Yes they could!" the man in the wheelchair said, intensely. "Maybe not this minute, but someday . . . We're just like a real family, Cyn. The father passes on to the sons. When we're done, you and me, there'll be someone else running things. But it will always be ours."

"So *that's* why!"

"What? Cyn, are you—?"

"*That's* why you want Lymon . . . gone. That's why you're not telling him wrong stuff, so he could pass it along to Shalare. You did that before, Beau. Remember, back when you found out Tiller Hawthorne was telling the Richardson brothers about . . . about what we were doing? When you had that big run, down from Canada, you gave Tiller the wrong route, and told him the disguise. So the Richardsons ended up hitting a post-office truck, and they all went to prison."

"Tiller wasn't really one of us. Just a guy who did work."

"I know. Lymon, he's . . . he's that 'family' you're always talking about, Beau. Still, you could use him the same way you used Tiller, instead of having Harley . . ."

"Lymon's fifty times as smart as Tiller. If I tried the same thing on him, he'd sniff it out in a second."

"Then just cut him loose, Beau. Kick him out."

"He's a dirty Judas, Cyn. Selling his own people for pieces of silver."

"He's just a weak man, Beau."

"Lymon? What's weak about him? He stood with us against Lenny Maddox, didn't he? He's handled a hundred jobs, and never showed yellow once."

"He's . . . changed, I guess. If he wanted to sell you for money, he could have done it a long time ago, Beau. Right at the beginning, even. How much would Maddox have paid if Lymon had given him warning about what you were planning to do that day? It's not . . . I'm not excusing him, Beau, but it's not as if Shalare wants you dead. He just wants . . . Well, we're not even sure what he wants, but it isn't what Dioguardi's been after. Now, if Lymon were talking to *that* man, that would be different."

"Look, Cyn, I can't—"

"Lymon wasn't going to take over anyway, Beau. He's the same age as we are."

"It's Harley," Beaumont said, firmly. "He's got the . . . vision, I guess you'd say. Look at how he came up with a way to make money out of that acreage we own out on Route 85. All we were getting out of it was a couple weeks' rent, once in a while, when the carny would come to town, or they'd have a tent revival. It was Harley who came up with the idea of a drag strip, and a track for those go-kart things."

"He's so young, Beau."

"I don't think that's such a bad thing, Cyn. He's more . . . in touch than a lot of our guys are. More forward-thinking. Remember when he first talked about selling marijuana? We thought that was just for those beatniks, but Harley said there was money to be made there, and he was right."

"He was right because it's kids smoking it. That's how he knew so much about it. Just like that drag-strip idea."

"We were all young once, Cyn. It's not how old you are that makes you a leader; it's how smart you are. But our kind of people, they won't follow a man unless he's been blooded."

"It doesn't have to be Lymon's blood!"

"I . . . All right, damn it. I'll feed Lymon a diet of baloney from now on, see if maybe we can't put a little sugar in Shalare's gas tank. And when this is over, I'll cut him loose," Beaumont said, making a ripping gesture at his chest, as if pulling out his heart.

1959 October 04 Sunday 15:48

"Your boss ready to talk to me now? Or does he need some more messages?"

"You!" Vito sputtered. "He'll . . . he wants to talk to you. Just hang on, I'll—"

"I'll call back. Fifteen minutes. If anyone but your boss answers this line, it'll cost you more men."

1959 October 04 Sunday 15:56

The panel truck that had delivered guns to the junkyard slowed as it came to an intersection of alleys north of Lambert Avenue. This afternoon it was beige, and each side had a plastic sign attached with magnets: FOSTER BROTHERS PEST CONTROL. The truck's license plate was mud-splattered; its window glass was heavily hazed.

"I don't like this," the driver said.

"What else is new?" the man in the passenger seat said, almost slyly.

"I mean it, Fred. We're supposed to be gathering intelligence. Surveilling, interviewing—"

"We pay informants, Milt," the shorter man in the passenger seat said, mildly. "That's right in the—"

"We pay *authorized* informants. These kids, they're not even—"

"We're not giving them money."

"Come on, Fred. What's the difference?"

"The difference is, like I told you before, *initiative,* okay? Just pull over there, by those garbage cans."

1959 October 04 Sunday 16:00

"When things change, people have to change, too," Beaumont said, lighting a cigarette. "There's whole towns that didn't understand that, Cyn. *Ghost* towns, now. A plant closes down, a mine stops operating, it's like somebody cut off the air supply. The town just . . . suffocates. Locke City was a fine place to live during the war. Everybody had work, everybody had money. But then it all dried up, like a farm with no rain for years. So we had to plant new crops."

"We always had gambling, Beau. Here, in Locke City, I mean. Even when we were kids, there was always places where you could find—"

"That was low-level stuff, honey. Not organized, the way we

have it now. There's a mountain of difference between a crap game on a blanket in an alley and a professional dice table, with a man in a tux raking in the bets and pretty girls walking around with trays of drinks. What makes Locke City special isn't the games. Or the girls. It's not just what you can get here; it's the *quality* of it.

"Look, there's places all along the river where you can buy a drink, dry county or not. And there's no town where you *can't* find a dice game, or a whorehouse. But those are rough places, where you're just as likely to wake up in a back alley with your wallet missing. A man comes to Locke City, he knows he's going to be protected, if he comes to the right places. *Our* places. We don't water the booze, and we don't serve Mickey Finns. Our houses don't get raided. If you bet on a horse, or a football game, or whatever, and you win, you *will* get your payoff. That's what we're really selling here. Not sin, safety."

"There must be plenty of places in the big cities where you could get the same—"

"Sure, if you're rich. There's always high-class places, with everything nice and protected. But Locke City, we built it for the workingman. The regular, average guy. The folks who live here now, they all make their living from the people who are passing through, see? Everyone's invested, one way or the other. That's why the water has to be calm on the surface. From the time we took over from Maddox, we've kept it that way."

"But now you bring in this . . . I don't know what to call him."

"Because we need him, Cyn. The prettier the flower, the more people want to pluck it. If Dioguardi was just going to keep nibbling at the corners, we could deal with him on the quiet. Do the kind of thing to protect ourselves that never makes the papers. But he's coming *hard* now, and we have to put him down for good. Close him up."

"Beau . . ."

"Cyn, I can smell danger like a mine-shaft canary. Dioguardi's just a gangster. And not even a smart one; he's like the guy who gets to run the family business because he married the boss's daughter. Whoever gave him this territory, they knew he couldn't do anything big with it. He's been around, what, three, four years? What's he ever had, that two-bit protection racket of his? I'm surprised he can even cover his payroll with what he takes in. Now, all of a sudden, a couple of months ago, he starts moving in on *our* places. Jukeboxes, punch cards . . . still just little stuff. What for?"

"I don't know."

"I don't know, either. Like I said, he's a stupid man. So, maybe, it could be no more than that. But Mickey Shalare, *he's* not stupid. Not even a little bit. Something's coming. And we're not going to sit here and wait for it. Hacker was the last one of us who's going to be taken by surprise."

"What are we going to do?"

"We're going to adapt. Find other ways. That's what we did with the . . . doctors, right?"

"You mean the—?"

"A girl needs an abortion—I don't just mean in Locke City, I mean *anywhere*—what's she supposed to do? Go visit one of those coat-hanger guys? Risk getting crippled for life, or even dead? Now we've got it all in one place: clean, safe, sterile. And never a whiff from the law. It's been a real moneymaker, too."

"And it all started with me," Cynthia said, choking back a sob.

"It didn't have to, sweetheart. I never wanted you to—"

"I *had* to, Beau! There was no way we could have—"

"Yes, we could," Beaumont said, clenching his jaw as he bit off the words. "Here in Locke City, in *our* town, there's nothing we couldn't do, Cyn."

"No," she said, firmly. "There's some things we could never do."

The man in the wheelchair closed his eyes, nodded his head a couple of times. His sister walked behind his desk and stood next to him, her hand on his shoulder.

"It was just you and me, from the beginning," he said. "You remember when Dad would come home? Stinking drunk? Remember when he used to think it was real funny, kick the braces out from my legs, watch me crawl?"

"Beau . . ."

"How many beatings did you take for me, Cyn? How many times did you throw your body over me when he came at me with the belt?"

"It didn't matter. I—"

"I never knew about the rest. Not until I saw—"

"I don't want to talk about . . . about that, Beau. You know I don't."

"You told Mom," he said, bulling through her refusal. "And what did *she* do, the dirty bitch? I wish they hadn't been asleep when I did it."

"Beau!"

"The cops never even took a second look," he said. "Why should they? A couple of drunks like them, falling asleep with a lighted cigarette, cans of kerosene right there in the house for the heater. The paper said you were a hero, carrying your little brother out of that fire just in time."

"You were the hero."

"I wish I could kill them both again," Beaumont said, unaware his hands had turned to claws. "For what they did."

"They were poison, Beau. That's why I could never—"

"Not because the baby would have maybe been—?"

"No. I could bear that. Look at Luther. He's not right. He never will be. But he's a lovely little boy."

"Luther's not a little boy."

"You know what I mean, Beau. I could have lived with a . . . damaged baby. But I could never carry on their seed. It would have been like spreading a filthy disease. I couldn't. . . ."

Beaumont took a deep, slow breath, then said, "I'm sorry I said what I did, Cyn. You were right—you were right then, and you're right now. I'll never speak of it again."

"Beau, do you think we'll . . . Do you think we'll go to hell?"

"Into the fiery pit? That's where *they* went, sweetheart. God wasn't around to save us, so we saved ourselves. I don't think there's anything after . . . this. But if there is, there's no hell for you. Not for you, Cyn. Everything you did, everything you *ever* did, it was only for love."

"You, too, Beau."

"Killing those animals? Sure, that's true. But there's been a lot marked down on my ledger since then."

"Wherever you go, I'm going with you."

"Then it doesn't matter where it is," the man in the wheelchair said, closing his eyes again.

1959 October 04 Sunday 16:04

When the phone in the back office of the restaurant rang, it was Dioguardi himself who picked up the receiver.

"Who are you?" he said, without preamble.

"I'm a businessman, just like you. I want to do business. So I sent you my card, and a sample of my work."

You're a very cute guy, Dioguardi thought to himself. "Okay," he said aloud, "what kind of business do you want to do?"

"The kind where I get paid."

"Paid how much? And for what?"

"Well, that's really your choice. You can either pay me for what I sent you a sample of, COD, or you can pay me to take my business elsewhere."

"Uh-huh. And how much payment would we be talking about?"

"For deliveries, it's a sliding scale, starting at a grand a head."

"Starting?"

"Starting. But if you want to make a deal for me to move my operation to another city, you can pay a onetime noncompetition fee. That'd be ten large."

"Just to go away?"

"Far away. And not come back."

"You, uh, ever do this other places?"

"Lots of other places. It's what I do."

"Maybe I don't want to do business at all."

"That's up to you."

"I can't just—"

"I understand. I'll give you some time to think about it, okay? Then I'll call again, and you can give me your answer."

"Hey! If you—"

The dial tone cut off whatever Dioguardi was going to say.

Five young men walked down the alley toward the panel truck. They were in a V-formation, two on each wing of their leader, whose slender frame made him appear taller than he was. He gave a hand gesture and the group halted. The leader approached on his own, hands open at his sides.

"How old is this punk, anyway?" the driver said.

"His DOB is six-ten-forty-one," the passenger said. "Makes him just past eighteen. Doesn't look it, does he?"

By then, the young man had closed the distance. He stepped to the passenger side as the window rolled down.

"Mr. White?" he asked.

"That's right, Myron," Fred said.

"I don't go by that," the young man said. "They call me—"

"Get in the back," Fred told him. "The door's not locked."

The young man felt his comrades close by, but he didn't look in their direction.

The passenger glanced at his watch. When he looked up, his eyes were as empty and flat as twin panes of brown glass.

The young man walked around to the back of the truck, opened the right-side door, climbed in, and pulled it closed behind him.

The driver started the engine and drove off, without a glance at the remaining Hawks.

The gang leader duckwalked toward the front of the truck. He knelt behind the seat, said, "Where are we going?" to the man in the passenger seat.

"Not far," Fred told him, his tone not inviting further conversation.

The gang leader watched through the windshield as the truck navigated familiar streets. As they turned onto Devlin Avenue, he mentally catalogued the changing neighborhood, clicking off stores he recognized like a priest working rosary beads. *I have to do this,* ran through his mind. *I'm the President. And this is our chance.*

The truck pulled into a gas station, but drove past the pumps all the way around to the back. The passenger hopped out and opened a garage door. The truck pulled inside.

"Let's go," the driver said, as he got out of the vehicle.

The gang leader climbed out the back and found himself in front of a collapsing-leg bridge table and three metal chairs.

"Have a seat," Milt told him.

All three sat down.

The gang leader reached in his pocket for his cigarettes, moving very slowly so as not to startle the two men. His hand was halfway to his jacket before he realized he was wasting the effort—they looked about as nervous as a pair of gardeners.

"You've got one on for Wednesday night," Milt said. "At the lot on Halstead."

"Yeah," the young man answered, not questioning how the men sitting across from him would know such a thing. "That's the best time—too many cops driving around on weekends."

"Fair one?" Milt asked.

"Supposed to be. But you can't trust the—"

"Who called it?"

"We . . . I guess we both did. Our warlord met their—"

"Whole mobs, or ten-best?"

"Nobody does ten-best anymore," the young man said, unconsciously dry-washing his hands. "The others always show up, to watch, like, and they end up getting in it, anyway."

"So you'll be outnumbered," Fred said.

"Not this time," the young man said, pride thickening his voice. "We have a treaty with the Mercy Street Gladiators. So some of them might even be there with us, maybe."

"That was pretty slick work," Fred complimented him. "Only thing is, we heard the niggers have reached out."

"Huh?" the young man said, puzzled.

"You ever hear of the Chicago Vice Lords?"

"I . . . I think I heard of them. But I never seen—"

"They started the same place the Hawks did," Fred said.

"In Truesdale?" the young man said. "Man, you don't know what you're saying. I spent more than two years locked up there, and I never saw any—"

"I don't mean the same physical location," Fred said, patiently. "I mean the same *place*. 'Locked up,' that's a place, understand? Only, for the Vice Lords, it was in the St. Charles Reformatory— that's up in Illinois, an hour's drive west of Chicago. That joint, it's run the same way they do it at the Truesdale Training School for Boys. Cottages, right?"

"Dorms," the young man said. "The cottages were only for the—"

"Right," Fred interrupted. "The point is, they kept you separated, mostly."

"Except for the sissies. They had their own dorm. That was the only place they mixed colors. But nobody cared about that. Even niggers got no use for—"

"That was a mistake," Milt said.

"What?"

"A *big* mistake," Fred took up the thread. "You leave niggers alone, they're going to plot. And that's what happened. What they call those places, it's all wrong. 'Reformatory.' 'Correctional Institute.' 'Training School.' What did they train you to do in Truesdale?"

"Uh, to be a farmer, I guess. That was all we did there, just get up in the morning and—"

"Yeah," Fred said, making it clear he wasn't interested in the young man's recollections of institutional life. "Look, Myron—I'm sorry, look, *Ace*—when you do a burglary, you're inside the house, you see a chest of drawers, where do you start?"

"With the bottom drawer," the young man said, promptly. "That way, you don't have to close each one to get to the next one. Saves time, you get out faster. But you gotta be sure to—"

"Where'd you learn that?" Fred said.

"While I was in— Oh, yeah, I see what you mean now."

"Learned some other things, too, didn't you?" the agent said. "And when you got out, it was like you earned your stripes, wasn't it?"

"My stripes?"

"Proved yourself," Fred said. "Showed you had what it takes. You were a Hawk before you went in, weren't you?"

"Just one of the Juniors."

"Sure. But by the time you came out of Truesdale . . ."

"That's when they first wanted me for leader."

" 'Leader,' now, *that's* the word we're looking for, Ace," Fred said, leaning in, flicking his lighter into life to start the youth's cigarette burning. " 'President,' that's just a title. Something you are. But 'leader,' well, that's something you *do*."

"The Vice Lords aren't just a club," Milt said. "They're more like an army. *Their* leaders, they call them 'generals.' They practically run the whole West Side of Chicago. You know how big a piece of turf that is? More than all of Locke City."

"I heard, in New York, the niggers got gangs so big they swarm like ants when they come to bop," Ace said. "But that's just what people say. Here, they got more men than us, but nothing like that."

"That's what I was telling you before, Ace. About the Kings reaching out," Fred said, extending his arm to illustrate his words. "The Vice Lords are thinking about expanding their territory. And, Wednesday night, they're going to have some men on hand. Not to fight. More like . . . observers. If they like what they see . . ."

"I don't get it," the young man said, dragging on his cigarette. "Why would they even care? It's not like anyone around here has got anything."

"Where do your boys get reefer?" Milt asked.

"From Fat Lucy," the young man said, wondering, even as he spoke, why it seemed impossible to lie to the self-assured men sitting on either side of him. "She runs the candy store over on—"

"Right," Fred said, approvingly. "And where does *she* get it?"

"I don't know," the young man said, shrugging. "She's always had it."

"If Fat Lucy was in Chicago, you know where she'd get reefer to sell, Ace? From the Vice Lords. You see the difference? That's the wave of the future. Consolidation. A little club like yours, no offense, you can hold your turf, a few blocks, maybe, but you can't make a living from it. So it's not really yours."

"Where we live, everything around there, it belongs to Mr. D."

"Yes. And where did *he* get it from?"

"Huh?"

"Pay attention, Ace. Sal Dioguardi didn't get what he has because he had a rich father, left it to him in his will. He *took* it. He took it doing the same thing you're going to be doing Wednesday night."

"Fighting."

"Yeah. But not fighting for . . . Do you even know what you're fighting for?"

"The niggers keep coming into our—"

"Christ!" Fred said, disgusted. "Look, that's the exact same reason you used to rumble with the Gladiators, isn't it? Before your 'treaty,' I mean?"

"We can't let—"

"This is why the whole white race is going to hell," Fred said, exasperated. "You can get just as dead rumbling over who gets to sell reefer in your part of town as you can over who stepped on a piece of sidewalk without permission. You take the same risks. You go to the same prison if you get caught. If the Vice Lords decide to come to Locke City, it'll be like someone spread hot black tar all over the North Side, and then brought in a steamroller. The only way to keep them out is to show them it's not worth the risk."

"I . . . How could we . . . ?"

"You got how many zips in your arsenal?"

"Three *good* ones. There's a few more, but I'm not so sure they'll—"

"And the niggers?"

"Who knows *what* they'll bring. Last time, they didn't even have one, I don't think. Nobody got hit, anyway."

"Wednesday, that all changes," Fred said. He took a chrome-plated revolver out of his jacket, laid it on the table in front of the gang leader. "Ever use one of these, Ace?"

"I once—" the young man began, then cut himself off to speak the truth. "No."

"Nothing to it," Fred assured him. "Now, this here is a quality piece. Smith and Wesson thirty-eight, exactly like the cops use. Soon as the niggers even *see* it, they're going to run. And when it goes off—*boom!*—it's not like hearing that little pop from a zip gun; this thing sounds like a cannon."

"It's beautiful," the gang leader said, not reaching to touch the pistol, willing his hands to calmness.

"Wednesday night, you walk toward each other, all in a line, right? Side to side? You in the middle, the leader. The leader from the Kings—what's his name, Preacher?—he does the same. You wait until you get *close* before you pull this out, Ace. And two seconds after that, the whole world changes. That is, if you've got the heart to—"

"Me?" the young man said, torn between anger and fear. "Me!?"

"Come on! What are you talking about?" Milt said to his partner. "Ace wouldn't be leader of the Hawks if he hadn't proved himself."

"Sure, that's right," Fred apologized. "I know you're the man for the job."

"How much for the pistol?" the young man said, tight-jawed.

"Consider it a gift," Fred said. "From your friends." He brought out a box of bullets. "There's twenty-four in there. More than enough for you to practice with, and have plenty left for Wednesday." He released the revolver's cylinder and sighted down the barrel, holding his thumb at the front end to reflect light. "That's how you check, to make sure it's clean, okay?"

The gang leader nodded, watching closely.

Fred loaded the pistol, each step a slow-motion demonstration. "You only put five in, okay? So the hammer always rests over an empty chamber." He snapped the cylinder into place.

"You with me?" he asked.

The gang leader nodded again, realizing that he wouldn't like the way his voice would sound if he spoke aloud.

Fred reopened the cylinder, turned the pistol upside down, and caught the cartridges as they spilled into his open palm.

"They come out real easy *most* of the time. But if they stick, you just use the extractor, like . . . this, see?"

Another nod.

"First thing, you get used to the trigger pull," he said, handing over the empty gun.

The gang leader hefted the pistol, surprised at its weight.

"Aim it over there . . . at the wall. Good. Now *squeeze* the trigger. One long, *steady* pull. Don't ever jerk it."

The gang leader felt the resistance of the trigger, pulled steadily. As the hammer came down, his face twitched, so slightly that it would have gone unnoticed if the others hadn't been expecting it.

"Now, you *could* cock it first," Fred said, taking the pistol back and demonstrating, "and *then* shoot." The hammer dropped—Ace flinched at the sound. "And that's more accurate, if you're only going to shoot once. But you don't want to be doing that. You want to be able to squeeze all five off, bang-bang-bang, nice and smooth. Understand?" he asked, handing the pistol back.

"Will it kick?" the gang leader asked.

"A little bit. Nothing much. That's why you have to practice. Get used to it. So it doesn't make you jump when you go into action."

"Okay."

"There's no safety on this piece," Fred said. "But if you don't walk around with it cocked, it's never going to go off accidentally. And, anyway, you're always on an empty chamber, like I showed you, all right?"

"Yes."

"This is it, Ace," the man he knew as Mr. White said. "After Wednesday, the Hawks aren't going to be small change anymore. You're going to be the real thing."

1959 October 04 Sunday 17:06

The knock on the hotel-room door pulled Dett from the easy chair as if attached by invisible wires. He said, "Yes?" in a calm, polite voice, slid the derringer from his pocket, and padded silently across the room so he was standing to the side of the door.

"It's me, sir. Rufus. Thought I'd just freshen up that ice bucket for you before I went off my shift."

Dett opened the door, his right hand in the pocket of his slacks. Rufus smiled his way inside, and made straight for the top of the bureau.

"Yes, sir, this one ain't but water now."

"Appreciate it."

"Yes, sir. You know, like I said before, anytime you want something, all you got to do is ask for me."

"Thanks."

"You okay with your liquor supply, sir? 'Cause it just take me a minute to—"

"I'll be fine," Dett said.

"Mix you one now, if you like?"

"Yeah, okay." Thinking, *He's working way too hard for a lousy dollar.*

"I notice, a lot of the gents, they like to have a little taste before dinner, 'specially if it's going to be a real spread."

"You must be a mind reader," Dett said, half-smiling. "I've got a big date later, and a big date starts with a big dinner, if you know what I mean."

"Yes sir, I sure do!" Rufus said, grinning as he handed over the drink he had prepared. "Gonna be out late tonight, I bet."

"If things work out the way I plan, *all* night," Dett said, holding up the glass of bourbon in a silent toast.

1959 October 04 Sunday 17:11

"In this life—*our* life, I mean—you know what's the best thing you can have going for you?" Salvatore Dioguardi said.

"People you can trust?" the scar-faced man sitting across from him replied.

Dioguardi nodded his concurrence. "I know guys, *you* know guys, right in this thing with us, been from the beginning, guys who wouldn't give you up even if they had to walk into the death house," he said. "We got a dozen men fit that description, right in our own outfit back home, G."

"More," the scar-faced man said.

"But that's not enough to make a man trustworthy," Dioguardi said. "A man could have a solid-steel pair on him, but that don't make him smart. Some guys, you couldn't beat their own name out of them, but you put them in the right situation, you could get them to tell you anything you want to know."

"You mean, like with a broad?"

"With a broad. Liquored up. Or even just plain okey-doked— tricked, scammed, chumped. They'd be spilling their guts, and they wouldn't even know it."

"So you're saying the best thing a man can have is a good brain?" the disfigured man asked, waiting patiently for the punch line.

"No, Gino. The best thing, for what we do, for our life, is when people think you're stupid. When they underestimate you."

"Nobody underestimates you, Sal."

"When did you turn into an ass-kisser, G.?"

"Hey!" the older man said, his voice dropping an octave.

"What else should I say, you pouring the olive oil over me like I'm a fucking plate of pasta, Gino? You know me all my life. I always looked up to you. When I started to make my own moves, you were the man I wanted with me, from the beginning."

"And I *been* with—"

"Yeah. Yeah, you have, G. The man I come to with my problems, that's you to me. Closer than my father—fuck him in his eyes—ever was. I don't keep you right next to me so you can jerk me off like some hooker."

"Sal, I don't have to take—"

"You'll take it, G. Because it's the truth. And that's what I want from you, *capisce*? The truth. I can't do what I got to do unless I see things like they really are."

"I never—"

"Ah, you just fucking *did,* G. 'Nobody underestimates you,' the fuck does that mean? Everybody thinks I'm a real genius, right?"

"No," the older man answered, chilly-voiced.

"No?"

"No, Sally," he said, heavily. "Everybody don't necessarily think you're a genius, that's right."

"Now we're rolling," Dioguardi said, smiling broadly, showing a gleaming set of perfectly capped teeth. "So what's the read on me, G.? Straight up, straight out."

"Cugliuna di ferro!" Gino said, as if taking an oath.

"And the brains of a parakeet, right?"

"It's not that bad."

"No?"

"What do you want me to say, Sally? That you're no Luciano? Who is?"

"*You* think I'm smart, G.?"

"Kind of question is that? Ever since you were a little kid, I knew you could be—"

"—a boss, with my own crew? Sure. But not the kind of man they ever ask to sit on the Commission."

"What do you care about that, Sally? You sit down with those people, you're in the room with the most crafty, devious, back-stabbing collection of men in the whole world. Like putting your hand in a basket of fucking rattlesnakes."

"I can handle—"

"You know what made Lucky what he was?" Gino interrupted his boss, gently steering him away from danger as he had so many times in the past. "Lucky wasn't like the rest of us. He was a prince," the scar-faced man said, worshipfully. "And a prince, he's not with one little group or another. He's with everyone."

"No tribes," Dioguardi said, listening.

"You got it! With a *real* leader, it don't matter who's your cousin. This thing of ours, it started with blood. Close blood. Maybe it should have stayed that way. Now you got 'families' what ain't families for real. And the bosses, they spend more time plotting against each other than they do thinking of ways to take care of their soldiers."

Dioguardi leaned back in his chair, cast his eyes at the ceiling, and recited, as if reading from a report. "Sal Dioguardi, that is one *vicious* motherfucker. Rip the eyeballs out of your head and eat them for appetizers. Kill you, your father, *and* your sons if you cross him. How many men did he kill before he even got a little crew of his own? A dozen? More? A stone *animale*. About as subtle as a sledgehammer. You got a problem with Sally D., he'd rather hit you in your fucking head than sit down and talk with you." He shifted position, pinned the man across from him with his eyes. "That sound about right, G.?"

"I heard people say that, yeah. All of it."

"And, see, G., that's all true. I *made* all that true. A rep like mine, it buys you some distance. One time, when I was just a young guy, back home, I made this nice score, and I was flush. I heard about this girl, Angel. Three hundred bucks a night, but she was supposed to be worth it. The best piece of ass in the whole city, what people said. I didn't have my button yet, but I was a comer. A sure thing. I wasn't ready for a Caddy—not in my position, not then—but I could have the best of *something*. Treat myself, you know?"

"Yeah."

"So I go see this girl. I mean, I called her, made an appointment, like she was a doctor or something. And she was gorgeous. Long black hair, boobs out to here," he said, gesturing, "an ass like a perfect ripe peach, a face like you could see what they named her after, everything.

"Now, all night means all night. After the first time, I was just laying back on her bed—silk sheets she had, G., *black* silk—and we're talking. Mostly her, the talking, I mean. I'm kind of half-listening—that broad almost put me in a coma—and I realize she's talking about a job. A job *she* wants done."

"On her pimp?"

"No. No, nothing like that. A woman like her, she never had no pimp, I bet. What she was talking about was one of her . . . clients, she called them. A guy who worked with diamonds. One of those Jews with the beards and the long black coats? What she told me was, they carry the ice around with them. And they deal all in cash. You understand where I'm going?"

"She had a plan to take this guy off?"

"Right. A *complicated* plan, G. But, listening to her, I could see how it could work. I remember, I sat up in the bed, and just . . . just *stared* at her. And you know what she said?"

"What?"

"She said, and I never forgot it, 'I just *look* like this. It's not all I am.' You see what I learned right there, G.? You look at this broad, you never think she could be some kind of mastermind. Only she was. And, right that minute, I swore to myself that I'd be just like her. It's the perfect camouflage. You look at her, all you see is a piece of ass. You'd never see how dangerous she is, because you wouldn't be thinking of her that way."

"Did you ever do that job? The one she wanted you for?"

"No. And I never went back to see her again, either. 'Cause even as I snapped to what she was telling me, I realized I was *already* playing the role I do now. I mean, if she hadn't thought I was a little slow, she wouldn't have picked me. I ever did that job with her, she'd own me, the cunt. Probably turn right around and sell me to the Jew she wanted me to rob."

"You got a plan, Sal? Is that what all this—?"

"I got a *lot* of plans, G. That's what makes me different from the others. They all got plans, but they're like a flock of pigeons on the ground, so busy pecking at the garbage that they never look up, see where it came from."

"You mean . . . what, Sal?"

"I mean the people who run the whole show, G. Not the Commission, the government."

"The feds?"

"Not them. They're just soldiers, too. They got bosses, they do what they're told. A boss—a boss by us—he gets clipped, what happens to his people? When I was in Japan—oh, the money you could make *there* after the war!—I made friends with this guy, Yasui. He told me the Japs had a thing like ours thousands of years before we did. Believe that! They had families, bosses, soldiers, territories, rackets . . . everything.

"So, anyway, my point, when one of their bosses got killed, his soldiers—'samurai,' they called them—they were just cut loose. After that, they were 'ronin,' which means, like, a man without a family. A bad thing to be. Like a mercenary. Take the money and do the job, but they got no . . . connection. You can never trust a man like that, because he's not tied to you: not by blood, not by honor.

"Our people, we do things different. Our way is better. With us, your boss gets taken down, you can catch on with another family. Not the one you was at war with, maybe—although even *that* happens— but you're still . . . connected. Still a part of something."

"Sure, Sal. But what does that have to do with—?"

"The president, he's just like a boss, G. And the feds, they're his soldiers. When the president's gone, the next guy who takes over, he gets all the soldiers, too. Now they're *his* soldiers."

"Maybe."

"Maybe? What're you talking about, G.? How else could it be?"

"If the feds are soldiers, *their* boss, it's not the president, it's that fucking Hoover. We changed presidents how many times? But it's still Hoover. It's like he's the boss-for-life."

"Batista," Dioguardi blurted out.

"What?"

"He was boss-for-life, too, right, G.? Down in Cuba. We had all *kinds* of things working there. It was perfect. Our own country. Then this guy comes out of the mountains and—*bam!*—before you can look up, everything's turned upside down."

"Sally, I'm not following you."

"The smart boys—the ones *think* they're smart—they've been looking over their shoulders so long, make sure one of the others isn't sneaking up on them, they forget how to look forward. The things we make our money from, they could disappear in a second, just like Cuba."

"I still don't see—"

"Like liquor, G. Remember when that was our gold mine? Every family in America today, that's where it got its stake. Everything started with booze. That's what took us to the big time.

"But what kind of money is there in liquor now? You got hillbillies running moonshine into dry counties, but that's a mug's game. The government saw how strong we were getting off the booze money. So what did it do? They cut us off at the knees. You make something legal, how do we make a profit off it? That's why the smart boys think drugs are the way to go."

"They're right," the scar-faced man said, flatly. "No way they're ever going to make dope legit. It'll be good for—"

"Don't say 'forever,' G. Because dope's not like booze. There was always outlaws in the booze racket, but they were small-timers. It wasn't even worth shutting them down. Drugs, that's different. Ten years from now, maybe less, you'll have niggers and spics and—who knows?—maybe the fucking Chinese in on the action.

It's their neighborhoods where it gets sold, what's to stop them from dealing themselves in?"

"They don't have the organization for anything like that."

"Yeah? How many niggers do *you* talk to?"

"Me? I don't talk to *moolingan*."

"I do."

"Huh?"

"I got a boy on the payroll. My personal payroll, out of my own pocket. Smart boy, too. He's like me, in a way. You see him working—he's a bellhop, down to the Claremont—you think, There's another mush-mouthed jungle bunny. But this one, he's slick. And he likes money. That's how I know about this man Beaumont's brought in. I got a watch on him like he's a fish in that aquarium over there."

"And this guy, the nigger, I mean, he's going to be dealing dope someday?"

"I don't know what *he's* going to be doing. Maybe saving the money I give him to buy a red convertible with leopard-skin seat covers, all I know. But we're not going to be in the dope game, G. Not us. I got something better."

"Yeah?" the scar-faced man said, tilting his head slightly, to show he was fully focused.

"You know the stag films, the ones we get made up in Calumet City?"

"Sure. But they don't bring in the kind of—"

"Not *yet* they don't. But they will. Someday, those are going to be a better racket than booze ever was."

"Come on, Sally. How much can we make on a stag film?"

"How much can we make on a load of dope?"

"Huh? That depends, right? On how much you got to sell in the first place."

"Right!" Dioguardi said, rapping the tabletop twice with his knuckles. "That's it, exactly, Gino! See, what they sell on the streets—I'm talking *real* dope now, heroin—it has to go through a lot of hands before it ever gets here. The poppy don't grow in America. Where they grow it, it starts out as opium. People, people who know what they're doing, they have to change it into heroin. And once the heroin's made, pure, it has to be cut, right?"

"Sure. So?"

"So how many times can you step on it before you got nothing? You cut it *too* much, it's worthless. And once you sell it, it's gone forever. You with me?"

"Yeah. But . . ."

"Gino," Dioguardi said, unconsciously flexing his biceps under his suit jacket, "listen. We put up the money for a stag film—not just some stripper playing with herself—the whole nine yards, fucking, sucking, anything goes. Let's say we ante, I don't know, five large into the whole production, okay? Do a real professional job, lights and cameras, everything. Maybe even in color. Now we sell copies for—what?—ten bucks? And even with everybody dipping their beak along the way, we net, say, five bucks a pop. So we need to sell—what?—a lousy thousand copies, and we're in gravy from then on. Because, and this is the beauty part, we never really sell it, see? We're selling *copies*. And we can make a million copies, we want to. Sell the same thing, over and over again."

"It would take a whole—"

"Network? Sure. But look how easy it would be to put one together, G. What are they going to hit you with for selling fuck-films? A fine? It's not like the way it is with dope—nobody's really taking a risk. And, for product, there's girls everywhere. I know a guy, out in L.A., he says he could get us a different girl, a *gorgeous* fucking girl, every day, we wanted. Get them to do anything, even the weirdo stuff.

"Let the feds go chase the dope, Gino. We'll be sitting on a gold mine, because all we're going to be selling will be *copies* of the gold."

"You really think it could work like that, Sal?"

"How could it not? There'll *always* be guys want that stuff. Just like there'll always be whores. But films, films like I'm talking about, that's the future.

"Look, the government, they're just another mob. A greedy fuck-ing mob, at that. So, you have to figure, they see *us* making money, they want to get in on it themselves. How long you think it's going to be before they got legal casinos in places besides fucking Vegas? They legalized booze, they could do the same thing with the numbers too, they wanted. But fuck-films? No way the government ever makes *that* legal, right?"

"Right, Sally. Any senator voted for something like that, it'd be Kaddish for him."

"See?" Dioguardi said, triumphantly. "Things are happening now, G. All around us. This whole truce thing, the election, everything. I don't know how it shakes out when it's done. I don't know if they're going to be able to get to Beaumont, even. But I know this. If we get into this film thing on the ground floor, we can build ourselves a mountain of cash, G. And cash, that's the locomotive that pulls the whole train."

"It's worth a try, Sal. The way you got it all doped out, it's no big risk."

"And no big-money investment, either. That's why I want you to go out to L.A., meet with this guy I just told you about, get things set up."

"But what about the wild card, Sally? This guy who knocked off Tony and Lorenzo? Don't you need me around for him?"

"Maybe down the road, but not now. I think this guy, whoever he is, he's about to make the same mistake about me everybody else does."

1959 October 04 Sunday 17:38

"You got it?"

"Right here," Ace said, patting his gang jacket.

"Let's see it, man," a sixteen-year-old with an acne-ravaged complexion said, eagerly.

"At the clubhouse," Ace said. "Tonight. Call everyone in."

1959 October 04 Sunday 17:41

"Hello . . ." The woman's private-line voice was lush with secrets, revealing nothing, promising everything.

"It's me," Sherman Layne said.

"Yes. When will you be—?"

"After it gets dark."

1959 October 04 Sunday 20:46

"We came a long way for these, brother," the neatly dressed, dark-skinned young man said. "We thought there would be more."

"Omar says we have to divide up what we have," Darryl told him.

"Yes, I understand all that," the young man said. "But we were told to expect five. And we came with the *money* for five."

"It's your decision to make, my brother," Darryl said.

"What decision is that?"

"You have to decide: Are we calling each other 'brother' to mean something? Or do you think we're just a bunch of gun dealers?"

"I wasn't saying anything like—"

"This is what happened," Darryl said, his cadaverous face spectral in the afternoon sunlight. "We made a deal for fifty weapons. We agreed to pay a certain price. When the man—the *white* man—came here, what he had, instead, was twenty-four. He said they were better than the ones we were supposed to buy. And Kendall, that's our armorer, he said that was true. The ones we ended up with, they're not semi-autos like we expected. *These* ones, you can switch them to full auto, like machine guns."

"Yes, but—"

"—but that still means less men with a gun in their hand," Darryl finished the sentence for the other man. "We know this. The man—the *white* man—he said he took what he could get, and twenty-four was what he could get. What he said was, it's the same time in prison for twenty-four as it would have been for fifty. And he wanted the same money for the load he *did* bring."

"And you paid him?"

"We paid him."

"So what are we supposed to do now?"

"You were supposed to get ten percent of the shipment," Darryl said. "You still can, if you want it."

"Ten percent of twenty-four is—"

"—two point four. Which rounds out to two."

"Two? Why doesn't it round out to three?"

"Because the units who took twenty percent, they expected ten. Now they're going to get five. We take their four point eight up to five, it means your two point four has to drop to two."

"So they get half of what they expected, but we get less than that," the young man said, his voice classroom-argumentative, reflecting his other life, a college student.

"These are guns, brother. Not poker chips. There's no way to divide them more fairly than what I just said."

"The man talks sense." The young man's companion spoke for the first time. "He talks sense about the whole thing."

"You could of told us about this," the young man said to Darryl. "Before we made the drive, I mean."

"You know how it works," Darryl replied. "We do not talk our business on the telephone, brother. That's the rules we were given; that's the rules we live by. Like I said, it's your decision."

1959 October 04 Sunday 20:59

"It's a beauty!"

"Brand-new," Ace said smugly to the lanky, red-haired youth. "The only way any of those niggers ever saw anything like this before was in a cop's hand."

Seven young men, ranging from mid- to late teens, were clustered tightly around a table made from pine planks set across a pair of half-barrels. The pistol lay on the bare wood surface before them: a rare jewel, amateurishly appraised.

The basement was divided into four rooms. Two had long, narrow, street-level windows, another housed an oil-burning furnace. The last, all the way to the back, was furnished with street-salvage: a couch so rotted that its exposed springs had been cut off at their base, with the jagged tips wrapped in black electrical tape; two kitchen chairs with no backs; a once-blue armchair now stained into virtual blackness; a child-sized desk; an army cot; two portable radios; and an assortment of ragged couch pillows strewn randomly on the floor.

No outside light penetrated the room. A single red bulb dangled from exposed overhead wiring, spliced from the adjacent building. Fat hurricane candles burned in several upturned hubcaps. The cement floor was an ashtray.

"This is just the beginning," Ace told the others. "After Wednesday, when people hear our name, when they see our colors, they'll pay attention. Because we're going to be stepping up."

"Stepping up to what?" a boy named Hog, whose bridgeless nose and wide nostrils had given birth to his name, asked.

"To the rackets," Ace said: an acolyte, reciting liturgy. "If we just keep on like we've been doing, where do you think we end up?"

"We . . ."

"Got no answer, right, Harold?" Ace said to the red-haired youth. "You think a man like Mr. Dioguardi didn't get his start the same way we are now?"

"But he's in the Mafia, right?" the acne-scarred boy said. "They have a whole . . . organization, and all."

"He was just an example," their leader said, smoothly. "You don't have to be Italian to be in the rackets. Look at Mr. Beaumont. Everybody knows how *he* got started."

"He was in a club?" Hog said, incredulously. "In a wheelchair? How was he going to—?"

"He was in *something*," Ace said, assuredly. " 'Cause he had men with him when he made his move. Same as we do."

"They was older guys," Hog said.

"How do you know that? I mean, none of us *really* knows. All we have is . . . stories. One person tells another person, that's the only way we ever know anything. But this part isn't no story: Mr. Dioguardi, he's got his stuff going, but Locke City, the whole thing, it belongs to Mr. Beaumont. And wherever *he* started out, it wasn't on top. It was small."

"I still don't see where we could—"

"This is all about rep," Ace said, confidently. "It's all about how people see you . . . us. Mr. Dioguardi even said to me, once, maybe someday he'd have some jobs for us. The Hawks, I mean."

"He said that to you—to you, personally?"

"That's right, Hog," Ace said, choosing to ignore the skeptical tone. He'd speak to Hog later, privately—it didn't look good for a Warlord to question the President in front of the others. "To me. Face to face. How do you think we got this clubhouse? Mr. Dioguardi owns this building. He owns a whole lot of buildings. On this block, he told me, you men—the Hawks, he was saying—are my eyes and ears."

"That's not doing a job," Harold said.

"Not a *big* job," Ace corrected him. "But how is a man like Mr. Dioguardi ever going to know that we *can* do bigger jobs, unless we grow our rep? After the meet with the Kings, he's going to know. Everybody's going to know."

"Yeah!" Hog said, crossing his arms to show he stood behind their leader.

"We don't have much of anything now," Ace told the group. "We've got a few blocks, our turf, that's it. When we bop, it's not to get new ground, it's to hold on to what we already got, that's all. The Gladiators, they've got a real clubhouse. A big apartment, over on Harrison. On the second floor, even. They've got cars, too. I'll bet they've got fifty members. When they walk down the street, it's like an army on the march. You don't see the Kings crossing *their* line. You don't see *their* debs going with outsiders."

"That's because they've got the reefer business," the acne-scarred boy said. "The money, that's what does it."

"That's *exactly* what the men who gave me this pistol said, Donny," the leader replied. "We should have a piece of that for ourselves."

"How?" Hog asked. "The Gladiators only signed that treaty

with us because of the niggers. They're not going to give us any of their—"

"They're not going to *give* us nothing," Ace said. "Wednesday night, it's *our* meet. We're the ones that called it. The Gladiators will be there, like to back us up, because of the treaty. But we know what that's really about, don't we? It's just to watch us, see how we handle ourselves."

Ace took a quick swig from the pale-green bottle of Thunderbird, passed it to the boy on his right, and addressed his audience.

"And remember, their President, Lacy, he fucking *hates* that nigger Preacher. And after Lacy sees what *I* do to him, he's going to think, Okay, those Hawks, they've got it. They're killers, man.

"I'm not saying we'll run the Gladiators off. They got the numbers. And there's the treaty, too. We have to respect that. But the reefer, in our territory, by rights, it should be us getting paid from Fat Lucy, not them. After they see how the Hawks have real firepower, I'll bet they see it that way, too. And Mr. Dioguardi, he'll know the Hawks can do a lot more jobs than just keeping an eye on things for him."

"We're doing all right without . . ." said a tall, well-muscled boy with a deeply underslung jaw.

"We're *not,* Larry," Ace said. "Not if we want to—"

"What *I* wanted, when I joined, was to . . . I don't know, be with a club. Have a place where we could bring girls, drink a little wine, smoke some gauge, you know what I'm saying. I mean, sure, bop with anyone who calls us out. But I don't want to be a gang man for my whole life."

"What do you want to do, then?" Ace confronted the challenger. "Go work in the plant, like your daddy did? The plant's fucking *closed,* man."

"I was thinking about the army."

"The army?"

"My brother went in. Oscar. He was—"

"Oscar didn't have no choice," Ace said. "He was a Hawk, too, remember? The judge told him it was the state pen or the army. A lot of guys went in the same way."

"Yeah, I know that," Larry said. "But Oscar ended up *liking* it.

He was supposed to go in for four years, but when that was done, he signed up again. He's a sergeant. He's always writing me, telling me I should do it, too. It's a pretty good deal. He never has to worry about losing his job. And he can even retire when he's younger than my father is right now. Have a salary for life. He's got a new car, and he's saving for a 'Vette. They get free doctors and free—"

"Free? He's not free, man. He's got to take orders."

"Everybody takes orders from somewhere," Larry said, stubbornly. "It doesn't sound so bad to me."

"That's because your brother, when he came up, it was a different time. He didn't have the . . . opportunities, like we're going to have."

"I don't—"

"What's your hurry, man? I know all about that army thing. You got to be seventeen to go in, even if your folks sign for you. Just wait until after Wednesday, okay? You'll see."

"I'm just saying—"

"Who gave you that gun, anyway?" Hog asked, deliberately redirecting the growing tension in the basement.

"All I know is Mr. White and Mr. Green," Ace told the others. "They said they'd been scouting us. Liked what they saw."

"You think maybe they were from Mr. Dioguardi's—?"

"Oh, man, come on!" Ace said. "Those guys, the way they talked, I know where they're from." He paused dramatically, waiting for everyone's close attention. "They were the Klan," Ace said, rapturously. "The way they talked, they got to be."

1959 October 04 Sunday 21:05

"It's your turn," Ruth told the busty girl in the white babydoll nightgown. "You want it or not?"

"What do you mean, my turn?" the girl who called herself Lola asked. Her dull-brown hair fell limply on either side of even duller-brown eyes.

"You know the trick," Ruth said, tapping a yellow pencil against the frame of her cat's-eye glasses. "I told you about it when you first

came here. And you've talked about it with other girls, girls who've
done it."

"I didn't—"

"Yes, you did. There's something else I told you, told you from
the beginning," Ruth said, sternly. "In this house, you can turn down
a trick—any trick—and still stay. But you lie to me, even one time,
and you're out on your ass."

"I'm sorry, Miss Ruth. I didn't mean to—"

"He's going to be here soon, all right? Now, either you say yes,
so we can get you down to the blue room, or you say no, and I get
someone else."

"I . . ."

"This isn't a punishment, you dumb bitch," Ruth said, sharply.
"It's a fifty-dollar trick. Ever get that much before? In your whole
life? There's girls here who never even *heard* of such a thing, except
when they're lying to each other. The way it works is, the man calls,
and I spin the wheel. Whoever's name comes up, they—"

"What wheel?"

"There *is* no wheel," Ruth sighed. "It's just an expression. What
I *actually* do, since it's so important to you to know, I write every
girl's name on a card, like this one," Ruth said, holding up a plain
white index card, with the letter "L" written on it in a composition-
book hand, "and I put them all in a bowl, face-down. Then I close
my eyes, mix them all around, and pull one out. That one, it's the
winner, not the loser."

"Does it . . . does it hurt?"

"You never . . . ?"

"No. I don't think it's . . ."

"And you never asked Barbara? Or Lorraine? They both—"

"I *did* ask Lorraine. But I know how some of the girls are.
They'll say things. . . ."

Ruth pointedly looked at her wristwatch, a black oval on a thin
gold band.

"Does he ever tip?" the dull-eyed woman asked.

1959 October 04 Sunday 21:20

"You better not be calling me from work," the voice said.

Cold and hard, Carl thought, *like a diamond. A perfect pure-white diamond.* "No, of course not," he said aloud. "I would never—"

"—disobey," the voice finished the sentence for him.

"Never!" Carl said, excitement rising in that part of him he kept buried under his many shields.

"Don't say 'never' to me like that, you sniveling little baby! I *told* you, no more notes. *Didn't* I?"

"Yes, but—"

"Yes?" the voice said, the undercurrent of threat closer to the surface.

"Yes, sir. I'm sorry. I only wanted to—"

"What *you* want isn't important. *Is* it?"

"No, sir."

"And you know what *is* important, don't you?"

"Yes. I . . . Yes, sir, I know. Please?"

"What time is your shift over?"

"Eleven. But then I have to close down the—"

"Oh four hundred hours," the voice said. "That will give you plenty of time to prepare yourself."

1959 October 04 Sunday 21:34

I got to get closer, refrained through Holden's labyrinth mind. *I got to get closer, so I can make my report.* He moved as cautiously as a weasel approaching a henhouse, his passage disturbing the underbrush less than a gentle breeze. The night creatures were used to Holden's presence—his scent didn't alarm them, his movements didn't send them scurrying. He was one of them: a resident, not a visitor.

That's the one, he said to himself. *That same '55 Chevy. That's why he didn't back all the way in, the way most of them do—he wouldn't want to get that beautiful paint all scratched up.*

Music drifted out onto the night air, so softly that even Holden's forest-trained ears could barely pick it up. Unlike the lumbering gait he automatically fell into whenever he had leave the safety of his forest, Holden moved with an almost sinuous grace as he closed the gap. The bruised-and-blue sounds of Bobby Bland's "I'll Take Care of You" floated over to him, but Holden didn't recognize the song. *He's going to run down his battery, playing the radio with the engine turned off like that,* he thought.

The moon refracted against the Chevy's windshield, blocking Holden's view of the interior as effectively as a curtain. *It's a warm night. Maybe they have the side windows down. I know that Chevy's a hardtop, so even if they're in the back seat . . .*

Holden was so close that he tested each footstep before committing to it. From long experience, he knew that hiding behind a tree wasn't as effective as standing in the open, blending with the night. His green-and-brown camouflage jacket and matching hat—gifts from his friend, Sherman—coupled with his ability to stand perfectly, soundlessly still, were all he had ever needed.

Holden didn't like radios. They masked the sounds he coveted. The secret sounds he replayed in his mind, back in his room. They were his, those sounds. He owned them.

Holden often wanted to tell Sherman about the sounds. He thought his friend would understand. But . . . but he couldn't be sure. Besides, Sherman was a policeman. A detective, even. Maybe there was a law Holden didn't know about. . . .

The side windows were down, just as Holden had wished. Sometimes, Holden believed he could wish things true. Like tonight. He had wanted the windows to be down, and . . . there they were. But when he tried it on . . . other things he wanted, it didn't work. There was something about this Holden yearned to understand. But there was no one he could ask—he knew what would happen if he did.

"I hate this."

A woman's voice came through the side window. Something about it was deeply familiar to Holden, but he knew better than to reach for the memory. Every time that happened, he ended up trying to grasp smoke. If you spook up a rabbit, and you don't chase it, just stay in the same spot, very still and quiet, sometimes, sometimes, the rabbit comes back.

"You think *I* like it?" A man's voice. A young man. Holden was sure he hadn't heard it before. "What am I going to do?"

"That's just it, Harley. It should be 'What are *we* going to do?' "

"You know that's what I meant." The man's voice was somewhere between angry and . . . something else. Holden searched his mind for the right word. *Sulky. That was it. Sulky like a little kid.*

"It's only a couple of months, Harley. A couple of months, and then I'm gone from here. I'm going to start second semester."

"You'll be back."

"You're so sure?"

"Kitty, why do you have to always be twisting everything I say? I only meant, college, it's not like you stay there forever. You'll be back, for summers and stuff, that's all I was saying."

"You could come with me."

"Come with you? To . . . what's the name of that school, again?"

"Western Reserve University," the woman's voice said, proudly. "And it wouldn't be to the school. We, the girls, we have to live in dorms. But it's in Cleveland, Harley. A big city. You could find work easy, I know. My father says the mills are still pumping like mad up there. There's plenty of—"

"A steel mill? That's what you think I'm going to do with my life, Kitty?"

"I didn't mean—"

"Let me ask you something," he interrupted. "Why are you going to that fancy college?"

"To get an education. It's the only way I could ever hope to . . . to make something of myself."

"Nobody just gets an education. You learn things so you can use them, don't you? I mean, nobody takes Drivers' Ed in school so they can learn all that crap about safety; they do it because they want to get a license. There's a teachers' college right over in—"

"I'm not going to be a teacher."

"What, then?"

"I . . . I don't know. But I know it's going to be something. Maybe a doctor. Or a lawyer."

"You?"

"Why not, Harley?" she said, her voice sharpening down to an ice-pick point. "Because I'm a girl? Or because I'm a—?"

A colored girl! flashed onto the screen of Holden's mind. *She talks just like a colored girl.* He shifted his stance, a leafy branch reacting to a faint breeze, and leaned in closer, straining to listen.

"I . . . I didn't mean what you think, Kitty. I just, I just know how people are."

"People change."

"No, they don't," he said, stolidly.

"I don't mean individual people, Harley. I mean society. The whole world is changing. Not as fast as I would like. Not as fast as it should. But things are changing. If you looked anyplace but Locke City, you'd see it for yourself."

"Things are changing here, too, baby. That's what I've been trying to tell you. You want me to go someplace like Cleveland, where we could be together right out in the open, don't you?"

"Of course I do. You think I enjoy sneaking around like I'm some kind of—"

"Cleveland, it's different from here, sure. But not for the reason you think."

"And what reason do *you* think I think?"

"Come on, Kitty. I drove up there with you once, remember? Sure, you can see couples, couples like us, walking around that little lake they have in the middle of the college. But a college, that's not real life. Sooner or later, you have to leave, go out in the world."

"There's plenty of places where we could—"

"Oh yeah. Like Greenwich Village, I suppose."

"What do you know about Greenwich Village, Harley?"

"My friend Sammy, he was there. During the war. I mean, he was on leave, in New York. Most of the guys wanted to go to Times Square, but a couple of them heard there was more action in Greenwich Village. So he went down there. Sammy said it's all beatniks and stuff. Everything all mixed together."

"Greenwich Village isn't a town, Harley. It's just a little part of a big city. New York. And my father says there's places there where a Negro can't even walk without some gang jumping on him. My father's from down south. And he says, up here, it's no better. It's only that people talk different, not that they *are* different."

"If you're strong enough, it doesn't matter what people say. Or even how they think."

"Are you saying you're ready to—?"

"Not yet, I'm not, Kitty. You think I've been stalling you. Not wanting to . . . I mean, like going to Cleveland. That's not because I don't want to work. I work. I work hard. But working in a mill, that means, every day you get up in the morning, you never know if you're going to have a job to go to. It's not anything you own."

"Like your own business?"

"Exactly like that. And that, that's where *I'm* going."

"In Locke City? What could you possibly—?"

"Someday I'm going to be where Mr. Beaumont is, Kitty."

"A gangster!"

"A businessman."

"Some business," she said scornfully. "Gambling dens and whorehouses and—"

"Those are just rumors. Mr. Beaumont, he's in real estate. If you knew how much of the county he owns, you'd be shocked."

"And that's what you want? For yourself, I mean?"

"For *us*. I want it for us. You think if we lived in a big house like Mr. Beaumont's, you think if I had all kinds of people working for me, people would say anything about you and me?"

"Of course they would! This is still—"

"Mr. Beaumont, he's in a wheelchair. He can't even stand on his own two feet. You ever hear of anyone calling him a crip, or a gimp?"

"I never did."

"Right! Maybe they did when he was a kid, before he . . . before he *made* himself something. But now he's a man that's got everybody's respect. Everybody wants to be Mr. Beaumont's friend. You wouldn't believe the people who come to his house. Like they're visiting a king!"

"And you're going to be a king, someday, Harley?"

"You're going to be a doctor, aren't you?"

Holden watched as the kerchief-covered head moved closer to the silhouetted flattop. He waited for the sex sounds, but they never came.

1959 October 04 Sunday 22:02

Dett drove slowly past a weak red neon VACANCY sign into a graded dirt clearing that housed a ramshackle collection of individual cabins. He parked the Impala in a patch of shadow and got out, a single suitcase in his hand. He walked toward a flat-roofed building with bilious lemony light spilling from its single window.

"Checkout's at noon," a wizened man in a stained blue vest worn over a faded-to-gray shirt said, placing a key on the countertop and palming the bill sitting there in the same motion. He studiously avoided eye contact.

Dett went back to the Impala, drove past Unit 11, into the unpaved darkness just beyond the parking lot. After taking a single suitcase from the trunk, he walked back to the empty cottage, turned the key, and let himself in.

1959 October 05 Monday 01:24

"He's back."

"Log him in, Dave."

"I already did, Mack. I wonder what that cop wants this time."

"Money," the older man said.

"How can you know that?"

"See how he's moving? Not parking where he did before. Not watching the house. He's going around back."

"Maybe he's just scouting."

"We know there's nothing back there—not one car or person since we've been sitting here. Shouldn't take him more than a couple of minutes to find out the same thing."

"So?"

"So," Mack said, "if he's gone more than that, he's doing business."

1959 October 05 Monday 01:29

"He's not going to hurt you," Ruth said to Lola, as she fastened the last of the straps on the leather harness. The girl was on all fours, positioned on a raised platform that had been covered with a deep shag carpet, backed with a heavy layer of foam. "But I'll be right outside the door. If there's anything, *anything,* that gets you upset, all you have to do is say something."

"You're not going to—?"

"Those bitches never *stop* gossiping, do they? No, there's not going to be any gag in your mouth. That's a different trick. The men who like that, they know who to ask for. Like Brenda. She's the one who told you, isn't she?"

"She was just trying to—"

"—scare you out of this session," Ruth finished for her. "You know why? Because she wants it for herself. When you're all done, you'll be *hoping* your card comes up next time, you'll see."

"Okay . . ."

"I'm going to put this on real loose," Ruth said, gently draping a black muslin hood over the girl's head. "You can breathe right through it, see?"

"I . . . Yes."

"I'm going to turn out the lights as I leave. You won't see him come in. And you won't hear him, either. He's not going to say a word."

"Do I have to—?"

"No, you don't have to say anything, either. I told you, he's not that kind of trick. All you have to remember is to relax. Don't tighten up. You cleaned yourself out, with what I gave you to take, yes?"

"Yes."

"All right, Lola. You be good, now," Ruth said. She patted the girl gently on her framed-and-displayed bottom, and left the room.

1959 October 05 Monday 01:54

"Can't sleep, Beau?"

"I tried, honey. But even with my eyes closed, I kept seeing things. Things I should be doing."

"What you should be doing is sleeping. It's almost two o'clock in the—"

"I thought I'd work on my charts, Cyn."

"You and those charts," she snorted, affectionately. "It's a good thing we've got so much room on the walls here."

"You want to help?"

"What could I do, Beau? I don't know any of the—"

"You help just by being here, Cyn. With me. Every time I have something to figure out, you just being there, it helps me. Makes things clear. Come on, what do you say?"

"I'll make us some coffee," Cynthia said, smiling.

1959 October 05 Monday 02:12

As Dett was eating directly from a white carton of chicken chow mein, chewing each mouthful slowly, Rufus was prowling Room 809 of the Claremont Hotel. In his hand was a flashlight, its face taped so that only a sliver of the beam shone through. He had left the door slightly ajar. *Every other guest on this floor already in his room,* he recited, comforting himself. *This hour, they all asleep. Any man get off that elevator at two o'clock in the morning,* got *to be Mr. Dett. And got to be drunk, too.*

Outside the room, two men waited, both dressed in what would pass for the maintenance coveralls issued by the hotel. If a white man, *any* white man, emerged from the elevator, one of them would alert Rufus. Then they would walk toward the man, waving their arms in silent, heated argument, blocking his view and delaying his passage. They were large, bulky men, so similar in appearance they could pass for brothers. Anyone getting off the elevator was not going to just stroll past them. And the back staircase was only seconds away, in the opposite direction.

Papers and numbers, Rufus thought, gingerly probing the contents of the chest of drawers. *No.* He shifted his attention to the desk, but again came up empty. The flashlight's softly focused light played over the largest suitcase, the one Rosa Mae had said contained the mojo. *Hoodoo bullshit,* Rufus said to himself, *like Silk thinking Mr. Dett's real name is Mr. Scratch.* But he didn't open it.

Where's the other suitcase? And that little case, too?

But a search of the closet drew a blank.

Never mind, Rufus assured himself. *I already got what I came for.*

1959 October 05 Monday 02:16

"He's always at the top, isn't he?" Cynthia said, pointing to a large rectangular piece of white oaktag, taped to the wall lengthwise. On its glossy surface was a collection of names, written in black grease pencil. Each name was circled, connected by lines to the others. The effect was as neat and orderly as a school presentation.

"Ernest Hoffman? Sure, honey. And he's always going to be. I remember a word I read once. I don't remember the book or anything, but that word, it always stayed with me. 'Kingmaker.' You see how strong that word is? There's been four different governors of this state since the war. Only Jake Moore has managed to hold two terms, and he's up again, soon. They come and go, but Hoffman, he's always there. He's the man who calls the shots."

"Because he owns the newspaper?"

"That's just a piece of it, honey. There's a lot of papers around the state. Here, we've got the *Compass.* But only the *Union Mes-*

senger goes statewide. Most people, they take two papers, the local and Hoffman's. Plus, he's got the radio stations, three of them. I'm pretty sure he owns Channel 29, too.

"And, see over there," Beaumont said, pointing to the extreme left side of his chart, "besides everything else, he's got the unions in his pocket. You know why? The same reason he's got the governor. Because he decides who gets to be president of the locals. A king-maker."

"But he doesn't touch anything of ours. Or of anyone else you have on that chart, Beau."

"Oh, he *touches* it, all right, Cyn. Maybe not with his own hands, but he pulls the strings, and everybody dances to the tune he calls. The man who controls the vote controls everything, one way or the other. We own a few cops; Hoffman, he owns the police *budget,* see? You know what it means, to control where a new plant opens up, where a road gets built, what a garbageman's salary is, which town gets a new school?"

"Everything."

"Everything," Beaumont echoed. "Shalare," he said, pointing to another chart, "he's trying to buy his way in, but he's not playing for the same stakes. Shalare can pay a state senator to vote a certain way, that's all. But that same senator, he ever crosses Ernest Hoffman, well, he's not a senator anymore. That means his son loses his job, too. His nephew doesn't get a promotion. His daughter's husband doesn't get to run for a judgeship. He's all done.

"You see what I'm saying, girl. That's *real* power. So, if a man wants to run for . . . even president of the United States, why, he'd have to come to Ernest Hoffman first. And he'd better come with his hat in his hand."

"How did he get so powerful, Beau? There's plenty of people with money. . . ."

"It was his father's money, first, and his father's before him. See where it says not just 'Ernest Hoffman,' but 'Ernest Hoffman III'? Like he really *was* a king—King Ernest the Third. His grandfather owned the big mines over in Stilton. That's where it started.

"His father was the one who brought in the state police to

put down the strikes. Crushed the union forever, people thought. But now, today, that union is back in power, a real force. What a comeback, huh? Only Hoffman, he owns it. It belongs to him. The president, McCormick? He's so deep in Hoffman's pocket that he probably thinks he's back down in the mine shaft.

"You know what a man like Ernest Hoffman could do, if he wanted, Cyn? It's *his* trucks that move goods; it's *his* factories that keep people working; it's his . . . his everything. During the war, why do you think they built that huge munitions plant down in Morgan County? Because, with Hoffman at the helm, the government had an ironclad guarantee that there wouldn't be any union nonsense getting in the way. In New York, on the docks, they had to deal with Luciano to keep things moving—in these parts, it's Ernest Hoffman. You see what I mean, honey? The real government isn't sitting in the statehouse. It never is."

"But it *could* be? Is that what you're saying, Beau?"

"I thought about this a lot," the man in the wheelchair said. "Some nights, when I can't sleep, it's *all* I think about. What you just said, it's the secret to . . . everything. Like a magic key, that unlocks any door."

"I don't under—"

"Remember when you said it *could* be, girl? That's what *they* think. Even what they *believe,* like in church. Let's say you're a politician, and you want to clean up Locke City, okay? Here's your plan. First, you start small. You go along to get along. You take the money, you look the other way, you wait your turn. Then, one day, you're in charge. The mayor, say. *Now* what do you do? You clean house. Top to bottom. The chief of police, the municipal judges, the commissioner of public works . . . You sweep them all out, then you bring in your own people. Honest men, every one of them. You make Locke City into the straightest town this side of heaven. And you know what that does, Cyn?"

"I can't even imagine."

"It kills the town. It kills Locke City like somebody put a bullet into the heart of every man, woman, and child who lives here. This town, it rose from the ashes once. When they closed down the mills, that should have been it. The only reason Locke City's not a deserted village right this minute is because of the same things this great 'reformer' would be wiping out."

Beaumont contemplated the tip of his burning cigarette—he couldn't remember having lit one. "And *that's* when the truth comes out, Cyn. Under pressure. The harder things get, the closer to the truth they are."

"If things happened like you say, people would see it, wouldn't they? They'd turn on him. And vote him out of—"

"The town couldn't wait for that to happen. It wouldn't survive. Takes too long for people to wake up, most of them. But not people like us. We know. A man who takes our money, our support, to get where he is, it's because we expect things from him. We have a deal. And if he doesn't keep up his end, all the new police chiefs in the world won't help him."

"People like us . . ."

"I don't make the mistake the others make," Beaumont said. "I know I'm no better than Dioguardi. Or Shalare. Or anyone else in our game. I may be smarter; I may have a tighter crew; I may be dug in deeper; but I'm the same as them. And you know what that means, hon?"

"No, Beau."

"It means Ernest Hoffman, he's the same as me," Beaumont said, his voice steeled with utter conviction. "I'm a boss; he's a bigger boss. He sees everything I see, but he's standing on top of a much higher mountain, so he sees more. Maybe all the way across the country."

"Why is he so important now?" Cynthia asked. "Because of the election next year you keep talking about? If you're right, what difference does it make who wins? Locke City will still be the same."

"It matters who wins because the power flows down through every political machine in every city in America, Cyn. I don't care about history; I care about right now. And the reason Hoffman's so important is because of this whole 'truce' thing. Shalare wants to meet with me. He says he's already got Dioguardi signed up. We're all supposed to be pals, put our weight into making sure the election goes the right way. Who could call for such a thing but Ernest the Third?"

"So you're going to meet with him? Shalare?"

"Sure. And I'm going to make the truce, too."

"Then why did you send for . . . that man?"

"Because it's all lies, Cyn," the man in the wheelchair said, coldly. "Every word out of every mouth is a lie now. When this is over, there's only going to be one man in charge. In Locke City, I mean. And you know who gets to pick him?"

"Ernest Hoffman."

"Yes. Ernest the Third himself. *That's* why he counts. That's why he matters. We can't have gang war in Locke City. The only way to have peace is for Hoffman to pick a boss. He only has to say the word, and the Italians would tell Dioguardi to pack his bags. Shalare, I'm not so sure. But there's other ways, and Hoffman, he'll know them."

"Why would he pick one over the other? Just to keep us from fighting?"

"Because it's more efficient. Things work better when there's one man in charge. You make a plan, you don't have to worry about someone else making a different one. That's all I think about now: how I can get Ernest Hoffman to see that it's our organization he wants to run Locke City after the election's over."

"Have you ever met him? Hoffman?"

"Never once," Beaumont said. "But I've been studying him for years."

"*That's* why you brought him in!"

"What do you mean, honey?"

"Dett. That man, he's here to do something about Ernest Hoffman, isn't he?"

"Not what you think," Beaumont said. "But once I meet with Shalare, we'll see if this Walker Dett's really worth what he costs."

"I had to tell him *something*," Ruth said.

Detective First Grade Sherman Layne leaned against the wall of Ruth's office, expressionless, arms folded across his broad chest. *Look at him,* Ruth thought. *Like a big piece of rock, covered with a thin layer of rubber.*

"You didn't *see* him," she said, a rush of indescribable fears creating a vortex in her chest. "He'd do it."

"Set this whole place on fire?"

"With everyone in it," she said.

"And he said he worked for Beaumont?"

"Yes. And that's what Beaumont himself said, too."

"You called him?"

"I called him myself," Ruth said, emphasizing the last syllable. "At a number I had, not one this man gave to me."

"And you know Beaumont's voice?"

"Yes," she said.

"Are you saying Beaumont . . . knows?"

"No! Nobody ever did. Not about . . . you. But this man, he . . . he knows how it works. One of the girls who left, that's who I think told."

"It doesn't matter," the big man said, dead-voiced.

"It does to me!" Ruth said. "You know why I—"

"I just meant, it doesn't matter how he knows," Sherman said, his detective's mind raising and rejecting possibilities. "He only knows about . . . what happens. He doesn't know it's me."

"No."

"And you didn't . . . ?"

Ruth lowered her face into her cupped hands.

"It's all right," Sherman said. "He hasn't got any—"

"You *bastard*!" Ruth snarled, lifting her tear-streaked face to stare up at Sherman. "You thought that I . . . that I would *ever* . . ."

"Oh Christ, Ruth. I'm sorry. I was just trying to . . ."

"What? Make me feel better for betraying you? After all, what could you expect from a whore anyway, right?"

"I never—"

"Yes you did, Sherman," she said, getting to her feet and moving over to where he stood against the wall. "You hurt me deep. You're the only man on earth who can do that. The only man who can make me cry. I hope you're proud."

"I'm not proud, goddamn it! I'm . . . sorry, Ruth."

"You *should* be sorry. Because I gave that foul man what he wanted, all right. A name. I told him it was Bobby Wyeth."

"Hah!" Sherman chuckled, despite himself. "That was perfect. The last man in Locke City Royal Beaumont needs to blackmail is Mayor Bobby Wyeth. He already owns him."

"And he *does* come here, Sherman," Ruth said, eagerly. "Plus, he's got his own . . . tastes. If a blackmailer just dropped a little hint—you know how they work; they're very careful what they say—he'd probably even pay up!"

"That was really slick," the big man said, admiringly.

"The man who came here, I wish you could have seen him, Sherman," Ruth said, glowing under the big man's praise despite herself. "He said he worked for Beaumont. But he said something else, too. He said he knew I didn't."

"Ruth, what are you talking about?"

"He said, this man, that he knew I was really in business for myself. Paying Beaumont was like paying tax. And if Beaumont was gone, I'd just pay someone else."

"Seeing if you were loyal, you think?"

"No, Sherman. Telling me, I *think* telling me, that he was in business for himself, too."

"That's why you think his . . . source wasn't Beaumont?"

"Yes. I've never seen him before. I don't think he's from around here, so I don't know where he could have found out. But it was more like he was fishing than . . . I mean, I think he's the kind of man who would hear a lot of things, but wouldn't have any way of knowing if they were true. So, when he came here, I think it was really to see if whoever told *him* was lying."

Dett, Walker, Sherman Layne thought, replaying the information he had vacuumed from the records of Ajax Auto Rentals. A gentle hint that someone who may have rented from them within the past month was a "possible suspect" in a bank robbery had been enough to get the clerk to turn over the ledger and step outside for a smoke that lasted a half-hour. *Date of birth: March 3, 1920. Height: 6'1", Weight: 175 pounds. Home address: Star Route 2, Rogersville, Oregon. No restrictions.*

"I can never come here again," he said aloud.

"I know."

"Ruth, I apologize. Not for what I said, or even for what I was thinking . . . because I wasn't. But if I hurt your feelings . . ."

"There's another way," she said, looking down.

"I—"

"If you want me, there is."

"Ruth . . ."

"I'd do it for you, Sherman," she said, tilting her face up to look at him. "I'd do anything for you."

"I . . ."

"Yes you *could*," she whispered.

1959 October 05 Monday 02:22

Carl stood under the shower in a cloud of steam, a safety razor in his hand. *Everywhere!* he repeated to himself, working with great care from the waist down.

When he finished, he rinsed off in an icy stream, shivering but determined. *As a Spartan!*

Carl turned off the shower spigot, parted the curtains, stepped out, and began to pat himself dry. While waiting for the mirror to defog, he worked baby oil into his skin with mechanical determination. Caressing his stiffened penis, Carl paused. *Purity!* he admonished himself, applying some of the oil to his swollen, hairless testicles. Then he coated his forefinger and penetrated his anus. *I resist!* By the time he was finished with his underarms and the soles of his feet, the mirror had cleared.

A cotton ball coated with a peroxide solution was Carl's next tool. Years ago, before he learned, he had attacked any emerging pimples with such ferocity that he caused angry red blotches to appear against his fair skin. Now he cleansed with delicacy. *If it's worth doing, it's worth doing right,* he heard his mother's voice in his head. He bared his teeth.

Perfect white teeth. Carl remembered the dentist, working the foot pedal of his drill during the excavation of a particularly deep cavity, pausing to compliment him. "You'd be surprised how a lot of big, strong men can't take this," the dentist had said. "They always want more and more novocaine. Now, you, young man, you've got the pain tolerance of a bull," he had said, approvingly.

If you only knew, Carl had thought. Dr. Gottlieb was the best dentist in all of Locke City. *The Jew has a natural capacity for intellect, just as the dark races have a natural capacity for strength. One would rule by insidiousness, the other by brute force. Only the Spartans bar the gates against them.*

Carl gargled with mouthwash, then brushed his teeth for the second time since he had arrived home that evening. He inspected his nails. *Why is it that a gangster can get a manicure without being thought . . . unmanly, but an Aryan warrior can never take such a risk?* he thought, regretfully.

Normally, Carl wore only white silk boxer shorts and matching undershirts. But tonight, plain white jersey briefs and a sleeveless cotton T-shirt went on beneath a dark, tailored suit.

As he knotted his muted blue tie, Carl gazed longingly at the pair of black boots, polished to a brilliant shine, standing in the corner of his closet. He sighed and shook his head. *Someday,* he promised himself, settling for a pair of wingtips.

He walked down the short flight of stairs from his private, converted-attic suite to the second floor, his footsteps silent in the carpeted hallway as he passed his mother's bedroom. Carl wasn't concerned about waking her—she always retired within an hour after he came home from work, taking a sleeping draught with her glass of warm milk. If the neighbors heard his car start up in the middle of the night, they would just assume he was working an extra shift at the hotel—he often volunteered for such duty.

Carl opened the padlock and spread the doors of his garage wide. Inside sat his immaculately black '57 Mercedes 190 sedan. It had originally been purchased in Germany, shipped home by a returning GI, and then offered for sale by a private party in Chicago. Fitting himself behind the wheel, Carl recalled that special trip. What a voyage of discovery that had been! *My journey to myself.*

His mother had argued ferociously against the purchase, persisting even after he pulled his prize into the driveway for the first time.

"I don't see why you need a *foreign* car, Carl. And it cost the earth! Why, for what you spent, you could have bought a—"

"It's my money, Mother," Carl had replied, calmly. "I saved it myself. Besides, it's not just a car; it's an investment. Ten years from now, it will be worth more than I paid for it."

"I don't see how that could be," she said, using that passively stubborn tone he hated so.

"Well, I guess we'll see who's right when the time comes," he said, attempting to dismiss the issue.

"It's just too much money. Especially on your salary, Carl."

"I don't really have much in the way of expenses, Mother. It's not as if I had to pay rent someplace."

Catching the implied threat, his mother had subsided.

But that was over a year ago. Tonight, Carl was alone in his perfect Reich car. He slipped the column shift into reverse, tenderly let out the clutch, and backed out of his driveway.

1959 October 05 Monday 02:51

Finished with his meal, Dett took a short length of rope from his suitcase and stood ramrod-straight. He held one end of the rope in his right hand, draped the length of it down his back, and grasped the other end with his left. Dett pulled at both ends of the rope, lightly at first. Then he increased the tension until the rope vibrated, the muscles in his arms and shoulders screaming in protest. He willed away the pain, breathing steadily and rhythmically through his nose, counting slowly to one hundred. He switched hands and repeated the exercise.

Dett stood under a hot shower for several minutes. Wearing only a towel around his waist, he took a small pair of steel springs from his suitcase. Placing one in each hand, he began to compress them, over and over, until his forearms locked and the springs dropped from nerveless fingers.

He stood up, rotating his head on his neck, first in one direction, then the other, making five full circles each time. Next, he un-screwed the top of a small hexagonal jar, dabbed his finger into the dark-red paste inside, and applied it to each of his hands. He dry-washed his hands until the paste was fully distributed and he felt a familiar tingling sensation.

Spreading fresh towels over the tatty carpet, Dett lay on his stomach, placing his hands, palms-down, on either side of his face. Then he raised his neck all the way back until his sternum was barely touching the improvised mat, and held the position for a count of six. He did four repetitions. Then he rolled over onto his back and slowly drew his body into a ninety-degree angle, sitting straight up, back perfectly aligned. He lowered himself to the mat, moving in small, smooth increments, feeling the tightening of his abdominal muscles with each repetition.

On arising, Dett walked to the far wall, placed his spread fingers against it, and pushed until his entire upper body cramped.

Dett stepped away from the wall, arms dangling at his sides, the middle finger of each hand barely touching his thighs. Slowly, he moved his hands behind his back until they met, and clasped them together. He took a deep breath through his nose, held it for a few seconds, then expelled it as he brought his hands up behind his back and over his shoulders in one smooth, continuous motion. When the arc was completed, his clasped hands were at his waist.

Dett held that position for a full minute, then repeated the entire exercise. He went back under the shower, toweled off, and lay down on the bed in the darkness, holding his derringer.

After a while, he closed his eyes. But he did not sleep.

1959 October 05 Monday 02:59

"What's all that you writing, brother?"

"It's what I found in that man's room," Rufus said. "Look for yourself."

Kendall stepped behind Rufus. He saw a grade-school notebook—white ruled paper, bound in a hard black cover with a random pattern of white splotches. Rufus opened the book, as if displaying a trophy. The right-hand page was divided by a lengthwise line, creating two columns:

X	50
D	25
J	10
L	10
R	5

Under the columns was a string of addresses, all public buildings: the city library, the police station, the post office . . . and three different banks.

At the very bottom of the page, in the far right corner, was a ten-digit number.

"I thought you said there wasn't nothing in his room," Kendall said.

"There wasn't," Rufus replied. "But when I meet with the boss greaseball, *Mister* Dioguardi himself, this is going to be what I tell him I copied down, see?"

"Does it mean anything?"

"Only the long number at the bottom. And that one's a pay phone, in a part of Chicago they call Uptown. White man's territory. Ivory picked it up one day, on his route, and it went right into our information book. Now we finally got a use for it. Only I wrote it backwards, like it was in code."

"You going to tell the man that, Omar?"

"What?"

"That it's in code, man. Otherwise, what good is—?"

"Brother, listen to me. The last thing I would ever do is explain anything to those kind of people. See, niggers is *stupid*. We don't know nothing. We just good little monkeys, taking orders, stepping and fetching. We smart enough to take money for stuff they tell us to do, but that's about it. You understand?"

"No," Kendall said, his voice tightening. "I know how you always be saying—"

"Yeah, K-man. I always be saying, but you don't always be *listening*. Look, we're not a 'minority' for nothing, understand? That means just what it says—there's more of them than there are of us. Always going to be like that, too. So we learn to slip and slide, hide what we got. And what we got the most of is brains, brother. Those 'race leaders' of ours," Rufus said, his voice clotting with disgust, "they're all about convincing the white man he's wrong about us. We're *not* ignorant apes that only want to fuck their women—with our giant Johnsons, don't forget—no, not us. We *good* boys. They should call us 'Negroes,' not niggers, or jungle bunnies, or spooks. They should let us go to school with them, work in their businesses, ride on their buses."

Rufus unconsciously shifted into his natural orator's voice, but kept the volume down. "But the 'good' whites, they don't see us as equals. No, to them, we're pets. And you got to take care of your pets. Make sure they get enough food and water, right? See, pets, they don't want to be free. No, they just want to be taken care of.

"So let them think we're *all* like that. Why do you think we're raising those puppies out back, brother? Whitey thinks we all scared of German shepherds, because that's the dogs they use on us down south. White man thinks, I got me a German shepherd, I never have to worry about no nigger burglar, okay? But dogs, they're like children. They don't have no natural hatred of any race. They have to learn that. So we're raising our own."

"Our own children, too," Kendall said, proudly.

"Yes, brother. But you can't *teach* a child if you can't *feed* a child. The child will not respect the father who doesn't take care of him and protect him. You got millions of black children in this country, and who's their father? Uncle Sam, that's who. The white man, the Welfare. Same thing.

"We got to have our own, K-man. Our own businesses, our own money. Our own land. And the only way we even get that *chance* is to sneak up on Whitey."

"But the NAACP—"

"Let them walk their own road, brother. Let them eat white rice, even though everybody knows the brown rice is better for you. Let them straighten their hair, bleach their skin. Let them marry whites, they love them so much. You know where the word 'nigger' comes from?"

"No, man. I don't."

"Me, neither. But I know what a 'spook' is. A spook is a haunt. A ghost. Something you *scared* of. The white man who calls us spooks, he's not lying. How many of our people got hung from trees? Shot like mad dogs? Dumped in graves nobody will ever find? All those dead niggers, *that's* their 'spooks.' I can hear them, calling to me."

"For real?"

"Real as life, brother. Real as death. You know how a preacher say he 'got the call'? Well, I did, too. Not to preach. Not to yell and scream and beg. Jesus ain't for us. If he was, he wouldn't be white. And he wouldn't stand by and let them do us the way they do."

Rufus's voice dropped a few degrees, in volume and in temperature. "Let *Mister* Dioguardi be happy with his tame nigger, Rufus Hightower. Nigger like Rufus, he be too stupid to make up some phony list and say he copied it down from what he seen in the man's room. He'll never see the real me, brother. You can't actually *see* a spook."

"Never see us *coming,* you mean!" Kendall said, holding up a clenched fist.

The man he called Omar tapped Kendall's fist with his own, a blood oath.

1959 October 05 Monday 03:10

Carl loved this time of night. Or, rather, morning, he corrected himself. On the other side of town from where he ruled the Claremont's front desk, it was as if he rode through a transparent-walled tunnel, watching the filth and degeneracy of the streets flare like a match just before it dies. He could feel the desperation just outside his steel-and-glass cocoon, the whores and junkies and con men and burglars and drunks and . . . all trying to make one last score, one final connection, one more try, before they were driven back by the coming morning, when the good citizens would take back the streets. Temporarily.

Carl wished they could meet at HQ. How glorious that would be, especially in the meeting room itself, with the crossed flags standing sentry to their cause. But he understood why this was never to be.

The warehouse district was a thing of such beauty that it sometimes brought moisture to Carl's eyes. Most, he knew, would look upon it as a cluster of abandoned buildings, symbolizing the death of the town's industries. But Carl saw a different symbol entirely. He saw . . . *Cleansing! This is how whole cities will look, someday. The streets empty, free of vermin, awaiting the occupation of the Master Race.*

1959 October 05 Monday 03:51

"Lights," the man seated behind the tripod-mounted binoculars said to his partner.

"Ready."

"Turning. Got a . . . I'm not sure *what* that is. Wait! It's the Mercedes."

"Romeo, Zulu, nine, two, zero?"

"Roger."

"Logged."

"Turning left into Sector Four. Hey! Hear that?"

"I don't hear anything," the other man said.

"Neither do I," the spotter said. "Even with all these windows open."

"So he's parked?"

"Yeah. Close by."

"This is our post."

"Come on! This is the third time. Whoever he is, he's not out for a night drive."

"We're not supposed to—?"

"We can go over the roofs," the spotter said. "They're all pretty much the same height. He can't be more than a block or two away, and we'd still have—"

"—the high ground," the other man finished. He unzipped a padded bag, removed a heavy-barreled rifle. "All right, but it has to be quick."

1959 October 05 Monday 03:54

The Commander's car was nowhere in sight, but Carl was unconcerned. He flashed his brights three times, quickly. A door next to what had once been the loading bay began to climb upwards, slowly exposing an empty slot. Carl knew the electricity to the warehouse had been cut off years ago, and the Commander was cranking the door by hand.

Carl backed his Mercedes into the open space. He watched through the windshield as the door descended, turning his whole world dark.

1959 October 05 Monday 03:59

"Now what?" the man holding the rifle whispered.

"Somebody opened that door for him. From inside."

"You want to try to get—?"

"No. We're in perfect position here," the spotter said. "Let's just wait. We only saw one come in. What we want is to see *everyone* who comes out."

1959 October 05 Monday 04:02

Karl climbed out of his Mercedes. He closed the door lightly behind him, but the sound was still audible in the empty building. Suddenly, a hand—a *powerful* hand, it always was, when Karl called up the image in the privacy of his shower—grasped the back of his neck. Obediently, Karl allowed himself to be propelled forward, his eyes now picking up the streaks of phosphorus that appeared on the concrete floor. Arrows, pointing the way to his destiny.

Around a corner, and there was light. Faint light, from a three-cell flashlight, positioned so close to the wall that only a pale aura was visible. But there was enough light for Karl to see the roll of carpet on the floor. And the blanket-covered sawhorse.

The hand on the back of his neck clamped tightly, but Karl never flinched. His hands were steady as he undressed.

"The Spartans never went into battle without the special strength they drew from their Boys of War," the Commander said, his lips an inch from Karl's ear.

1959 October 05 Monday 04:44

"Car number one—"

"The known."

"Right. Car one—the known subject—entered Sector Four at oh three fifty-one. Entered Building 413 at oh three fifty-four. Exited oh four thirty-six. Car number two—unknown subject, Foxtrot, Echo, Bravo, eight, eight, one, local plate—exited oh four forty."

"He must have come in from across the open ground to the east," the rifleman said. "That's why we haven't see him before, I bet. But now, whoever he is, he won't be *un*known in a few hours."

1959 October 05 Monday 05:58

"Nice time for a briefing," Special Agent David L. Peterson said grumpily to his partner. "Six in the morning."

"The Bureau never sleeps," Mack Dressler replied laconically.

"Nothing ever bothers you, does it, Mack?"

"Not anymore, it doesn't," the older man said, settling himself in a metal folding chair.

A tall man in a navy-blue suit suddenly strode into the large room. He had dark hair, worn slightly longer than current Bureau fashion, and an aristocratic face.

"I'm betting Yale," Mack whispered. "He looks a little too loose for Harvard."

"Gentlemen," the man at the podium addressed the thirty men seated before him. "My name is M. William Wainwright, Special Agent in Charge of the Organized Crime Task Force, Midwest Branch. I've called you in this morning to review our objectives and bring you up to speed on the current initiative."

"The Invisible Empire," Mack muttered sarcastically.

"The Klan?" his younger partner whispered.

"Pretty hard to be invisible when you're walking around with a sheet over your head, partner," the older man answered, his voice as soft and dry as sawdust. "This guy's talking about the Mafia. You know, the mob the boss said didn't exist until a couple of years ago."

"As you already know," the speaker continued, "there exists within America a tightly organized network of criminals. Originating in Sicily, this . . ."

As the speaker droned on, two assistants entered from the side, one carrying a large easel, the other several sheets of poster board. When they completed their setup, the speaker unclipped a pen-size object from his breast pocket. With a snap of his wrist, a professorial pointer emerged.

"This," he said, "is the overall structure, at the national level." A brief biography of each individual followed. "As you can see, there is a quasi-military structure to the organization, with a distinct chain of command."

"Jesus," Mack said, very softly.

His partner moved a few imperceptible inches away from the heretic.

"But that's just background," the speaker said, his tone indicating he was about to say something important. "In this region, our specific target is one Salvatore 'Sally D.' Dioguardi. Originally a member of the Mondriano family in Brooklyn, New York, Dioguardi was dispatched to Locke City approximately four years ago, with orders to wrest control of local rackets from one Royal Beaumont."

The speaker's assistants placed charts of the two organizations side by side on the easels.

"Beaumont is a local product, with no national connections. However, he is well entrenched, with deep roots in local politics, and Dioguardi has not been successful in dislodging him. The Bureau has been aware of the situation since its inception. However, as activity was relatively stable, and, presumably, well-known to local law enforcement, no Bureau role was envisioned."

The speaker paused to gauge the impact of his presentation on the audience. His quick glance took in a wall of attentive postures and flat faces—a tabletop full of face-down cards.

"Recently, one member of the Dioguardi gang was severely beaten. He is still comatose. Two other members were assassinated. No arrests have been made. According to our sources within the Locke City Police Department, there are no suspects.

"Note, Dioguardi himself appears to share the view that Beaumont is not responsible for the attacks. Our profile of Dioguardi indicates that he is a rash, impulsive individual, with a violent temper. And hardly an intellectual," the speaker said, chuckling.

None of the assembled agents joined in.

"Therefore," the speaker went on, unfazed, "we do not believe we are facing a gang-war situation as has occurred in larger cities around the country. In fact, several of our RIs have reported rumors of an impending truce of some sort. Any potential alliance of criminal organizations is of great interest to the Bureau, especially one that involves Mafia families and outsiders. We have no record of this occurring previously, although, of course, nonmembers have worked with Mafia organizations on many occasions, and even formed working partnerships."

"So pay close attention . . ." Mack said, just below a whisper.

"Every agent in this room has been working in a remote surveillance capacity of some sort," the speaker continued. "Placing undercovers inside either of the organizations in question is not a viable option. So the information provided by our Registered Informants is, admittedly, secondhand. The purpose of the Task Force is, therefore, to begin the process of information sharing. The Bureau is *extremely* interested in these 'truce' rumors. So, once weekly, we will

be meeting. Same time, same place. And once all the new information is assimilated and correlated, we'll have—"

"—more fucking charts," Mack said, under his breath.

"—a clearer, more comprehensive picture of whatever the various parties hope to gain from a joint enterprise."

1959 October 05 Monday 06:44

"He never even mentioned the Irish guys," the spotter said to the
rifleman, as they drove back to their base in the warehouse district. "You think that means Shalare's not a player?"

"No," the rifleman said, "it means that kid in the fancy suit—
Wainwright?—*he's* not."

1959 October 05 Monday 07:09

"I got it, boss!"

"You sure?"

"Boss, mebbe I ain't sure 'xactly *what* I got, but I got *something*,
I knows that much."

"What we were talking about?"

"Yes, *sir*. Just like you said there was gonna—"

"That's enough. When can I see it?"

"I'm at work, boss. I don't finish till six. I could—"

"Too much traffic then. Make it eight."

1959 October 05 Monday 09:39

"You wasn't in your room last night, suh," the elevator operator
said to Dett. "Even though it looked like you was."

"How do you know all that, Moses?"

"Know it looked like you was, 'cause the maid said the bed all
messed up when she came in to do your room earlier this morning.
Knew you wasn't, 'cause somebody else was."

"Who?"

"Can't say, suh. But I thought it might be something you would want to know."

"Much obliged," Dett said, offering his hand to shake.

The elevator operator hesitated, then grasped hands with Dett, felt the folded-up bill inside, and pulled it back with him. "Hope you didn't give me too much, suh."

"I don't catch your meaning."

"What I told you, wasn't no big surprise to you."

"How do you know that?"

" 'Cause other peoples knew you was gonna be out real late, suh, if you came back at all. And I figure, a man like you, that can't be no accident."

"You're an even sharper consultant than I first thought, Moses."

"There's a room I got here, suh. Not no room like *you* got, not a sleeping room or anything. More a big closet, like. Down in the basement, off the boiler room. Got me an old lock on it, but I don't need it. Nobody would go in and mess with old Moses's junk."

"Why not?"

" 'Cause, all the years I been here, I got a lot of friends. And I know a lot of things. Plus, I'm an old man, so, sometimes, I forget to lock that room for days on end. People got themselves plenty of chances to look inside, see what I keep in there."

"And what's that?"

"Got me a nice easy chair. Came right from this here hotel. They was going to throw it out, but I rescued it, like. I got a little table, a big green ashtray on it. And a picture of my wife, when she was a young girl. Most beautiful girl in Tulia, Texas, she was. I like to sit there, all by myself, just smoke me a sweet pipe of cherry tobacco. When I look at the picture of my Lulabelle through the smoke, it's like she's right there, still with me."

"She's gone, then?"

"Left me it'll be twenty-eight years this December, sir. Just before Christmas."

"I'm sorry."

"She was took with the cancer," the old man said. "It came at midnight, the Devil's time. When she woke up the next morning, it had her in its clutches. And it never did let her go."

"I . . . I don't know what to say."

"That says a lot about you, suh."

"I don't—"

"This little room I got," the old man went on, as if Dett had never spoken, "it'd be a perfect place if a man wanted to keep something outside his own room. That is, if the man trusted old Moses enough to do it."

"What time do you get off today?" Dett said.

1959 October 05 Monday 10:06

"You know what the other cops call you? 'The Great Sherman Layne.' What do you think that means?" Procter said, sardonically.

The calculated dimness of the bar was perfectly suited to morning drinkers. Even the mirror facing the two men was a murky pool of misinformation.

"It means you've got something on Chet Logan," the detective said, the image of the jowly cop coming readily to mind. "Same as you got something on the chief. And probably half the people in this town."

"You think it's only Logan calls you that?"

"I've got no idea," the big detective said, indifferently. "But he's the one who caught the Nicky Perrini case, and with you nosing around the way you always do . . ."

"You think that's a bad thing?"

"What?"

"To go nosing around."

"It's always a bad thing for *somebody*," the detective said. "Sometimes, the guy who gets found out; sometimes, the guy who does the finding."

"That sounds like a threat," Procter said, tapping his glass on the counter for a refill.

"Good advice usually does," Layne said, unruffled. "When I

was in uniform, we'd get these radio runs to what they call a 'domestic.' Always means the same thing: somebody beating up on his wife. What you're supposed to do, a case like that, is take the guy aside, talk to him like a Dutch uncle. That is, unless he went too far, and the woman's nearly dead. Or just plain dead—that happens sometimes."

Procter raised his freshly refilled beer glass and his eyebrows at the same time, asking the detective if he wanted another. Sherman Layne shook his head "no," and went on with his story. "Now, what you tell a guy in a situation like that is, he keeps it up, he's headed for trouble. See, there's things in life the law just can't allow to go on, because they always end up ugly. You keep beating on your wife, one day you're going to hurt her so bad that you're going to jail, even if she won't press charges—and they never do, not that I can blame them—or kill her, which means the Graybar Hotel, for sure. And there's other nasty possibilities, down that same road. Maybe your wife, she's got a father with a short fuse and a long rifle. Or a brother who's handy with a baseball bat. See what I mean?"

"Yeah."

"Anyway I remember one night, I've got this guy outside, and I'm telling him all this. But he doesn't listen good. He takes it like *I'm* the one who's going to come over there and hurt him if he keeps on doing like he was."

"What happened?"

"Well, like I said, he was a bad listener. He was so damn sure that what I was telling him was a threat instead of good advice, he hauled off and took a swing at me."

"Do I have to guess the rest?"

"I don't think you do. You see what I'm saying, here?"

"Sure. You're telling me about a self-fulfilling prophecy."

"Those happen," Layne affirmed. "And they're never accidents."

"I'm not interested in you," Procter said, throwing back half of his beer in a single gulp.

"That's funny," Layne said. "Because I'm sure as hell interested in you."

"Me? Why?"

"Because you're a real lone ranger, Jimmy. You don't have friends, you've only got sources. And that's the way you want it, I think. See, you're an addict. Been one your whole life, I'm guessing. Only it's not dope you need, it's information. You don't get your fix, you get . . . Well, we all know what a junkie will do for his dope."

"You've got my job confused with my personality, Sherman. How would you like it if I said you *needed* to solve crimes?"

"I might not like it," the big man said. "But that wouldn't make it a lie."

1959 October 05 Monday 10:11

Back in his room, Dett checked the top drawer of the bureau, not surprised to find that the hair he had plastered across the opening with his own saliva had been disturbed. But the medicine chest in the bathroom was open the exact same half-inch he had left it, the sliver of toothpick holding it open still firmly in place. And the suitcase he had left behind had not been touched.

Nobody's that good, he thought. *But Moses wasn't lying, either.*

Dett drew the shades and the curtains, then lay down on the bed, fully dressed. He drifted off to *Five o'clock!* flashing behind his eyes like the VACANCY sign at the motel where he had spent the previous night.

1959 October 05 Monday 11:17

"You see that guy, over at the corner table?" the pudgy man behind the counter said.

Harley Grant looked over at a tall, rail-thin man in doeskin dress slacks and a black Ban Lon short-sleeved shirt, which displayed pipestem forearms that tapered to narrow wrists and pianist's hands. He was fox-faced, with a night-dweller's complexion and feral eyes. His dark hair was combed into a high pompadour.

The man was playing alone, beneath a large NO GAMBLING

sign. Harley watched him lightly tap a solid-red ball into a side pocket—the cue ball hopped slightly, then gained traction and flew backward, caromed off two cushions, and settled in the same place it had started from. The shooter stalked the table, eyeing the green felt with the hyper-focused concentration of a diamond cutter; his split-second hesitation at the full extension of each metronomic backstroke reminded Harley of a round being chambered.

"Yeah," he said, expressing no interest. "So?"

"That's R. L. Hollister, Harley. They call him Cowboy."

"*Who* calls him Cowboy?"

"Everybody does. Supposed to be the best one-pocket man east of K.C."

"Yeah? Well, I never heard of him."

"Which of the top players *have* you heard of, Harley? Shooting stick, that's not your game."

"Fair enough, Benny. But I know enough to know if you recognized him other people will, too. So how's he going to make any money here?"

"The Cowboy's no hustler," Benny said, almost indignantly. "He's a professional. Like the men who sit in on the big stud game at Toby Jesperson's club. They don't come in wearing disguises; they come to take the other guy's money, right out in the open.

"That's the beauty of the games Mr. Beaumont runs, Harley. You guys supply the dealer, you supply the cards, the tables . . . everything. So a man can concentrate on playing without worrying about someone pulling a fast one. The house takes its tolls from the pot, so it doesn't care who wins. Nice and clean. People come from all around just to—"

"That's poker, Benny. Not pool. We don't have anything like that for—"

"But you *could,* right?" the pudgy man said.

"What do you mean?"

"Harley, I'm kind of . . . sponsoring, I guess you call it, a little tournament here. Starts Wednesday night. In the back room, I got a brand-new Brunswick table. Just the one. It's absolutely perfect, that table. Dead level. Nobody's ever played on it, not one rack."

"How are you going to have a tournament on one table?"

"That's just for the *championship*. The final match. See, every player antes five hundred bucks, and they play double elimination."

"Benny . . ." Harley's face matched the "get to it" tone of his voice.

"Okay, look, I'll make it simple. Nine-ball. Race to five. Nine racks, max. First guy to win five games, he moves on. You lose two matches, you're out. And the action's *quick*. Just the way people like it."

"What's the prize?"

"Five grand for the winner," Benny said, flushing with pride as Harley raised his eyebrows, "and a deuce for the guy who comes in second. Whatever they want to side-bet between them, that's their business. But we'll have a board up here, too, so anyone can get a bet down, anytime he wants."

"With you?"

"Well, they place the bets with us, but they're really betting against themselves. Parimutuel, like at the track. See, we keep the records, we hold the money, and we make the payouts. So we—"

"—take your piece off the top."

"Exactly! Just like when you run a dice game. Only, here, *we're* the house, see?"

"When were you planning to tell us about this, Benny?"

"Today!" the pudgy man exclaimed, one hand over his heart. "You always come Mondays, don't you? Listen, Harley, this could be big. Action like what we're planning on, it brings people in. The place will be packed for a week. And the back room, it's all fixed up special. Wait'll you see it. Got this beautiful blue carpet on the floor, a couple of girls to serve drinks, leather chairs to sit on, everything. People'll be proud to pay twenty-five bucks, have a ringside seat for a championship match like this one. Tell their kids they once saw Cowboy Hollister himself play. The final, it's going to be *five* games. Five *sets* of games, I mean. First man to win three sets, the money's his. We can handle bets on every game. Hell, every *shot,* if people want. We've even got a little kitchen back there. When people drink, they want to eat."

"You've been planning this a long time."

"A *real* long time. Harley, I'm telling you, the day will come when Benny's Back Room—that's what I'm calling it—is famous. Just like Ames's in Chicago or Julian's in New York."

"How much is it going to cost you?"

"*Cost* me? I'm going to be making a bundle. You'll see, when you get your cut."

"How much did it cost you, get this Cowboy guy to come and play?"

The pudgy man took off his steel-framed glasses and polished them with a clean white handkerchief. "I can see why people say what they say about you, Harley."

"And what's that?"

"That you're going be the boss around here someday."

"Try it without the Vaseline, Benny. Just tell me what I asked you."

"Five," the pudgy man said, not meeting Harley's eyes.

"You mean you paid his entry fee, or you . . . ?"

"Five large. But, look, Harley, it's an *investment,* okay? You know how many boys, think they're holding hot sticks, already entered? Thirty-one, and we still got two more days to sign people up."

"That's fifteen five, and you're paying out twelve," Harley said, acknowledging the wisdom of the math.

"Not counting our cut of the wagering pool, the money from the drinks and the food, and . . . we'll make another bundle just from tickets to see the final. I'm telling you, Harley, this thing's a mortal lock."

Harley lit a cigarette, leaned back, and exhaled a puff of smoke, thumb under his chin. He was the very image of a man considering a complex proposition, wanting to be scrupulously fair about it. "If this guy is so great, how come so many people want to try him?" he finally said.

"A guy I knew in the army, he once fought Sonny Liston."

"Yeah?" Harley said, drawn in despite himself. "What happened?"

"What happened? Sonny knocked him out, what do you think happened? Only man ever to beat Sonny was Marty Marshall, and that was when Sonny got a broken jaw in the middle . . . and he *still* finished the fight, lost on points. Now, Marshall, he could *bang.* But when Sonny got him back in the ring, six months later, it was lights-out for that boy."

"Why are you telling me this, Benny?"

"Jesus, Harley, don't you get it? Just being in the ring with Sonny Liston, that's something that you can brag on forever. Makes you special. Sonny, he's going to be world champion as soon as he gets a title fight. *Nobody* beats him, so it ain't no disgrace to lose to him, see? I love that guy. Why, it'd be an honor just to shake his hand, wouldn't it?"

"Yeah, okay, I get it," Harley said, thinking, *Be an honor just to shake his hand, huh? Long as it's not happening in your living room. Maybe Kitty's right. No matter how big I ever got in Locke City . . .*

"Well," Benny continued, "if you're a pool player, that's what playing Cowboy Hollister would be like. Now, I don't mean a *pro* player. Some of them, I'm sure, they think they can take him, any given night. And with a game like nine-ball, they could be right. But when it comes to one-pocket—"

"Uh-huh," Harley said, absently, looking around the poolroom.

"Someday, people are going to talk about the great matches they seen in Benny's Back Room like they talk about when they seen Stan Musial go up against—"

"You've been real up-front about all this, Benny."

"You know I'd never do nothing without what I cleared it with you, Harley. But, see, I *knew* you'd love this."

"That's a lot of money you'll have around, Benny. Are you going to need any extras?"

"Nah. Everybody knows this place has Mr. Beaumont's protection. Who'd be crazy enough to try and rob us?"

"Somebody who was crazy," the younger man said.

"Well . . . maybe you're right. We're not that far from the South Side. Can I get a couple of men for finals night?"

"We'll send you three," Harley said. "Two at the usual rate, the other on the house."

"Hey, thanks, Harley!"

"Yeah. The third man, we'll put him right on the cashbox. All night long. Just to be on the safe side."

"Put six men on it, all I care," the pudgy man said, grinning. "I'm not doing this for the money."

1959 October 05 Monday 11:23

"I was just trying to be a gentleman," Mickey Shalare said into the phone. "I asked for the meeting, so it's only right that I come to you, at your convenience."

"Is tomorrow afternoon all right with you?" Royal Beaumont replied, his voice as steel-cored courteous as the Irishman's.

"Well, that would be fine indeed. Anytime at all, just say the word."

"Four o'clock?"

"Just the time I would have chosen for myself."

"Anything special I can have for you here? What do you drink?"

"Ah, Mr. Beaumont," Shalare said, chuckling, "if you have to ask that question, I can tell you're not familiar with my reputation."

"Oh, I think I am," Beaumont said. "Do you need directions to my place?"

"I surely do," Shalare said. "I know it's way out in the country, somewhere, but I could be wandering around for hours. You won't mind if I bring a driver? He wouldn't be sitting in on our meeting, of course."

"Bring whoever you like," Beaumont said. "We'll take care of them."

1959 October 05 Monday 11:38

"Daddy Moses, could I talk to you?"

"You can always talk to me, gal. You know that."

Rosa Mae scuffed the toe of her flat-heeled white shoe against the just-vacuumed mauve carpet that covered the eighth-floor hallway. She looked at her shoes as if fascinated by the sight.

"What is it, child?" Moses asked her. "You in some kind of trouble?"

"No. I'm not . . . No! I wouldn't never—"

"There's all kinds of trouble," the elderly man said, soothingly. "I wasn't thinking about . . . what you was."

"I . . . I need to ask your advice about something. But I'm a little scared."

"Scared of Moses? How that going to be? You know I'm—"

"That's what I mean!" Rosa Mae said, plaintively. "You're like a father to me. Since I come to work here, you always look out for me, and . . ."

"And what, child?"

"And I couldn't bear it if you was to think . . . if you didn't think I was doing right."

"You call me 'Daddy,' and it does two things, Rosa Mae," the old man said. "It makes me proud, 'cause if I had been blessed with a child, I'd want her to be just like you. And it makes me . . . makes me responsible, too. A good father, he don't judge. If there's something you need, I help you. That's all there is to that. I ain't no preacher. Whatever you got yourself into—"

"Oh, Daddy," Rosa said, eyes shining with barely restrained tears, "it's nothing like that. Nothing like you think. Can I come down to your office later, and just . . . talk?"

"Sure you can, honey. We do it at lunchtime, all right?"

1959 October 05 Monday 11:44

The dull-orange '53 Oldsmobile pulled up in front of a fire-gutted building on Cardinal Street, barely inside Hawks territory. Five teenagers in black-and-gold jackets were lounging on the stone steps; three sitting, two standing.

The front passenger door of the Oldsmobile opened, and a well-proportioned youth stepped onto the sidewalk. He was wearing a mustard-yellow satin shirt and black peg pants, saddle-stitched to match his shirt. The pants were sharply creased, billowing at the knee before tapering to a tight cuff as they broke over pointy-toed alligator-look shoes. Dark aviator-style sunglasses concealed his eyes.

"Who's Ace?" he asked.

One of the standing Hawks pointed without speaking, recovering some of the face lost when their leader had not been recognized.

"Let's go," Sunglasses said.

The leader of the Hawks got to his feet. Slowly, making it clear he was not responding to a summons but accepting an invitation. As he started toward the Oldsmobile, two Hawks moved next to him, one on each side.

"Just him," Sunglasses said, pointing.

"It's all right," Ace told the others. "There's no room in there for any more of us, anyway."

Sunglasses opened the back door. A heavyset young man, dressed identically to Sunglasses, stepped out, gesturing with his head for Ace to climb in.

The Hawks watched as the Oldsmobile pulled away, their leader sandwiched between two Gladiators in the back seat. Hog turned to Larry. "Wait'll they see," he said, nodding his head to notarize the promise.

1959 October 05 Monday 11:56

"I'll be seeing him tomorrow," Shalare said into the phone.

He listened for a few seconds, then said, "Yes, I know how important this is, Sean. I'm not a man who has to be told the same thing twice."

Another pause, then Shalare said, "You'll know as soon as I do. Or as soon as I can get to a phone."

Shalare hung up. "Brian," he said to the man seated across from him, "sometimes I wonder about some people."

1959 October 05 Monday 12:00

Dett awoke at noon. He brushed his teeth, then opened the brass canister and washed down several crimson flakes with two glasses of water, taken slowly and deliberately.

From his closet, he selected a dove-gray suit, an unstarched white broadcloth shirt with French cuffs, and a blue silk tie. He placed all three on the bed, and looked at them critically for several minutes.

From a small jewelry case, Dett removed a pair of silver cufflinks, centered with a square of lapis, and a pewter tie bar.

Picking up the phone, he called the front desk.

"Would I be able to get a pair of shoes shined?" he asked.

"Of course, sir," Carl answered. "Shall I send a boy to your room to collect them, or would you prefer—?"

"If you'd send someone up, that would be great."

"Ten minutes," Carl promised. "And you would need them back . . . ?"

"In a couple of hours?"

"Absolutely!"

1959 October 05 Monday 12:22

Wedged between the two Gladiators in the back seat, Ace resisted the urge to touch the talisman concealed in his jacket. He was torn between relief that he hadn't been searched and anger that the rival gang hadn't even bothered.

Sunglasses puffed on a cigarette, flicking the ashes out the open window. None of the other Gladiators smoked. Nobody offered Ace one.

Instead of turning east, as Ace expected, the Oldsmobile crossed Lambert Avenue, motoring along slowly. *Kings turf,* Ace thought to himself. *And they're just driving through it, like it was theirs.* He kept his hands on his thighs, hoping his expression showed how profoundly unimpressed he was.

The Gladiators' Oldsmobile did a leisurely circuit of the area, even driving right past the block of attached row houses on South Eighteenth, where the Kings had their clubhouse.

Look at all the niggers, standing there on the corner like they owned it, Ace thought. *If you had a machine gun, you could just mow them down, like cutting the grass.*

The Oldsmobile finally turned east, then headed back across

Lambert, and into Gladiator territory. As the driver parked in front of an apartment building on Harrison, all four doors opened in unison, and the Gladiators stepped out. Ace slid across the seat cushion and followed, feeling the presence of the others surrounding him as he walked.

1959 October 05 Monday 12:26

"Why are you always pulling stuff like that?" Dave Peterson asked his partner.

"Like what?"

"You know what I mean, Mack. Wisecracks and all."

"What are we doing here?" the older man asked, suddenly.

"Here? You mean here, on surveillance? Or here, like . . . our purpose in life?"

"Dave," the older man said, wearily, "I thought we came to a gentlemen's agreement on that stuff. I know you're a good Christian. Hell, anyone who gets to listen to you for ten minutes knows that. And you, you know I'm a sinner, going straight to hell."

"I never said—"

"Yeah, I know. Never mind. Look, what we're doing here, we're doing our job."

"You always say that."

"What else do you want me to say, kid?"

"I wish you wouldn't call me that."

"Why not? I'm old enough to be your father, aren't I? Doesn't that make you wonder?"

"I don't under—"

"Come on. You know I've got more than thirty years on this job. I go back to the days when Capone was running things. So how come I don't have an 'SAC' after my name? How come I'm partnered with a rookie?"

"I . . . don't know. I guess, maybe, to teach me some of the—"

"You don't *know,* but you've *heard,* haven't you?"

"I'm not a gossip," the younger man said, stiffly.

"I know you're not," Mack said. "You don't smoke, you don't

drink, you don't gamble, you don't cheat on your wife, and all you want to do is serve your country."

"Why do you have to—?"

"I'm not mocking you, kid. I mean it," Mack said, his voice just short of affectionate. "Okay, look, I'm going to answer my own question. What are we doing here? Our job. And what is our job? We're blackmailers, kid. You, me, and the entire Federal Bureau of Investigation."

"Mack!"

"That's the way things get done," the older man said, calmly. "That's the way people stay in power. Because there's one thing on earth that's more valuable than gold or diamonds, Davy. Information. The most precious commodity of all. You get enough on a man, it's like there's a handle growing out of his back. And whoever's hand is on the tiller, he gets to steer."

"That's not blackmail; that's just . . . law enforcement."

The older man leaned back in his seat and lit a Winston, ignoring the younger man's frown. "Law enforcement means keeping tabs on people who are breaking the law, kid. But the Bureau watches *everybody*. If the boss had his way, he'd have a file on every man, woman, and child in America. Wouldn't be surprised if he already did."

"Well, the way things are today—"

"Don't start with that 'Communist' nonsense, again, Dave. That's just a cover story. We're supposed to be cops, not spies. That's the CIA's job."

"But the CIA can't work in America. It was the FBI that caught the Rosenbergs. And it was the Bureau that—"

"The Bureau spies on people because that's what it does, kid. And they'll be doing it long after Communism's dead and gone."

"You're . . . you're wrong, Mack. We're not spies, we're crime-fighters. America's most important—"

"Yeah, I know. Doesn't it strike you as unfair that we have to play by the rules and the bad guys don't?"

"Well . . . sure. But if they *did* play by the rules, there wouldn't be any need for us at all."

Mack tossed his still-burning cigarette out of the side window of the plain-Jane sedan. "Want me to tell you a story, Dave?"

"I . . . don't know," the younger man said, warily.

"Oh, it's a good one," Mack promised. "You want to hear the inside scoop on how we nailed Al Capone?"

"I already know that. The Chicago police weren't ever going to stop him. Probably half of them were on his payroll. But the Bureau got him on income tax, and that finished him and his whole empire."

"Not a word of that's true, kid."

"Al Capone *didn't* go to prison for tax evasion?"

"Of course he did. That's not what I'm talking about. You want to hear the story or not? We've got another four, five hours to sit here and wait, anyway."

1959 October 05 Monday 12:29

"Take the chair, child."

"Oh, no, Daddy. That's *your* chair. I'll be fine on this," Rosa Mae said, carefully perching herself on an upended crate.

"Bother you if I smoke my pipe?" Moses asked, holding up a long-stemmed white clay model as if for her inspection.

"Daddy, you *know* I love the way that cherry tobacco smells."

"Never hurts to have manners," the old man said.

"Yes, sir."

"Come on, gal. I know you didn't give up your lunch break for no reason. What you want me to help you with?"

"Daddy Moses, what do you think of Rufus Hightower?"

"That boy? Why you be asking—? Oh, I see. . . ."

Rosa Mae lowered her head for a moment, then turned her amber eyes on Moses. "That's what I want to know, Daddy," she said, very softly. "What *do* you see? Because, sometimes, *I* see him . . . different than the way other people do. At least, I *think* I do."

"Rufus is a very intelligent young man," Moses said, cautiously. "A lot smarter than he let most folks know. But that's nothing so strange, gal. Our people been doing that since we was on the plantations."

"Oh, I know that," Rosa Mae said. "But that's for dealing with white folks, not our own. Rufus, he . . . Daddy, sometimes, it seems like he is two different people. Do you understand what I'm saying?"

"One minute, he all diddybop, right?" Moses replied. "Got his mind on nothing more than a bottle of wine, some sharp clothes, a nice car, and a piece of—excuse me, gal—and as many women as he can catch. Next minute, he all serious. Not preacher-serious, all righteous and stiff: serious like he got plans."

"That's it!"

"He been talking to you, child?"

"Well, sure. I mean—"

"Don't go all country-girl on me, Rosa Mae," the elderly man said, sternly. "You know what I mean when I say 'talking to you.' "

"Yes, Daddy," she said, meekly. "He's been talking to me."

"Both parts of him?"

"Yes! Oh, Daddy, I *knew* you'd understand. Sometimes when Rufus talks to me, he's like all the others. You know what I mean."

"Wants to be the boss rooster."

"That's him. That's him *sometimes*. But other times, it's like he really, truly . . . sees me. Not just . . . you know. Me. The real me."

"You know what they say about a good burglar, little girl?"

"No, Daddy."

"He can't get in the door, he'll try the window."

"Yes," Rosa Mae said, sadly. "My momma always told me that, only she said it different."

"Your momma was done wrong by a man, honey. She just don't want you to make her same mistake. That's natural."

"You know my momma?"

"Know her story, is all. She's a whole lot younger than I am. We don't be going to the same places."

"My momma goes to church," Rosa Mae said, tartly, smiling to take the edge off her words.

"So did I, child. Went every day when my Lulabelle had the cancer. Prayed and prayed. Spent so much time on my knees, I wore out the pants of my good suit. I promised God, You let my woman live, You can have whatever you want from me. Take me instead, You want that. But He didn't listen to me then. And I don't listen to Him now."

"I'm sorry, Daddy," Rosa Mae said, eyes misting. "I was only playing. And I should know better."

"That's all done, gal," Moses said, drawing on his pipe. "Now it's time for you to tell me."

"Tell you what?"

"Whatever Rufus asked you. Or told you. Whatever it is that's got you all upset."

"You know the man who stays in 809? His name is—"

"Yeah, that's Mr. Dett."

"Yes. Rufus, he is *very* interested in that man. And what he asked me . . . what he asked me, would I look around his room. Not take anything," she said, unconsciously putting her hand over her heart, "just tell him what I saw while I was cleaning."

"Rufus don't steal," said the elderly man, surprising himself with his spontaneous defense.

"Oh, *no*, Daddy. It wasn't *nothing* like that. I know it wasn't."

"So you did it."

"Yes, sir. Yes, I did. And Rufus paid me, too. So I figure someone must be paying him."

"Now, *that* sounds like the boy."

"You mean, a hustler? I know he does that, Daddy. I know he brings things to men in their rooms. Even . . . you know. But that isn't why he has me so confused. See, other times when Rufus talks to me, it's . . . it's like I said, he's got plans."

"And you *in* those plans?" Moses said, catching on.

"I . . . I *think* that's what he's saying. Daddy, did you know Rufus was a race man?"

"A lot of those young boys *say* they race men, but that's just putting on a show for the girls."

"I know. But Rufus, when he talks, it feels like truth to me, Daddy. I don't know what to do."

"Well, at least you told me something, child."

"What's that?"

"You got feelings for that young man. Real feelings. And you know what that means?"

"No . . ."

"Means I got to make it my business to take a closer look at him."

1959 October 05 Monday 12:34

This is beautiful! Ace thought, as he was escorted into a large room with freshly painted white walls, furnished with a couch and two easy chairs, all covered in the same tan leatherette. A blond wood coffee table was set in front of the couch, a matching set of red glass ashtrays positioned at each corner.

"This is the President's office," Sunglasses said. "Just have a seat," indicating one of the easy chairs. "He'll be here in a few."

The escort team positioned themselves at various points around the room.

"This is some setup you got here," Ace said.

Nobody answered.

Like that, huh? he thought to himself. *Okay, motherfuckers. You want ice, you got ice.* He lit a Camel, leaned back in the chair, half-lidded his eyes.

As Ace ground out the butt of his cigarette in the red glass ashtray, a man of average height entered the room. He was wearing a fingertip-length black leather jacket over a black dress shirt, buttoned to the throat. His dark-blond hair was worn long on the sides and square-cut across the back. He looked to be in his early twenties, with what Ace thought of as a hillbilly's face—narrow, long-jawed, with suspicious brown eyes. *Lacy Miller himself,* Ace thought. *President of the Gladiators. Should I . . . ?*

The man in the leather jacket crossed the room and held out his hand, interrupting Ace's thoughts. Ace got to his feet, and they shook. Lacy's grip was perfunctory. *Got nothing to prove to the likes of me,* Ace thought, resentfully.

The President of the Gladiators stepped back and took the unoccupied armchair. As he settled in, the other gang members took seats, too. All except for Sunglasses.

"It's still on for Wednesday night?" Lacy asked.

"The Hawks will be there," Ace assured him.

"How *many* Hawks?"

"Well, I can't say exactly. We've got seventeen *counted,* but there could be more. There usually is."

"The Kings have got at least thirty men," Lacy said, his tone indicating that he would not entertain a contradiction.

"Thirty niggers," Ace said.

Sunglasses snorted.

"You think a nigger's blade doesn't cut as deep?" Lacy said, his voice mild and unthreatening.

"I didn't mean nothing like that. Just that, well, the Hawks can hold their own, even if we're outnumbered. We done it before. Plenty of times."

"You know what that comes from, 'holding your own'?" Lacy asked.

"Comes from?" Ace said, confused.

"Where it started," Lacy said, patiently. "It came from the pioneers. The ones who went out west, a long time ago. They went out there to farm, or ranch, or pan for gold. To do that, you had to stake a claim. Sometimes, people would try and take it from you. Indians, maybe. Or white men too lazy to work for what they wanted. You had to fight them off your land. Hold your own, see?"

"Yeah," Ace said, thinking, *This guy, the President of the Gladiators, he talks like some faggy schoolteacher. Jesus.*

"So—you see what I'm telling you?" Lacy said, smiling as if he read Ace's thoughts . . . and forgave him the mistake. "You—the Hawks, I mean—you never really did hold your own."

"The niggers wouldn't dare to move against us on our own turf," Ace said, hotly.

"Why should they?" Lacy countered. "They don't want your territory; it's on the wrong side of town. But that lot on Halstead, that's No Man's Land, right?"

"Well . . . well, sure it is. I mean, it's just a whole block of dirt and junk. Nobody even lives around there."

"Uh-huh. Last time you rumbled there, who won?"

"We did," Ace said confidently, knowing each side would tell a different story. *Hell,* he thought, *when a rumble's over, everyone tells a different story . . . 'specially those who weren't even there.*

"So you won . . . what, exactly? A fight?"

"What else is—?"

"There's the *land,* is what I'm telling you. When you win a war, you get the land, right?"

"Nobody *wants* that land, man. It's just a—"

"Yeah, I know. But, see, if you control land, you can do things with it."

The same thing those Klan guys were telling me, Ace thought. "I see what you mean," he said, aloud.

"We've been thinking about that property ourselves," Lacy said. "So we're going to send along a few men Wednesday night. Just to make sure the Kings don't try anything extra."

"That's cool."

"And after it's over, that lot on Halstead, it's going to be Gladiator turf," Lacy said, his voice subtly downshifting to a tighter gear.

"Well, I guess. I mean, we got this treaty—"

"The treaty means you don't move on us and we don't move on you. It means you can walk through our turf flying your own colors and you don't get jumped. It doesn't mean we're partners."

Ace felt his face flush. He lit another cigarette, quickly glancing down to satisfy himself his hands were steady. "If your club went to war, we'd be right there with you," he said.

"That's not going to happen," Lacy said. "You see what it says on our jackets now?" He nodded to his right.

Sunglasses plucked a white satin jacket from the seat of a straight chair in the corner. He held it up in both hands, displaying the back, with its ornate red script yoked across the shoulders:

Gladiators SAC

"Social and Athletic Club? You're going collegiate!?" Ace blurted out. "The Gladiators always been the strongest bopping club in the whole—"

"Relax," Lacy said, holding up his palm like a traffic cop. "What we're doing is moving up. Rumbling, that's for kids. We've got bigger plans. Who needs the cops looking over your shoulder every minute?"

"They don't bother us," Ace said, struggling with what he was hearing.

"No offense, but why should they, unless you're getting it on with some other club?"

"Yeah, I can see that, but . . ."

"But what?"

"It's like . . . I don't know, not what I expected, maybe. What do you want us to do?"

"Do? Nothing. You have your meet Wednesday night. After that, it's over."

"No warring with the—?"

"Listen, when it comes to other clubs, you guys do whatever you want. But not on Halstead. Wednesday night is going to be the last rumble in that lot. On that whole block, in fact. The Kings cross your border, it's okay with us, you kill every last one of them. And if you decide to go down on them, jump them in their own territory, that's your business, too. Wednesday, we'll have enough men there, make sure you guys come out all right. But after that, the lot on Halstead, it's Gladiator turf. Understand?"

"We'll come out all right," Ace said, sullenly.

"Because they're niggers?" Lacy said.

"No," Ace told him, pausing dramatically, "because they ain't got nothing like what we got."

"What's that?"

"This," Ace said, slowly taking the pistol out of his jacket.

Nobody moved.

"It's not loaded," Ace said, thrilling inside at the silence he had produced. "I'd never bring a loaded piece inside your clubhouse."

"Y̶ou know how old Capone was when he went to prison?"

"Fifty?" Dave guessed.

"Just a little past *thirty,*" Mack told him. "And when he was re- leased, he was barely forty. So how come he didn't move right back in, take over the rackets again?"

"He was sick, I thought."

"He was sick all right, kid. Paresis, you know what that is?"

"Like, cancer?"

"No. His brain was all rotted out. From syphilis."

"Ugh. That's . . ."

"What? A nigger disease?"

"I didn't say—"

"I'm not accusing you of being prejudiced, Davy. But that *is* what you heard, isn't it? That only coloreds get it?"

"No. That's not true at all. In the army, they showed us this film—"

"And gave you the short-arm inspection when you got back from leave, sure. But that's for the clap, gonorrhea. Syphilis, it's what the colored people call 'bad blood.' Compared to the clap, it's like a howitzer against a rifle."

"How come you know so much about this?"

"That's another story. Now you're hearing this one. So pay at- tention. Syphilis, it's a special disease. When you got the clap, you know it—it burns like hell when you take a piss. But the syph isn't like that. When you first get it, what they call the primary or the sec- ondary stage, you get these sores on your body. Right at the same spot where you . . . made contact. They look like all holy horror, like leprosy or something, but they don't hurt. And here's the special thing about them: they go away. All by themselves."

"You only get it from having sex?"

"Yeah. No matter what else you might have heard, that *is* the only way. And it doesn't matter *what* kind of sex, okay? So even queers get it. Anyway, if you ever go into a neighborhood where it's all colored—not just a place where they let them live, where it's wall-to-wall black, businesses and everything—you'll find some of what they call 'men's doctors.' They're not real doctors. Not even witch doctors," Mack said, making a sound of disgust. "They're just con men. You come to one of them with syphilis sores and they'll sell you some potion supposed to be just the thing for it. So, when the sores go away—and they always do—you think you're all cured. Only you're not."

"But if the—"

"There's a third stage. They call it 'latent' or 'tertiary.' What that means is that you can't pass it along to anyone else. You're not what they call 'infectious.' But you're sure as hell infec*ted*. It's a freakish disease. The worse it looks, the less it's doing to you. And when you think it's gone, it's actually eating you alive."

"Killing you?"

"One way or the other, yeah. Sometimes, it goes after the heart. Sometimes, the liver. Paresis, what Capone had, means it went after the brain. By the time he got out of prison, he was a walking vegetable."

"With all his money, why didn't he just go right to the hospital?"

"He did," Mack said. "But by then it was too late. See, in those days, they used to treat it with all kinds of different drugs, like '606.' Sometimes they worked, sometimes they didn't. Today, we have penicillin. For syphilis, that's the KO punch. Kills it, every time. But even if they had had it back then, it wouldn't have mattered. Because all it can do is stop the disease in its tracks—it can't repair any damage already done. Once syphilis gets to the brain, that's the end."

"Where would Al Capone get syphilis?"

"Well, the story is, he got it when he was working muscle for Johnny Torrio back in New York, when he was just a kid himself. Torrio was a major pimp, had a whole string of whorehouses, so Capone could have been dipping his wick anytime he wanted."

"Then he thought it went away, but, all the time, it was—"

"—killing him, yeah. That's the story. But it's not the truth. See, Al Capone had syphilis, all right. But he didn't get it when he was a kid—he got it in the federal penitentiary."

"How? If he was—"

"When he first got busted for taxes, he made some kind of a deal to plead guilty. According to him—and I *mean* him, not some rumor; that's what he *said*—he was supposed to draw a deuce in the pen, and cover all the charges with that. But he bragged to the papers about it, and the judge—a *federal* judge, remember—said he wouldn't go along. Hell, with all that press, he *couldn't* go along, or it would look like he was on the mob's payroll, too. Get him*self* investigated. So Capone went to trial. And he ended up with eleven years."

"You think, if he had kept his mouth shut—?"

"We'll never know. Anyway, they put him in the Cook County Jail while he was waiting to see how his appeals came out. And, kid, let me tell you, he *ran* the place. Had three private cells to himself, fixed up like a hotel suite. He ate steak and lobster, drank the best bonded booze, had all the 'visitors' he wanted, too.

"When he lost his appeals, he was sent to the federal pen in Atlanta. And he ran that place just like he ran Cook County. The man was a king inside those walls. And that's when it happened."

"The syphilis."

"Yep. Girl named Noreen Tisdale. Most gorgeous blonde you ever saw in your life. Face like a schoolgirl, and a body like Candy Barr—never mind, trust me, she was a real stunner. Visited that scar-faced greaseball five times, just to make sure."

"Wait! You're saying she knew—"

"Knew? That's what she was paid for, kid. First, she had to fuck a guy who had the syph—early stage. Then she had to be checked by a doctor, make sure *she* had it. And then she goes and lets Capone fuck her, any way he wanted it. By the time she was done with him, that was it."

"But couldn't a doctor—?"

"What? Fix him? Maybe . . . *maybe* . . . if he'd gotten to one in time. But, soon as they were sure they had him infected, they boxed him up and shipped him to Alcatraz. That's when Big Al stopped running the show. No more special treatment. No privileges, no nothing. And the only thing the doctors they had in *there* ever treated was stab wounds."

"Why would any woman do . . . all that?" Dave said.

"Her husband was sitting in the Death House at the Georgia State Pen. Bank robbery, and a guard got killed. He got a pardon from the governor when another guy confessed to the crime. Turned out her husband was innocent all along."

"Jesus Lord!"

"Yeah. She was some kind of woman."

"Her? I meant . . . an innocent man on Death Row. It's so . . ."

"He was guilty as sin, Davy."

"But you just said—"

Mack drew a long, deep breath. Let it out slowly. Turned to the younger man and said, "It was a business deal, son. All the way around. Noreen did the job, and she got paid what she wanted for it. And what *we* got, we got Capone."

"We? You don't mean—?"

"Yeah, I do. That was just an experiment, at the time. And it worked. Nobody knew exactly *what* would happen if a man got syphilis and never got any treatment at all. Not for sure, anyway. Can you imagine what you could do with something like that? A disease you get from sex? The Krauts had their mustard gas in World War I. This, this could be bigger than that by a thousand, a million times. If you knew how to keep it under control, use it only when *you* wanted to use it, you could own the whole damn world."

"Mack, how could you know all this?" Dave demanded.

"Because that was my job then."

"Al Capone?"

"No, kid," the older man said deliberately, as if the words were too heavy for his breath to carry them. "Noreen Tisdale."

1959 October 05 Monday 14:49

"Benny's Poolroom," the pudgy man answered the phone.

"I want to leave a message for Harley Grant."

"Shoot," the pudgy man said.

"Tell him that part he wanted for his Chevy just came in. The one he's been waiting for."

"Sure. Who's—" Benny started to ask. But Lacy Miller, President of the Gladiators, had already hung up.

1959 October 05 Monday 14:51

"The car wasn't satisfactory, sir?" the clerk at the rental agency asked.

"No, it was fine," Dett said. "Only I believe I need something a bit . . . nicer."

"Well, we do have a Buick Invicta available. It's a real beauty. Brand-new, really. But it's quite a bit more than—"

"I'll take it," Dett said.

1959 October 05 Monday 15:28

Tussy's bedroom looked as if it had been freshly burglarized, by a ham-fisted drunk. Drawers hung open, their contents strewn about the room. The bed was hidden under a blanket of discarded dresses, sweaters, and blouses. The back of the room's only chair was draped in brassieres, its seat covered with panties.

All this . . . junk! she admonished herself, surveying the mayhem. *The red one is too tarty, the black one is for funerals, and that blue one is for an old lady. What am I going to—?*

Surrendering, Tussy went into her kitchen and poured herself a cup of coffee. "You want something, too?" she asked the enormous gray-and-black cat who was perching regally on one of the padded chairs.

When the animal responded with a rumbling noise, Tussy poured a dollop of cream into a saucer and set it out on the floor. The cat calmly strolled over to her offering, sniffed it suspiciously, then lapped it up.

Tussy sat down at the chrome-legged kitchen table and lit a smoke. Glancing at her watch, she realized she still had a couple of hours to go before her date. *After all this aggravation, I'll need an-*

other shower before I get dressed, she thought, absently patting the curlers in her hair.

Dett inspected his newly polished shoes with a jeweler's eye.

"Those look all right to you, sir?" Rufus asked, anxiously. Thinking, *Those shoes, they're just like the man himself. Nice and smooth on top, but they got rubber soles and steel toes.*

"They look better than when they were new," Dett told him. "Whoever you've got doing shoes at this place is an ace."

"Did them myself, sir. Not to be downing the boy who usually do them, but I wanted them to be perfect. And I know, you wants a job done right, you does it yourself."

"Why do you talk like that?" Dett asked, suddenly.

"Huh? What you mean, boss?"

"That's what I mean," Dett said. "You're an educated man. Why do you talk like you're not?"

"Educated man? Me? No, sir. I ain't got no education, 'cept for up to the tenth grade at Lincoln—that's the high school over in—"

"Help you get bigger tips?" Dett asked, as if Rufus had not spoken.

"No, sir, I don't believe it do."

"I don't blame you for not trusting me," Dett said, handing Rufus a folded five-dollar bill. "Thanks for the shoes. You did a beautiful job."

"Fuck!" Hog said to Ace. "Why'd you show it to them?"

"You weren't there, man."

"What's that mean?"

"It means, the way they talked, it was like *we* were the niggers."

"But the treaty—"

"You're not listening, man. The treaty, all it means is, the Gladiators aren't going to move on us. But, see, what they were saying—and this is from Lacy himself—they wouldn't be doing that *anyway*. Bopping, that's kid stuff to them now. Big shots."

"I thought Lacy hated Preacher."

"Maybe he does, but he sure didn't act like it. It was . . . like they didn't give a fuck, one way or the other. The only thing they cared about was the lot on Halstead. After Wednesday night, that's theirs. Maybe if the Kings tried to claim it—'hold their ground' is what Lacy said—that'd make him call an all-out. But it doesn't matter anymore. The plans we had, they're no good now."

"We still gotta show. Otherwise . . ."

"You think I don't know that, man? But no matter how it comes out, we're never going to end up part of the Gladiators, not now. Remember how we had it figured? After the meet, after they see what we can do, we get asked to come in with them? Sure, I don't be President anymore. And you wouldn't be Warlord. But men like us, we could move up in the organization, be a part of something big. That's all gone, now. So I'm thinking about what those Klan guys told me."

"About Fat Lucy's and—?"

"Yeah. See, it's like someone talked to the Gladiators, too. About the same thing, only bigger."

"What are we going to do, Ace?"

"First, we're going to take care of the Kings," the young man said, grimly. "Then I'm going to ask to see Mr. Dioguardi. He'll know what we should do."

1959 October 05 Monday 17:21

Dett shaved slowly and meticulously. He patted witch hazel onto his cheeks, and started to dress. His face was a frozen mask, his mind a cloudless night sky.

1959 October 05 Monday 17:29

Tussy grunted as she tugged a panty girdle over her hips, finally letting out a breath when it was in place. She attached her stockings—a brand-new pair, purchased earlier that day—to the garter clips, then shrugged into a pale-pink bra trimmed in lace around the top of the cups. Next came a dark-gray pencil skirt—her earlier attempts to fit into it had necessitated the girdle—a lightly ruffled ice-blue silk blouse, and a peplum jacket that was a mate to the skirt. Finally, ankle-strapped black pumps with three-inch heels.

Tussy walked over to the full-length mirror and surveyed the result of her handiwork. Her makeup had been applied before she dressed herself. The glass reflected a radiant beauty. *Fatso!* she said to herself, sticking out her tongue at the mirror.

1959 October 05 Monday 17:40

When the elevator car opened on the eighth floor, Dett entered, carrying a leather shaving kit in his right hand.

"I wonder if you'd mind holding on to this for me until I get back," he said to Moses.

The old man pulled a folded brown paper bag from inside his uniform jacket. He snapped open the bag, inserted the shaving case, rolled the bag closed tightly, and deposited it atop the padded stool next to the brass control lever. He moved the lever to the right, and the car slowly descended.

Neither man spoke until the car opened in the lobby and Dett stepped out.

"You have yourself a good evening, suh," the operator called out.

Dett walked over to the front desk, waited patiently as Carl finished speaking with one of the maintenance men, then asked, "Do you know where I can find a good flower shop around here?"

"At this hour?" Carl said, glancing at his watch.

"Yeah," Dett said, his voice shifting tone so slightly only a human mine-detector like Carl would have noticed. "Right now."

"Give me a moment," Carl said. He picked up the desk phone, dialed a number from memory. "Laurel," he said, to whoever answered, "we have a guest who needs some flowers. Yes, I *know* you close at six. But this is a VIP request, Laurel. The Claremont would very much appreciate . . . Hold on," he said, turning to Dett. "Did you have any particular flowers in mind?"

"Just nice ones."

Covering the receiver with his hand, Carl leaned toward Dett ever so slightly, said, "Forgive me if I seem intrusive, sir. But there are flowers one brings to a lady, flowers one leaves as an offering, although that would be more a floral *arrangement*. . . ."

"I've got a date," Dett said, the spaces between his words so measured, the effect was just short of mechanical. "I want to bring her some flowers."

"Ah! Excuse me. . . ." Carl removed his hand from the receiver, said, "Laurel, we can make do with American Beauties. I know you still have some *very* fresh ones from earlier. Of *course* long-stemmed. And, I think"—glancing over at Dett—"some whites, too." Catching Dett's confirmatory nod, Carl went back to the phone: "No, Laurel, not a dozen. That's so . . . ordinary. Let's have six white, with three red, centered, of course. Wait. . . ." Turning to Dett, he said, "Their boy has already gone for the day; they won't be able to deliver. Shall I send someone over to collect them for you, or would you prefer—?"

"I'll pick them up myself," Dett said. "Just tell me where I have to go."

"He'll be there in, say, ten minutes, Laurel. We won't forget this."

Carl hung up. "It's really not even five minutes from here by car," he said to Dett. "I'll just draw you a little map."

1959 October 05 Monday 18:45

Tussy peered out from behind the living room curtains. It was six-forty-five in the evening, past dusk, but the street was alive, as if the unseasonably warm weather had turned back the calendar.

The men in work clothes had been home for a while; the ones in business suits always came later. A man played catch with a boy wearing a blue baseball cap with a white bill. Tussy didn't need a telescope to read the embroidered logo on the cap—anyone in her neighborhood would recognize the colors of the Beaumont Badgers, the Little League team sponsored by Beaumont Realty.

Some of the men were doing what Tussy always thought of as weekend work—washing their cars, mowing their lawns. A pack of kids were playing touch football in the street, making the kind of noise that quiets every mother's anxiety. A little girl jumped up and down excitedly in front of her parents, telling them something wonderful. The neighbor's beagle—a notorious escape artist no fence could contain—charged across a backyard, chasing an invisible rabbit.

Parents watched as a bronze Buick came slowly down the block, silently approving of the driver's cautious approach. It was more than his being alert to the ever-present possibility of a child or an animal darting into the street—somehow, it felt as if he was showing respect for their neighborhood, like a man who knew enough to take off his hat in church.

They all watched as the Buick pulled to the curb in front of Tussy's house. Tussy watched, too. And when a tall, neatly dressed man emerged from the car, a bouquet of roses in his hand, and started up her flagstone walk, she thought, *Now they'll have something to talk about for weeks!*

Dett felt eyes on his back. He didn't feel endangered; he felt . . . appraised. Squaring his shoulders, he tapped the brass door-knocker gently, the sound barely registering.

He counted to seven in his head, and was just reaching for the knocker again when the door opened.

Tussy.

"Hi!" she said. "You're right on time. I'm almost ready. Come on in."

Dett stepped across the threshold, holding out the flowers. "These are for you."

"Oh, they're just lovely! I never saw roses like that, so . . . perfect."

"Well, I—"

"I have to put them in something. I think I have . . . Oh! I'm sorry; I have no manners. Please sit down; I'll be back in a minute."

Dett looked around the small living room, dominated by a large couch made of some dark wood, with an ornately carved frame into which sky-blue cushions with a white fleur-de-lis pattern were inset. In front of the couch was a simple slab of white-veined pink marble, standing on wrought-iron legs. The floor was wide pine boards, with knotholes showing through a gleaming coat of varnish. Against one wall was a small hutch, backed by a mirror. Its shelves held framed photographs, some hand-painted porcelain figurines, and what looked like military medals.

He took a cautious seat on the edge of the couch, back ruler-straight, unsure of where to put his hands, eyes trained on the door through which Tussy had departed.

The gray-and-black cat entered the living room, regarding Dett with unflinching yellow eyes. His thick tail twitched twice, then he effortlessly launched himself onto the seat of an armchair upholstered in the same fabric as the couch. The cat curled up comfortably, his bulk covering the cushion completely. His eyes never left the intruder.

"Oh, you met Fireball," Tussy said, smiling as she came back into the living room.

"He looks like someone should have named him *Cannon*ball," Dett said, making a face to show he was impressed.

"Yes, he's a big fat load now, aren't you, boy?" Tussy said, scratching the monster behind his ears, a move instantly rewarded with a sound like a trash compactor. "It was my dad who named him. Even when he was a little kitten, he was the laziest cat on earth. 'A real ball of fire,' my dad said one day, and it just stuck."

"I never saw one that big. Is he part bobcat or something?"

"I don't know *what* he is. My dad brought him home one day from work. I had been asking for a kitten for the longest time, and it was my birthday, so . . ."

"But that had to be when . . ."

"When I was a little girl, yes. Well, twelve, anyway. Fireball's been with me ever since. Guess how old he is?"

"I . . . uh," Dett struggled, trying for the right number, ". . . thirteen?"

"I don't know who you're being nicer to," Tussy said, "me or Fireball. He's twenty-one—old enough to vote."

"Really?"

"Why are you so shocked? Didn't you ever hear of a cat who lived that long?"

"I . . . I don't know much about cats. I never had one. But if he's twenty-one, and you got him when you were—"

"I'm thirty-three years old," Tussy said, hands on her hips, as if daring him to deny it.

"You don't look . . . I mean . . . I don't know how to say things sometimes. I thought you were . . ."

"Younger? Don't look so distressed, Walker. I took it as a compliment."

"I didn't mean it as one. Damn! I'm sorry. What I meant to say was, I wasn't just saying it. You *look* like you're maybe twenty-five. Anybody would say the same thing."

"Well, me and Fireball are a lot alike. We're both overweight, and we both don't show our age so much."

"You're not . . ." Dett felt his face burn as his voice trailed away.

"I'm just having fun with you," Tussy said. "Look, it's only a half-hour drive to the restaurant. I've never been there, but I know where it is. Would you like a cup of coffee?"

"No, thank you."

"I *should* have tea in the house. My girlfriend Gloria does; it's ever so elegant. But I don't drink it, and I don't have people over very much."

"Could I have a glass of water?"

"With ice? Boy, listen to me!" Tussy laughed. "You can take the girl out of the diner, but you can't take the diner out of the girl, I guess."

"I would like some ice water," Dett said. "Very much."

He studied the cat, who affected great boredom, until Tussy returned with a pair of tall blue glasses, one in each hand.

"Here you go," she said, handing one to Dett, and seating herself on the opposite end of the couch.

Dett took a sip. "It's great," he said. *It's water, you fool,* he thought to himself.

"Oh, just put it down on the table," Tussy said, sensing his discomfort. "We never used coasters in the house. Mom always said they were for people who put on airs."

"With a house like this, you wouldn't *need* to put on airs," Dett said. "Your furniture is really something. It looks too good to buy in a store."

"It is!" she said, delightedly, clapping her hands. "My father made it. All of it. My father and my mother together, actually. Dad did the woodwork, Mom did the upholstery. It took them forever. And when it was finally all done, Mom said she wasn't about to cover it with plastic, the way some people do."

"Your father makes furniture? I mean, for a living?"

"No. He worked at the plant. Woodworking, it was like his hobby."

"Hobby? He's a real artist. I'll bet he could sell stuff like this for—"

"My parents are gone," Tussy said. She opened a little black purse, took out her pack of Kools. Dett reached for his matches as she said, "They've been gone a long time. My dad had a workshop. Out in the garage. There wasn't even room for the car in there. And my mother, she sewed for money, sometimes. She made dresses, like for proms or weddings." She leaned toward Dett, accepted the offered flame, inhaled deeply. "She never got to make one of those dresses for me."

"Christ, I'm sorry," Dett said. "I didn't know. I never would have—"

"They've been gone a long time. Eighteen years, this December. It's all right, Walker. I love this house. I love everything my mom and dad did to make it beautiful. It didn't make me sad when you said what you did—it made me proud."

1959 October 05 Monday 19:00

"I didn't know who else to talk to," David Peterson said.

"You did the right thing," SAC Wainwright assured him.

"Exactly the right thing," the man standing next to Wainwright's desk seconded. He was a stranger to Dave, dressed in a matte gray alpaca suit which draped softly over his lithe frame, and a white silk shirt, buttoned at the throat. The man's skin was the color of rawhide, emphasizing the artificial whiteness of his too-perfect teeth. His eyes were shallow pools of dirty water. "What is it this time?" he said. "Nazi scientists, working in a secret lab to send rockets to the moon? A plot to test new vaccines on military personnel? Flying saucers?"

"Giving syphilis to Al Capone," Dave said, relieved when the unnamed man barked a laugh.

"Mack Dressler used to be a top agent," Wainwright said, solicitously. "But a number of years ago, he began experiencing what psychiatrists call 'paranoid ideation.' It's not as uncommon as you might think, Agent Peterson. A man spends his life following people, opening their mail, listening in on their phone calls—he starts to think people are doing the same thing to *him*."

Wainwright paused, looked into Dave's eyes to emphasize his concern, paused a couple of heartbeats, then went on, as if responding to a question: "Well, of course, we arranged for Mack to get treatment. Had him in a government hospital for almost a year. Unfortunately, the treatment wasn't a complete success. He no longer believes he's under surveillance, but he . . . ruminates a lot. And he constructs bizarre, highly detailed scenarios in his head, to 'explain' things."

"Sir, could I ask, how come he's still . . . ?"

"Working? Well, there's two reasons, Agent Peterson. The first one is that Mack Dressler, for all his . . . well, we might as well call it what it is, craziness . . . is an excellent investigator. He has superb skills, and we use him in sort of a training capacity, always partnering him with new agents. You've learned a few tricks from him, I'll bet."

"I sure have," Dave said, loyally. "He's shown me how to—"

"Yes," the unnamed man interrupted. "Exactly so. And the other reason we keep Mack Dressler on staff is the most important one. The Bureau always takes care of its own, Agent Peterson. Never forget that."

"I won't, sir."

I never saw a Bureau man who didn't wear a tie before, Dave thought to himself on the drive back to his apartment. *And he wasn't carrying a weapon, either—you couldn't even hide a wallet under a suit like that.* He wished he could ask Mack what it all meant.

1959 October 05 Monday 19:13

"This is a swell car," Tussy said, touching the overhead sun visor of the Buick with a freshly painted fingernail.

"It's not mine," Dett told her. "It's just a rental. For while I'm in town."

"That must be fun, driving different cars all the time."

"I . . . I guess it could be, if you did it only once in a while. But when you do it all time . . ."

"When you're home, do you have a car there?"

"I don't really have a home."

"How could you not have a home? Everybody has to live *some-place,* don't they?"

"I suppose most people do, but me, I'm like a high-class hobo. I sleep in hotel rooms instead of boxcars, and I eat good, but I don't have a real home of my own."

"Well, you have a home*town,* don't you? I mean, a place you're from."

"I used to live in Mississippi."

"You don't talk like you're from the South."

"I haven't been back in a long time," Dett said. "I guess I lost the accent. Besides, I wasn't born there. I was born in West Virginia, and we moved to Mississippi when I was a kid. Then I went in the service, and when I got out, I never went back."

"Wow. I've been in the same place my whole life."

"Locke City?"

"The same house. I was born there. I mean, I was born in the hospital, but my folks always said they bought that house for me. As soon as Mom got pregnant, they went out and got it."

"But when they—"

"Turn up ahead," Tussy interrupted. "The road we want is just past the next intersection, on the right."

1959 October 05 Monday 19:29

"See?" Wainwright said to the man in the alpaca suit. "He's harmless. We know what he's going to do. And every single man we've partnered him with has come to us with the same report."

"So you think that's a good test?"

"Don't you? Now, if one of the rookies *didn't* come to us with one of Mack's famous stories, then maybe we'd have something to worry about."

"What do you think turned him?"

"He's not *turned*," Wainwright said, forcefully. "He's nuts. There's reports on him going back to way before I signed on."

"Fine," the other man said, patiently. "What's the read on why he started giving those little lectures of his, then?"

"The McCarthy business."

"He was in on that?" the man in the alpaca suit said, tonelessly.

"Not in on the end-game, no. But he was . . . told certain things, during the briefings, when we were still in the process of selecting the . . . technicians."

"Christ."

"It's nothing to worry about," Wainwright said, making a flicking motion at his lapel. "He was a drunk then. Everyone knew it, but there was a lot of pressure to get things moving, and there was a personnel shortage. Anyway, Dressler's been telling his wild yarns for so long, who'd ever take him seriously? As you just heard for yourself, he always sounds exactly like what he is—a crazy old man."

"That's the Bureau's take on it? Officially?"

"From the top," Wainwright said, firmly. "And there's no reason for you people to look at it any differently. If Mack Dressler's a problem, he's *our* problem, not yours."

1959 October 05 Monday 19:51

"That's it," Tussy said, pointing through the windshield to a château-style building standing at the top of a rise. "Even the cars in the lot are all foreign. It looks like it was transplanted right from France, doesn't it?"

"I've never been there," Dett said.

"Well, neither have I, silly! Don't you ever just *imagine* the way things would be, things you've never seen yourself?"

"Sometimes I do," Dett said, feeling the bluestone under his tires turn to pavement as they drove up to the entrance. He got out, leaving the engine running, and walked around to open the door for Tussy. A uniformed man beat him to the job.

Tussy put her hand on Dett's forearm as he handed the uniformed man a folded bill.

They walked to the door together. Dett stood aside to open it for Tussy, regretting the loss of her hand on his arm the second it occurred.

Inside, a man in a tuxedo checked a register, confirmed the reservation Carl had called in Saturday afternoon, then personally showed them to their table, already set for two. It had banquette-style seating. Dett stood aside as Tussy slid in first, then he settled himself next to her.

"The sommelier will be with you momentarily, monsieur," the man in the tux said.

"Is that French for 'waiter'?" Tussy said, biting softly into her lower lip.

"I don't know," Dett replied. "I was never in a place like this."

"In your whole life?"

"That's right."

"Well, for goodness' sakes, how come you picked this one, then?"

"The hotel, the one where I'm staying, they said it was the best place in town."

"Do you always do that? Go to the best places?"

"Me? I *never* do. What for?"

"I don't under—?"

"I only wanted to come here because I was with you, Tussy," he said, heavily conscious of her name in his mouth.

"You don't have to put on a show for me, Walker."

"I—"

"Our wine list, monsieur," the red-coated sommelier said, presenting a grape-colored leather packet with a gold tassel.

Dett and Tussy looked at each other. The corners of her mouth lifted slightly. *Even her eyes smile,* Dett thought.

"Perhaps I might be of some assistance?" the sommelier said, unctuously.

"I don't like wine very much," Tussy said, speaking only to Dett. "I drank some at a wedding once, and it tasted like . . . I don't even know how to say it, but it wasn't . . . fun."

"I don't like it, either," Dett said. Turning to the sommelier, he said, "I think we'll pass."

"Pass, monsieur?"

"Not have any," Dett translated.

"Oh. Well. *Votre garçon—pardon,* your 'waiter'—will be with you very shortly."

"I think we made him mad," Tussy said, giggling.

"At least we know how to say 'waiter' in French now," Dett said.

1959 October 05 Monday 20:12

"This is what you got?" Dioguardi said, holding the list Rufus had concocted in one hand, reading with a flashlight.

"That's what I wrote down, boss. But that be '*xactly* what the man had on his own paper. I copy as good as a camera. Checked it over twice, just to be sure."

"Where did you find the paper? The one you copied this from?"

"In his room, boss. Just like you—"

"*Where* in his room, goddamn it?"

"Oh, I see, boss. It was in the pocket of one of his suits," Rufus said, patting his own chest. "Nice suits he got, like the one you wearing."

"What made you look there?"

" 'Cause I couldn't find nothing nowhere else, boss. Looked in his shoes, too. Sometimes, people be hiding things there."

"That was slick thinking," Dioguardi said, soothing over any problem he might have caused by his earlier flash of temper. *You have to watch the way you talk to these people,* he counseled himself. *They can get all sensitive on you, clam right up.*

"Thank you, boss."

"Let me ask you another question, Rufus." *They like it when you call them by their name, not "boy" and stuff like that.* "When you were looking around, did you see anything that might give you a read on the man? You know, something about his personality?"

"Well, he didn't have no magazines, boss. That tell you something, you see what some people be looking at. You be surprised what some people keep in they rooms. No letters, neither. Had him some whiskey, but I was the one that went out and got that for him. I tell you this, though. That one, he a *serious* man."

"You say that why?"

"Man had him a straight razor, boss."

"So? Lots of people shave with a—"

"Yes, sir. I knows that. But the man, he had him a *safety* razor, besides. Nice new Gillette. And plenty of blades for it, too."

"I see what you're saying."

"That's right, boss. Some of the baddest men I know, they never walk out they house without one."

"No guns?"

"Not a one, boss. And a gun, that ain't something you can hide in a hotel room. Not from Rufus, noways."

"You did a good job, Rufus. Like you always do."

"Thank you, boss." *Nah, massah, Mr. Dett, he don't keep no gun in his room. That's 'cause he carries it around with him. Just ask Silk, you greaseball motherfucker.*

"Now, that list you saw, it's probably not worth anything," Dioguardi said. "But remember when I explained to you that time the difference between flat-work and piece-work?"

"Yes, sir! I remember that like it was yesterday, you told me."

"You ever see a hundred-dollar bill before, Rufus?"

"I *seen* them, boss. But I never *held* one."

"Well, now you are," Dioguardi said, smiling in the night.

The two men shook hands—*Niggers love it when you do that,* buzzing through Dioguardi's mind—and Rufus slipped out of the Imperial and into the welcoming shadows of the vacant lot on Halstead.

1959 October 05 Monday 20:32

"Do you know what *any* of this stuff is?" Tussy asked Dett, tapping a red-lacquered fingernail against the placard on which the various dishes were listed.

"The only French I know is *à la carte.*"

"And all I know is *à la mode,*" she said, making a face. "Do you think we should ask him?"

"The waiter?"

"Or we could just take a guess at something. I mean, how bad could it be, in a place like this?"

"I did this wrong, didn't I, Tussy?"

"What? You haven't done anything—"

"I should have asked you where *you* wanted to eat. Instead of, like you said, putting on a show."

"You just come out and say what you think, don't you?"

"Not usually. I'm not that much of a talker."

"But in your business . . ."

"Oh, I talk all the time," Dett said, deflecting. "But that's, like you said, business talk. Negotiations and all. I meant . . . with women."

"You don't seem like a shy man to me."

"I just don't spend a lot of time going out on dates and stuff. I'm always working."

The waiter hovered.

Tussy and Dett looked at each other.

"Could I have this?" she said to the waiter, touching a line on the menu.

"*Certainement,* madame. And for monsieur?"

"I'll try this one," Dett said, following Tussy's example and pointing at random.

"What's your favorite?" she said, as soon as the waiter departed.

"My favorite?"

"Your favorite *food.* I know it's not . . . whatever we just ordered. If you could have anything you wanted, what would it be?"

"Lemon pie," Dett said, unhesitatingly.

"That's no meal!"

"You said whatever I wanted."

Tussy turned in her seat so she was looking directly in Dett's eyes. "All right, let's say it would be lemon pie—*my* lemon pie—for dessert. What would the main course be?"

"Well, I guess . . . I . . . I guess I don't think about food much. Maybe a steak?"

"Uh-huh. And what else? You can't just have steak and pie!" she said, mock-indignantly. "You need a vegetable at least. You like baked potatoes?"

"Sure."

"You don't sound all that excited about it."

"I like the skins. Not the inside, so much."

"Do you like salads?"

"I like the stuff they put *in* salads, but not all mixed together, with dressing all over it."

"Lettuce and tomatoes?"

"Lettuce. And celery. And radishes. And those little onions."

"Pearls."

"Pearls?"

"Pearl onions, that's what they call them, but I never heard of anyone eating them raw. You like real crunchy stuff, huh?"

"I guess I do. Like I said—"

"—you don't think much about food," she interrupted, smiling. "You don't go out on a lot of dates. And you said you weren't a gambler. What do you do for fun? Watch television?"

"Not so much," Dett said.

"How old *are* you, anyway?" Tussy said, laughing.

"I'm thirty-nine. I was born in—"

"Oh, I was just playing," she said, a touch of anxiety in her voice. "I didn't mean anything by it."

The waiter arrived, and ceremoniously presented the food. Tussy and Dett ignored him until he went away.

"This kind of looks like a little steak," Tussy said, poking dubiously at the meat on her plate. "And yours, it looks like . . ." She bent over Dett's plate and sniffed. "Well, I *think* it's some kind of fish, but there's wine in that sauce on it, that's for sure."

"The bread's good," Dett said, chewing a small morsel he had removed with his fingers. "Anyway, I don't care. I didn't come here for the food."

"Well, *I'm* not leaving here without tasting everything," Tussy said. "Gloria, that's my best friend, she'd *kill* me if I didn't describe every square inch of this place, never mind the food." She resolutely cut off a small piece of the meat on her plate, and popped it into her mouth, chewing thoughtfully for a few seconds before swallowing, and saying, "It's not steak. It's . . . lamb, I think. What about yours?"

Dett forked a morsel into his mouth, swallowed it without chewing. "It's all right, I guess."

"Can I try it?"

"This?" he said, nodding at his plate.

"Yes. That way, I can say I had two *different* meals here. Besides, it might be good."

"Sure," Dett said. He reached for his plate, intending to put it before Tussy, but she had already speared a portion with her fork.

"This *is* good!" she said.

"Let's switch," Dett immediately offered.

"Don't you like—?"

"Like I said, it's okay. But it's not what I came here for."

Tussy held Dett's eyes for a long second. Then she reached over and switched their plates with professional skill, blushing furiously.

1959 October 05 Monday 21:02

The Gladiators' dull orange Oldsmobile made its third circuit of the lot on Halstead.

"I know that car," Sunglasses said to Lacy, as he pointed with a black-gloved finger. "That dark-blue Imperial. It's Dioguardi's."

"You're sure?"

"Yeah," Sunglasses said. "I seen it plenty of times, right in front of that restaurant he owns."

"You think he's meeting with that Ace kid?"

"In that spot, who else? It sure as hell isn't any of the Kings, right? You still want us to drop you off? Two blocks away, it's their turf. If they spot you . . ."

"Nobody's going to spot me," Lacy said. "That's why the jacket stays in the car. You know how people are always saying niggers all look alike?"

"Yeah."

"Well, you know what? I think it works the same way for them when it comes to us. Without my jacket, I'm just . . . a regular guy. A nothing."

"Without the jackets, maybe that's what we all are," Sunglasses said.

1959 October 05 Monday 21:54

The check was presented in a natural-calfskin case, open on three sides. Dett unfolded it like a book, glanced at the tab, put a hundred-dollar bill inside the folio, and closed it.

"It cost *that* much?" Tussy said.

"No. There'll be change."

"I'm sorry. I know you're not supposed to—"

"You could never do anything wrong," Dett said. "Not with me."

The waiter returned with the portfolio. Tussy seemed relieved to see several bills inside when Dett opened it again. He took some of the money, left the rest, and closed it again.

"I trust you found everything to your satisfaction," the man at the front said, as they walked to the front door.

"Oh, it was just wonderful!" Tussy assured him.

The valet drove Dett's Buick to where they were waiting. An attendant reached to open the passenger door for Tussy just as Dett stepped forward to perform the same act. The attendant bounced off Dett as if he had hit a wall. Dett closed Tussy's door gently behind her, and handed the breathless attendant a pair of dollar bills with his other hand, all in the same motion.

Dett walked around to where the valet was holding open the driver's door. "Your partner's got your half," Dett told him, and pulled his door shut.

1959 October 05 Monday 21:58

A s if beckoned by the red glow of Lacy's just-lit cigarette, Harley Grant's Chevy glided up. Lacy tossed his cigarette away and got in.

"What was so important, you had to see me?" Harley asked him.

"There's a meet Wednesday. Between the Hawks and the Kings," Lacy answered.

"A real one?"

"Yeah. Supposed to go down in the big lot on Halstead, a little ways from where you picked me up."

"Kids," Harley said. "What's that to me?"

"Kids, yeah. Only, we got a treaty with the Hawks."

"I told you, Lacy. We've got big plans now. You can't be getting into any—"

"I *know* that. I know what the plan is. We wouldn't be fighting with them—on their side, I mean—but they wanted to be sure we'd be around, back them up, in case the Kings bring too many men. Extras, like."

"We talked this over, Lacy," Harley said, in the same quietly commanding voice he used with Benny, a voice Royal Beaumont never heard. "If you get your guys into any—"

"We're *not*," Lacy assured him. "But that isn't what I had to tell you, the important thing. See, the Hawks, they've got guns."

"So do the Kings. It'll be like it al—"

"Not zip guns, Harley. Real ones."

"How do you know that?"

"Ace, the President of the Hawks, he showed it to us. Brought it right into our clubhouse."

"What, exactly, did he show you?" Harley asked, enunciating each word to emphasize its importance.

"A pistol. A real pistol."

"One like this?" Harley said, pulling a snub-nosed revolver from inside his leather jacket and holding it below the dash.

"Like that," Lacy said, "only bigger. And it was all bright, too, not like yours."

"You're sure?"

"I seen plenty of real guns," Lacy said. "This was just like the ones the cops carry."

"He say where he got it? Or if they have any more?"

"He said he got it from the Klan," Lacy snorted. "But I don't think so. I think I know where he got it."

"Where?"

"From Dioguardi."

"Dioguardi?" Harley said, consciously keeping his voice level. "Where'd you get *that* idea?"

"Where they have their clubhouse, that's Dioguardi's building," Lacy said, defending, but not defensive. "Dioguardi's got a storefront real close by, too—the one with the windows painted black? And tonight, just before you came, we saw his Imperial, parked in the exact same lot where the meet's going to go down."

"This . . . Ace is his name? . . . He was with him? With Dioguardi?"

"We couldn't see inside the car. But it figures, right? I mean, where would the *Klan* have heard of some little club like the Hawks?"

"Did you mean what you said before?" Tussy asked Dett.

"What?"

"That I couldn't do anything wrong. With you, I mean?"

"Yes. That's the truth."

"Walker, how could you say such a thing?"

"I don't know how I could say it," Dett told her, as he turned onto Route 44, heading back toward town. "But that doesn't mean it isn't true. When I said it, I knew it was. I don't know how else to explain."

"I guess we'll find out," she said, drumming her fingers lightly on the dashboard.

"What do you mean?"

"I want to keep talking to you."

"I want to, too," Dett said.

"I know. I just don't want you to take what I'm going to say the wrong way."

"I promise."

"If you take me home now, I can't invite you in. The neighbors . . . Some of them, they've known me since I was a little girl. And the others, they know I was divorced, so they all think I'm . . . you know."

"I would never want you to—"

"And the only place I know in town—the only nice place, I mean—where we could sit quietly and talk this late is the diner, and I could never bring you *there*."

"Oh," Dett said, not understanding, but unwilling to say so.

"I know someplace. It's out in the woods. Where some of the kids go to park. You know, like to—"

"Sure."

"I want to go there," Tussy said, firmly. "We could be alone, and talk some more. But I don't want you to think I'm one of those—"

"I wouldn't," Dett said, solemnly. "Never."

1959 October 05 Monday 22:16

"Are you crazy, calling me here? At this hour? What if my father had answered the phone?"

"I would have hung up," Harley said to Kitty. "But I had to take the chance. I have to talk to you."

"Talk?"

"Kitty, please. This is serious. Real serious. It's about your brother."

"If you're just—"

"I'm not. Please, Kitty. I can't tell you this on the phone. Can't you just meet me by the back of—?"

"No! And if you come by here, everyone in the neighborhood will hear those loud mufflers of yours."

"I already traded cars. For the night, I mean," Harley added, hastily. "It's a black Caddy."

"Fit right in around here, huh?"

"Kitty, now's not the time to be doing that. Will you meet me or not?"

"I could go over to Della's house for an hour, maybe. But that's all, Harley. When could you—?"

"I'm only a couple of blocks away," Harley said, speaking urgently into a pay phone, one hand inside his leather jacket. "Just walk to the end of the block, I'll pick you up."

1959 October 05 Monday 22:43

"I haven't been here in . . . God, I can't even *remember* the last time I was here. But it is beautiful, isn't it? You can see the moon right through the trees."

"Want to sit outside?"

"Outside? I'm all dressed up, and we don't even have a blanket or . . . or do you?" Tussy said, a faint hint of wariness edging her voice.

"A blanket?" Dett said. "No. Where would I get a blanket? I thought, maybe, you could sit on the hood of the car. On my jacket, I mean, so you wouldn't mess up your dress."

"You'd ruin your coat," Tussy said. The little smile at the corners of her mouth seemed to reach inside her words.

"No, I wouldn't. And that way, I could . . . see you better. They didn't even let us sit across from each other in that restaurant."

"Yes. Wasn't that—?"

"I thought you'd feel better that way, too. Outside, I mean."

"Me? Why? Oh!"

"Did I say something wrong?"

"What you said was just right, Walker. Come on, let's do it, just like you said."

Dett spread his jacket on the Buick's broad hood. Tussy took his hand, put one foot on the heavy chrome bumper, and stepped, turning as she sat down. "It's warm," she said, giggling.

"It is," Dett agreed. "More like summer than—"

"I meant, where I'm sitting," Tussy said, hiding her face behind her hand. "From the engine."

"Oh. Do you want to—?"

"It's fine," she said, fumbling in her purse.

Dett moved close to her, matches ready.

As he leaned in, Tussy kissed him on the cheek, so butterfly-soft that he couldn't be sure if it had actually landed.

"You want to know all about me, don't you?" she said.

"Yes."

"That's so strange."

"What is?"

"Just that you'd want to know, for real. When people ask, they really don't, mostly. They're just being polite. But what's so . . . strange is that I know it myself, somehow. That you truly want to, I mean."

"You don't have to tell me anything you don't—"

Tussy blew a jet of cigarette smoke to stop Dett from talking. "After my mother had me, she couldn't have any more children, the doctor said. She used to tell people that was fine with her, because I was more than enough for anyone to handle.

"I had such a lovely life. I never knew how lovely it was until it happened. When I was fifteen."

Dett watched Tussy's face intently, silently willing her to go on.

"My parents were killed," she said, quietly. "People said it was an accident, and I guess it was. But I say 'killed,' because that's what happened to them. They were coming home from the movies. It was pretty late, but I was up, because I was waiting for people to come home from the movies, too. I was babysitting, for the Taylor kids. I was a great babysitter. Everybody wanted me, because I was so reliable. I'd been doing it since I was eleven. I bought all my own clothes for school with the money I made, and I even had extra left. I was so proud of that."

"Drunk driver?" Dett said.

"They were *all* drunk," Tussy said, pain and sorrow twisted in her voice, "every single one of them in that car. It was just before Pearl Harbor. Everyone knew we were going to war, sooner or later. My dad had been in World War I. He always said that was supposed to be the last one, but there would never really be a last one, not with the way people are. . . ."

Tussy's voice trailed off. Dett descended into the silence with her; he stood immobile, as if any movement would frighten her away.

Tussy took a deep drag of her cigarette, blew the smoke out in a vicious jet of anger. "They were all college boys," she said. "Seven of them, in one car. They were going like maniacs. My folks were stopped at a light. They came right through the red and just . . . smashed them to pieces."

"What happened to them?"

"I told you," she said, sharply. "They were kil— Oh, you mean, what happened to the college boys? Nothing. They didn't even get *hurt*. The driver walked away. I mean, he walked right out of his car. His big, huge new car. It crushed my dad's little Ford like it was made of paper."

"Did he go to jail? The driver, I mean."

"Jail?" she said, bitterly. "I told you, they were rich boys. Maybe they got a ticket or something, I never knew. When the Taylors got home, we waited for my folks to come by and pick me up. But they never came. It got real late. There was a knock on the door, finally. It was the police."

"Christ."

"You know what? I didn't believe them. No matter how many times they said it, I wouldn't listen. They took me to the hospital. They had my . . . they had my mom and my dad there. When I saw them, all . . . I don't remember what happened after that."

"Did people take you in?"

"Nobody took me in," Tussy said, fiercely. "I quit school. I got a job. The same job I have right now today. And I never missed one single payment on our house."

"Didn't anyone . . . make trouble or anything, you being all by yourself?"

"Well, they sure *tried,*" Tussy said, leaning back and supporting herself with one palm against the hood. "The Welfare people said I had to go to a foster home. Even the school, they said I was too young to drop out. I could get working papers, for part-time, but I couldn't leave school entirely, is what they said. And the bank said I couldn't take over the mortgage, because I wasn't of age."

"But . . . ?"

"But Mr. Beaumont—he's the biggest man in Locke City—he saved me. With everybody acting like I was a baby, I was so scared. I thought I would lose . . . every last trace of my mom and dad. But this one policeman, he told me, 'Miss, you go and see Mr. Beaumont. He can fix things.' And that's just what I did," she said, reflectively. "I knew the proper thing would be to write him a letter, but I couldn't wait. I was too terrified. I couldn't just sit in my house and have them come for me. So I started walking."

"You walked to—? I mean, was it far?" Dett hurriedly amended.

"It was *real* far. The policeman, the nice one, he told me where it was, but I had never been way out in the country. I mean, we went out there, for picnics and stuff, but not to where Mr. Beaumont lives. That's a different kind of country, you know?"

"Sure. Rich country."

"Yes! First, I hitched. I knew that was stupid. If my dad had ever caught me pulling a stunt like that, he would have . . ."

Tussy tossed away her cigarette, put her face in her hands, and started to sob. Dett held her against him, protectively, not moving his hands, his face as flat and blank as a slab of stone. He felt his own heart—a fist-tight knot in his chest, pulsing hate.

1959 October 05 Monday 23:01

"What do you make of it, Sally?"

"It's a list of some kind, G. Maybe the letters are the jobs he's been hired to do, and the numbers are the payoff?"

"Could be, I guess. But what's with the buildings? I mean, banks, I could see. Even the post office, there's money there, if you know where to look. But the police station? That don't make any sense."

"I know. But let's say those letters, they stand for people, okay?"

"Okay," the scar-faced man said, noncommittal.

"One of them, the letter is 'D.' What's that tell you?"

"The truth, Sal? Nothing. Not a damn thing. Those numbers, they're not right. See where the 'D' is on the list? Second, not the top. And the number next to it, that's half of the number across from the 'X.' Even if it *was* a hit list, nobody gets fifty grand. Nobody. Even the guys who did the job on Albert, they got ten apiece. And those guys, they were *famiglia,* not some outside contract men. If you're the 'D' on that list for twenty-five K, then who's 'X,' for fifty?"

"I'm not saying that's what it is, G. But I know this: it means *something.* This guy, Dett, it's more like he's a fucking Russian spy than a hit man."

"In Locke City?"

"You making a joke, G.?"

"No, Sal."

"No? Good. Because I got news for Mr. Walker Dett. Sal Dioguardi's not some fucking *cafone;* he's a man with a mind. See this number, here?"

"Yeah."

"Mean anything to you?"

"Not to me."

"It's a *phone* number, G. You know how I know?"

"How?"

"The last three numbers, that was the tip-off."

"Two-one-three?"

"Yeah. Look, I cover those numbers with my finger—see?—what do you have left?"

"Sally, I swear I'm not—?"

"You got *seven* numbers," Dioguardi said, excitedly. "That's a *telephone* number, G. Now, if you want to call long distance, you need an area code, right?"

"Right."

"Which is *how* many numbers?"

"Three. Huh! So you think the whole thing, it's a phone number?"

"Those last three numbers? Two-one-three? That's the area code for L.A., Gino."

"And this guy, we know he didn't have a car when he came in; he had to rent one here," the scar-faced man said. "It all adds up, Sal."

"Yeah," said Dioguardi, thoughtfully. "We talked about you going out to L.A. anyway. For that other business. Okay, this moves things up a bit: I want you on the next plane out, G. Tomorrow, okay?"

1959 October 05 Monday 23:06

"I didn't mean to just . . . let go like that," Tussy said, her voice muffled in Dett's chest.

"It's okay," Dett said. Knowing it was, trusting the knowledge.

"You really want to hear all this?"

"More than anything."

Tussy pulled back slightly. She examined Dett's face in the moonlight for a long minute, making no secret of what she was doing. Finally, she nodded to herself, swallowed, and went on with her story: "I got three rides, one after the other. By then, it was already afternoon. I knew I wasn't going to get anyone to pick me up on the side roads—I didn't even *see* anyone for a long time—so I walked. It was almost dark by the time I got there.

"Mr. Beaumont's house, it's like a castle. All stone. I never saw anything like it before, even in a book. There's a gatehouse at the entrance to the property. Not a fence, a little house, like, where you have to stop before you can go in.

"The man there, the guard, I guess he was, he was very nice, but I told him I would only talk to Mr. Beaumont. Like I was *insisting* on it, isn't that ridiculous? But, finally, he told me to move away. Not get off the property, just step back. Then he picked up a phone thing and he talked into it. After he hung up, he told me someone would be out to get me.

"I just stood there. A man came up. He was one of those . . . slow ones. I don't like the names people call them, but I don't know the polite thing to say. He just said to come with him, and I did.

"Inside the building, it was just like the outside. I mean, like a *palace* or something. I don't even have the words to tell you how . . . stupendous it was. The foyer, where I waited, it was bigger than my whole house.

"The man who brought me, he said to just sit down—there was a hundred places you could do that—and somebody would come and get me.

"I guess I expected it would be Mr. Beaumont himself, I don't know why. But it was a lady. She told me her name was Cynthia Beaumont, and she was Mr. Beaumont's sister. I went with her into this place like an office, and she sat behind a desk and told me to tell her everything I came to tell Mr. Beaumont.

"That's what I did. She had a hard face, Miss Beaumont did. Not a mean one, but hard. Like policemen have. I never saw her smile, not once, all the time I was talking. But I guess I didn't tell her anything to be smiling about. I was crying. A lot.

"When I was all done, she said, 'Mr. Beaumont will set things right for you, young lady.' Then she just got up and left. In a minute, that man, the one who you could see was kind of slow, he came back, and he took me outside.

"There was a car sitting there. A big black car, like you see in gangster movies. The slow man, he said to get in. So I did. And the man in the car—a different man—drove me straight to my house, like he knew exactly where it was."

"That's some story."

"That's not even the end," Tussy said. "After that, everything stopped. No more Welfare people, no more truant officer, no more talk about a foster home. I got my job at the diner, working for Armand. And I still did babysitting—I didn't work nights then. One of the other girls, she was a few years older than me, she had a car, and I rode to work with her.

"I only made sixty cents an hour—fifty for the babysitting—but I got my meals free. And the tips were very good. The mortgage is thirty-seven dollars and forty-nine cents a month, so I could pay it with plenty left over, for the electricity and the oil man and everything."

"Why do you think this Mr. Beaumont did all that for you?" Dett asked.

"Oh, I think he does it for *everybody*. Not the same thing, of course. But everyone in Locke City knows Mr. Beaumont is the man you go to if you have a problem. There's only one thing that makes me sad, every time I think about it."

"What's that?"

"I never had the chance to thank him. Oh, I wrote him a letter, of course. But he never answered it. I never even met him. People say he's a cripple, in a wheelchair. I wish I could do something for him. Fix him, like he fixed me. But that's just being silly. What could someone like me ever do for a man like him?"

1959 October 05 Monday 23:12

I *don't know her,* Holden Satterfield thought. *I don't know him, neither. And I never seen that car before. I have to write it down, so when Sherman—* Holden's forest-trained ears picked up the sound of another car pulling in, just on the other side of the embankment. *They're not going to do nothing. They're just talking. I better go see who else is here. . . .*

"All right, tell me," Kitty's voice floated out the car window. *I know this one,* Holden said to himself. *She's been here before. In that pretty red Chevy. But it's a different car tonight. A Cadillac. She must be one of those girls who . . .*

"Wednesday night, there's going to be a rumble. In that big lot on Halstead."

"Harley, what Uriah does has nothing to do with me. With any of our family. He hasn't lived at home for—"

"You know people call him 'Preacher'? You know he's the President of the South Side Kings?"

"Yes. Yes, we all know. Everyone in town knows. Every family has its disgrace. That's why my father—"

"This won't be one of those kiddie rumbles they're used to having, Kitty. Not this time."

"What are you saying?"

"The Golden Hawks, the ones your brother's gang is going to clash with, they have guns. Real guns."

"You mean like the army?"

"No. Pistols. But real ones. Your brother, he's the leader. He's got to go first. Walk right up to the leader of the other side and start throwing. Only, your brother, he's going to be expecting bicycle chains and tire irons and baseball bats . . . stuff like that. If he walks up on a man holding a pistol—a real pistol, Kitty, not a little zip gun—he's going to get killed."

"Oh my God."

"You see why I had to tell you? I know you and your brother don't—"

"Uriah got shot once. In one of those rumbles. He didn't even have to go to the hospital, he said."

"That was with a zip gun, Kitty. They only take twenty-two shorts, and most of the time they don't even—"

"I don't want to know about guns! I hate them. I don't . . . Why do you even know how they . . . how gangs fight, and everything?"

"That was me, once," Harley said. "I didn't know it then, but gangs, they're like the minor leagues. In baseball, I mean. The big boys, they have scouts. They know what they're looking for. And when I got picked, that's when I got my chance. The chance for everything I've been telling you about, Kitty."

"But you work for Royal Beaumont. How could he—?"

"It doesn't matter. Not now, anyway. What matters now is, you've got to tell your brother."

"What good would that do?"

"Do? It would save his damn life, if he called this off."

"Harley, sometimes I don't know where you were raised. If you were in a gang yourself, you know my brother could never do anything like that."

"Then he should use different—I don't know—tactics."

"Like what?"

"Maybe, while the Hawks are going over to the lot, your brother's gang sneaks over to their clubhouse and waits for them. Then, when they come back, ambush them or something."

"Wait around in *that* neighborhood? They'd all end up in jail."

"So? That would be the best thing, wouldn't it? *Let* someone call the cops, and say a lot of . . . Negroes are congregating. If your brother and his boys have to spend the night in jail, it's a lot better than being dead."

"I . . . I'll tell him. About the guns. I can cut lunch tomorrow and go over there. But I don't know if he'll—"

"You have to at least give him the chance."

"You're only doing this because of me, aren't you?"

"Kitty, I don't give a damn about your brother, and I'm not pretending to."

"If anyone ever found out you told, wouldn't you get in a lot of trouble?"

"More than a lot."

Holden watched as the voices stopped and the bodies came together.

"I don't know why I told you all that," Tussy said, sliding off the hood of the Buick to stand next to Dett. "Some date, huh?"

"This wasn't a date."

"What do you mean?" she asked, a tincture of misgiving in her voice.

"I mean, a date, it's like you . . . it's just something to do," Dett told her, struggling to express himself. "You go out on dates a lot, don't you? But they don't mean anything."

"I *don't* go out on dates a lot, for your information. But you're right: they don't mean much."

"This does," he said, gravely.

"This?"

"Being with you. To me, I mean."

"You don't even know me, Walker. For all you know, I could be—"

"Pure."

"What?"

"That's what you are," Dett said. "Pure. A pure person. I knew it the minute I saw you."

"I thought I heard every line there was," Tussy said, chuckling hollowly, longing for him to say something to banish her skepticism.

"It's not a line. I know you think . . . I don't even think you *do* think it is," Dett said. "You know, just like I knew."

"That you're a pure person?"

"I'm not. I'm nothing like that. I never was; I never will be."

"You mean, like the church says, about sin? I already told you I was divorced. You know what they say about—"

"There's no church. Not for me, there isn't. A turned-around collar doesn't make you a good person, no more than wearing a black robe makes you an honest one. I wasn't talking about that. You say I don't know anything about you. Well, I'm saying that I do. What I said is true. And so are you. True. I know this. And what I said about you knowing me? I only meant, you know I'm not lying now."

"I thought 'pure' meant you were a virgin."

" 'Pure' is your heart, not your . . . I don't know how to say what I want to, Tussy. You know what? I've been all over. Not just in America. All over. And the world, it's rotten. Like, if you could look all the way into the center of the earth, it would be this . . . ugly, evil thing."

"There's bad people and there's good people," Tussy said, in a schoolmarm's tone. "I found that out for myself, like I just told you about. Just because you had some bad experiences, that doesn't mean the whole world's—"

"No, no," Dett said. "Can I . . . ?" He reached out his hand. Tussy took it, as trusting as a child.

Dett felt her hand, small and work-roughened, pulsing faintly, like a heart at peace.

"I wasn't talking about people," he finally said. "Not . . . individuals. I meant the world. The people who run it."

"Like kings and presidents?"

"Not them. Well, *maybe* them, but even that's not what I mean. I mean the people who run *them*."

"I don't understand. Nobody runs the president of America. And nobody runs an evil man like . . . like Hitler was, right?"

"No."

"No, I'm right? Or no, I'm wrong?" she said, looking up at him.

"No, you're wrong. But you're right about people. Most people, anyway. They're sheep. They go wherever they're herded."

"Walker?"

"What?"

"You're not some kind of . . . religious man, are you?"

"I already told you—"

"When I was nineteen," she said, suddenly, "I got married. He was twenty-five, just back from the war. He had been wounded in Italy. He was a hero, people said. He was a very handsome man, especially in his uniform. That's what he was wearing when I met him. In the diner. I thought he was the man I had been waiting for."

"But he wasn't . . ." Dett said, fearful she would stop talking, desperate beyond his own understanding to hear the end—to know what had gone wrong.

"Joey didn't have any trouble getting work. The war was still going on—this was right after VE Day—but everyone knew we would win by then. The plants were running double shifts. And, with him being a veteran and all . . .

"We got married in the church. And then we came back ho—to my house. For a little while, it was good."

"And then . . . ?"

"It started . . . I don't know exactly *what* started it. So many things happened at once. Joey didn't like Fireball—which was a dirty trick, because when we were going out he *said* he did—and he . . . drank a lot. I thought that was because he hated his job. He wasn't a war hero at the plant. He was always coming home in a temper because the foreman had chewed him out or some supervisor didn't like the way he did something."

"You said there was plenty of work. . . ."

"There *was*. Joey would quit one job and get another, but it was always the same story. And even with him hating *his* jobs, he was always after me to quit *mine*."

"Why didn't you want to quit your job?"

"I *did*. You think being a waitress is a wonderful career? I always wanted a baby, ever since I was a little girl. I thought it would be so wonderful, to be a mom like mine was. Help my husband, be a family, together. But I knew if I quit my job I couldn't make the payments on my house."

"But when you got married, wasn't it his job to—?"

"No!" she said, hotly. "I mean, it *would* have been, maybe, if I did what he wanted. Sell the house, and move into an apartment. Then Joey would have paid the rent, sure. But I wouldn't sell my house. So he moved in there, with me."

"What's wrong with that? I mean, couldn't he just as easily pay the mortgage? It would be cheaper than renting an apartment, especially right after the war."

"He wanted to do that, too. After I put his name on the deed."

"You did that?"

"I was going to," Tussy said, almost apologetically. "But I was . . . I don't know, nervous about it, kind of. So I went to see a lawyer. Mr. Gendell, he has an office right over the bank where I have my account. Everyone says he's the best lawyer in town. He even does some things for Mr. Beaumont, that's how important he is.

"But he turned out to be the nicest man you ever met, except for those horrible cigars he smoked. The air in his office, it was just *blue*. I was a little scared of him. He's very big and he talks very loud. I wanted to know how much it would cost for him to explain the law to me. About mortgages and deeds and things. And he said I should just tell him what I wanted to know, and he'd figure out what it would cost. That scared me even more, but I went ahead and did it.

"Mr. Gendell listened to everything I told him. And then he said, 'Young woman, if you put your husband's name on that deed, you will never be able to get it off.'

"I asked him why I would even *want* to get it off. And he said, 'Things happen.' That's just what he said, 'Things happen.' He said the house would be half Joey's. And Joey was the man. So, if he wanted to sell it, for example, well, he could just *do* it. Mr. Gendell didn't say anything about divorce, but he asked me how long I'd known Joey before we got married, and stuff like that, so I understood what he was really saying.

"He gave me a real lecture. Not like a scolding, but like I always imagined college would be, if I had ever went. He told me about the Married Women's Property Act, and how hard it had been for women to get the vote, and how the courts treated women when they got divorced, and . . . Well, anyway, when *he* was done with me, that was the end of me putting Joey's name on the deed to the house."

"How did Joey take that?"

"He walked out of the house. He came back late at night. Drunk. And he beat me up. Ow!" Tussy squealed, as Dett's hand clamped down on hers.

"Oh God, I'm sorry," Dett said. He felt hot lava suffusing the artificially tightened skin of his face, threatening to erupt. He quickly bent forward and kissed her hand. "I'm sorry, Tussy. I didn't mean to—"

"It's all right," she said. "You just . . . startled me, that's all."

"When I heard you say he—"

"I understand," she said, realizing, as she spoke, that she did, and not questioning it.

"What happened?" Dett said, clipping each syllable.

"I told you. He—"

"*After* that."

"Oh. The next morning, he apologized. It was the liquor that made him do it, he said. But I couldn't forget him . . . punching me, screaming how could he be the man of the house when it wasn't even *his* house? I didn't go to work the next day. I was too ashamed. My face was all . . ."

"He never did it again?"

"Can I . . . ?" Tussy said, gesturing.

Dett handed over her purse, lit the cigarette he knew was coming.

"He did do it again. And again. He even kicked Fireball."

"Your cat? Why would he—?"

"Fireball tried to tear him up. Scratching and biting. Joey couldn't get him off."

"I didn't know cats did that. Dogs, sure. But—"

"Well, Fireball did. He was a little tiger. When Joey kicked him, he went flying into the wall. I thought Joey had killed him. If he had . . ."

"But he was okay?"

"I took him to the vet. They said he was fine, but that's when everyone found out."

"Found out?"

"About Joey . . . beating me. I *had* to take Fireball to the doctor; I thought he was hurt real bad. I did my best to cover up my . . . I put on a lot of makeup, but it didn't do any good. I had a black eye, and my nose was all swollen."

"You think the vet told people?"

"Maybe. I mean, I *guess* so. Because, when the police came, it was like they already knew."

"The police came to the vet's?"

"No, no. To my house. It was the very next night. Joey was drunk, and he slapped me. I punched him back, as hard as I could. Then I tried to scratch his eyes out, like Fireball would have, if he could. A window got broken. Someone must have called the police. One of my neighbors, I think. Nobody ever said.

"When they got there, Joey looked worse than me, I think. But I was the one with the broken ribs. We all went to the hospital. The police asked me what happened, and I told them. They said if I pressed charges Joey would go to jail, and then he'd lose his job, and there'd be no one to take care of me. I couldn't even explain to them that I didn't *need* anyone to take care of me; I was too busy crying. I felt like everything was just . . . gone."

"Did you press charges?" Dett asked, shallow-breathing through his nose.

"What happened was, Sherman Layne came in. I didn't know his whole name back then, but I remembered him, from the time my parents . . . he was the one who told me to go and see Mr. Beaumont He remembered me, too. I asked him, what should I do? He said the best thing would be for Joey to just leave and not come back. I told him Joey would never do that. But Sherman—everyone calls him that, Detective Sherman—he said he would."

"Did he?"

"Yes," Tussy said, as if still surprised at the memory. "That's just exactly what he did. He moved out. He didn't really have that much stuff to take, anyway, all the furniture—what you saw—it was mine. And then he had a lawyer send me some papers saying we were going to get divorced. I showed the papers to Mr. Gendell, and he started laughing. 'Stupid punks,' is all he said. Then he took the papers from me, and said not to worry about anything.

"A few weeks later, Mr. Gendell came into the diner. He gave me some legal papers, with seals on them and everything, and said I was divorced, and Joey had to pay me sixty dollars a month for alimony! I told him I didn't want any money from Joey, and Mr. Gendell just smiled. He told me he *knew* I was going to say that. Joey was never really going to pay me a dime—the alimony was just for insurance, he said. In case Joey ever made trouble for me, I could have him locked up for nonsupport.

"I was so grateful. I asked Mr. Gendell how much money I had to pay him, and he said *Joey* paid him. He laughed when he said it. Like it was this terrifically funny joke."

"He sounds like a good man, especially for a lawyer."

"Oh, he *is*. But, you know, the way he laughed that day, I wouldn't ever want him to be mad at *me*. Do you know what I mean?"

"Yes."

"Well, now you know. My whole sad story. Still think I'm so pure, Walker?"

"Even more," he said, holding her hand.

1959 October 06 Tuesday 00:13

"It didn't even hurt, Daddy," Lola whispered.

"You sound like you mad about it, sweet girl," Silk said.

"Well, those other girls, they *said* it did. They said it burned like fire, and they couldn't—"

"So you think they was gaming on you, playing you off the trick, so they could have him for themselves?"

"It was fifty dollars, Daddy!" Lola said, proudly. "Who gets that kind of money?"

"You do, little star. And that's the truth. Be the truth forever," Silk said, pulling his whore closer to him on the leather seat of the Eldorado. "Now tell Silk what you remember. Every little thing, right from the beginning."

1959 October 06 Tuesday 00:41

As Dett nosed the rented Buick out of the clearing, a black Cadillac Coupe de Ville flashed past. *Moving too fast for these dirt roads,* Dett thought. *He'll put a lot of chips in that paint job.*

"Anyone you know?" he asked Tussy, keeping his voice casual. Back where they had been parked, Dett had felt another presence. A lurker of some kind. *Probably kids, looking for a thrill,* he had thought at the time, not picking up any sense of danger. And, whatever it was, it had moved on quick enough. But now the Caddy . . .

"Why would I know anyone who comes here?" Tussy said, more angrily than she intended.

"I didn't mean . . . that," Dett said, holding his hands up help-lessly. "I meant the car itself. It looked pretty fancy for a teenage kid to be driving."

"Oh. No, I . . . I mean, it just looked like a car to me. I can't tell them apart, the way some people can."

"Sure. I thought it looked like it belonged to one of the people I've been talking to. About buying property."

"Well, it was a *big* one."

"Yeah. A Cadillac. But there's no shortage of those around."

"I guess that depends where you live," Tussy said, chuckling. "You won't see any on *my* block."

"That's sensible," Dett said, seriously. "Some cars cost so much, you could buy a nice little house instead."

"I can't understand why *anyone* would do that. Have you ever noticed how some colored people buy big cars? I'm sure they buy them on time, but that's the same way you'd buy a house, isn't it? I mean, either way, you have to make payments every month. So why do you think they do that?"

"Well, what if you *couldn't* buy a house?"

"I don't understand. I, well, maybe *I* couldn't, with what I make, but some of them—"

"No, I mean, what if nobody would *sell* you one? You walk into a showroom, I don't care if you're black or white or purple they'll sell you a car. But if you want to buy a house . . ."

"Oh. I see what you mean. I never thought of it like that."

"I didn't, either," Dett assured her. "Not until someone pointed it out to me."

"And now you pointed it out to me," she said, seriously. "I guess that's the way people learn things."

"It's only learning if it's the truth, Tussy. If a lie gets passed from person to person, they're not learning, they're being tricked."

"Did you get this way from the business you're in?"

"What way?"

"Thinking so . . . black all the time. Like everything is crooked and rotten. Is that from being in real estate? I heard, from people who come in the diner, it can be a real cutthroat business, real estate."

"No. I learned it . . . a long time ago. And not in any one place."

"I . . . Oh, good Lord! Do you know what time it is?"

"It's . . . almost one o'clock."

"In the *morning*."

"I didn't realize."

"Neither did I. My goodness."

"I'm sorry if I—"

"Oh, you didn't do anything. I just got . . . lost. In talking. And I don't have to go to work tomorrow, anyway."

"Right. No Mondays or Tuesdays. I was hoping . . ."

"What, Walker?"

"That you would let me see you again."

"Tomorrow, you mean? Well," she said, grinning in the darkness of the car's interior, "later *today,* actually."

"Yes. Anytime at—"

"Would you like to come over for lunch? In the daytime, it would be perfectly fine."

"With your neighbors?"

"You think I'm silly, don't you? I'm just not a . . . flashy person. My girlfriend—"

"—Gloria."

"Oh, you *really* listen, don't you?"

"I listen to you. Every word you say."

"I *guess.* Anyway, to show you what a flop I am at being, well, not *wild,* exactly, but . . . one time, Gloria talked me into trying out at the Avalon."

"What's that?" Dett asked, images of strip joints stabbing his mind.

"It's a dance hall. You know, one of those dime-a-dance places. It's very classy, actually. The men had to wear ties. And they didn't serve liquor. Gloria said it would be fun. Plus, we could make some money."

"But you didn't like it?"

"Well, I was a little afraid of it, at first. I mean, can you see me as a dance-hall girl? I'm way too short, and way too . . . plump."

"No you're not."

"Oh, you have a lot of experience with dance halls?" she said.

"I was never even in one," Dett told her, truthfully.

"I was just clowning around, Walker. I know you were being nice. I'm no good at taking compliments—I never know if someone's just being polite."

"I wasn't. I mean—"

"Oh, stop it!" Tussy said, smacking him playfully on his right arm. "I understand. Anyway, one night in that place was enough for me. At first, I was afraid nobody would ask me to dance, and I'd just sit there, a little wallflower, until Gloria was ready to go home. But a man came over right away. And then another. I could have been on my feet all night."

"What didn't you like, then?"

"You know."

"Being grabbed?"

"Yes. When I was in high school—I was only a freshman, so it was my first year—I used to love to dance. But this, it wasn't dancing at all. The men couldn't dance. Or, more likely, they *wouldn't* dance. All they wanted to do was paw. Some were nicer about it than others, but . . . one man, he just reached down and grabbed my bottom! Right out on the floor."

"That's when you slugged him?"

"I wish I had! But I was too . . . shocked to do anything but pull away from him. I went right over and told Gloria we were leaving. And she didn't argue."

"I'll bet she didn't," Dett said, admiringly.

1959 October 06 Tuesday 01:40

"I figure, whatever *that* man wants to know, might be something *we* want to know," Silk said.

"You figured right, brother," Rufus said.

"So—what *do* we know?" Kendall asked, a shade softer than hostile.

"My woman, Lola, she told me everything. But, the way they do it, there ain't a single clue about the man who comes by for that kind of taste."

"You came all the way over here, tell us that?"

"Ice up, K-man," Darryl said, quietly. "Let the man say what he come to say."

Silk nodded gratefully at Darryl, then said, "But here's what we *do* know. The woman who brings the girls to that 'blue room,' she's the one who sets the whole thing up. Puts the girls in that leather thing to hold them, tells them how to get ready, how to act . . . all that. Now, any madam might do that for her girls, especially for a high-paying regular. But *somebody* got to know when the trick is coming, 'cause it take time to get everything ready for him. *Somebody* got to let him in. So *somebody* got to know his car, see his face, hear his voice. . . ."

"The madam," Rufus said.

"That's the one, Brother Omar," Silk confirmed. "This Ruth girl, she knows. She knows all of it."

1959 October 06 Tuesday 01:44

"I wish you could come in," Tussy said, as Dett's rented Buick turned off the main road. "For coffee, I mean," she added, quickly.

"But it's so late. . . ."

"It's not that," she said. "I'm wide awake. I usually don't even get home from work until past midnight."

"Your neighbors—"

"Oh, they're probably asleep. Who stays up this late if they're not working? It's just . . ."

"The car, right? Standing in front of your house."

"How did you know?"

"People," Dett said, shrugging.

"I don't see where what I do has to be so much their business," Tussy said, defiantly. "It would just be for—"

"I can drop you off," Dett said. "Walk you to your door, and drive off. And then come back."

"But what difference would that make? You'd still—"

"Nobody would see me coming," Dett said, so softly Tussy had to lean toward him to be certain she heard. "The back of your house, there's nothing there except a big ditch and some empty land."

"That's where they stopped working," she said. "The builders, I mean. They cleared all the land behind us after the war. It was supposed to be the next Levittown. But it was a stupid idea."

"Levittown?"

"No, silly. That was a *great* idea. I read where it sold out in just a few weeks. But that was because they built it where there was work. Maybe not right there *in* Levittown, but close enough to where people could commute.

"What was there like that around here? It was all factory work back then. Plants and mills. The men who worked in them *already* lived here. So, when everything dried up after the war, so did the big 'development.' I don't know who owns that land now, but it can't be worth anything."

"You know a lot about land, huh?"

"Well, not like you. I mean, not like a real-estate person. But I love reading about houses. Little ones, not big mansions. I like looking at pictures of houses in faraway places, and thinking about the people who live in them."

"Like Levittown?"

"Yes. But, you know, those little houses, they're not like mine."

"What do you mean?"

"Well, they're all alike. They look different from the outside—I think they have five or six different fronts—but inside, they're all the *exact* same. It would be like living in one of those housing projects, only all on the first floor."

"No, it wouldn't," Dett said, steering onto Tussy's block.

"Why do you say that?" she asked.

"I've never been to Levittown. But it's all individual homes, isn't it? They may be all the same, but each little house, somebody *owns* it. It's yours. You don't have people on top of you, or below you. You have some . . . privacy."

"I've never seen a project, except in magazines. They look like awful places to live."

"They are."

"Oh," she said, as Dett pulled the car to the curb in front of her house.

He shut off the ignition, climbed out, walked around behind the car, and opened Tussy's door. She held out her hand. He gently took her elbow as she exited, then dropped his grip when she stood up. They walked to her front door, shoulders touching, hands at their sides.

"It was a lovely evening," Tussy said, facing him. "I'll never forget it."

"Neither will I."

"I . . ." Tussy looked around furtively, then whispered, "Could you really do it? Come back so nobody would see you?"

"I promise," Dett said. "But it'll be at least an hour, maybe more."

"I'm not sleepy," she said. "There's a back door. But it's pitch-black dark out behind the houses. Are you sure you can—?"

"I'm sure, Tussy. I promise I am."

1959 October 06 Tuesday 02:00

"Lights," the spotter called from behind his binoculars. His partner waited, notebook in hand.

"On-off . . . two, three, four. Brights. Off."

"That's him, then."

"Yeah."

"What should we do?"

"Nothing," the rifleman said. "He knows how to find us. He only signaled so we wouldn't mistake him for a hostile."

"He's off the screen. Now where did he—?"

"He's inside," the rifleman said, gesturing for silence as he swung his weapon around to cover the doorway.

Thirty seconds later, the man in the alpaca suit stepped onto the top floor of the warehouse. He held a small flashlight, the beam aimed at his face, as if holding out his passport to border guards.

When Tussy heard the tap at her back door, she opened it instantly.

"You shouldn't do that, not without looking first," Dett said, gently. "How could you be sure it was me?"

"Well, who *else* would be knocking at my door in the middle of the night?"

"I don't know. But still . . ."

"Oh, come on in," Tussy said, pointing at the kitchen table. She had changed into a pair of jeans, rolled up to mid-calf, and a man's flannel shirt, the sleeves pushed back to her elbows. She was barefoot, and her face had been scrubbed free of makeup. "How do you take it?" she asked, as Dett sat down.

"Take . . . ?"

"Coffee. My goodness."

"Oh. Black, please."

"Why are you . . . staring like that."

"I'm sorry," he said, dropping his gaze. "It's just . . . Remember, before, when I was off by so much? When I was guessing how old you are? Well, now you look like you're not even *that* old."

"That's very sweet of you to say," she said, laughing. "But if I had to spend another minute in that girdle, I'd get blood clots, I swear."

Dett ducked his head, not saying anything.

"You changed, too," Tussy said. "Boy, I can understand why nobody would see you, dressed like that. Where did you get all that black stuff?"

"They're work clothes," Dett said. "Uh, for when I have to walk around certain kinds of property. Sometimes, you can't wear good clothes. They'd get ruined in a minute. Stuff like this, even if I get them all dirty, it wouldn't show."

"I know what you mean. Some nights, my uniform looks like I'm wearing what everybody had for dinner."

She placed a steaming mug in front of Dett. He sipped it, said, "This is really good."

Tussy sat across from him. She lit a cigarette, and left it smoldering in an ashtray while she went to the refrigerator for a small bottle of cream. "Fireball," she called. "Come on, boy. I've got your favorite cocktail."

"I thought cats don't come when you—" Dett interrupted himself when he saw Fireball enter the kitchen and stalk haughtily over to the saucer of cream Tussy had placed on the floor.

1959 October 06 Tuesday 02:48

"You're out pretty late tonight, Holden."

"Well, there was a lot going on, Sherman. 'Specially for a Monday night."

"Is that right?"

"Yes, sir! I got my logbook all ready for you," Holden said. "See?"

"You do a beautiful job, Holden," the big detective said. "I wish I had ten men like you. Let's have a look. Hmmm . . . a couple of new ones, huh? Never saw these before."

"The Buick? There was a man and a girl in it. Well, not so much *in* it. They was standing around, talking."

"You hear what they were talking about?"

"Sort of. It wasn't any of the stuff you said to be sure and listen for, Sherman, I know that. Just about growing up and things. The girl told him about her parents being killed."

"Killed?" Sherman Layne said, taking care to keep his voice level.

"By a drunk driver," Holden said, proud that he had remembered. "It was a long time ago."

"A blond girl? Kind of short? Chubby?"

"That's right! Boy oh boy, Sherman. You must be as smart as Sherlock Holmes in the movies."

Tussy Chambers? He repeated the name to himself, as he copied down the license number of the Buick Holden had discovered.

"And I got something else, too!" Holden said, excitedly. "About the Cadillac? I never seen it before. And I couldn't see the people inside, neither. Where they were parked, I couldn't get close enough to hear what they was saying, but I know the voice, Sherman. Of the girl, I mean."

"Who was she?"

"I don't know her name, Sherman. But I know her voice. It was a colored girl."

"Out here? In your section?"

"Yes, sir! And that's not all, Sherman. I know her name. Part of her name, anyway."

"Slow down, Holden. Easy . . . That's right. Let's you and me go sit in the car, where we can discuss this like professionals."

"In your car, Sherman? The police car?"

"The *unmarked* car, Holden. Detectives don't use black-and-whites, right?"

"Right!"

The two men walked over to Sherman's Ford and climbed in. Sherman let Holden devour the interior with his eyes for a couple of minutes, then said, "Tell me about the girl, Holden."

"She was a colored girl, Sherman."

"Yes. I wrote that down, Holden. But you said you knew her name . . . ?"

"Kitty," Holden said. "That's what the man called her."

"You sure he didn't say 'kitten,' now? That's what some guys call their girlfriends. You know, like 'honey,' or something like that?"

"No, *sir.* I heard it plain. 'Kitty.' He called her that a lot. 'Kitty.' Plain as day."

Might be a street name, Sherman thought to himself. *But I can't see any Darktown working girl coming way out here to turn a trick.*

"But, listen, Sherman. There's something else. See, the man she was with, I heard his name, too."

"And what was that, Holden?" Sherman said, feeling his interest fade. Holden always tried his best, but . . .

"Harley," the forest prowler said. "Harley was what she called him."

1959 October 06 Tuesday 05:41

As Carl showed up for work, early as always, Dett and Tussy were falling asleep together, she in her beloved house, Dett in Room 809.

Dioguardi was at his weight bench in the cellar of his restaurant, stripped to a pair of gym shorts and sneakers, seeking that almost-exhausted physical state that unleashed his mind.

Rufus daydreamed of fire.

1959 October 06 Tuesday 08:01

"Come on, Beau. It's a real Indian-summer day. We won't have many more like this before it gets cold out."

"Not today, Cyn. I've got too much work to do."

"You always have work to do. So do I. So does everyone else. But you never get any sun, Beau. That's no good for you. Remember what Dr.—"

"I haven't believed a doctor since I was a kid," Beaumont said, flatly. "Why should I?"

"Oh, forget the doctor, then. But you need to get out, get some fresh air. You could play a few games of horseshoes with Luther. You know he loves it when you do."

"Luther's fine."

"Beau, please."

"Cyn, you know how long it takes to roll this damn wheelchair out of here?"

"Well, you *could* go straight out the back, through that little doorway, if you'd only let me—"

"What? Tear the cellar apart, rip out the stairs, build a whole bunch of . . . We can't have that kind of work done on this house, honey. We can't let outsiders down there. And if we just used our own men, it would take months. The garage, that's our escape hatch, remember? We could leave from there and never go near a main road for miles. So it was worth whatever time and money it took to get that built. But just so you could wheel me straight out to the backyard? No."

"Well, even if you won't let me build what it takes to make it easy, that doesn't mean you can't go at all," Cynthia said, walking behind Beaumont and pulling the wheelchair toward her. "Now, come on!"

1959 October 06 Tuesday 08:19

"You know full well I'm meeting Royal Beaumont himself this very afternoon, Sean," Shalare said to the bulky man seated across from him in his upstairs office.

"I do, Mickey. And your timing is a thing of beauty, as always."

"So I need to know," Shalare went on, as if the other man had not spoken, "what it is, exactly, I'll be offering him."

"Offering him? Why, this whole town, son. And everything in it. Dioguardi's been told, and he'll *do* as he's told. Once the election's over, for all we care, they can go at each other like rats and terriers."

Shalare templed his fingertips, touched the tip of his nose, then said, "The way Beaumont looks at it, offering him this town, Sean, that's like offering a man sex with his own wife."

"Oh? You *did* say Beaumont's worried enough about Dioguardi that he's brought in a specialist."

"I did."

"Doesn't seem to have actually *done* anything, this man, does he?"

"There's those two of Dioguardi's men that—"

"Ah, you're not telling me that Beaumont had to send for outside help to handle something like *that,* are you?"

"No. You're right there," Shalare admitted. "But, just because you can't see the miners, it doesn't mean the coal's not being dug."

"Let me tell you something about trains, Mickey Shalare," the bulky man said, pointing a stubby finger for emphasis. "You can control the conductor, you can control the engineer, but it's the men who lay the tracks who get to say where it ends up going."

"That's all well said," Shalare replied, unruffled. "But we've been watching Locke City a long time, now. Getting the feel of the land before we plant our crops. And this is what I know about Royal Beaumont: he's one of your hard men. The genuine article. Hear me, the man's a pit bull, veteran of a hundred fights. You pull his teeth, he'll still try and gum you to death. A man like him, he may come at you like a locomotive, but it'll be on tracks he laid himself."

"That's the way he negotiates? Or is he—?"

"All in," Shalare said, as if reluctantly proud of his adversary.

"I should hope it wouldn't come to that," Sean said, judiciously. "But there's too much riding on this for any one man to be allowed to derail *our* train. Should it come to it, your Mr. Beaumont's not the only one who can call in a specialist."

1959 October 06 Tuesday 10:12

"A ringer!" Luther yelled. "Look, Roy! I got one!"

"Go for the six-pack, Luther," Seth urged him on. "You can do it."

The slack-mouthed man hesitated, one of the custom-made "turn shoes" the Beaumonts had given him last Christmas steady in his hand.

"Bring it home, Luther," Beaumont said. "One more and we've got forty. That'll teach these young bucks to mess with old stags like us."

Luther stood at the edge of the platform, sighted down the length of the pit to the stake, exhaled slowly, and delicately rainbowed the shoe through the air.

"Damn!" Harley said. "You nailed it, Luther. We're done."

Luther's slack mouth flopped into a wide grin. Beaumont rolled over to him, and extended his hand.

"Easiest hundred bucks I ever made," he said. "A pure slaughter. You and me, Luther, we're a hell of a team."

"Well, you got most of the points, Roy. Nobody pitches as good as you."

"Yeah? Well, it wasn't me that went back to back and slammed the door on them, Luther."

The slack-mouthed man pumped Beaumont's hand, speechless.

Cynthia caught her brother's eye, and beamed her approval. Their love arced between them, as palpable as an electric current.

1959 October 06 Tuesday 10:28

"Yes?" Dett said, his voice as inanimate as the receiver he was holding.

"He'd like to see you." Cynthia's businesslike voice.

"When?"

"That would depend on your . . . schedule. He knows you're working on an important project."

Dett felt the muscles in his neck unclench. *If he wants it for lunch today—anytime today—I can't do it. But if you don't come when they call, they start thinking you've slipped the leash. . . .* "How would tomorrow be?" he said.

"If that's the soonest you can make it, that would be fine."

Was there something in her voice?

"I'm still collecting some of the information he wanted," Dett said. "I expect to have a good bit more of it come in sometime today. Tomorrow, my report would be more complete."

"I understand. Tomorrow then. You have no time preference?"

"No."

"Sometime in the evening, then. Say, eight?"

"I'll be there," Dett said.

1959 October 06 Tuesday 10:33

Tussy stood before her bedroom mirror, studying her face for the tenth time that morning. *Oh, what is* wrong *with you?* she thought. *I don't care if you only got a couple of hours sleep, you don't gop on the war paint in the daytime. Stop stalling and start cooking!* She brushed her tousled hair vigorously, then gave herself a sharp crack on the bottom with the hairbrush. *All right, now!* She nodded briskly at the mirror, grabbed a fresh pair of dungarees and pulled them on, holding her breath to fasten the waist.

"And what are *you* looking at?" she said to Fireball, who was curled up on her bed, inspecting her.

What would he want for lunch? she mused, as she walked through her kitchen, idly opening and closing the overhead cabinets. *Some men like a big steak. I still have time to go out and—No, wait! That's too much for lunch. Maybe tuna salad and some . . . Oh,* damn*! I should have just asked him. . . .*

1959 October 06 Tuesday 10:42

"Where does a man take a girl like you?" Rufus said to Rosa Mae.

"*Take* me? Rufus Hightower, I—"

"I didn't mean for it to come out like that, Rosa Mae. I was trying to ask, when you go out, a woman like you, where does a man take you? I know you're not going for some juke joint, but you don't seem like you're the nightclub type, either. I . . . I guess I don't know much—hell, I don't know *anything*—about where a respectable woman would go on a date. The movies, maybe?"

"Are you taking a survey, Rufus? Because, if you are, there's a whole lot of women at my church you could go and ask. I'm sure they'd be happy to talk to you."

"Why you want to make this so hard, Rosa Mae?"

"Me?"

"You, girl. You know how I feel about you. I . . . declared myself, didn't I?"

"You said some things. But am I supposed to know you . . . like me just because you talk to me?"

"Because of what I talk to you *about*," Rufus said, earnestly. "About what's important to me. What I hope will be important to you, too."

"Rufus, if you want to go out on a date with me, why can't you just ask me, like any regular man?"

"Because I'm *not* a regular man, Rosa Mae. You know that. You know that because I showed it to you. That's what I was trying to say, before. I asked you about . . . where you go and all because that's where I want to take you."

"Like a real gentleman? That doesn't sound like—"

"Like Rufus? Like the Rufus you *think* you know, even after all the times I've talked to you? I swear, little sugar, if your daddy was around, I'd go and ask him before I asked you, if that's the way you wanted me to be."

Rosa Mae stepped back from Rufus, her amber eyes flashing, as if in sync with her pulse. "You would?"

"On my heart," he said.

"Then you go and talk with Moses," she said, turning on her heel and walking off.

1959 October 06 Tuesday 11:08

Dett drank four glasses of tepid tap water, then did his exercises, his mind taking him to that colorless no-place he could induce at will.

He dressed slowly. A fresh-pressed pair of chinos, a dark-green chambray shirt, oxblood brogans whose heavy construction concealed their steel toes.

Dett slipped his brass knuckles into the side pocket of his leather jacket, and dropped his straight razor into a slot he had sewn in just for that purpose. The derringer, chambered for the same .45 caliber as his other pistols, fit snugly inside his left sleeve.

He locked his room door behind him, and rang for the elevator car.

"Morning, suh," Moses said.

"Morning to you," Dett replied.

As the car descended, Dett asked, "You're not going to say anything about that package I left with you?"

"Package, suh?"

"You could teach some of these young men think they're so sharp a thing or two," Dett said. "Another day okay with you?"

"One day the same as the other round here, suh."

"How are you enjoying Locke City so far, Mr. Dett?" Carl called out, as Dett stepped off the elevator car and started across the lobby.

"It seems like a good place to do business," Dett said, not breaking stride.

1959 October 06 Tuesday 11:11

"Time for another coffee break," Sherman Layne told the clerk at the car-rental agency.

"How long a break?" the young man asked, worriedly.

"Ten minutes, tops," Layne promised him. A quick phone call earlier that day had identified the plate on the Buick logged in by Holden as belonging to the agency. The clerk would have pulled the matching paper for him, but Sherman Layne was a man who believed in collecting information, not giving it away.

Him again! he said to himself. *Changing rides, are you, Walker Dett? And what does a man like you want with Tussy Chambers?*

He strolled out behind the agency building, where the clerk was puffing on a cigarette. "Ever get yourself stopped by the police?" Layne asked the young man. "For speeding, maybe. Or being parked where you shouldn't be?"

"No, sir," the clerk said, nervously.

"Next time you do, you give them this," Layne said, handing over one of his business cards, with "OK/1" handwritten on the back.

1959 October 06 Tuesday 11:22

"He driving a Buick now, boss," Rufus said into the pay phone. "Brand-new one. Shiny brown color. Let me give you the plate."

"Who was that, Sal?" a scrawny man in a white shirt and dark suit pants asked, when the phone was put down.

"That was the future, Rocco," Dioguardi told him. "For anyone smart enough to see it."

"No flowers today?" Tussy said, as she stood aside for Dett to enter.

"I didn't think—"

"Oh, don't be such a stick!" she said, grinning. "I was only teasing you."

"I guess I'm no good at telling."

"Well, when I make this face," Tussy said, turning the corners of her mouth down, "that's the tip-off."

"But you weren't—"

"Walker, what am I going to do with you? That was teasing, too!"

"I . . ."

"I wish you could see the look on your face. Honestly! Well, come on, let's get you some food. Just put your jacket over the back of the couch there, if you like."

"Where's Fireball?" Dett asked, sitting down at the kitchen table.

"Who knows?" Tussy said, airily. "He comes and goes just as he pleases."

"You mean he can get out by himself?"

"Sure," she said. "The back door's got a hole cut in it for him, down at the bottom. My dad did that, a long time ago. He used to go out a lot more than he does now, but he still likes the idea that he *can,* you know?"

"Yeah," Dett said. "I do know. Sometimes, all you have is the things you think about."

"What do you mean?" she asked, her eyes alive and attentive.

"Well, things can happen. The bank can take your house—not *your* house, not with you never missing a payment," Dett added immediately, seeing a dart of fear flash across Tussy's face. "But . . . well, you can lose *things*. Like a car being repossessed, or a business going bad. But the *idea* of things, those you get to keep, no matter where you are."

"Like dreams, you mean? Wishes?"

"No. More like . . . When I was in the army, some of the men I served with, what really kept them going was letters from home. But not everybody got those letters. The guys who didn't, some of them built their own. In their head, like. The *idea* of a girlfriend, or a hometown, or people that cared about them—I don't know— things that *could* have been. Or things that could come true, some-day. Some guys, that was all they could talk about."

"But if those things never happened—"

"They *could* happen," Dett said, insistently. "I don't mean fools who dreamed about being millionaires—or . . . there was this one guy, Big Wayne, he was always talking about how he was going to write a book. Not like that. I mean, things that really could happen, if you got lucky enough."

"Fireball, when he goes out, I don't think he . . . chases girl cats, anymore," Tussy said. "He used to come back just *mangled* from some of the fights he got into with the other toms. But with that door still there, maybe he thinks he *could* go out and . . . be like he was before. Is that what you mean, Walker?"

"It's exactly what I mean," Dett said.

1959 October 06 Tuesday 12:36

"You have to listen to me, Uriah."

"That's not my name. Not no more," the tall, rangy youth said to his sister. He was wearing a long black undertaker's coat and matching narrow-brimmed black hat, with three orange feathers in the headband.

"I don't care what you call yourself," she said, firmly. "I didn't cut out of school and come all the way over here to listen to any more of your foolishness."

"*My* foolishness? It ain't me saying those mangy-ass little white boys got themselves some real guns. Where'd you hear that, any-way?"

"I can't tell you," Kitty said. "But it's from someone who knows."

"I *know* you ain't keeping company with none of those—"

"I'm not one of your little gang boys, Uriah Nickens," she said, facing him squarely, "so don't you dare use that tone of voice with me."

"You heard it at school?"

"What if I did?"

"Yeah. What I thought. Those white boys think they slick, spread the word they got cannons, maybe we don't show up tomorrow night. Punk out. Wouldn't they fucking love *that*!"

"Do you have to talk that way?"

"I'll talk . . . I'm sorry, Kitty-girl. You my baby sister. Always will be, no matter what the old man say. Look, I think I got it scoped out, what happened. It's just a bluff, like I said."

"Uriah, you know I don't lie. Just because I can't tell you where I heard it, that doesn't mean it's not true. If you go and fight, you could end up . . ."

"You don't know nothing about our life, the life we live, Kitty. Some people got farms, some people got houses, some people got cars. What *we* got is that we're the South Side Kings. And every King knows, when we roll on another club, he might not be coming back. But if one of us punked out, *ever* punked out, then we're *all* dead, or might as well be."

"You could always come back home, Uriah. Daddy didn't mean those things he said. I know he didn't. You come back, and I'll stand right there with you, I promise."

"I know you would, Kitty-girl. And I hope you find the life you want for yourself. College and all. But me, this is my life. Back there, I'm Uriah Nickens, the nigger-boy dropout nothing. If I'm lucky, maybe I get me a job cleaning some white man's toilets. Here, I'm Preacher, President of the South Side Kings. And you know what, baby sis? I'd rather die where I stand than live back where I came from."

1959 October 06 Tuesday 12:52

The sky had broken its morning promise. A dull, leaden rain slanted down with the self-assurance of an experienced conqueror. A pink-and-black '58 Edsel Corsair swayed down the two-lane blacktop, yawing badly at each curve. The turnoff was unmarked, but the driver had been thoroughly briefed, and recognized the lightning-scarred trunk of what had once been a magnificent white-oak tree.

The Edsel slowed considerably as the blacktop turned to hard-packed dirt, passing ramshackle houses so deteriorated a stranger to the area would have thought them abandoned. The houses were scattered carelessly, like garbage tossed from the window of a passing car. *Just like home,* the driver thought. *Only I don't live here anymore.*

The house at the top of a rise was little more than a cabin, but it looked well maintained, with a fresh coat of barn-red paint and a cedar-shake roof, faded to a soft gray. The surrounding yard was more forest than lawn, with a wide swath of macadam laid through it, branching off to a detached two-car garage.

The Edsel pulled up to the garage, and Ruth Keene, proprietress of Locke City's finest whorehouse, stepped out.

The door to the cabin opened; Detective Sherman Layne stood there a long moment. Then he walked over to her.

1959 October 06 Tuesday 13:31

"Can I talk to you?"

"You talking to me now," Moses said to Rufus.

"Not like this. I want to sit down with you."

"After work," the elderly man said.

"You want to meet me at—"

"You know where I got my little office?"

"There?"

"After work," Moses said, again.

"I don't like talking business with so many white people around."

"When's the last time you saw any white people down there?"

"Fair enough, what you say. But . . . this is private, man."

"So's my office."

Rufus looked into the old man's eyes. *Stubborn old mule,* he thought. *But he's holding the case ace, here. And he knows it.* "Thanks, Moses," he said, humbly.

1959 October 06 Tuesday 13:33

"What is this?" Dett asked Tussy, touching a dark-green leaf lightly with his fork.

"That's basil leaf. Sweet basil, they call it. When I make my tuna salad, I always put some across the top. It adds something to the flavor. And it looks pretty, too, the way parsley does. I always put a sprig of parsley when I serve anything. See that pot on the windowsill there? I grow the basil myself. You have to keep it indoors; it won't survive a good frost."

"It's good," Dett said, chewing the basil leaf slowly.

"Oh, you're not supposed to *eat* it."

"Why not?"

"I . . . I don't know, now that you say it. That's just what the waiter told me."

"Where?"

"In this place where I went out to eat. An Italian restaurant. I had a veal cutlet, and this leaf was on it. I asked the waiter what it was, and he told me. So, later, I tried it myself. Putting it on food, I mean. I like to do that, try new stuff. Don't you?"

"I guess I never think about it."

"Maybe, working at the diner, I get the idea that food means a lot to people. They're always talking about it, aren't they?"

"Not the people I deal with."

"Well, I guess people are different around here—we even have a Businessman's Special at the diner. I had dinner with a man once, and he said it all went on his expense account."

"Big spender," Dett said, dryly.

"That's what Gloria said! I mean, not the words, but the same way you said them."

"Well, I thought women liked it if a man spent money on them."

"Some girls do. You know what my mom always said? She said the man who spends a lot of money is all well and good to go on a date with; but the man who's careful with his money, that's the one you want to marry."

"But the man you married—"

"Joey wasn't careful with anything," she said, sorrowfully. "But, by then, my mom wasn't around for me to listen to."

"Your father wouldn't have liked him, either."

"No, he sure wouldn't," Tussy said. "Daddy was always joking that I wouldn't even be allowed to go out on dates until I was twenty-one. He didn't mean it—I went to school dances with boys—but he looked them over *careful,* you can bet on that."

"I don't blame him."

"Would you be that same way? If you had a little girl, I mean."

"I'll never have a little girl."

"Why not? Plenty of men get married at—"

"I'll never get married, Tussy," he said.

In the silence that followed, Dett plucked the sprig of parsley from his plate and put it into his mouth.

"You're a strange man," Tussy finally said.

"Because I'll never get married?"

"No, because you eat basil!" she snapped. "I think plenty of men are never going to get married. It's probably more fun being a bachelor. But you're the first man I ever met that I was . . . that I had a date with, that ever came right out and said it like that."

"Why wouldn't they?"

"Well, come on! If you were a girl, and a man said he was never going to get married, would you go on seeing him? I mean, I know *some* girls would, if he was . . . generous and all. One of the girls who works at the diner, her boyfriend is *already* married. But . . ."

"I have to tell you the truth," Dett said.

"Why?" Tussy said, getting to her feet and starting to clear the dishes. "Why do you have to tell me the truth?"

"I . . . I'm not exactly sure, Tussy. But I know I have to."

"But you still ask me to go out with you? Even though you're never going to be my . . . boyfriend, even? Because, if you want a girl just for . . . fun, I'm not her."

"I know that."

"How?" she demanded. "How do you know all these things?"

"I promise to tell you," Dett said. "I *have* to tell you, or this would all be for nothing. But I can't do it now."

Tussy snatched Dett's empty plate from the table and brought it over to the kitchen sink. She stood there, with her back toward him, and said, "You're never coming back again, are you? To Locke City, I mean?"

"No."

"It would be easy to lie. Just say you *might* be. In your business, that's always possible. Something like that."

"It would be a lie."

"What do you want from me, then?" she said, turning to face him. Her mouth was set in a firm line, but her green eyes glistened with tears.

"I want to tell you my story," he said. "I waited a long time."

"For what?"

"To find you," Dett said.

1959 October 06 Tuesday 13:38

"This place is really . . . impressive," Ruth said. "I never saw a house built like it, one huge room, with no walls."

"I did it myself," Sherman told her. "It started out as kind of a hobby. I bought the land when I was just a kid. It was a few years into the Depression. I was already a cop, so I wasn't worried about having a job, but I couldn't afford to buy a house. And what does a man living alone need a house for, anyway? So I thought I'd invest in a piece of land and sell it someday. Like the big shots do, only just this little bit.

"I started out by clearing the land. Coming up here on my days off. I guess that's when the idea came to me."

"How long did it take you to finish it?"

"It's still not finished," Sherman said, ruefully. "At the rate I'm going, it may never be. But it's good enough to live in. For me, anyway."

"Where did you learn how to do all the . . . things you have to do? To build a house, I mean."

"I just read about it. At the library. They've got books on everything there. Plumbing—you can't get city water out this far; I've got a well—electricity, everything. I didn't always get it right the first time, but I just kept worrying at it until I solved it."

"Like one of your cases?"

"That's *exactly* what it's like," Sherman said, looking at Ruth with open admiration. "You collect as much information as you can. Then you take whatever you want to test—it doesn't matter if we're talking about a plumbing line or a theory—and you try it out, see if it'll hold up.

"You put a lot of pressure on it," the big man explained. "Work slow and careful. Keep good notes. Check and recheck. Never let your emotions get in the way. Just because you *want* something to turn out a certain way doesn't mean it will. If you let what you want . . . influence you, the whole thing falls down."

Ruth made a complete circuit of the big room, then seated herself elegantly on a couch made of wide, rough-hewn pine planks, covered with a heavy Indian-pattern blanket.

"How did you learn the carpentry part?" she asked. "Was that from books, too? Or did your father teach you?"

"The only thing my father ever taught me was to fear him," Sherman Layne said, his voice as quiet as cancer. "Until the day I taught him to fear me."

1959 October 06 Tuesday 13:47

"What do you mean, 'find' me?" Tussy said.

"Would it be enough if I promise to tell you everything?" Dett replied. "Not now, before I leave. If you don't want to see any more of me until then, I'll understand. I wouldn't blame you."

"I thought you were going to take me out again tonight," she said, making a pouty motion with her mouth.

"I *am*. I mean, I'll take you anywhere you want to—"

"You know where I'd like to go? The drive-in. I haven't been there in a million years. But I looked in the paper this morning, and *North by Northwest* is playing. I really wanted to see that one."

"Sure. What time should I—?"

"Well, if we get there by seven-thirty, we'll have plenty of time to eat and everything."

"Do you know a place?"

"To eat? No, I mean right there at the drive-in, silly."

"Oh. Okay."

"Haven't you ever done that? Eat dinner at a drive-in?"

"I've never been."

"In your whole life?"

"Not even once."

"Oh, you'll *love* it. It's so much nicer than in a movie theater. Like having the show playing just for you."

"If you like it so much, how come you don't go more?"

"It's really for kids. Or people *with* kids. For the teenagers around here, the drive-in's just another place to make out. They wouldn't care if the screen was blank."

Dett was quiet for a few seconds. Then he said, "That tuna was delicious, Tussy. The best I ever had."

"You're just saying that."

"I'm not. I don't do that. Just say things, I mean. Every time I have tuna salad, from now on, I'm going to ask for basil on it. And a little piece of parsley on the side."

"Well, most places have parsley. We serve it at the diner with certain dishes. Like it always comes with the meatloaf. But basil, I don't know."

"I can just buy some. In a store, I mean. And take it with me."

"Oh, people *do* do that. One old man, he's a regular, a real sweetheart, flirts with all the girls, he always brings his own bottle of sauce. I don't know what's in it, but he puts it on *everything*. Meat, fish . . . even eggs. I don't know if the basil would stay fresh, though."

"It would if you bought it that same day."

"I guess it would. But it seems like a lot of trouble."

"No," Dett said. "That isn't trouble."

1959 October 06 Tuesday 13:56

"Do a lot of people know you live out here?" Ruth asked.

"I'm . . . not sure. My mail comes to the post office; I've got a box there. But this place, it's not a secret."

"It doesn't look like you get a lot of visitors. Or else you have a woman come in and clean for you."

"I never have visitors," Sherman said.

"Until me," Ruth said.

"You're not a visitor."

"What am I, then?"

"What you've been for a long time," Sherman Layne said. "The person I trust. The only one."

1959 October 06 Tuesday 13:57

"You ever get tired of all this?" the man behind the binoculars asked the rifleman.

"This?"

"Waiting. Waiting all the time."

"Any job there is, there's always some waiting in it," the rifleman said.

"You never get bored, just sitting around, doing nothing?"

"What we do, it only takes a couple of seconds," the rifleman said. "But waiting to do it, that's part of doing it right."

1959 October 06 Tuesday 14:04

"Would you like to see my garden?" Tussy asked. "You couldn't have seen much in the dark, last night."

"Yes," Dett said, getting to his feet.

Tussy led him out the back door. She pointed to a neat square of plowed and furrowed earth. "My mother started it," she said, "before I was even born. That parsley you had? I grew it right here. I've got fresh carrots, onions, radishes, all kinds of vegetables. Better than anything you could buy in the store. My dad always said he was going to put a beehive back there. One of those you build yourself. We'd have fresh honey then, too. But Mom said she wasn't going to have a bunch of bees buzzing around her every time she went outside."

Fireball left the house, moving slowly and purposefully.

"He's playing like he's stalking a bird," Tussy said. "He hasn't caught one since my thirteenth birthday. He brought it home. For me, like a present. I cried and cried. My dad explained it was just him being a cat—he couldn't help himself. But I think he—Fireball, I mean—I think he understood how upset he'd made me, because he never brought one home again."

1959 October 06 Tuesday 14:09

"Is there a basement?" Ruth asked.

"Well . . . no. The foundation is really just some big pieces of rock I hauled myself."

"Oh. And the garage, it doesn't have heat, does it?"

"The garage? No. It's all wired, for when I have to see what I'm doing when I work on my car, or put some project together, but you wouldn't want to go out there in the winter without your coat."

"It's all so . . . open in here."

"You don't like it, Ruth?"

"I *love* it. It's beautiful, Sherman. I was just looking for a place where you could . . . build me something?"

"Build you . . . I don't understand."

"Like in my blue room," she said, looking him squarely in the face. "Only right here."

1959 October 06 Tuesday 14:11

"You sure I'm the man you want with you for this, Mickey?"

"Ah, Brian, how many times is it I'm to be telling you the same thing? Now, just drive, boyo. You be the pilot; I'll be the navigator," Shalare said.

"Not to drive the bloody car, Mickey. I mean that other thing you said."

"All you have to do is use your eyes, Big Brian. Make them into little cameras. Whatever you see, it's gold for us. I don't know if they're going to let you in, keep you outside, stash you someplace else . . . but it doesn't matter. Wherever they take you, wherever they let you be, it's going to be someplace we've not ever seen before."

"Why is that so important, then?"

"Because we may have to come back someday, Brian. Only without the invite."

1959 October 06 Tuesday 14:16

"Why?" Ruth demanded.

"Why what?" Sherman said. Knowing he was evading her question; knowing she knew.

"Why can't you trust me the way you say you do?"

"I do trust you, Ruth. You know my . . . you know things about me nobody else does."

"That's not trusting, Sherman. That's trusting not to tell. There's a big difference."

"What would be trusting you?" the detective asked. A wave of depersonalization washed over him. He could see himself, seated across from Ruth. *Lean back to invite a confidence; lean forward to intimidate; work the middle distance to assure the suspect that whatever he's about to say is going to stay between us.* His shoulders trembled as he shook off the wave. Sherman Layne knew how to do that. He had been practicing since he was a child.

"Building me what I asked you for would be a start."

"Ruth, I don't think of you like that."

"But you *said* . . . I mean, when I said I'd do anything for you, I meant it. And when you asked me out here, I thought . . ."

"You don't understand," he said, in the hushed tone used for sharing secrets. "What you . . . think I do . . . out at your place? You're wrong."

"But I don't *care* what you—"

"Just listen, okay?" Sherman said. "Please?"

1959 October 06 Tuesday 14:55

"Damn, I'd hate to find this place after dark, Mickey. Are you sure we're going right?"

"If the directions he gave us are true, we are," Shalare said.

"Are you thinking . . . ?"

"Ambush? No, Brian. I'm not saying Beaumont's not capable of it, mind. But he's too smart for such a stunt now."

"Now?"

"He'll be wanting to hear what we've got to say first," Shalare said. "That's what I'd be doing myself."

1959 October 06 Tuesday 15:03

"You got a call, Rufe. On the pay phone, down in the kitchen. Man say you should call home. Hope nothing's wrong, bro."

"Thanks, Earl. Probably just one of my dumb-fuck cousins. Got a couple of them staying at my crib. Probably can't figure out how to turn on the stove or something. Country boys, you know?"

1959 October 06 Tuesday 15:41

"*There* it is," Shalare said, pointing at the black boulder. "The perfect landmark, isn't it? Looks like God himself tossed a giant lump of coal into those birch trees."

"Aye," the prizefighter said, steering carefully. "And here comes the . . . curves, just like he said."

"Remember what I told you, Big Brian."

"Eyes like a camera."

"Yes. And ears like a pair of tape recorders."

"I doubt they're going to be talking to me, Mick. They'll probably just put me in some—"

"Lymon's been good for more than helping us see the future, Brian. He's told us a bit about some of Beaumont's boys, too. And if luck smiles on us today . . ."

1959 October 06 Tuesday 15:49

"What?" Rufus said.

"You know that boy, Preacher? He's the head of the—"

"I know. Come on, man. I'm at work."

"He's been around," Darryl said. "Wants to buy something. Thought we might have it."

"We?"

"At the yard. Look, I told him, come back tonight."

"Why you do that?"

"When you come by, I tell you, brother. But, hear me, this is a decision we got to make. Tonight."

1959 October 06 Tuesday 15:51

Seth emerged from the guard cottage and walked slowly over to Shalare's Chrysler, a shotgun in his right hand.

"Help you folks?" he said, as the driver's-side window descended.

"I've got Mr. Shalare here," Brian said, "to see Mr. Beaumont."

"Right on time, too," Seth said, glancing at his wristwatch. "Hey!" he said, suddenly. "You're not Brian O'Sullivan, the fighter, are you? I could swear—"

"That's me, for true," Brian said, grinning broadly. "Hard to mistake a mug like mine, once you've laid eyes on it, I'll bet." He extended his hand.

Without taking his eyes off the men in the car, Seth tossed the shotgun from his right hand to his left, and used the gentle momentum to bring his open hand up to take Brian's offered grip. "I was at the Paladium in Akron the night you fought Buster Blaine," he said. "You've got one of iron and the other of steel, just like people say."

"I sure needed *both* that night. Fighting Buster was like punching smoke."

"That's right! I told my pals he could dance all night but sooner or later Brian O'Sullivan would land one. And that was all it took."

"Did you bet on me, then?"

"Didn't I? A double sawbuck, I went for. The odds were . . . well, they were pretty good," Seth said, embarrassed.

"Well, they should have been," Brian assured him. "Buster Blaine is a better boxer in his sleep than I ever was awake."

"Faster, maybe," Seth said, stoutly. "But sure not better. You were never a man to get a break from the judges. I thought you got jobbed when you fought John Henry Jefferson. By rights, they're supposed to give you points for being aggressive."

"Nah, he won that one," Brian said. "My own mother would have scored it for him. If I could have caught him, even one time, maybe it would have ended otherwise, but—"

"No 'maybe' about it," Seth said, conviction ringing through his voice. "If you'd of ever caught him, it would have ended, all right!"

1959 October 06 Tuesday 15:59

"Oh! I'm sorry," Tussy said, belatedly covering her mouth as she yawned. "I didn't realize how tired I am."

"Are you sure you still want to go out tonight?"

"I am *absolutely* sure. All I need is a little nap."

"All right. Should I come back in—?"

"Just a catnap. Only an hour or so," she said. "I'd rather you stayed . . . if you want."

S eth walked beside Shalare's Chrysler as it slowly crept along the curved drive.

"You can leave it right here," Seth told Brian. Directing his voice to Shalare, he continued, "And you, you can go right in the front door. Just give a knock, and Luther will take care of you from there on."

"Many thanks," Shalare said, opening his door.

"We'll have a wait," Seth said to Brian. "If you like, you can come back and share my guard duty with me. Or I could get you a—"

"Ah, it isn't every day that I meet a man I can talk boxing with," Brian said. "That little house of yours, it wouldn't by any chance have a little refrigerator in it?"

The door opened before Shalare could knock. The slack-mouthed man on the other side of the threshold stared blankly, as if waiting for someone to throw his switch.

Good sweet Jesus, Shalare thought. *The man's a blessed dummy.*

"Come on," Luther said, turning and walking away.

Doesn't search me, lets me walk behind *him—what kind of people does Beaumont have working for him, anyway?*

It took almost a full minute for Luther to wend his way through the house to their destination. *Like a bloody damn museum,* Shalare thought. "Beautiful place, this is," he said aloud.

Luther didn't respond.

They came to a double-width door, the entrance ramp telling Shalare that the room inside was higher than the floor he had been walking on.

Luther strode through the doorway, Shalare three steps behind him. Beaumont was at the other end of the room, seated behind a modern, kidney-shaped desk. Shalare crossed over to him. "Thanks for having me," he said, holding out his hand.

"Thank you for coming," Beaumont said, with equal formality.

Here comes the bone-crusher, Shalare thought, steeling himself as they shook hands. To his surprise, Beaumont's grip was just firm enough to be masculine-polite. One quick, dry squeeze, and it was done.

"Please sit down," Beaumont said. "Can I get you anything? Coffee? A drink?"

"Well, since you're offering, an Irish coffee would be a treat."

"Jameson's good by you?"

"I see you've been doing your homework," Shalare said, grinning broadly. "Good by any son of Erin, and good anytime."

"No homework necessary," Beaumont said. "I fancy it myself. The Jameson's, I mean, not in coffee. That one's an acquired taste, I believe."

"Well, that may be," Shalare said, touching two fingers to his lips. "But I acquired it quite early on."

Luther reappeared, handed Shalare his drink, placed a heavy tumbler full of ice cubes and a fifth of Jameson's on Beaumont's desk, barely moving his head in a "no" gesture as he did, indicating the Irishman was not armed.

Beaumont poured himself a shot of the whiskey, held up his glass. "To friendship," he said.

"To friendship," Shalare echoed.

Each man sipped at his drink. Noticing the black marble ashtray at his elbow, Shalare lit a cigarette. Nodding, as if this confirmed still another point of understanding between them, Beaumont opened his silver cigarette case and lit up himself.

"So," he said.

"I want you to know I appreciate this," Shalare said. "I feel we've a lot to discuss, you and me. And I'm thinking, Royal Beaumont is a man you want to talk with face to face, not over some phone, or through intermediaries."

"As I would have thought of you."

"You'll forgive my bluntness, then," Shalare said. "I wouldn't have you think me impolite, or without proper respect. But I know your time is valuable. So, with your permission, I'll lay out my cards, and let you tell me if you think I've got a hand worth playing."

1959 October 06 Tuesday 16:33

"I'll just wait here," Dett said, tilting his head in the direction of the armchair in the living room. "Okay?"

"Perfect," Tussy said, and walked out of the room.

Dett was halfway through a cigarette when Tussy came back, carrying a pink blanket. Without a word, she curled up on the couch, and pulled the blanket over herself.

Fireball immediately launched himself onto the couch, nestling himself at her feet.

"I think that's why they call them 'catnaps,' " Tussy said, closing her eyes.

1959 October 06 Tuesday 16:58

"There's going to be an election next year . . ." Shalare said. Getting no response from Beaumont, he went on, "The biggest one in the history of this country, from where we sit."

Beaumont said nothing.

Those eyes of his, they look like the sky just before it rains, Shalare thought. "We've all got a stake in this one," he said. "Yes, sure, we all have a stake in *every* one, but this one, it's going to change . . . business, for all of us. Forever."

Beaumont raised his thick eyebrows, but stayed quiet.

"That is, of course, if the right man wins. It's my job to see that he does."

"Your job?" Beaumont said.

"Ah, you're right to put me in my place," Shalare said, with a self-deprecating smile. "It's not my job to make such a grand thing happen, of course. It's my job to do my part. To do what I can do. Whatever I can do. There's people all over this country—all over the world, truth be told—that have the same job. The trick is to make sure all the horses are pulling in the same direction, so that none of us cancel out the others."

"That *would* be quite a trick," Beaumont said.

"Aye. But it's one that can be done, provided each man sees what's in it for himself. And for his people, of course."

"And that's your job? To tell me what's in it for me and my people?"

"It is."

"What are you looking for, exactly?" Beaumont asked.

"Well, the simple answer is . . . votes. Not local votes—we don't care who's the next mayor or city councilman or governor, even. The only thing we care about is the presidential race."

"What makes you think I could—?"

"Because you *do*," Shalare interrupted. "Your machine runs this town like the engine in my car. You built it, you maintain it, and you control it."

"Are we still taking about votes here?"

"That's my point, Mr. Beaumont—"

"Roy."

"And I'm Mickey," Shalare said, bowing his head slightly to show his appreciation of the gesture. "And it's *only* votes we're talking about. Not the casinos, not the clubs, not any of the . . . enterprises that your people control. Rightfully control, I might add. A man's entitled to the fruits of his labor."

"There's some around here who don't agree with you."

"I'll get to that, I promise. But let me just finish—about the votes, I mean. We need every single one, Roy. Come election day, we can't allow anyone inclined to go our way to stay home. And we won't be encouraging visits to the polls by any of those who might be opposed, either."

"It's not going to be a landslide," Beaumont said.

"Right you are! And that's why I'm here, hat in hand, to ask you for this special favor."

"Exactly . . . what?"

"Exactly? I'll tell you exactly, Roy. This is a Republican town, isn't it? On paper, anyway."

"On paper?"

"Well, if someone was to take a poll, right? The local Republican club is the power in Locke City. Everything gets run out of there. The mayor's a Republican, the—"

"And it would be better, for this one election, if they weren't?" Beaumont cut in.

"Much, *much* better," Shalare said, not smiling. "And that's where your organization comes into play. Sure, you've got the judges, the city council, the mayor. But they're not what we're after. To Mr. Royal Beaumont, those are just chess pieces. You've got the ward healers, the precinct captains, the ground-level troops. You've got them all. Not that tool Bobby Wyeth. You. On your payroll, in your debt, following your lead, because that's the way it's always been, here. What we need is for this whole area to turn around."

"Vote Democratic?"

"For this one election *only,*" Shalare said, leaning forward.

"That's a huge effort."

"Yes. Way beyond our reach. But not beyond yours, Roy. You could make it happen. Especially if you started laying in the foundation right now."

"Even so, it would cost a fortune, in time *and* money. Because, from what you're saying, I don't think you want to leave this up to speeches and posters."

"That's right. We need the voting machines to work properly, too," Shalare said, flatly. "But the more the final tally reflects how people in the area actually know they voted, the less . . . attention is drawn."

"So, all over America, there's men like you meeting with men like me," Beaumont said, nodding his head thoughtfully.

"There are. There are areas of entrenchment we can rely on, we believe. The people in power there, they're *already* committed to our side. Nothing but gold and gravy for them if things come out right. Each side can count heads. And each is going to try and poach off the other's land."

"Politicians poach with promises."

"And they all make the same ones," Shalare agreed. "That's why our strategy is to go right into the heart of those places the opposition isn't going to waste any time or money on. Places where they believe they already can count on the vote."

"Locke City."

"Not just Locke City, Roy. We know your reach goes out way past the city limits."

"You may be giving me too much credit."

"More likely, you're giving us too little. No offense, but we've done our homework, too."

"It's a massive move you're proposing."

"We've no dispute about that, Roy. But this game is worth the candle, no matter if it's all burnt by the end."

"More like a stick of dynamite than a candle, Mickey."

"I've had *those* in my hands, too. They work just fine, so long as you throw them quick enough."

"And accurately."

"Yes. That's why we wouldn't even try this area without going to the man who controls it."

"Like I said before, there's those who seem to have a different idea. Or a different ambition, I should say."

"Dioguardi," Shalare said.

"I would have put you on that same list," Beaumont retorted, calm-voiced. "You've been coming from different directions, is all."

"We've never interfered in any of your—"

"No. No, you haven't. And, now that you've laid out your cards, I can see why you've been buying up people in the statehouse."

"And I'll not deny it," the Irishman said. "But it was never the plan to try and move in on—never mind take over—your operations. Hell, man, when it comes to this part of the state, I'd rather have Royal Beaumont in my corner than the governor himself."

"That's what they told you, was it?"

Shalare took a sip of his drink, then raised his eyes to Beaumont's. "That *is* what they said, for a fact," he said, frankly. "We thought there was a hierarchy of some kind. A pyramid, like. So, of course, you start at the top, if you can. But we found out, soon enough, that this state isn't one pyramid, it's a whole row of them. And when it comes to picking your pyramid, you don't look for the tallest one, you look for the one with the broadest base, the one that's been standing the longest. Because that's the one that'll weather any storm."

"That's on the money," Beaumont said. "No matter who wins, we'll still be standing at the end. So what good would it do me and mine for your man to win the next election? It wouldn't change anything around here."

"Ah, that's exactly it! You don't *want* things to change around here. And we're in a position to help you see that through."

"That brings us back to Dioguardi, doesn't it?"

"I do mean Dioguardi. But I don't mean it as you think I do. We both understand that Dioguardi doesn't stand among his men as you do among yours. If he vanished like *this*," Shalare said, making a hand-washing motion, then flinging his hands apart, "his people would just put another pawn on the table, and keep the game going. We can reach past him. In fact, we already have."

"The men he recently . . . lost. That was your work?" Beaumont said.

Oh, this man is a master of his trade, Shalare thought to himself. "It was not," he replied, sincerely. "We've no idea what that was about, but it has nothing to do with this conversation. When I say we reached past Dioguardi, I mean all the way to the people who sent him to Locke City in the first place."

"Reached past him for what?"

"For a lesson in reality," Shalare said. "As of the minute I walk out your door, Dioguardi's intrusions into your affairs are going to stop. Not slack off, not change target—*stop*. As if they hit a brick wall."

"When I was a kid, there was a guy, for a dollar, he'd run right into a brick wall," Beaumont said. "Butt it with his head like a ram."

"Probably ended up with mush for a brain," Shalare said.

"Yeah," Beaumont said. "That's exactly what happened to him. He started out stupid, and he got stupider. Only thing is, he kept right on doing it . . . butting that wall."

"I must be missing your meaning, Roy."

"This guy, the one who rammed the wall? He kept right on doing it, usually when he was drunk. Until, one day, he must have hit the wall wrong. Dropped dead, right there on the spot."

"Ah."

"See, before this guy got all mushy in the head, he thought he could keep hitting that wall forever, and nothing would happen to him," Beaumont said, speaking slowly and deliberately. "Then, when his brain turned soft, he wasn't smart enough to stop. Oh, you could get him to stop *temporarily*. But, soon as he got drunk, he'd go right back to it."

"Dioguardi's bosses, they want this as bad as mine do," Shalare said, underscoring his understanding.

"So you came here to tell me Dioguardi's going to back off until the election . . . ?"

"He's not going to be a problem for you, Roy," Shalare said. "Not now, not ever. And we'll give you any assurances you want on that score. Any at all."

1959 October 06 Tuesday 17:29

Tussy awoke to find Dett still in the armchair, watching her. *He looks like he hasn't moved a muscle,* she thought, finding the feeling oddly comforting. "That was just what I needed," she said, throwing off the pink blanket, so that it landed across Fireball. The big cat struggled out from underneath, gave Dett an annoyed look, as if the entire episode had been his fault, and marched off.

"You feel better?" Dett said.

"I feel *great,*" Tussy said, stretching her arms over her head. "Sometimes, when I'm feeling just . . . beat, I take one of my little naps, and it always works."

"Your cat didn't seem too thrilled."

"Oh, Fireball thinks this is *his* couch. But I never take naps in the bed. That's too much like sleeping. When I use the couch, I never seem to sleep long, even without an alarm clock."

Dett got to his feet.

"Are you sure you want to drive all the way back to the hotel just to change clothes?" Tussy asked. "It's . . . why, it's after five. I never realized. . . ."

"I didn't, either. The time, I mean. I wish I could stay here. . . ." Dett's voice fell into a pit of such despair that Tussy felt the vibration as it landed.

"Well, you certainly don't have to get all dressed up just to go to a drive-in movie, Walker. I'm not going to change. I mean, I *am* going to take a shower, but I'm not going to get into a dress or anything."

"I want to do the same thing."

"The same . . . Oh, take a shower? Well, you could do that here, couldn't you?"

"I . . . I never thought of that. But I . . . I mean, I . . . I don't have fresh clothes to change into, not with me."

"Well . . . all right, then," Tussy said. She stood on her toes, kissed Dett lightly just to the side of his lips. "I'll see you later, okay?"

1959 October 06 Tuesday 17:31

"I wonder," Beaumont said. "You're not just doing a job, are you, Mickey?"

"What do you mean?"

"When people spend money, it's either a purchase or an investment."

"Aye. And, if you're asking me, is Mickey Shalare some sort of mercenary, the answer is no. I've got—*all* my people have got—a huge stake in this."

"Yes?" Beaumont said, inviting an explanation.

Shalare took a slow, deliberate sip of his drink. "Yes," he said, evenly, rejecting the offer.

"Have you ever been beat down?" Beaumont asked, suddenly. "Getting pounded on so bad, by so many people, that you can't hope to win?"

"Aye," the Irishman said, gravely.

"So, when I tell you that, sometimes, the best you can hope for is just to get one in, you know what I'm talking about, don't you?"

"I do."

"And it doesn't matter if you walk away afterward," Beaumont said. "Look at me, Mickey; how long do you think it's been since I could walk at all? It doesn't matter if you crawl, just so long as you survive. Stay alive, so, someday, you can return the favor."

" 'Getting your own back,' we call it," Shalare said, holding his glass in a silent toast to a shared value.

"And we call it 'payback,' " Beaumont said, raising his own glass. "But it doesn't matter what something's called, only what it is. Have you ever just . . . nourished yourself with that thought, with *only* that thought? 'Getting your own back'?"

"Sometimes," Shalare said quietly, "it was more than food and drink to me. Without it, I would have starved."

"I must have some Irish blood in me, then," Beaumont said, solemnly.

1959 October 06 Tuesday 18:12

Rufus didn't change out of his bellhop's uniform when his shift was over. Though acknowledging the truth of what Moses had told him—he had, in fact, never seen a white man in the basement of the hotel—he reasoned that even a chance encounter with any of the white staff would go unnoticed if he was in uniform. *Makes us look even more alike to you,* he thought, as he made his way down the back stairs.

Walking past the kitchen, Rufus heard the the intimate caress of Charles Brown's sultry voice drifting out of the radio, crooning his signature "Black Night." "Oh, Charles!" a kitchen worker implored him, to the rich laughter of her girlfriends.

Moses was in his chair, his pipe already working.

"Leave it open," he said, as Rufus entered. "People see a closed door, they got to find out what's on the other side of it. We keep our voices down, with these walls, might as well be in a different town, all anyone could hear. Besides, this way, we see them coming."

Nodding his head at the wisdom, Rufus glanced around the room, not saying a word.

"Ain't got no other chair," Moses said. "But you could probably get something to sit on out of the—"

"I can stand, say what I got to say."

"Go ahead, then."

"It's about Rosa Mae."

"What about her?"

"I got feelings for her. Not what you think," Rufus said, holding up his hand as if to ward off those same thoughts. "I got . . . I'm deep in love with her, and I told her so."

"So what you need to talk to me about?" Moses said, puffing slowly on his pipe.

"Rosa Mae's got no father. Not even one of those Christmas daddies, come around once a year, bring some presents, get a fuss made over them, and then go back to their trifling little hustles. So, when I told her if she had a real father I would go and talk to him first, she said I should talk to you."

Moses drew on his pipe again, his body language that of a man waiting for something. A patient man.

"I know she wasn't just . . . messing me around," Rufus said. "Everybody here knows you just like her father. Look out for her and all, I mean. And she listens to you like a father. Respects you like one, too. So . . ."

"So I'm like a roadblock you need to run, that about right?"

"No, sir. Not something to get around, that isn't what I was saying. I mean, I got to *show* you something, same way any man would have to show a girl's father something."

"Not many young men think like that, not today."

"Not many young *black* men think at all. All they want to do is get themselves some fine vines, a sweet ride, and tear it up on Saturday night."

"And that's not you, what you're saying?"

"That's not any kind of me, Mr. Moses. I don't smoke, I don't drink, and I don't eat swine. I don't want to make babies for the Welfare to feed. I *save* my money. And I got plans."

"Everybody around here knows you've got a brain, Rufus," the elderly man said, calmly. "But there's a world of difference between smart and slick."

"Fair enough. Just ask me what you want to know, and I'll tell you. Then you can make up your own mind."

"Let me give you an example," the old man said, unruffled. "You've been knowing me for years, from your first day on the job. Before today, you speak to me, you call me 'Moses,' right? Or 'man' or some other kind of jive talk. Today, what comes out your mouth? It's all 'sir' and 'Mr. Moses.' Like, all of a sudden, lightning struck you and you got all this respect. Now," he said, drawing on his pipe unsuccessfully, then pausing to relight it, "that's either get-over game, or you got another reason."

"Rosa Mae—"

"—been calling me 'Daddy Moses' for a long time, Rufus. She didn't start today."

"I know that. But it wasn't until I . . . knew I had feelings for her that it . . . meant anything to me. I'm not going to lie."

"Because you got no other reason to show me respect."

"You're just like she is," Rufus said. "Making things hard. What do you want me to say?"

"The truth. Like you promised."

"All right," Rufus said, moving closer to the old man. "Here's some truth: I was raised to respect my elders, but that was all about manners—what you say, not what you feel. Why should I respect someone just because they're older than me? That never made any sense."

"Don't make no sense to me, neither," Moses said, surprising the younger man. "You know what experience is?"

"Of course I know what it is."

"Yeah? So, you got something wrong with your car, you want to take it to an experienced mechanic?"

"Sure . . ." Rufus agreed, warily.

"Let's say the man been working on cars for thirty years. You call a man like that 'experienced,' right?"

"Yeah."

"Okay, now let's say he been working on cars for thirty years but he never was no good at it. In fact, he so lousy a mechanic that he had himself a hundred different jobs. Kept getting fired, one place after the other, because he couldn't do a job without messing it up. He got a lot of experience, but no knowledge. Lots of old people like that. If they ain't learned nothing, just being old don't make them people you should be listening to."

Rufus stared at the old man for a long time. Moses looked back, unperturbed, at peace within himself.

"Can I sit down? On that crate, there?" Rufus asked. "I got some things I need to tell you."

1959 October 06 Tuesday 18:20

"It's going to be Nixon for the Republicans," Beaumont said.

"Sure, and who else? But he's no war hero, like Ike was. And our guy, well, he is."

"You're positive that's such a good thing?" Beaumont challenged his visitor. "If the voters think your guy's going to get us into another mess like Korea, he's dead in the water."

"No, no, no," Shalare answered, quickly. "That's all been talked over. We know how to wrap a package, Roy. Our man's going to be a tiger on national defense, sure, but that'll be *self*-defense, not sticking our nose into another meat-grinder like Korea."

"Nixon's no Eisenhower in more ways than one," Beaumont said, warningly. "And one of those is, he's a whole lot smarter."

"An election's not an IQ test. If it was, Stevenson would have won the last couple of times, wouldn't he?"

"There's all kinds of smart," Beaumont said. "I never met the man, but, with television, you can get a read on someone even at a distance. I'll tell you this: you're not going to find a craftier man in all of politics than Richard Nixon."

"He's a ferret-faced schemer, no doubt," Shalare said. "And that's a plus for him. The minus is, he *looks* like what he is. And, like you said, television. That's going to play a big role in what's to come."

Beaumont nodded his concurrence.

"The timing is right," Shalare continued. "The Taft machine pretty much died off when Ike got the nomination away from them. A lot of them crossed over after that. Look at Warren. They took care of him, and, soon as he got on the Supreme Court, he ambushed the lot of them."

"That was Eisenhower's mistake. Nixon wouldn't make the same one."

"If we all pull together, Nixon won't get the chance."

"Tell me again why I should be part of that," Beaumont said, lighting another cigarette.

"Didn't I already?"

"Dioguardi? He's not such a problem, for what you're asking."

"It's not the person, it's the . . . situation. Look at this Castro, over in Cuba. The great revolutionary he is, freeing his people from the yoke of oppression. Mark what I say: he'll be the same as the man he removed. He'll use different words, dress different, maybe. But he didn't take over that country to free it, Roy. He took it over to *rule* it."

"So, even if Dioguardi . . . disappeared, there'd be another to take his place?"

"You know that's true as well as I do," Shalare said. "It's not Dioguardi himself who has to disappear; it's the reason he was sent that has to go."

"Here we're talking about elections, and you want to make me a promise," Beaumont said, smiling to take some of the sting out of his words.

"That's right, I do," Shalare said, not rising to the bait. "For starters, there won't be any more squabbling about jukebox rents. Nobody else trying to handle the pinball machines or the punch cards, either."

"Pennies."

"Pennies add up to dollars, don't they? And nobody likes to pay the same landlord twice. Dioguardi's people are going to stop selling protection insurance, too. For starters," Shalare reminded Beaumont.

"Because . . . ?"

"Because he's going to be *told* to stop. And he will. Everything. This whole town will go back to its rightful owner. You, Roy."

"He never took it. And he never could."

"He never did. But he was coming, and you know it. Now he stops."

"One door opens and another one—"

"He stops *everything,* Roy. The only thing Salvatore Dioguardi's going to do in Locke City from now on is pay his taxes."

"How's he going to keep his men, with no income?"

"Then I guess he'll lose some of them."

"The way he already has?"

"I told you, we had nothing to do with that," Shalare said. "Anyways, losing a few men wouldn't keep him off you—that's just the cost of doing business."

"I don't know how that whole Mafia thing works. Is Dioguardi some kind of big shot, or just their stalking horse?"

"I'm not sure. What difference does it make?"

"If he's a stalking horse, one they put in here to see if they could find a soft spot, they'll learn soon enough that they made a mistake. But if he's a big shot, and this was his own idea, that's different."

"Because, if he's a big shot, he might be too stubborn to pull out? Or even big enough to call in more troops?"

"There's that. But I was thinking of something different."

"And that would be . . . ?"

"You know how they sell cattle? Price them at so much a head?"

"Yeah . . ." Shalare said, cautiously.

"Well, with people, it's not like that. Because some heads are worth a lot more than others. Especially when there's a gesture of good faith involved."

"Ah."

"My sister always tells me, when someone gives you a gift, it's low-class to look at the price tag. It's the thought that counts, you've heard that?"

"Sure. I was raised the same way."

"But that's gifts, not business. In business, a man never wants to get shorted on a deal."

"So, if you traded for a . . . single head of cattle, you'd want to know if you got the best bull of the herd?"

"Wouldn't you?"

"I would. In an undertaking as big as this one, there's a lot that has to be overlooked. You deal with men you wouldn't have in your home," Shalare said, glancing around the spacious room as if to underscore the bond between them. "The Jews killed Christ, and we're dealing with them on this. What's going further than that?"

"What did the coloreds ever do?" Beaumont said.

"I don't under—"

"You deal with the coloreds, too, don't you? Maybe not you, personally, but this whole 'effort' you've been talking about, the people running the show, they had *better* be doing that, if they want to pull this off."

"Well, sure and you're right," Shalare said. "I didn't mean we only deal with our enemies, just that we have to go outside the tribe—*all* of us do, to make this happen."

" 'Tribes.' That's just a word, too. Like 'blood,' " said Beaumont, contempt strong in his iron eyes. "Wasn't it one of your own that shopped the Molly Maguires to the Pinkertons?"

"Huh!" Shalare said, surprised. "You're a historian, for sure. But he was a—"

"—Protestant? So am I, I suppose. I know I'm not a Catholic or a Jew, so what's left, being a Buddhist? You're right, Mickey. I *am* a man who studies the past. I studied Centralia. I studied the trial of the McNamara brothers. Sacco and Vanzetti."

"They were—"

"What? Italians? Anarchists? Catholics? Innocent? What does it matter? My point is, when you try and change governments, whether you're assassinating a dictator or winning an election, you've got to be able to carry through after you take over."

"We'll have our own—"

"All I care about is *my* own," Beaumont interrupted. "Dioguardi getting out of my hair isn't a fair trade. But getting his people to stay out of Locke City forever, now, *that* could be one."

"You have my word, Roy," Shalare said. "My sacred word. And if that's not enough, I'll throw in a head of cattle, if you want. The finest of its kind for many miles around."

1959 October 06 Tuesday 18:29

"You know what a pilgrimage is?" Rufus said.

"A holy journey," Moses answered, as if he had been expecting the question.

"That's right," Rufus said, surprised. "And I took mine on September 3, 1955. On that day, I went to Chicago. So I could see that little boy, Emmett Till. See him in the coffin where the white man had put him."

"I remember that."

"His mother left the casket open so people could see—so the whole world could see—how they had tortured her child before they murdered him," Rufus said, his voice throbbing. "It was supposed to be because the boy had whistled at a white woman. Not raped her, not killed her—whistled at her. Men came in the night and took him; didn't make no secret about it. Everybody knew who they were. And they bragged about it all over town, too. Took some cracker jury about ten minutes to find them not guilty. Probably some of them on that jury, they were along for the ride that night themselves."

"Mississippi," Moses said.

"Yeah, Mississippi. And then the men who did it, they got *paid* for it. I read it in *Look* magazine, the whole thing. After that jury cut them loose, some reporter paid them to tell the true story, because you can't try a man twice for the same crime. Every cracker's dream, kill a black boy and get paid for it, too. Like a bounty on niggers."

"I read that story," Moses said, evenly.

"Didn't it make you want to . . . kill a whole lot of whites?"

"I don't believe in killing by color."

"What do you mean?"

"I mean, if I could *pick,* there'd be a whole lot of whites I've met in my life that needed killing. But I wouldn't go kill a bunch of white men for what some *other* white men did."

"You mean, like they do us?" Rufus said, every syllable a challenge.

"That's not why they kill us," Moses said, a teacher correcting a pupil. "Not for anything we *ever* did. That's just their excuse. Like that 'wolf whistle' the Till boy was supposed to have done to that white woman."

"There's plenty of them would kill all of *us,* they had the chance," Rufus said.

"Sure. Or put us back on the plantations. Or ship us back to Africa. But no matter how much they hate us, things is never going back to the way they was—the way they liked it. If things was going backwards, then that evil Faubus bastard would be running for president. I'll bet he thought he *was,* when he stood there on the steps and barred our children from his schools. But he guessed wrong. All the crackers in this country put together couldn't put their own man in the White House, not today."

"You're right about that," Rufus said, thinking, *This isn't just an old river, it's a damn deep one.* "There's too many of us now. Too many that vote, I mean. Maybe not down there, but up here, the white people—the bosses, I'm talking about—they got to pay attention. That's why Eisenhower sent the troops in. It wasn't for our people in Arkansas, it was for our people in Chicago. And Detroit, and New York, and Cleveland, and . . . everyplace we migrated to. That's the way the NAACP wants us to think, too. Wait our turn. Be good Negroes, so the good white people can see they should be letting us go to their schools."

"So they can learn how Lincoln freed the slaves."

"Yeah!" Rufus said, his voice thick with hate. "And whatever other lies they want to put in our nappy little heads. You know a lot more than I thought, Moses."

"You can't tell what a man knows until you get with him," the elderly man said, puffing on his pipe. "Just watching, that's nothing. Ofay been watching *us* since we were picking his cotton, under the lash. But he never *knew* us, 'cause we learned to keep our thinking off our faces. That's what I was telling you before, Rufus. The difference between experience and knowledge. I know about the Scottsboro Boys, too. And a lot of other things."

"But you Tom it up, man. I see you, every day."

"And you don't?"

"I don't do it because that's me, man. I'm not just surviving, I'm playing a part."

"How do you know I'm not?"

"Because you never . . . I mean . . ." Rufus sat silently for a moment, then admitted, "I . . . I guess I don't."

"I was born on the seventeenth day of August, in the year 1887," Moses said, a resonant timbre entering his voice. "Does that date mean anything to you?"

"The Civil War was over, but your parents, they were slaves?"

"They were, but that's not what I'm saying. A great man was born on the same day as me. Marcus Garvey. You ever hear of him?"

"Well, damn, man, of *course* I heard of him. Marcus Garvey, he's our spiritual father."

"I was in that," Moses said. "The Universal Negro Improvement Association. Before they came and took it all down. But I never forgot. And I was with Wallace Fard Muhammad himself, when I was in Detroit, back in '34."

"Then you're a Muslim?"

"No, son," Moses said, sadly. "I didn't say I *met* Wallace; I said I was *with* him. It was just too neat, him signing everything over to Elijah and then just vanishing, like the earth swallowed him up. The night Wallace disappeared, I caught the first thing smoking. Been right here in Locke City ever since."

Rufus got slowly to his feet. "I was going to tell you something today," he said. "But I got a better idea. That is, if you're willing to take a ride with me, later on tonight."

Moses leaned back in his chair, reading the face of the young man before him. Decoding.

"I'd be honored if you would," Rufus said, holding out his hand.

Moses grasped the younger man's hand for a long second. Then he rose from his chair.

1959 October 06 Tuesday 18:44

As Luther was escorting Shalare back to the front of the house, a sliding panel behind Beaumont's desk opened, and Cynthia stepped out.

"What do you think?" Beaumont asked, without preamble.

"He's the kind of man they used to call a silver-tongued devil, Beau. Two-faced, with a lie in each mouth."

"For all that, he was being honest with me . . . to a point."

"Yes. The point about what *he* wants. The only question is, is that *all* he wants?"

"From us? It just might be, girl. Shalare's outfit was never after our rackets. He's a political man."

"You mean, the elections?"

"No. I mean, yes, sure, that's what he wants—*now*. But Mickey Shalare's a man who plays the long game, Cyn. His roots aren't here."

"In Locke City?"

"In America, honey. Remember what he said about getting his own back? That's what Mickey Shalare's all about. I'm sure of it."

"So you think he would take care of—?"

"Dioguardi? I think he's got the horsepower to make him back off, no question about that. I mean, what's the point of lying to us about that? We'd see the truth of things in a few days, anyway. It's the rest of his promise—you know, that after the election Dioguardi, or another of his kind, won't come back. That one I'm not so sure about."

"That he can deliver?"

"Or that he even intends to. Shalare's a man who understands power. And he knows, if our organization puts together the landslide he needs here, we're going to leave our own people in place for the *next* time. Even stronger, we'd be. This is America. Nobody gets elected president for life, not since Roosevelt."

"It's still a puzzle, isn't it, Beau," she said, her tone making it clear she was pondering the situation.

"A big one."

"So now you're glad you've still got Lymon," Cynthia said, smiling wistfully.

1959 October 06 Tuesday 18:50

"You had a fine old time, didn't you, Big Brian?"

"Didn't I just, Mick! You don't often run across a man who follows the fight game the way Seth does."

"The man at the guardhouse?"

"Yeah. He got someone else to cover for him, and we just strolled the grounds, talking."

"And had a couple of cold ones?"

"Sure did. Pretty decent, too. Although it's not Guinness they brew over here, that's for sure. I told Seth he'd have to come by sometime and I'll draw him a real—"

"You invited him to our place?"

"Well . . . sure I did, Mickey. I thought you'd be pleased."

"I am, Brian. What did he say, when you asked him?"

"He said he would. And I hope he does. He'd fit right in. With the fellows, I mean."

"Not like Lymon, hey?"

"Lymon? He's a bloody tout, isn't he? Grassing on his own. Seth wouldn't do that."

"You can tell?"

"That man would step in front of a bullet for his chief, Mickey. Same as I would for you. I could see it in him, strong and clear."

"You saw the grounds, too, Brian?"

"Well, I don't know as I saw them *all*. That's a huge spread Beaumont has got. Big enough for a man in training to do his road-work and never go off the property. Did get a long look at the house, though. Looks like it could take a direct hit from a mortar and laugh it off, it does. Solid stone, all around."

"When we get back, you can draw us a map, Brian. It's good work you did today."

"Aye, Mickey. And thanks. Did your own work go well?"

"Well, I met the man. And I believe we took the measure of one another. But as for whether we have a deal, that I don't know. We have to show him something first."

"But that part's easy, isn't it? Dioguardi already said he would—"

"Starting tomorrow, we'll just see about that, Big Brian," Shalare said. He tapped the fingers of both his hands lightly on the dashboard, playing a song only he could hear.

1959 October 06 Tuesday 18:56

"Like I said, I came of age right in the middle of the Depression," Sherman said to Ruth. "It was hard times."

Harder on some than others, Ruth thought, remembering. She was next to Sherman on the couch, hands clasped in her lap. Her burnt-cork eyes never left his face.

"There wasn't any work," Sherman went on, "except the WPA stuff. Didn't bother my father much—he'd been a drunk all his life, so he just *stayed* drunk. It was my mother who fed us."

It was me *who fed us,* Ruth thought. *Only I wasn't the mother, I was the child. The rented child.*

"My mother wasn't a church person, but she had a sense of right and wrong that would have shamed a preacher. There were only two ways a man could go back then. Get on with the government, somehow. Or pick up the gun."

"So you became a policeman?"

Sherman made a sound Ruth had never heard before, but instantly recognized. *He's calling home,* she said to herself.

"Not at first," Sherman finally said, holding her soft brown eyes with his own pair of faded-denim blues. "The only way to become a cop in Locke City back then was . . . Well, it's the same way it is today: you have to buy your job. Today, you can buy it with things other than money. If you know someone, someone political, I mean, you can go to them, make the right promises, and they'll maybe take you on. But back then it was always done in cash.

"It was all a crazy circle," he said, nodding his head as if agreeing with some unseen person. "If you had enough money to buy a job, well, you didn't *need* a job. Not a job as a cop, anyway. People didn't just want that job for the paycheck, Ruth. There were always plenty of extra ways to make money. . . ."

"I know," she said, whisper-soft.

"So I made . . . I guess you'd call it kind of a bargain. I knew there was only one way for me to get the money to become a cop. So I swore, if . . . He let me get away with it, I would be the most honest cop there ever was. I'd never steal another dime as long as I lived."

"So you did pick up the gun, but just one time, is that what you're saying, Sherman?"

"Yes."

"Why are you telling me this now?"

"Because I never told anybody else."

"Oh," was all Ruth said. She felt as if a malicious nurse had just given her an injection of sadness. *I get it now. Once you get past the dollar tricks in alleys, once you start dealing with a higher class of customer, they all have a story they need to tell.*

"It's not that," Sherman said, sharply.

Ruth sat up as if she had just been slapped. Her cheeks darkened, but she didn't say a word.

"You're not . . . Whatever you think you are, you're not that to me," Sherman told her. "I don't have any need to tell my secrets, like going to confession. What I . . . trusted you with, what I come . . . used to come . . . to your place for, that's nothing. I don't mean it's not a secret—sure it is—but it doesn't tell you anything about me. This . . . what I'm saying, it does. I hope it does, anyway."

"I already knew," Ruth said.

"How could you? It was almost thirty years—"

"I don't mean about what you did to get the money to become a policeman, Sherman. I mean, I already knew you. I'm ashamed of myself. For what I was thinking before. I don't know how you knew, but . . ."

"I know you, Ruth. Like you say you know me. I don't know how I know, or how you know. But . . . I want you to hear . . . what I have to say. It's important to me."

"It's important to me, too," Ruth said.

Sherman watched her eyes for a long moment, polygraphing. Ruth dropped her curtain, let him in. Sherman nodded slowly and heavily, as if taking a vow.

"Remember what I said about my mother?" the big detective began. "Remember what I said about her shaming a preacher? Well, that's the opposite—the reverse, really—of what happened. The preacher, in the church we used to go to, he shamed *her*. That sanctimonious dog stood up before everyone and denounced my mother. For the crime of feeding her child, he said she was going to burn in hellfire for all eternity."

"What could possibly have made him—?"

"My mother went with men for money," Sherman said, tonelessly. "It started when I was little. When my father wanted to bond me out. You know what that is?"

"Yes," Ruth said. *Some children get sold to farmers,* she thought. *And some get sold to pimps.*

"My mother knew what that would mean. She and my father fought about it. I could hear every word. In that house, you always could. She told my father she was going out to get some money. I didn't know what she was talking about, but I knew it was a bad thing. My father didn't say anything."

Sherman lowered his head, dropped his voice.

"When my mother came back, it was real late. Almost morning. I remember my father calling her that word. 'Whore.' He whipped her. With his belt. Then he took the money she brought home."

"Filthy pig," Ruth whispered.

"No pig would do what he did," Sherman said. "My mother kept me from being bonded out, but it cost her . . . everything."

"What happened to him?"

"How do you know something did?" Sherman asked.

"I just know, Sherman."

"He had an accident. Out in the barn. He was drunk. Must have tripped and fell down from the loft. Hit his head against an anvil. Right after that, he ran off."

"Oh."

"That was when I was thirteen. I wanted to quit school, but my mother wouldn't let me. I pleaded with her, but she wouldn't budge, and I couldn't go against her. You know what she told me, Ruth? She said she was already damned. I couldn't save her; nobody could. But if I ever became a . . . bad person, then all her sacrifice would have been for nothing."

"You really loved her," Ruth said.

"I always will. My . . . I was going to say 'friends,' but that would be a lie . . . the kids I went to school with, they knew what my mother did. So I turned into a pretty good fighter. Everyone said I would end up in reform school, but we made them all eat crow at the end. My mother was so proud when I became a cop."

"Is she still—?"

"She died a couple of weeks after I got sworn in," Sherman said. "She'd been sick for years. It was like she was holding on, just waiting for that."

"Is that why you . . . ?"

"Feel the way I do about you?" the big man said, meeting the challenge head-on. "No, Ruth. Listen, my mother never was a whore. I don't care what people called her, or called what she did. She was a mother, protecting her child. My father was the whore, selling his honor and his name for a few dollars, then drinking up all the money because he couldn't look himself in the mirror.

"My father wasn't a man," the big detective said, "but my mother, she was a woman. A real woman. And so are you, Ruth. Understand?"

"Yes," Ruth said, between her tears.

1959 October 06 Tuesday 19:04

"Wow! Where did you get this jalopy?" Tussy said, as Dett held the door of the '49 Ford open for her.

"I just borrowed it," he said. "From a guy I met. Actually, we traded. He had a big date, and he thought the Buick would help him impress the girl."

"And you don't want to impress me anymore?" Tussy said, smiling.

"I wish I could," he answered. "Only I know you. And I know a car would never do the trick."

"Even after I got you to take me to the most expensive restaurant in town?"

"Well, that was like . . . an adventure, right? It wasn't how much it cost, it was just that you hadn't done it before."

"Yes! And now this," Tussy said. "I feel like a teenager. I mean, in a car like this—boy, those mufflers are *loud*—dressed like we are, going to the drive-in . . ." Her voice trailed away into the silence. "Do you feel like that, too? A little bit?"

"No," said Dett. "But I don't *look* like it, either."

"What do you mean?"

"I mean, *you* do, Tussy. You look like you're sixteen."

Tussy pulled a cigarette from her purse, put it in her mouth. Before Dett could react, she reached over and patted his jacket pocket, then extracted his little box of wooden matches. *Christ!* Dett thought, his mind on what else he was carrying. *I didn't expect that.*

"You know what?" Tussy said, thoughtfully, once she got her cigarette going. "If I *was* sixteen, and my folks were still . . . with me, I wouldn't be going to any drive-in."

"Your father wouldn't let you?"

"I don't think he would have. I never asked . . . never got the chance to ask him. A couple of boys asked *me,* when I was around fourteen, but I didn't even dare to mention it. Dad would have hit the ceiling."

"Nice girls don't go to drive-ins?"

"I don't think that was how he felt. He took *us,* and there were always plenty of girls there. But he never said anything, except . . ."

"Except what?" Dett asked, as his eyes swept the mirrors for any disturbance in his visual field. He could not have explained what he was looking for, but the years had taught him to rely on his sense impressions, and the scanning habit was now so encoded he wasn't aware he was doing it.

"Well, he *did* say that nice girls didn't wear skirts to a drive-in. I didn't even know what he meant until I was older."

"And you're still taking his advice," Dett said, nodding at Tussy's jeans.

"Well, it's not *that,*" she said, blushing in the darkness of the front seat. "It's just more comfortable than a skirt. I should know: I have to wear one every day. But at least they're nice and loose."

"The skirts?"

"The *waitress* skirts. In some places, they make the girls wear tight ones. And you know what happens: men get all . . . grabby."

"Where you work?"

"Oh, no. We get a very nice crowd. Families, mostly. Or couples, on dates. Now, my girlfriend—"

"—Gloria?"

"Yes!" she said, laughing softly. "Gloria used to work over at the Blue Moon Lounge. They made her wear these outfits that were just . . . scandalous, my mother would have called them. Gloria said, some nights, when she got home, she was too sore to sit down, from all the men pinching her."

"Is that why she quit?"

"No. She was . . . Well, you have to understand Gloria. I'm not saying she *liked* strange men pinching her, but she would have been pretty annoyed if none of them even tried. I don't mean she's like a . . . loose woman, or anything, but she likes it when guys notice her."

"I'll bet you don't go out together much."

"Why would you say that?"

"I know girls like her. Gloria, I mean. It's like you say, they're not . . . sluts, but they want the attention. And, standing next to you, she wouldn't get any."

"Oh, stop it! You don't even know what she looks like."

"It wouldn't matter."

"You make out like I'm Marilyn Monroe or something, Walker."

"You're prettier than she is."

Tussy turned to face Dett's profile, curling her legs onto the seat so she could move close despite the floor shift lever. "I know I'm not so gorgeous, okay? But I also know you're not lying. I mean, *you* mean what you're saying."

"You could be on one of those calendars," Dett said, defensively, looking through the windshield. "You know, like they have in gas stations. I've seen plenty of those."

"You know, a man once asked me to."

"Be on a calendar?"

"He sure did. Right in the diner. He was a professional photographer. With a business card and everything. He said I'd be perfect for . . . well, he said 'glamour shots,' but I figured out what he really meant."

"So you didn't do it?"

"Of course not!"

"Those girls . . . in the calendars, I mean . . . they have their clothes on."

"I didn't think he was talking about those kind of pictures, Walker."

"I don't, either," Dett said. "I just didn't want *you* to think . . ."

"What?"

"That I was saying . . . you know."

"You are the strangest man, Walker Dett. That never even occurred to me. I knew all along what you meant. And it was very sweet."

Dett exhaled, without realizing he had been holding his breath. "Is up there where we turn off?" he asked.

1959 October 06 Tuesday 19:29

"Y ou sure we can do this on the phone?" Dioguardi said.

"And why not?" Shalare replied. "All I have to tell you is that I spoke with our friend, and he agreed that these petty business disputes are getting in the way of the bigger objective."

"So he's going to play ball?"

"I believe that he is. But, first, we have to make a little good-faith offering."

"What we talked about before?"

"That. And *all* of that, mind you. The best way to prove you don't want what another man has is to step away from it."

"I get it."

"A *big* step," Shalare said. "Right out of his field of vision."

"I said, I get it," Dioguardi said, cold-voiced.

"How long to make it happen?"

"No later than tomorrow. There's people out now, working. I have to wait until they come back to give them the word."

"That would be lovely, indeed," Shalare said.

1959 October 06 Tuesday 19:34

"S ilk's not going to be around tonight?" Rufus said to Darryl.

"I could say 'no,' brother, but that would be a guess. The man *does* come around, you know. And the nighttime's his time."

"Who gets along with him best?"

"Gets along? None of the men want anything to do with—"

"This is a *job,* Darryl. Understand?"

"If it's a job, I'll do it myself. I'll take him over to the—"

"Can't be you, brother."

"Why not? All you need is for him to be someplace else, right? So, if he shows, I'll just slide in and—"

"I need you there tonight," Rufus said. "There's someone I need you to talk with. I'm going to get him, right now."

"This the man you don't want Silk to see?"

"Don't want him to even know about. Now, who we got to babysit a pimp?"

1959 October 06 Tuesday 19:41

"Where would you like to park?" Dett asked, as he steered the Ford over the pebbled surface toward the giant screen.

"Not too near the refreshment stand," she said.

"Okay," Dett said, creeping along in first gear, "is over there too far to the side for you?"

"No, it looks perfect."

Dett slid into the last spot in a left-side row, rolled down his window halfway, and attached the speaker. As he twirled the knob to make sure it was working, a dull orange Oldsmobile sedan went by, heading down front.

"Would you like anything to eat?"

"Well . . . I guess I could go for a hamburger. And a Coke."

"French fries?"

"You know, I serve so many of those—people eat them with *everything*—I can't bear to look one in the face. Besides, they're supposed to be the most fattening food of all."

"What difference would that make?"

"That they're fattening? You can't be serious," she said, putting her hands on her hips. "You might not believe it, but I exercise every day. Just sit-ups, and touching my toes, and jumping jacks, like we learned in gym, but I do. And I watch what I eat—which is not the easiest thing. If I wanted, I could just swipe something from every plate Booker puts out. If I didn't watch myself, I'd turn into a whale. I wish I could lose ten pounds, just like *that*," she said, snapping her fingers.

"You don't have to—" Dett quickly interrupted himself, seeing the look on Tussy's face. "I exercise, too," he said, quickly.

"It's not the same for you," Tussy said. "You'll never get fat," Tussy said.

"How can you know?"

"Because you can tell from a person's body type. You've got a naturally lean build. You could probably eat anything you wanted, and you wouldn't gain weight. But me, I'm naturally . . . plump. If I didn't put up a fight, I'd—"

"Okay."

"Okay? Okay, what?"

"Okay, I can't win. If I say you look perfect, you're going to say I'm an idiot. Or, worse, lying. But I'm not going to agree with you, either, so I'll just shut up."

"Oh, go get the food!" Tussy said, flashing a smile.

1959 October 06 Tuesday 19:54

"I've known you a long time," Ruth said. "But I never understood you. Not until now."

"If you didn't understand me," Sherman said, "why did you—?"

"—come out here? Make the promise I did?"

"Yeah. When you said you . . . would, I . . . I never expected that."

"I couldn't bear not to see you again, Sherman."

"And that's what you thought, that you wouldn't?"

"I . . . guess I didn't know."

"Why do you think I came out there?" the big man said, abruptly. "To your place?"

"So you could . . . you know."

"No, I *don't* know," Sherman said, thick-voiced. "Tell me."

"Have one of the girls," Ruth said, looking down at her lap.

"I'm sorry."

"Sorry? What are you sorry about? You didn't do—"

"I thought . . . Ruth, we made that . . . arrangement years ago. When I visit your place, how long does it take me to . . . do it?"

"I don't know. I don't—"

"Five minutes? Ten?"

"I guess."

"And how long do I stay, afterwards?"

"You mean, when we talk? Sometimes it's for . . ." Ruth's voice trailed off, as the truth of what Sherman was telling her penetrated.

"Hours, isn't it?"

"Yes," Ruth said. She felt her eyes start to glisten, kept her head down.

"All those . . . preparations, you know what they were for?"

"Because of what you . . . the way you wanted to . . ."

"So, when you said you'd do anything for me, that was what you were thinking of?"

"No," she said, lifting a tearstained face. "I mean, it was. I *would* do that, but that isn't what I meant. It wasn't *all* I meant."

"I'm lonely," Sherman Layne said, heavily. "I'm always lonely. You're the only one who makes a difference, Ruth. You're the one I talk to. The other . . . thing, all that stuff, it was just an excuse. I don't even . . . do what you think."

Ruth stood up, turned to face Sherman, and studied him for a long moment. Then she turned sideways and nestled herself into the big man's lap.

"Tell me now," she said, gently.

"I told you . . . what I wanted to do, so you could tell *them*. But that wasn't what I did. I just did it the . . . regular way."

"But why did you let me think it was . . . ?"

"Because, if that's what the girls were expecting, and it *didn't* happen, I knew they'd never say anything. For fifty bucks, they'd make it sound like it was the hardest thing they ever did, so the other girls wouldn't want to do it, see? The rest, it was all so they would never see my face. Or hear my voice. Or even feel my . . . I always use a rubber, and I take it along with me when I'm done. Like I'm a phantom."

"Why didn't you tell me, Sherman?"

"I didn't think it would matter. Until you . . . said what you said, I never thought you . . . I never thought you cared about me that way, Ruth. I knew you were my friend. I knew you were the one I trusted. But I was being a cop. The kind of cop I taught myself to become."

"I don't understand."

"You know how cops are supposed to be 'brothers in blue'? All for one, and one for all? Well, that's a lie. The police department in Locke City is just like those apartments they build for poor people—the projects. The bids are always rigged, and there's too much sand in the concrete. You can't see it to look at them, but those buildings are rotting from the inside. One day, they're going to just fall down, like a tornado hit them. They tolerate me because I do my job. I do it better than anyone they ever had. And someone's got to solve the crimes."

"Don't they usually solve crimes?"

"Most crimes don't *need* to be solved," Sherman said. "Most murders, for example, you don't have to look further than the family of the dead person to find out who did it. Most robbers, they keep doing the same thing, the same way, until they stumble into getting caught. And a lot of crime in Locke City *isn't* crime, if you know what I mean?"

"Like my house?"

"Like your house. Like the casinos. Like the punch cards and the jukeboxes and . . . all the rest. And there's other kinds, too, Ruth. There's rich man's crimes, which means just about anything a man does, as long as he's got the contacts and the connections. And then there's the crimes nobody gives a damn about."

"What kind are those?" she asked, snuggling deeper.

"A guy beats his wife half to death, what's going to happen to him?"

"Nothing."

"Nothing is exactly right. And his kids, unless he actually *kills* one, that's on the house, too. To get away with crimes like that, you don't even have to be rich."

"All you have to do is be a man."

"Yeah. A man can't go to jail for burning down his own house. The only way he gets in trouble for that is if he tries to claim on the insurance. He can do what he wants with what he owns. The law says a man can't rape his own wife. I mean, he *can,* but it's not a crime. I had one of those, once."

"A real rape? Not just . . . ?"

"A real rape. This guy, he broke her jaw, snapped her arm like a matchstick from twisting it."

"And nothing happened to him?"

"He wasn't even arrested," Sherman said.

Ruth caught something in his tone, shifted in his lap, whispered, "That doesn't mean nothing happened to him."

"You think that's wrong?" he said, almost in a whisper.

"No, Sherman," Ruth replied, shifting her weight again. "No, I don't."

1959 October 06 Tuesday 20:46

"Darryl, this is Mr. Moses," Rufus said, almost formally. "He's been in the struggle for longer than you and me have been alive, brother."

"Yes?" Darryl said, his tone noncommittal.

"I would like it if you would talk. To each other," Rufus said, his gesture encompassing both men. "In private."

1959 October 06 Tuesday 21:01

"I know it's just a movie, but this is *scary,*" Tussy said, sliding in close to Dett.

"I guess so," he said, dubiously.

Tussy turned to her left, reached across Dett, and flicked the ash off her cigarette out his window. Her breast brushed lightly against his chest, firing a synapse that radiated through his groin. Her hair smelled like flowers he couldn't identify.

1959 October 06 Tuesday 21:02

"What do you say?" Rufus asked Darryl.

"He's what we been looking for, Brother Omar. A true elder."

"You think he should sit in when that boy comes around?"

"He's got the wisdom," Darryl said, "and he's ready to share it with us. I be proud to have him."

"No sign of Silk?"

"No, brother. But if he shows, Kendall's going to ease him off—he'll never see nothing."

1959 October 06 Tuesday 21:03

"Sherman, can I ask you a question?"

"You can ask me anything," the big detective said.

"When you were with those girls. In my house, I mean. Did you ever think about me?"

"You mean, think about you that way? Or . . . think about you while I was . . . ?"

"What's the difference?"

"When you came out here, what did you expect?" Sherman countered.

"I expected to . . . I expected to prove my promise. About doing anything for you. So I didn't know *what* to expect, but it didn't matter."

"You thought what I wanted, it was the same thing I did down in your basement, didn't you?"

"Yes," she said. "But it wouldn't matter if you—"

"I *do* think about you that way, Ruth," Sherman said. "Having . . . being with you. But not with you tied up, or blindfolded. I always wished, when I was coming out there, when we were talking, that it would be . . . in bed. Like . . . afterwards, you know?"

"Start by kissing me," Ruth said, locking her hands behind Sherman's neck.

A boxy '51 De Soto moved slowly through the night-shrouded junkyard, every rotation of its tires recorded by watchers' eyes.

The car came to a halt. A young man with a tall, rangy build got out. He was wearing a long black coat. The three orange feathers in the headband of his hat looked like candle flames in the night.

Two men approached, bracketing the young man.

"I'm here to see someone," the young man said.

"Who?" the men asked, with one voice.

"I don't know no name. Don't *want* to know no name. I'm here to buy something. This is where they told me to come."

"You come alone?" one of the bracketing men asked.

"Just me."

"I don't mean in the car," the man said. "I mean, you got anyone waiting for you, close by?"

"No."

"Come on," the man said.

The young man followed the speaker; the silent man walked behind them, maintaining the bracket.

"In there," the lead man said, pointing to a shack.

The young man entered. The room was shadowy, illuminated only by the distant glow of the junkyard's arc lights coming through a single, streaked window. But he could make out a table, three seated men, and an empty chair.

"Sit down," said the man seated directly across from the empty chair.

The young man did as he was instructed, resting his hands on the table.

"Say what you come to say," he was told.

"My name is Preacher," the young man said. "I'm the President of the South Side Kings."

His statement greeted by silence, the young man continued, "We've got one on for tomorrow night with the Golden Hawks. At the lot over on Halstead."

More silence.

"I heard that the white boys got cannons, this time. Pistols. Real ones. That never happened before."

The young man took a breath, said, "I heard the white boys, they got guns from the Klan. We need guns, too. That's why I came here. To buy some."

"How much money you bring?" Darryl asked.

"I got three hundred dollars," Preacher said, proudly, hoping his voice concealed that he had emptied his gang's treasury for this purpose.

"You say 'guns,' you mean pistols?" Darryl asked.

"That's right. 'Cause that's what they got."

"You 'heard' this, about the white boys having pistols?" Rufus said. "You didn't say *where* you heard it."

"From a lot of different places," Preacher said, evasively. "Word's out, all over."

"What happens when the fight is finished?" Moses said.

"When it's finished?" Preacher asked, puzzled. "I don't know what you mean."

"What changes?" Moses said. "What will be different?"

"Oh, I see what you saying. What'll be different is that those white boys will know the South Side Kings don't play."

"And now they think you *do*?"

"Hey, man, no! Everybody knows our club is—"

"So what would be different?" Moses said, implacably.

"I guess . . . I guess it depends on how the bop comes out."

"No, it doesn't," Moses said. "Before you go out tomorrow night, you going to pour an 'X' out of wine on the sidewalk, right?"

"Sure. You got to—"

"What? Show respect for the dead? *That's* what they get, for dying? The people who *ain't* dead, they get together and say, 'Oh, that boy, he had a lot of heart'?"

"What else could they get?" Preacher said, as surly as a corrected child. "Tombstone wouldn't make no difference."

"You don't mind dying, do you, son?" the old man said.

"No, I don't. I *can't*. The only way a man can—"

"Courage is a good thing," Moses said. "You can't be a man

without it. But getting killed don't make you brave. And dying over a piece of ground that'll never be yours—"

"It *will* be ours," Preacher said. "After tomorrow night, that'll be Kings turf."

"Yours?" Rufus said, caustically. "Does that mean you going to build houses on it? Open a gas station, maybe? Could you sell it, get money for it?"

"That's not what I'm—"

"Fighting for land, that's what this country's all about," Rufus said. "White men killed a whole bunch of Indians, for openers. When they got done with the Indians, they started on each other. And they still doing it. But that's land that's got a deed to it, see?"

"You're saying it ain't worth it, over a little piece of vacant lot?" Preacher said. "But that's not what this is about. If we let the Hawks take that lot, it's like they took a piece of us."

"Rep," Rufus said.

"Rep," Preacher agreed. "When I was in New York . . ." He paused, but if he was waiting for some indication that he had impressed the seated men, he was disappointed. "When I was just thirteen, I stayed with my uncle for the summer. He lives in Harlem. They got gangs there the size of armies. They *run* the city. When people see them coming, they get out the way."

"That's where you took your name?" Rufus said.

"Huh?"

"The biggest gangs in New York, the Chaplains and the Bishops, right? So . . . 'Preacher,' that would be like . . . representing what they are."

"You know a lot," Preacher said, not disputing Rufus's intuitive guess.

"You know what? Those big gangs, those *armies,* they don't own nothing," Rufus said. "They got no real power. Only reason the Man hasn't stepped on them is, right now, they making things easy for Whitey. Got half the folks in the big cities scared out of their minds, so the politicians, nobody cares what crooks they are, long as they protect them from the crazed hordes of niggers. It's all a shuck, son."

"How do you know so much?" Preacher said. Not disputing,

wondering. Whatever these men were, they were a lot more than gun dealers.

"We're going to tell you," Rufus said. "And I hope you listen."

1959 October 06 Tuesday 22:39

"Walker?"

"Huh?" Dett said, opening his eyes.

"You were asleep!"

"Me?" he said, noticing, for the first time, that his right arm was wrapped around Tussy.

"Yes, you!" she said. "I've heard of boys who take girls to drive-ins for all *kinds* of reasons, but I never heard of one who fell asleep on the job."

"I didn't . . . realize. It was just so . . ."

"What?" Tussy demanded.

"It was so peaceful," Dett said, quietly. "Like when you come back in off the line—"

"You mean, in the war?"

"Yeah," he said, quickly. "For days before, you *can't* sleep. Not really sleep, I mean. You're . . . tensed up, like there's little jolts running through you. Guys talk, at night. Some do it just to pass the time, but mostly so you don't think about what's out there, waiting for you. They say, 'Soon as I get back, I'm going to . . . get drunk, or get a woman, or . . .' You know what I mean. But what happens is, when you finally do get back, it's like someone slipped you a Mickey Finn. You go out like a light. Sleep for days, sometimes."

"Like someone turned off your electricity?"

"*Just* like that," Dett said. "And, here with you, it was like I . . . I don't know what it was, Tussy."

"Well, I'm not mad now," she said, making a face. "But I know what would make me feel even better."

"What? Just tell me and I'll—"

"Talk, talk, talk," Tussy murmured, her lips against his ear.

1959 October 06 Tuesday 22:47

Sherman entered Ruth as gently as a man defusing a bomb. She opened delicately, a dewy blossom, offering the secret purity she had defended against the rapists of her childhood.

Like a key in a lock, radiated through Sherman's mind. *Only it's me who's opening.*

Ruth whispered words no customer could ever have paid her to say. Then shuddered to an orgasm she didn't believe could exist.

Sherman followed right after her, as they mated for life.

1959 October 06 Tuesday 23:12

"You think this'll do the trick, Gar?" Rufus said to a bespectacled man standing at a workbench.

"It *should,*" the man said, cautiously. "It's just physics. What we're after is dissipation of force. We can't build a thick enough wall, so we get the same effect with layers. Each one absorbs some of the energy, so, by the time you get to the last one, it holds."

"How much is that thing going to weigh, brother?" Kendall asked, skeptically. "Remember, the boy got to *walk* in it."

"He's a strong young man," Moses said. "And he won't have to walk far."

"Far enough," Rufus said. "The Kings' clubhouse is way over on—"

"We can drive him over," Moses said. "Drop him off at the side."

"That's not the way it works," Kendall said. "I was a gang fighter, in Detroit. Years ago, before I got . . . conscious. The leader has to *lead.* He's got to walk at the head, all the way down to wherever the meet is."

"If that boy's got a strong enough rep—and my guess is that he does—he tells his men this is strategy, him coming in at the last minute—and they'll buy it," Rufus said.

"Long as he first across," Kendall cautioned.

"I think it's ready," Garfield said, pointing to what looked like a thick blanket attached to heavy canvas straps.

"Let's find out," Darryl said, pulling a pistol from his coat.

1959 October 06 Tuesday 23:49

"Can you . . . can you do that thing you did before?" Tussy asked, as they approached her house.

"What thing?"

"You know. Go away and come back."

"Yes."

"Walker, I swear, how clear a picture do I have to paint for you?"

1959 October 06 Tuesday 23:57

"Is this how you imagined it?" Ruth asked. She was lying in Sherman's arms, nude, the black lace teddy she had brought with her still in the trunk of her car—in a makeup case that also contained a pair of handcuffs and a black blindfold.

"I didn't imagine it, I dreamed it."

"What's the difference?"

"I . . . never thought it could really happen."

"I never thought a lot of things could happen. Good things, I mean. Bad things, those you can count on."

"Not anymore," Sherman said, grimly.

"What do you mean, Sherman?"

"You'll see."

"Sherman, don't frighten me. Please."

"Christ, I'm sorry, Ruth. I just meant from now on bad things aren't going to happen to you."

"Not when I'm with you, anyway."

"More than just then," the big detective said, his voice lush with love and menace.

1959 October 07 Wednesday 00:54

Another man entering the back door to Tussy's house would have seen only darkness. Dett's nightman eyes quickly registered the vague shapes and outlines, and his memory supplied a map of the living room.

Tussy sat on the edge of the couch, knees together primly, hands in her lap. She was wearing a soft pink nightgown.

"Walker," was all she said.

Dett approached the couch. He dropped to his knees next to her.

"I told you I was chubby," Tussy said, throatily. "Do you still think you could pick me up and carry me?"

1959 October 07 Wednesday 00:59

"Does it make you happy, putting criminals away?" Ruth asked.

"Happy? Not really. It's a good thing to do, but it doesn't mean much."

"Why doesn't it?" Ruth said, turning so she could watch Sherman's eyes.

"Because fighting criminals isn't the same as fighting crime, Ruth. It's like . . . a garden, okay? If you have weeds, what do you do?"

"Pull them out."

"Yeah. *Pull* them out. Not chop them off, because that wouldn't do any good, right? They'd just grow back."

Sherman rolled onto his back, then shifted position so that he was sitting up, his back against the headboard of the bed. Ruth spun onto her knees, facing him.

"You know what people say about Dobermans?" Sherman asked.

"That they turn on you?"

"Yeah, that. It's a lie."

"Why would people make up lies about a dog?"

"I'll tell you why," Sherman said, eyes glinting with unforgiveness. "A man gets a Doberman puppy. Now, he's heard that Dobermans are really tough dogs, and he's going to make sure this one knows who's boss. So he beats the dog, that puppy. Until the dog does everything he wants it to.

"This goes on and on. But, one day, the dog realizes he's not a puppy anymore. And when the man picks up the stick to beat him that day, the dog nails him. You know what the guy he bit is going to say? He'll say, 'My dog turned on me.' You see what I'm telling you, Ruth? The dog didn't turn on him. The dog was never *with* him. He was just biding his time, waiting for his chance."

"Oh."

"But if he had been good to that dog, from the beginning, I mean, the dog would never have done that."

"And you think people are like that, too?" she said.

"No. People aren't as good as dogs—some *will* turn on you. I see it happen in my job, every day. And there's men I've known, they had every chance in life, but they were criminals in their hearts. Like rich kids who steal just for the thrill of it.

"But the thing is, the one sure thing is, the truly . . . sick ones, like the rapists and the child molesters, they all were like those Dobermans, once. Only once they got stronger, instead of turning on whoever hurt them, they went looking for weak people to hurt themselves. Like, once they learned how to do it, they got to love it."

"Some people are just born mean," Ruth said.

"That might be so," Sherman said, "but I don't believe anyone's born to murder a whole bunch of people for the hell of it. You don't get to be Charlie Starkweather from reading comic books, no matter what those idiot professors say."

"I remember that. Everybody's still talking about . . . what he did. You're not saying a man like that, he didn't deserve to die?"

"He deserved to die a dozen times over, Ruth. I'm just saying, well, he didn't get that way overnight."

"What about the girl? That little Caril?"

"What about her?"

"She went to prison. People say she did some of those murders, don't they?"

"Yeah. And I don't know what the truth of her is. I don't think anyone's ever going to know. Starkweather, he wasn't one of the hard men, he was just a freak."

"What do you mean, one of the hard men?"

"A professional. A man who does crime the way another man does whatever *his* job is. A man with . . . a code. If he'd been one of those, you can bet he would have taken the weight. Said it was all his fault, that he had forced the girl to go along. He was going to die anyway; he might as well have gone out with some class. Sat down in that chair and rode the lightning like a man. Starkweather, he was nothing but a degenerate. A piece of garbage like that, he doesn't care what other people think of him, even his own kind."

"You know what, Sherman?" Ruth said, curling into him. "Even if you're right, even if his family did . . . horrible things to him, he didn't have to do what he did. He had choices. Everybody has choices."

"Everybody?"

"Yes," she said, her voice as soft as gossamer. "Sometimes, the only choice is to live or to die. But you always have that. Like a bank account no one knows about, one that you can always go to if things get bad enough."

"You're not talking about Starkweather now, are you?"

"No, sweetheart. I was talking about that little Caril girl."

1959 October 07 Wednesday 02:02

"Are you sure?" Dett said. "You don't even—"

"If I wasn't sure, do you think I would dare to do it here? In my own house?" Tussy said, indignantly. "I already know you're not going to be with me when I wake up."

"But you're . . . crying."

"So what?" she said, defiantly. "Just because I'm a big enough girl to know my own mind doesn't mean I can't cry if I feel like it."

1959 October 07 Wednesday 02:09

"Night desk. Procter."

"I've got a story for you."

White male, mid-to-late-fifties, Midwest accent, but not local, flashed through the newsman's mind, as he reflexively reached for his reporter's pad. "Go," he said.

"There's a pay phone outside the Mobil station on Highway 109, just past the—"

"—exit. So?"

"I'll give you an hour," the voice said.

1959 October 07 Wednesday 02:13

Tussy's kisses tasted like peppermint and Kools. Dett was lost. He cupped her breast gently, as if testing its weight.

"I don't know how to do this," he said.

"It sure *looks* like you do," she chuckled, her hand trailing lightly between his legs.

"I don't mean . . . that. But I never . . ."

"Oh, Walker," she said, pushing him onto his back, "don't tell me you've never been with a woman before."

"Not with a woman I . . ."

"What?" she said, fitting herself over him.

Dett looked up at Tussy's face, haloed in the reflected light from the hallway. His life fell into her eyes. "Love," he said.

1959 October 07 Wednesday 02:20

"Do you hate them all, Sherman?"

"Who, honey?" he asked.

"The . . . bad people, I guess you'd call them."

"There aren't that many *truly* bad ones, girl. Most of them, they're just . . . dopes. You know how we catch them? They start throwing money around, brag to some girl they meet in a gin mill. Or one of them gets arrested for something else, and he turns informer to save his own skin."

"Some of them . . . you know the kind I mean . . . they're nothing but animals."

"No, they're not," Sherman said, with sad certainty. "But they all *practice* on animals. When they're still kids, I mean. Every single one I ever talked to, he started out hurting animals. They loved the feeling. So they went after more of it. They all loved fire, too." *Holden loves animals,* flashed into his thoughts. *And, just like them, he fears fire.*

"When they were kids?"

"Yeah. And, sometimes, even after. You show me a kid who tortures animals and sets fires, I'll show you a man I'm going to have to hunt someday."

"You think they're born like that?"

"No," he said, watching the candlelight dance in Ruth's dark hair. "It takes a lot of work to make them turn out that way."

1959 October 07 Wednesday 03:01

Procter pulled into the Mobil station with eight minutes to spare. He left his car at the pumps and walked inside. "Where's the restrooms?" he asked the attendant, covering his tracks to the pay phone.

"Around the side," the young pump jockey told him, pointing.

"Thanks. I'll just get some gas first."

"I can fill it for you, mister," the kid said. "If you're not back, I'll just pull it over in front for you, okay?"

"You got a deal," Procter said.

He ambled out of the station, walked around to the side of the cement-block building and into the darkness between the two restrooms.

The pay phone was hanging on the wall, sheltered by the overhang of the flat roof. Procter lit a cigarette, hunched his shoulders, and waited.

1959 October 07 Wednesday 03:03

"Oh God!" Tussy moaned, falling face-first against Dett's chest. Dett's arms encircled her, as rigid as steel bands, but not quite touching her back.

"It's all right, Walker," she whispered against him. "Come on."

1959 October 07 Wednesday 03:08

When the pay phone rang, Procter snatched it before the pump jockey could react. As he lifted the receiver to his ear, he heard, "That was a nice piece you did for *The Voice of Liberation*."

"Oh, *you're* the guy who read it," Procter said.

"How come you never did another?"

"I didn't care for the company."

"You knew they were Commies before you—"

"I drove a long way," Procter said. "So where's the big story you promised, whoever you are?"

"You never wrote another article for them because you found out that the man in charge of that paper wasn't Khrushchev, it was Hoover," the voice said. A statement, not a question.

Procter felt the hair on the back of his neck flutter, and he knew it wasn't the night breeze.

"Want more?" the voice said.

"Not on the phone, I don't," Procter said, dropping his cigarette and grinding it out with the heel of his shoe.

"They ran you off once," the voice said. "But I've been studying you. And I don't think they could do it again . . . if the story was big enough."

"You're doing all the talking," Procter said.

It was another few seconds before he realized he had been speaking into a dead line.

1959 October 07 Wednesday 03:21

A lone in his room, Carl angrily tore another sheet of heavy, cream-colored stationery into strips. *It has to be perfect!*

He stood up, went to his closet, and spent several minutes precisely aligning his clothes until a familiar calmness settled over him. Then he sat down and began to write.

Mein Kommandant, I am yours to . . .

1959 October 07 Wednesday 03:59

A s Ruth and Sherman slept in each other's arms, Walker Dett slipped through the darkness behind Tussy's house to where he had hidden the Buick and a change of clothes.

Driving back to his two-room apartment, Procter was thinking, *This one's no crank. And he knows about that time the G-men paid me a visit in Chicago.*

Holden felt the darkness lifting around him, felt the night predators retreating to their dens, felt the forest respond to the not-yet-visible sun. He checked his notebook one more time, then headed back to his cave.

A maroon Eldorado crept around the corner on Halstead, then turned up the block.

"One more pass," Rufus said to Silk. "Then we'll have it all mapped out."

1959 October 07 Wednesday 06:11

"You're up early, Beau."

"I can sleep when I'm dead, Cyn."

"Why do you always have to say things like that?"

"I'm sorry, honey. I just meant there's so much to do and there's never enough time."

"I know."

"And I'm never really sleepy, you know? A couple of hours, that's all I ever need."

"At least have a good breakfast, for once. I'll make some bacon and eggs, and maybe some potato pancakes?"

"I'm really not so—"

"You know how much Luther loves it when we have breakfast together, Beau. We can all eat at the big table. What do you say?"

"Sounds good," Beaumont said, smiling at his sister.

1959 October 07 Wednesday 07:12

"What?"

"Oh, Walker, I'm sorry! I woke you up, didn't I?"

"Tussy," Dett said, as if to reassure himself. "I thought it was . . . business. No, you didn't wake me up at all. Is anything wrong?"

"No! Nothing at all. I was just . . . I . . . well, I remembered you were staying at the Claremont, and I don't have to be at work until three, so I thought . . . I mean, I know you're busy, you have business and all, but I thought, I mean, if you wanted to come over for lunch, I could . . ."

"I never wanted to leave," Dett said.

1959 October 07 Wednesday 07:13

"You can pay six hundred dollars for a suit," the man with the rawhide skin and dirty-water eyes said, fingering the sleeve of his alpaca jacket. "And it could still be a bargain. A real work of art, all hand-tailored. Takes a whole team to make something like that. You have to see the design in your head, draw a pattern, cut the cloth perfectly, sew each stitch by hand, fit it and refit it until it hangs on you just right. . . ."

The spotter sat behind his tripod, listening with the patience of his profession. The rifleman's eyes watched the speaker's hands.

They're not two men, they're one man with two bodies, the man in the alpaca suit thought to himself. *Put them next to each other in a lineup, you couldn't tell one from the other.* "But one loose thread," he said aloud, "and the whole thing could be ruined. It's not the thread itself, you understand; only if someone were to pull on it the wrong way. The thing about a loose thread, dealing with it is no job for an amateur."

The speaker glanced around the top floor of the warehouse, as if waiting for one of the other men to speak. The spotter didn't change position. The rifleman breathed shallowly, dropping his heart rate as offhandedly as another man might wind a watch.

"Now, even the best professionals can disagree on something like that," the speaker continued. "One member of the team looks at the suit, says, 'We can fix it.' Another one, he says, 'No, we need to snip it clean.' The first tailor, he says, 'You do it my way, there won't be a trace—we can weave it back in; it'll be as good as new.' But the other one disagrees. He says, 'That loose thread, it's like a cancer. Just because you can't see it, that doesn't mean it won't eat you alive. Only thing you can do is cut it out, at exactly the right spot, or the whole beautiful suit, the one we all worked so hard on, could get ruined.' "

The rifleman and the spotter listened, growing more and more immobile with every word.

"Now, let's say the tailors, they're partners," the speaker said, his low-pitched voice just a shade thicker than hollow. "Equal shares in the business. They both worked on the suit; they both want it to be perfect, but, now that something's gone wrong—*potentially* gone wrong—they can't get together on how to fix it. It's like America: you let everyone vote, but, somewhere along the line, the big decisions come down to one man. So, with a suit like I just told you about, it's not up to the tailors to decide how to fix it. No, that's up to the customer, the one who ordered it made in the first place."

The man in the alpaca suit shifted position, moving his hands behind his back.

"You're a minute-of-angle man, aren't you?" he said to the rifle-man.

"I'm better than that," the rifleman said, "and you know it. I can do a hundred yards on iron sights and a bipod. Give me the right scope, I could work a quarter-mile."

"You have everything you need?" the man in the alpaca suit asked.

The rifleman and the spotter nodded together, synchronized gears, meshing.

1959 October 07 Wednesday 09:10

"What may I tell Mr. Gendell this is in reference to?"

"A legal matter," Dett said into the phone.

"Yes, sir, I understand," the receptionist said. "But if you could be more specific, so we would know how much time to set aside for your appointment . . . ?"

"Fifteen minutes is all I'll need," Dett said.

"Well, sir, we often find that the client's estimate is—"

"It's a real-estate transaction," Dett interrupted. "A very simple one."

"Well, let's say a half-hour, shall we?" the receptionist said, brightly. "Mr. Gendell won't be available until around four this afternoon. Would that be—"

"Perfect," Dett said.

1959 October 07 Wednesday 09:13

"You come see me on your lunch break, Rosa Mae."

"I will, Daddy. Did you speak to—?"

"I tell you all about it then, girl."

1959 October 07 Wednesday 09:15

"What we need is a fulcrum," Beaumont said.

"What's a fulcrum, Roy?" Luther asked.

"Well, let's say you got a big rock that you need to move," Beaumont replied. "Way too heavy for even a few strong men to budge. What do you do?"

"Put something under it," Luther said, promptly, making a fist of one hand and placing stiffened fingers beneath, at a forty-five-degree angle. "Then you push down," he said, bringing his stiffened fingers parallel to the ground to raise his fist.

"And you put a barrel under the stick, so you can lever it up easy, right, Luther?"

"Right!"

"Well, that's exactly what a fulcrum is, see? The balance point everything turns on, so you can move a big weight."

"What weight are you talking about, Beau?" Cynthia asked.

"Ernest Hoffman," the man in the wheelchair said. "Because, right now, we're against the wall. Shalare says he'll get Dioguardi to back away, and, after the elections, *stay* away. Maybe he will; maybe he won't. That's the future. If we say 'no' now, if we *don't* promise to deliver, there's no 'maybe' left. So we have to go along. But even though Shalare's been working the whole state, I don't think he's gotten to Hoffman."

"Why not?" Cynthia said.

"Because, if he had, he wouldn't have come here *asking* us for anything, Cyn. A man who's holding all the cards doesn't have to deal a hand to anyone else."

1959 October 07 Wednesday 09:19

"Put him on."

"Put *who* on? You must have the wrong—"

"Put Procter on, Elaine. And don't be afraid: I'm not working for your husband."

The leggy redhead who had once been a pageant contestant carefully placed the telephone receiver under a pillow, then rolled onto her side. "Jimmy," she whispered.

"Uh," Procter half-grunted.

"There's a man on the phone. He asked for you."

"You think your—" Procter said, instantly alert.

"No. He, the man on the phone, he said not to be afraid of that. What should I do? If Bobby—"

Procter sat up, pulled the redhead over his lap, and took the phone from under the pillow.

"What can I do for you?" he said, coldly.

"It's what I can do for you," said the voice Procter last heard six hours ago. "I just wanted to show you that I know things, so you'll listen to me when the time comes."

"Maybe you don't know as much as you think you do."

"You'll see for yourself," the voice said. "Need more proof first?"

"Just get to it," Procter said.

"Soon enough," the voice promised.

1959 October 07 Wednesday 10:15

"Who wants him?"

"He's expecting my call," Dett said. "You got thirty seconds to get him."

The hum of a live line was broken by Dioguardi's distinctive voice. "You called for your answer?"

"Yes."

"That's your answer, pal. Yes."

"Yes to what?" Dett said.

"Yes to the noncompetition fee. The ten large. Just come by my—"

"You're a funny guy," Dett said.

"Yeah. Yeah, I guess I am. All right. How do you want to do it?"

"Just put it in the mail," Dett said. "I'll give you the address."

1959 October 07 Wednesday 11:33

"Oh, I'm so glad to see you," Tussy told Dett, her arms wrapped tightly around his chest.

"Why? I . . . I don't mean that, Tussy. You just seemed, I don't know, so surprised."

"It's all my fault," she said, taking his hand and pulling him toward the kitchen. "Even though it was me saying you couldn't stay all night, I kept thinking about all those stories you hear. You know, how the man's not there in the morning. . . ."

"You're crying," Dett said, touching her face.

1959 October 07 Wednesday 12:06

"Rufus is a good man," Moses said. "I don't mean that the way you young folks talk, child. I mean, he's a righteous man."

"Rufus? You know he's got all kinds of hustles, Daddy."

"That's just for now, Rosa Mae. He's got plans. Big plans."

"Every man who ever talked to me, that's what he had," the young woman scornfully said. "Big plans."

"Not those kind of plans," Moses said. "Not . . . personal plans. Not for himself. For all of us."

"You and me?"

"Our people, child."

"Oh. You mean, he's one of those . . . ?"

"Not *one* of those, girl. He might be *the* one."

"The one for me?"

"Ah, that's the thing, little girl. Rufus, he wouldn't run around on you. Wouldn't get drunk and beat you up. He wouldn't toss the rent money across no poker table. But he's a bound man. He's bound to what he's going to do."

"I don't understand, Daddy."

"I got to be truthful with you, Rosa Mae. You put your trust in me, I got to do that. Rufus, the kind of man he is, you might only see him when you come to visit. Maybe the jailhouse, maybe the graveyard. Understand?"

"No!"

"Yeah, I think you do, child. I think you do. Rufus, he's a leader. A brave man. You been in this world long enough to know what happens to a brave colored man."

"You don't think I should . . . see him?"

"I think you got to make up your own mind on that, Rosa Mae. But I tell you this: Rufus, he's no halfway man. He wants you for his woman. Not his girlfriend, his wife. I know he'll be a good man, loyal and true. I know he'll take care of you. But, a man like Rufus, you can't go to be his wife without knowing you got a good chance to be his widow."

1959 October 07 Wednesday 12:16

"I invited *you*," Tussy said.

"Sure, but . . ."

"But what, Walker? You don't have to run around spending money on me every second. When I asked you for lunch, I wasn't asking you to *take* me to lunch. I can make something right here."

"That would be great."

Tussy walked around behind the kitchen chair where Dett was seated. She put her hands on his shoulders, and leaned forward so her lips were against his ear.

"There's another reason I want to stay here," she whispered.

1959 October 07 Wednesday 12:33

"Tonight," Dioguardi said.

"Ah cain't do it, boss," Rufus replied, holding the mouthpiece of the phone a few inches from his lips, projecting his voice. "No, sir, Ah jest cain't."

"Why not?"

"I got business, boss," Rufus said, putting a sly veneer over his servile voice. "You knows what I'm talking about."

"You can always get pussy, boy. One's the same as the other. Take it from me—there's no such thing as a golden snapper."

"Yessir, I know you saying the truth. But I done promised—"

"You know the car wash out on Polk?"

"Yeah, boss," Rufus said, resigned.

"I'm getting my car washed at seven o'clock. You just stand over to the side, you know, where the cars come out. They got nothing but— Uh, nobody'll even notice you; they'll think you work there. Everything I have to tell you, it'll take five minutes, then you can go get your pussy . . . with money in your pocket."

"All right, boss," Rufus said, allowing his voice to brighten.

1959 October 07 Wednesday 13:04

"Do you think I'm . . . you know what I mean," Tussy said. She was seated before her mirror, wrapped in a towel, brushing her hair vigorously.

"No, I don't," Dett said, standing behind her.

"Walker! Yes, you do. I'm asking, do you think I'm a nymphomaniac or something, asking you over for lunch just so we could . . . you know?"

"How could you be . . . what you said, Tussy? You never did anything like that before."

"Like . . . Oh! How could you know that?" she said, smiling into the mirror. "For all you know, I invite men over to take me to bed all the time."

"No, you don't."

"But how could you *know*?"

"I'll tell you," Dett said to her reflection. "I promise you, Tussy. Not today, but soon, I'll tell you everything."

1959 October 07 Wednesday 13:41

"I talked to Daddy," Rosa Mae said.

"Then you know I did, too," Rufus replied. "Like I promised."

"He scared me, Rufus."

"That's his job. That's what fathers do with their daughters."

"I don't know what to do."

"Why, girl?"

"Because . . . it's not a date you want, like you said. I'm standing in front of a door, and I don't know what's behind it. But I can't find out unless I open it."

"If you want, I can show you."

"What if it still scares me, after you show me? What if I don't want . . . If I can't . . . ?"

"Then you walk away, Rosa Mae. If I can't have you with me, I'll understand that."

"Would you, Rufus? Would you really?"

"Honeygirl, you have to listen to every word. I could understand it, sure. A woman like you, you could have . . . other things than what I got to offer. I'm not saying it wouldn't hurt my heart. But, yeah, I'd understand."

"If something hurts your heart enough, it might make you change your mind."

"No, little Rose," Rufus said. "If you counting on that, you got the wrong man. I've got a road to walk. I wish you would be walking it with me, right at my side. But even if you say you won't, I still got to walk it to the end."

1959 October 07 Wednesday 14:04

"Isn't it cute?" Tussy said, pointing at the little car in her driveway. "It's a Henry J; they don't make them anymore. I got it from a customer for twenty-five dollars, and Al deKay—he's a wonderful mechanic—fixed it all up for me. Someday, when I save enough money, I'm going to get it painted. Pink. I always wanted a pink car."

"Is it reliable?" Dett said, slowly walking around the car, his mind clicking off potential defects.

"Oh, it's very good. It never overheats in the summer, and it always starts in the winter, even when it's real cold. Mr. Bruton—he owns the Chevy dealership—he's always after me to get a new car. But those payments . . . I would be so scared to miss one. Besides, I like my car. At least it's not like every other one you see."

"I know you have to go," Dett said, glancing at his watch. "And I know you won't get back until late. But could I—?"

"It doesn't matter how late it is," she said, standing close to him.

"Just be sure to call before you come. I'll leave the back door open, okay?"

"Yes."

"I wish I didn't have to work tonight."

"That's okay," Dett said. "I have to work, too."

1959 October 07 Wednesday 15:56

"Good afternoon," Dett said to the stylishly dressed woman seated at a small desk behind a wooden railing. "I have an appointment."

She looked up from her typewriter, adjusted her glasses, smiled professionally, said, "Mr. Dett?"

"Yes."

"You're certainly on time," the woman said, approvingly. "Please have a seat." She stood up, tucked a ballpoint pen into her lightly frosted hairdo, and walked into a back office.

Dett remained standing. The woman returned, said, "Come this way, please."

Dett walked past the railing and followed the woman's pointing finger into a spacious corner office. The man behind the desk was wearing a navy-blue suit with a faint chalk stripe. A heavy gold wedding band on his left hand caught the sunlight slanting through the high windows.

"Mr. Dett," the man said, getting to his feet and extending his hand. He was slightly above medium height, with a bearish frame. Thick, tightly curled brown hair topped a clean-featured face. His eyes were the color of rich Delta soil.

"Thanks for seeing me on such short notice," Dett said, shaking hands.

Both men sat down. Gendell spread his hands, his gesture an invitation to speak.

"This is about a mortgage," Dett said.

"Oh?"

"You seem surprised."

"You're not from around here," the lawyer said. "So I assumed what you told my secretary was a pretext of some sort. And, now that I've had a look at you, I still think so."

"It's not about my mortgage," Dett said. "Someone else's."

The lawyer's expression didn't change.

"Let's say I wanted to pay off someone's mortgage," Dett went on. "How would I go about it?"

"You mean if you wanted to acquire the property for yourself?" the lawyer asked, his hands working expertly with a cigar cutter.

"No, nothing like that. Just pay off someone's mortgage. So they'd own their house, free and clear."

"Give them the money, let them walk down to the bank," the lawyer said, the corners of his eyes tightening.

"I can't do it like that."

"Because . . . ?"

"I don't want them to know. . . . I mean I want it to be a surprise."

"You want to be someone's mystery benefactor?" Gendell said, using a long match to distribute flame evenly around the tip of his cigar.

"There's nothing shady about what I want to do," Dett said, calmly. "There's someone I care about. A woman. If I just offered to pay off her mortgage, she'd never accept. So I want it to be a surprise. For after I'm not around."

"Oh, I get it. You want to leave her the money in your will, so when you—"

"No," Dett said, slowly. "After I've gone from *here*. From Locke City."

"And that would be . . . ?"

"In a few days."

"What, exactly, would you want me to do?"

"I want to leave the money with you. Enough to pay off the mortgage. A month from now, I want you to go to the bank, get the mortgage canceled, and give the papers, the free-and-clear papers, to her."

"Well, I'd need a power of attorney, together with—"

"Just the money," Dett said. He reached into his overcoat and took out several stacks of neatly banded bills. "There's a thousand in each one," he said. "Six thousand total. The mortgage is thirty-seven dollars and forty-nine cents a month. It's at least twenty years paid. That'll be more than enough to cover it. And your fee, too."

"You don't need a lawyer for this," Gendell said, puffing on his cigar. "All you need is a messenger boy."

"I *do* need a lawyer," Dett said. "To be sure she doesn't get cheated, make certain the deed they give her is what it's supposed to be. I don't want anyone at the bank pulling a fast one."

Dett got to his feet.

"Wait a minute," the lawyer said. "You come in here talking about the bank pulling a fast one, but you drop six grand on my desk and don't even ask for a receipt. How do you know I won't just pocket the money?"

"Because I know what kind of man you are, lawyer or not," Dett said. "The mortgage I want you to pay off, it belongs to Tussy Chambers."

1959 October 07 Wednesday 19:03

"The address is a bottle club in Cleveland. On East Seventy-ninth. In what they call the Hough area. It's all colored there; a white man would stick out a mile away."

"I never been there, boss."

"But you got people there, right? A cousin, a friend, something?"

"Well, I *knows* people there, sure. But what you want, that's pretty tricky stuff. Like being a spy."

"It's not tricky at all," Dioguardi said, soothingly. *Don't want to spook the nigger,* he thought, grinning inwardly as he realized his unintentional pun, vowing to use it later, when he got back to his headquarters. "The package is going to look like this," he said, holding up a nine-by-twelve-inch manila envelope with thick red bands running both horizontally and vertically to form a cross.

"Looks like a Christmas package, boss."

"That's right," Dioguardi said, encouragingly. "You could spot it at fifty feet. Now, we'll make sure it gets delivered this coming

Monday. All you have to do is watch for a white man coming out of that club, with this envelope in his hand."

"What if he don't pick it up on Monday, boss?"

"I told you; this is a colored place, in a colored neighborhood. A rough one, too. The guy I'm interested in, he's a white man. So he's not going to want to hang around. The way I have it figured, whoever he's got working for him—inside the place, I mean—that person is going to call him as soon as the package gets delivered. And the guy I want you to watch for, he'll be close by, ready to make his move."

"I don't think this is something I could do for you, boss. I mean, I *wants* to do it, sure, I do. I know you pays good. But I be worried that . . . well, they's just too many things that could go wrong. And then you be mad at me. If this was Locke City, in Darktown, I mean, I could follow any man you say. But Cleveland, I ain't never even been there myself. How I gonna chase after a man, I don't even know the streets?"

"I was counting on you, Rufus."

"That's just it, boss. I *wants* you to count on me. I got a good reputation with you, don't I? You ask Rufus to do something, it gets done. For a long time now, ain't that true? Well, this time, something go wrong, now Rufus ain't so reliable anymore, see? I can't have that, boss. Now, you got a slick plan, find out who's going to pick up your package. I know you a big man. You could probably make one little phone call, get a dozen good men to watch that place, if you wanted."

Dioguardi leaned back in his seat, staring at nothing.

Rufus waited, silently.

"You make good sense, Rufus," Dioguardi said, grudgingly. "You're right. I'll have it taken care of."

"Thank you, boss. You said there was *two* things. . . ."

"Yeah. And the other one, it's right up your alley. All I want you to do is tell me if Walker Dett leaves town."

"I gonna do that anyway, boss. I watching that man like a hawk for you."

"You understand, I don't just mean if he checks out, right? If he leaves town at all, even if he comes back. You can tell if he spent the night at the hotel, right?"

"Yes, sir. Easiest thing in the—"

"It's a long drive to Cleveland," Dioguardi said. "But it could be done in a day, easy. You watch him *close,* hear?"

1959 October 07 Wednesday 20:17

"How come you won't be needing that shack you asked me about before?" Beaumont asked.

"I changed the plan," Dett told him. "After I sapped that one punk, and that didn't work, I took out two of his other men. That got him on the phone. I offered him a bunch of options, but, bottom line, either he was going to pay, or more of his men were going to die."

"You shook down Sal Dioguardi?" Beaumont said, grinning. "A one-man protection racket, huh?"

"He couldn't know how many people were involved," Dett said. "All he knew was a voice on the phone."

"How did he even know you were the same one who—?"

"I mailed him that souvenir. From the first one."

"So what was the shack supposed to be for?"

"I figured he'd make some deal, say he had work for me. He'd know I wouldn't come into his place, so he'd promise to meet me wherever I said. That's why I wanted it local, so he'd think it was someone from around here. Like I said, he couldn't know how many people were involved at my end. So he'd send a whole bunch of his best men to storm the shack."

"And then?"

Dett gestured pushing a plunger with both hands. "Boom," he said.

"Christ," Beaumont said, exchanging a quick glance with Cynthia. "What kind of 'strategy' is that?"

"The kind that would make him deal with me the next time he heard my voice on the phone."

"I guess it damn well would. But . . . why do you think he paid you off, instead?"

"I don't know," Dett admitted. "It wasn't what I expected.

Probably he thinks he's going to snatch me when I go to pick up the money."

"But there's no chance of that?"

"None."

"Maybe he's doing just what Shalare promised he would," Cynthia said. "Backing off."

"Maybe," Beaumont said, musing. "But maybe he's got something else he's thinking about."

"I don't think he runs that tight an operation," Dett said. "I could just hit him, be done with it."

"That's just it," Beaumont told him. "I don't think that would put an end to anything. When I first sent for you, I thought Dioguardi was our problem. And he still *is* a problem, unless, like Cynthia says, he moves off, like we've been promised."

"By Shalare," Dett said, quietly.

"Yeah," Beaumont agreed. "So now it's Shalare that's the problem. I . . . think. It's like we're watching a puppet theater. All we can see is the puppets; we can't see who's pulling their strings."

"What do you want?" Dett said.

"Huh? You know what we want. The reason we brought you in here—"

"You thought there was going to be a war," Dett interrupted. "Now you're not sure. If you can't say what you want, I can't get it done."

"I'm paying you—"

"—to *do* something. Or get something done. That's what I do. Then I move along. No trouble for you; no trouble for me. I'm not looking for a salary."

Beaumont sipped at his drink. Cynthia got up and stirred the logs in the fireplace. Luther watched from the corner.

Dett lit a cigarette. He took a deep drag, then looked pointedly at the cigarette, as if to say the fuse was burning down on his patience.

"You're supposed to be a master planner," Beaumont broke the silence. "So plan me this: how can we get Ernest Hoffman to back us?"

"Who's Ernest Hoffman?"

"Ernest Hoffman is the most powerful man in the whole state. I've been studying him for years. Probably know more about him than he knows about himself."

"Tell me," Dett said, settling back in his chair.

1959 October 07 Wednesday 21:54

"Where Preacher at? We supposed to *go,* man!"

"How many times I gotta say it?" a round-faced youth with a shaven skull said. "Preacher gonna meet us at the corner. He say he got a surprise for those motherfucking Hawks. One they never gonna forget."

"It don't seem right, Buddha," another youth protested.

"You see this?" the round-faced youth said, getting to his feet, and pointing to an embroidered orange thunderbolt on the sleeve of his long black coat. "This says I'm the Warlord of the South Side Kings. Preacher called this meet, but I'm the one who set it up. And you know what? Me, I'm going down on the Golden Hawks if I got to do it by my motherfucking *self.*"

Buddha opened his coat, to display a heavy chain draped through his belt. From his pocket, he took a switchblade. As the others watched, he thumbed it into life.

"South Side! South Side Kings!" he chanted.

"South Side, do or die!" another youth picked up the cry.

"Walk with me," Buddha commanded.

1959 October 07 Wednesday 21:56

"After tonight, everything changes," Ace said. He held the pistol aloft, like a torch. "And this, this is what changes it."

"What about the Gladiators?" Larry said, tapping a length of lead pipe into his open palm.

"We don't need them," Ace said, quietly. "But I hope they show. I want them all to see this."

Hog took a final swig of blackberry wine, tossed the empty bottle onto the ratty couch, and stood up. "Hawks!" he shouted to the waiting gang. "Mighty, mighty Hawks! Tonight's our night. Pick up your weapons, men. Time to roll."

1959 October 07 Wednesday 22:03

"They're moving," Sunglasses said to Lacy. "Looks like . . . maybe twenty men. More than we thought."

"Cut across Davenport, so we can come in from the side," Lacy told the driver, from the back seat. "We're not driving through nigger territory. Not tonight."

1959 October 07 Wednesday 22:05

A battered silver truck with RELIABLE MOVERS stenciled in black letters on its sides slowed to a stop underneath a streetlight whose bulb had been shattered earlier that same evening. Inside the back of the truck, Rufus spoke urgently to Preacher.

"We got a ramp all ready, walk you down nice and easy. Four men going to go with you, right up to the lot, just to make sure you get there all right. But then it's all you, young brother. Be the boss!"

"I'm ready," Preacher said, grim-voiced.

"After tonight, nobody be calling you Preacher no more," Rufus said. "You going to be the Magic Man. And people, they going to *follow* you, son. Understand?"

"Yes, sir!"

"All right. Now, remember what we went over. You just stay there when it's done. Don't even try and get up. Everyone else's going to be running away, but we going to be running *at* you, get that stuff off, and bring you with us, just like we planned."

"It's hotter than a damn oven in all this," Preacher said, sweat pouring down his face and into his voice.

1959 October 07 Wednesday 22:10

"Spread out!" Hog ordered the bunched-up Hawks. "Corner to corner. Don't let any of them past the line, no matter what. Long as we keep them in front of us, we got control, no matter how many of them there are."

"Here they come!" the acne-scarred boy hissed.

The Hawks moved to meet their enemies, shuffling forward in a ragged line. Some carried sawed-down baseball bats. Others had lengths of lead pipe, bicycle chains, tire irons, car antennas. One brandished a glass whip—a length of rope coated in white glue, rolled in broken glass, and allowed to harden. Two held zip guns. Every youth had a knife of some kind, from cane-cutters to switch-blades.

1959 October 07 Wednesday 22:11

"There's Preacher!" one of the Kings yelled.

"Fuck, he walking *slow*," another said. "You think he hurt?"

"No, man. Remember what Buddha told us?"

"Behind me," Preacher called out, as he joined the Kings and merged with the night.

1959 October 07 Wednesday 22:12

"He's doing it," Darryl said, quietly. "Boy got himself a ton of heart."

"Ton of trust, too," Rufus said. "And he brought it to the right people."

The gangs closed the ground between them, moving in a silence so deep it vibrated, their wine-and-reefer courage already starting to fade.

"Rush!" shouted Hog, breaking into a run.

The Kings immediately fell back a few paces, creating an arrow formation, with Preacher at its apex. As the Hawks charged in, one of the Kings screamed "Ahhhhh!" and leaped ahead of Preacher, swinging a chain over his head like a mace.

In seconds, the vacant lot was a swirling vortex of violence, punctuated by the sounds of blunt objects against flesh, screams when knife blades found homes, the popping of zip guns.

Ace and Preacher stood apart, in the center of the chaos, seeing only each other.

Ace pulled his pistol.

Preacher walked directly toward him, hands in his pockets, moving stiffly.

"Die, nigger!" Ace screamed.

Preacher kept coming.

Ace leveled his pistol and fired.

Preacher dropped. His black-coated body disappeared into the deeper darkness of the ground.

Ace stood frozen, his hand locked to the salvation-promising pistol. His mouth opened like a hinge. A shock wave hit his stomach. He closed his eyes and fired again.

"They got cannons!" one of the Kings shouted.

Sirens ripped the night. Closing fast.

"Rollers!" someone screamed.

Like contestants hearing a referee's whistle, both gangs immediately started back the way they had come, dragging off their wounded.

Ace was rooted in place. He tried to sight down the barrel of his pistol, but his hands were in spasm. Suddenly, Buddha loomed out of the blackness, arms spread wide as if embracing whatever was to come. He dived to the ground, flinging his body over Preacher. Startled, Ace turned and ran, firing randomly over his shoulder. *I was the last to go!* blazed through his mind. *They all saw it.*

From the far side of the lot, Rufus, Darryl, Kendall, and Garfield raced toward where they had seen Preacher go down.

Buddha saw them coming, struggled to his feet. "Come on, motherfuckers!" he shrieked his war cry, standing over the body of his fallen leader, twirling his chain in one hand. "I got something for all of you!"

"Back up, fool!" Rufus snarled at him as they closed in. "We look like white boys to you?"

Buddha staggered backward. He watched in stunned amazement as the four men skillfully turned Preacher over on his stomach. Garfield used an industrial shears to cut Preacher's long black coat off, then quickly unbuckled a series of straps. The other men gripped together and pulled in unison, rolling Preacher out of his wrappings.

"You all right, son?" Rufus said, bending down.

"Got my . . . rib, I think," the young man gasped. "Like I was hit with a sledgehammer."

"Let me see," Darryl said. He felt with his fingers. "There?"

"Yeah!" Preacher grunted in pain.

"Never got in," Darryl said, triumphantly. "You got to walk a little now, brother. Going to hurt, but you can do it." He draped Preacher's arm over his neck, helped the young man to his feet.

"What about . . . ?" Garfield said, gesturing in Buddha's direction with the shears. The round-faced youth hadn't moved.

"Got to take him with us now," Rufus said. "We used our own sirens to get them all to run, but the real cops'll be here any minute now. You!" he snapped at Buddha. "Come *on!*"

1959 October 07 Wednesday 22:18

"I think I see a way to do it," Dett said. "If everything you've got here"—pointing to stacks of paper and the maps taped to the wall—"is accurate."

"I'd bet my life on it," Beaumont vowed.

"That's up to you," Dett said.

1959 October 07 Wednesday 22:41

"You see it?" Ace demanded, for the fifth time. "You see me drop that nigger like a sack of cement?"

"We got to get rid of that pistol," Hog said, urgently.

"Fuck that! This baby is what's going to make the Hawks—"

"Are you nuts? Once the cops dig that slug out of Preacher in the morgue, all they have to do is match it up with your gun, and you'll end up getting the chair."

"Why should they even—?"

"Oh, man," Hog said, despairingly. "I know you're all jazzed from what happened, okay? But you're not thinking, Ace. You asking people if they saw it. Well, they *did* see it, man. *Everybody* out there saw it."

"None of our guys would ever—"

"The *niggers,* man. You think they're not going to squeal?"

"Never did before, when we—"

"We never *killed* one before. This time, the cops are really going to look, man. That pistol has to go. Tonight."

"Damn, Hog."

"Hey, man, when the Klan hears what you did tonight, they'll give you another one. Maybe more than one . . ."

1959 October 07 Wednesday 22:43

"White boys got to burn for this," a coal-colored youth with a red bandanna around his neck said. "Gunned down Preacher like he was a dog. He never had a chance."

"Firesticks!" another youth said. "I got a cousin, works on a construction site all the way up in Gary. We get a couple of sticks of dynamite, go down to their clubhouse, blow those cocksucking Hawks all to hell. *Bang!*"

"Shut up, all of you," a squat, coffee-colored young man said. He swayed on wide-planted feet, blood still running from a gash next to his right eye. "This ain't what Preacher would want us to do. We got to be *cold,* not crazy. Cops gonna be all over this place. Everybody that needs patching up, get out. All the weapons got to go, too. Have the debs take them away. Now! When the rollers show up, we all want to be—"

"Dancer's telling it like it should be told." The voice penetrated the darkened room.

"Buddha!" A joyous yell. "Thought you got it, too."

"White boys can't kill no man like me," Buddha said, grinning.

"Is Preacher gonna make it?" one of the youths called out.

"Make it? Shit, motherfuckers, he gonna do a whole lot better than that. Everybody split now, like Dancer say. We meet back here, tomorrow night."

"You in charge now?" another youth asked, not a trace of challenge in his voice, only awestruck respect for the man who had stayed behind while all the others had run.

"*Preacher* in charge, fool!" Buddha said, laughing infectiously. "We all meet, tomorrow night, right here. And you gonna see for yourselves."

1959 October 07 Wednesday 22:50

"I have to look it over by myself," Dett said. "How far a drive is it?"

"To the estate?" Beaumont asked. "Probably take you only about—"

"Not there. To the daughter's house."

"The daughter? Why her? I thought it would be his son. He's the one named for him. Not Ernest Junior; Ernest the Fourth. Like he was a goddamned king. And I guess he will be, someday."

"You said the daughter had a baby."

"So? *That* kid's not going to be named for Ernest Hoffman. What makes you think—?"

"Hoffman himself's seventy-seven years old, right?" Dett said, pawing through some of the papers in front of him. "Had his own son, this Ernest the Fourth, when he was a young man, so *that* one's in his middle fifties already. And he's been married three times, no kids. What does that tell you?"

"He's had some bad luck picking women," Beaumont said, ticking off the possibilities on his fingers. "He can't make babies himself. Or he's a fag, and the women are just cover."

"If you've been looking as hard as you say you have, for as long as you have, you must have narrowed it down past that."

"If he's a fag, he's the best faker I ever heard of," Beaumont said, chuckling. "Ernest the Fourth has been in half the whorehouses in the state. And he's had a woman on the side every time he's been married, too. In fact, the one he's married to now, she used to be the lady-in-waiting."

"And if he wasn't shooting blanks, he would have gotten *one* of them pregnant by now," Dett said. " 'Specially when he knows any kid of his would inherit a fortune."

"Right," Beaumont agreed. "Got to be something wrong with his equipment."

"There's a lot more wrong with him than that," Cynthia said, disgustedly. "No man ever had more opportunities in life than Ernest Hoffman's son. And he's squandered them all. He's just a wastrel and a failure. If I was his father . . . Oh!"

"Sure," Dett said. "The line is going to die out, without anyone to take over. The daughter, Dianne, she's out of Hoffman's second wife, after his first one died. Twenty years younger than the son, and *still* pretty old to be having a baby."

"You think she was pressured into it?" Cynthia asked.

"It adds up," Dett said, moving his hands in a wide-sweeping gesture, as if to include all the material Beaumont had gathered. "Hoffman knows his own son isn't going to take over for him. But his grandson . . . I don't care what the name on the birth certificate says, that's the *real* Ernest the Fourth."

1959 October 07 Wednesday 22:59

Sherman Layne entered the precinct house at the beginning of his shift. He strolled through the squad room, back to the area reserved for the detectives. "I heard there was a rumble earlier, Chet," he said to a jowly, white-haired cop in a houndstooth sport coat, making the statement into a question.

"There was *something*," the plainclothesman answered. "Call comes into the precinct, says they're having World War III out there. Heavy gunfire. Everybody saddles up and rides, but, time the first cars are on the scene, it's back to being a vacant lot."

"That doesn't make sense," the big detective said, slowly. "There's always some of them left, either from wanting to be the last ones to run, or not being able to run at all."

"They got tricked," the jowly cop said, making a jeering sound with his rubbery lips. "Looks like someone in the neighborhood had their own police siren. Some of our guys heard it in *front* of them, as they were heading to the scene."

"That was pretty damn slick, whoever thought of it," Sherman said, furrowing his brow in concentration. "Those kids hear a siren, they're going to bolt. They wouldn't stop to figure out where it was coming from."

"Yeah. But you know that area. Nobody knows nothing. One old lady, lives a few blocks from the lot—on Halstead, where it went down—she said the sirens were coming from a couple of different cars."

"Cars?"

"That's what she said."

"But not squad cars?"

"Nope. Just regular cars. Driving around, blasting sirens."

"That's a new one on me. Never heard of anything like that before."

"Me, neither. But it wasn't her imagination, Sherman. 'Cause the gang boys heard them, too. That's what made them cut and run."

"I think I'll go out there myself," Sherman Layne said. "Take a look around while it's still dark."

1959 October 07 Wednesday 23:04

"Did you see it?"

"Not up close," Lacy said into the phone. "But we were there. Saw one of them go down. We split soon as we heard the sirens."

"Tomorrow morning, come over to Benny's place. We'll shoot a game of pool."

"What time?"

"I'll be there sometime between ten and eleven," Harley Grant said.

1959 October 07 Wednesday 23:08

"Dianne lives right here," Beaumont said, pointing to a large map. "Not in Locke City proper, but just outside. They have a place on Carver Lake."

"Summer place, you mean?"

"No, it's year-round. Her husband, he works for . . . well, he works for Hoffman, I guess. He's the manager of a half-dozen different businesses in town: couple of bars, Trianon Lanes—that's the bowling alley that's not ours—the movie house—the Rialto, not the drive-in—things like that."

"Sounds like a lot of work."

"It isn't *any* work," Cynthia said, making a snorting sound. "Every one of those places has a full-time manager. All the husband—Parsons is his name, Mark Parsons—has to do is make his rounds and collect money. He's like a little kid with an allowance."

"Is he paying anyone off?" Dett asked.

"With Ernest Hoffman for a father-in-law? You've got to be joking," Beaumont said. "Those businesses, they're all legit. And nobody'd be crazy enough to try and shake him down for protection."

"All he's good for is driving around in that fancy sports car of his," Cynthia said, dismissively. "And making babies. That he knows how to do."

"They only have the one kid, right?"

"*They* do," Cynthia said, her mouth twisting in disapproval. "But before that child was born, two of his girlfriends visited Dr. Turlow."

"He does abortions," Beaumont explained.

"If you know all that . . ."

"It's not a lever," Beaumont said. "The son-in-law is . . . well, he's a son-in-law. That's what he is; that's what he does. He's not running for office."

"What if he thought his wife was going to find out?"

"Even if that *was* worth something, it's not what we need," Beaumont said. "All the son-in-law could do is pay some money to hush it up. Probably already did. But he can't make anything happen, not the way we need it to.

"Hell, his wife probably *already* knows. And you can bet Hoffman himself does. If Hoffman wanted him to stop running around, he'd take care of it himself. There's nothing there for us."

"But if someone had the baby . . ."

"A *kidnap*?" Beaumont said. "You have to be insane."

"Who kidnaps kids?" Dett replied, calmly.

"I don't know. Psychos, I guess. It's, I don't know . . ."

"Dirty," Cynthia finished for him, her mouth twisted in disgust.

"Rich people's kids get kidnapped all the time," Dett said, calmly. "Bobby Greenglass, Peter Weinberger . . ."

"Those kids got *killed,*" Beaumont said.

"You're going to do a snatch, you might as well," Dett said, shrugging his shoulders. "It's the death penalty no matter what. They're going to execute that guy out in California . . . Chessman, and he didn't kill anyone. Ever since Lindbergh . . ."

"I don't see where you're going with this," Beaumont said, feeling Cynthia's anger fill his own chest. "We can't snatch Ernest Hoffman's grandson. Even if he'd play ball—and we don't know that he would—he'd know it was us. That's not strategy. That's suicide."

"Have to be pretty stupid to try and pull a stunt like that, wouldn't you?" Dett said, as if struggling to understand a complex proposition. "Extortion's for money, not for politics. I mean, what kind of a man thinks he can kidnap a kid to make the kid's grandfather do him a bunch of favors?"

"An idiot," Beaumont said, his voice as iron as his eyes.

"Exactly," Dett said, very quietly. "A real animal. The kind you can't talk to. You know anyone like that around here?"

1959 October 07 Wednesday 23:59

"Tussy! Call for you."

"Thanks, Booker."

"You know Armand don't like it when—"

"Armand won't mind," she said, innocent-eyed.

Tussy went through the swinging doors, picked up the phone, said, "Walker?"

"Yes."

"Do you want to come over after I—?"

"I can't," he said. "I'm a long way out of town. But I thought maybe you'd like to go for a drive with me tomorrow."

"A drive?"

"Yes. A long drive. I thought we could maybe find a nice place, have a picnic all to ourselves."

"Oh, I'd love that. I'll pack a—"

"No, I didn't mean for you to have to do anything. We can pick up some—"

"Oh, don't be silly," Tussy said. "Just tell me what time you're picking me up. I can be ready anytime after nine."

1959 October 08 Thursday 04:14

"He's going to go for it," Lymon said, shielding the telephone receiver in one cupped hand.

"You're sure?" Shalare said.

"He told me so. Late last night. A few hours ago."

"Just you?" Shalare asked, glancing over at Brian O'Sullivan.

"No. He called a meeting. Faron was there, too. And Sammy. And—"

"Okay."

"But he's going to wait for—"

"I know," Shalare said, and cut the connection. He turned to face his friend. "The curtain's coming up, Brian. Now it's time for the Italian to show everyone how good he can play his role."

1959 October 08 Thursday 09:29

"Where are we going?" Tussy asked, brightly. "I hear there's a lake not so far from here . . . ?"

"You mean Carver Lake? Did you want to go out on it?"

"Go out on it?"

"In a *boat,* silly. You can rent them there."

"I wasn't thinking of doing that."

"Oh, good!"

"You don't like the water?"

"I don't mind it myself," Tussy said. "But we'd never get Fireball into a boat."

1959 October 08 Thursday 10:13

"Those pills really did the job," Preacher said. "I slept like I was dead."

"Don't get used to them," Darryl told him, not unkindly. "Use them on pain, real pain, and they work just fine. Use them for anything else, you end up a junkie."

"I won't need any more of them," Preacher said, resolutely.

"Just make sure nobody punches you there," Darryl said, touching the young man lightly. "Or even gives you a hug. Cracked ribs, they heal by themselves, so long as you keep them taped. But you can't be jumping around, not even with a woman, understand?"

"Sure."

"Just rest," Darryl said. "We get you back home after it gets dark tonight. But, first, Brother Omar wants to talk to you."

1959 October 08 Thursday 10:15

"What did you see?" Harley asked Lacy.

Lacy leaned over the pool table, sighted down his cue. "There was a little light, from the street, but when they closed on each other, it was like they all stepped in a puddle of ink. You couldn't tell black from white. But one of the Hawks had a pistol, all right, a real one. We heard the shots."

"Anybody get hit?"

"Oh yeah. We saw him fall. Then everyone started running."

Harley picked up the orange five-ball and the black eight-ball, one in each hand. He placed them together on the green felt so that they were angled toward the corner pocket, then tapped them down with the cue ball. "Sometimes," he said, "a combination shot, it's the easiest one of all. It looks hard, but when everything's lined up right, all you have to do is hit it, hit it anyplace, and it goes. You know what they call it, when the balls are lined up like that?"

"Dead," Lacy said. "They call it dead."

"That's right," Harley said. Without taking aim, he casually slammed the cue ball into the five—the eight drove straight into the corner pocket. "Just that easy."

1959 October 08 Thursday 10:41

"I know you're not responsible for my recent losses," Dioguardi said. "So I wanted to tell you this personally. I'm pulling up stakes."

"What does that mean?" Beaumont said, into the phone.

"What's it sound like? I thought you were expecting this call."

"It sounds pretty complicated," Beaumont said. "And it sounds like business, too. Not the kind of business we discuss on the phone."

"So come on over, and I'll tell you to your—"

"It's not exactly that easy for me to get around," Beaumont said, stiffly. "You don't have any problem coming out here one more time, do you? I mean, since we're going to be partners and all."

"Nobody said anything about partners."

"Not until now, maybe. Is it worth an hour of your time to hear more?"

1959 October 08 Thursday 10:48

"I think one of our investments is going sour," SAC Wainwright said.

"Which one would that be?" asked the bland-looking man seated on the other side of Wainwright's bird's-eye maple desk. Only the thick weal of a repaired harelip rescued his features from total anonymity.

"The Führer."

"Him? He's a nothing. Just some freak who likes to dress up and play Nazi."

"No," Wainwright said. "No, he's not. Maybe he has only ten, twelve 'followers,' but he's got something else, too. Something we helped him get. He's got a platform."

"I thought that was what we *wanted* him to have."

"That's right. But the chain of command is now . . . rethinking the whole scenario. If he *does* go ahead and announce he's running for office, where do you think he's going to get votes from?"

"Mohr? What's he going to run for, state rep? He'll get the . . . I don't know what you'd call it, the votes from people who hate the coloreds. And the Jews, I guess."

"Don't forget the Catholics. They're on Mohr's list, too."

"So? Those kind of people wouldn't be voting for our guy, anyway."

"That's what we thought, what *everyone* thought, when the operation was launched. But that's not what we've been hearing lately."

"I don't understand," the man with the harelip said, a faint sprinkling of hostility edging his words.

"It's the chickens coming home to roost," Wainwright said.

"During the war, men like Mohr, they were very useful, especially in dealing with union problems. Instead of focusing on things like wages and hours and working conditions—you know, stuff the Commies could organize around—they had the men ready to riot if they had to work next to coloreds on the assembly lines.

"But some people fell asleep at the switch. What our intelligence says now is, if a man like Mohr ran for office, he'd be pulling his votes from some of the same people—the same *white* people—who would have voted Democrat."

"*Our* intelligence? Or do you mean—?"

"In-house," Wainwright said, carefully enunciating each syllable. "And our . . . friends don't know any more about it than they do about you working for us."

"Why don't you just tell Mohr to—?"

"We can't tell him anything. He's not on our payroll. And all the money we spent on his group just made him worse."

"Then . . ."

"Can't do that, either," Wainwright said. "The last thing we need is another Jew conspiracy. We don't want to make him a martyr. We need him neutralized. Discredited."

"How the hell can you discredit a guy who runs around calling himself a Nazi? What's left?"

"This," Wainwright said, sliding a blue folder across the glossy surface of his desk. Clipped to the outside of the folder was a photograph of Carl Gustavson.

1959 October 08 Thursday 11:17

"It's so beautiful," Tussy said. "I was never out here before except in the summer."

"If you're cold . . ."

"Not me," she said. "I'm pretty well insulated. Or haven't you noticed?"

"I . . ."

"Some men just like women who're . . . hefty," she said, hands on hips. "Gloria told me—"

"Gloria may know a lot about men," Dett said. "She might even be an expert, maybe. But she doesn't know me. She doesn't know anything about me."

"So they're both fruits," the man with the repaired harelip said, putting down the dossier. "What can we do with that?"

"That's a good question," Wainwright replied. "After all, Mohr says he's a Nazi, and *they* marched fags into the ovens right along with the Jews. We've got a tape of a speech he made. Mohr said there's no room in the party—that's what he calls that collection of pathetic misfits he's got, a 'party'—for fags. 'A man that can't fuck can't fight,' is what he said. So you'd think, we threaten to release what we've got, he backs off, plays along like he's supposed to."

"Only . . . ?"

"Only we've got men inside, like I told you. Sometimes, I think all of these freak-show organizations would dry up and die if we pulled our informants out—they're probably the only ones who ever pay their dues on time. Anyway, we had one of our assets get into a conversation with Mohr about it. The subject, I mean. Nothing confrontational, just sounding him out.

"This asset of ours, he spent time in prison—that's like a credential to those people—so it was a natural subject for him to bring up. What our man did, he admitted butt-fucking some boys while he was doing time. But he didn't say it like a confession; he said it like, what would you expect a real man to do when there were no women around?

"And Mohr never blinked. In fact, he said he'd do the same thing himself. He said a true member of the master race is a master of his situation, too. Fucking a man doesn't make you a fag, only *getting* fucked."

"But Mohr's . . . relationship with this Gustavson fruit, that's not because he's in prison," the man with the harelip protested.

"Mohr's got a line that covers that, too. He has this whole long story about ancient Greek warriors—"

"Greeks aren't Aryans."

"You know that, and I know that," Wainwright said, smiling thinly. "But these homegrown Nazis don't. Anyway, Mohr told our guy that part of being a real man is doing whatever you want. He didn't come right out and say he was doing . . . that with anyone, but it's easy to see how he expects it to come out someday. And he's ready for it."

"So where's our edge?"

"Our boy Carl. He's not a fraud like most of them. He's the real thing. A true believer."

"So?"

"So that's where the finesse comes in," Wainwright said. "And that's why I sent for you."

1959 October 08 Thursday 11:29

Tussy bent at the waist and scooped a flat piece of slate from the ground in the same motion, as agile as a gymnast.

"Want to see something?" she said, holding the stone with her forefinger curled around its edge.

"Sure."

"Come on," Tussy said, tugging Dett toward the water's edge with her free hand. Fireball followed at a judicious distance, eyeing the water distrustfully.

"Watch," she said. She stood sideways to the water, her right arm extended. Then she took a step forward, twisting her hips as she whipped her arm across her body, releasing the flat piece of slate. It hit the water, skipped, flew through the air, skipped again, and continued until it finally sank, a long way from shore.

"Damn! That must have gone a couple of hundred feet," Dett said.

"I can do long ones with just a couple of skips, or I can make it skip a whole bunch of little ones," she said, grinning.

"Where did you learn how to do that?"

"My father taught me. I was watching him do it one day, when I was just a little girl, and I wanted to do it, too. Mom told me girls didn't throw rocks, and I told her, well, *I* sure did, every time boys threw them at me. She said she'd better not *catch* me doing that. Then my dad said we'd make a deal. He would show me how to skip stones, the way he did, and I wouldn't make my mother frantic by throwing them unless we were at the lake."

"That sounds fair."

"It was. And I kept to it. I never threw any more stones. I did throw a dish once, though."

"At someone?"

"I sure did. At the diner, one time, this man—well, a boy really, he probably wasn't old enough to vote—he put his hand right under my dress and kind of . . . squeezed me. I dumped a bowl of hot soup on him. It didn't scald him or anything, just got him mad.

"I was going back behind the counter to tell Booker when I heard someone yell. I turned around, and he was coming right at me.

"Later, they told me he had just been coming over to apologize. But that's not what it looked like to me then, so I just picked up a dish—a little one, like you serve pie on—and slung it right at him."

"Did you hit him?"

"Right in the head. Or, anyway, it *would* have been right in his head, if he hadn't put his arms up. He was *real* mad. I guess I was, too."

"What happened?"

"Well . . . not much of anything, really. His friends started razzing him, and he just stalked out."

"He never came back?"

"I never saw him again," Tussy said. "Wanda took over my table—the one where he had been sitting. They gave her a good tip, too. I remember, because she wanted to give it all to me, but I made her split it, instead."

"How long ago was this?"

"Walker, what's wrong?"

"With me? Nothing. I was just—"

"Your face, it got all . . . I don't know, scary. Your eyes went all . . . black. Like someone turned off the light behind them. It was *years* ago, okay?"

"Okay."

"Let's eat some of the sandwiches I made," she said. "That'll make you feel better."

"I hope they're tuna."

1959 October 08 Thursday 11:36

"It's coming to an end, Cyn."

"What, Beau?"

"All of this. I can feel it."

"But why? Everything's going just like—"

"Like what, honey? Like *we* planned? It doesn't feel that way to me. Not anymore. We're riding the train, all right. But we're passengers, not the conductor. The best we can do now is hang on and keep from falling off."

"You're just tired, Beau. You've been working so much. . . ."

"I am tired, girl. But not from work."

1959 October 08 Thursday 11:44

"That's such a lovely place," Tussy said, from the front seat of the Buick. They were parked on a slight rise, looking down the slope toward a three-story brick house surrounded by a terraced garden. A turquoise '57 Thunderbird with a white hardtop and matching Continental Kit was visible at the side of the property, at the end of a long driveway.

"It's pretty big, all right."

"It's too big," she said, firmly. "Unless they have about a dozen kids, who needs a place like that? I wonder who lives there."

"There's no way to do it," Dett said. "The house is too big. They probably have a nursemaid living in, and I'm guessing the baby sleeps on the top floor, too. We'd have to have people watching for weeks even to find an opening. Plus, it's a long run from where they live to anyplace safe."

"That's it, then?" Beaumont said.

"Maybe not. Do you own any local cops?"

"We have . . . friends on the force," Beaumont said, concentrating. "Men who would do us a favor, men who owe their jobs to the organization . . ."

"The chief?"

"Jessup? He's a sideline man, like most of them are now. Chalk players, watching to see who's the favorite before they make their bets."

"There's a way to hit them all," Dett said. He was looking at Beaumont, but his eyes were unfocused, somewhere in the middle distance. "If it worked, you'd be the only one standing at the end."

"I don't like gambles."

"Then you won't like what I came up with."

"Maybe I should hear it, first."

"You have another place you could meet Dioguardi in?"

"Another place besides this house? I'm not going to any—"

"Another place *in* this house. A place not so fancy. A place we could fix up the way we wanted."

Beaumont exchanged a glance with his sister. "We have a meeting room. But you have to walk right past a car to get in there. Anyone who sees it would know what it's for."

"If you decide you want to do this, that won't matter," Dett said, snapping his eyes into focus.

"Well, what do you think now?" Ace said to Lacy. "Did we show you something or not?"

"Yeah," Lacy said. "You showed me you don't know what the fuck you're doing."

"What!? I iced that—"

"Only thing you iced was your own club. You're finished, all of you."

"Hey, man, come on. The cops haven't even been around. They don't have any clue about who—"

"You're the one with no clue, sucker," Sunglasses said. "Preacher's as alive as I am."

"He didn't die? But I—"

"Die? He didn't have a scratch. I saw him myself, strutting around with his boys like a . . . well, like a fucking *king,* man. Get the joke?" Sunglasses laughed, harshly. "I hope so. Because the joke's on *you,* chump."

"I'm telling you—"

"You ever check that pistol? Fire it yourself?" Lacy said.

"Hell, yes, man. It works perfect."

"Then it was the bullets. I guess the 'Klan' gave you a box of blanks."

"Those weren't no blanks."

"Yeah? Better give it to me, let us see for ourselves."

"You're not taking my gun," Ace said, pulling the pistol from his jacket. "This is mine. I don't know what your fucking game is, but I'll find out. I'll find that nigger Preacher, too. See if I don't."

"Relax," Lacy said, holding out both hands in a calming gesture.

At that signal, one of the waiting Gladiators smashed a length of rebar into the back of Ace's skull.

Ace crumpled, still gripping his sacred pistol. The Gladiator holding the rebar bent over and raised his arm.

"Never mind," Lacy told him. "He's not getting up."

Lacy slipped on a pair of thin leather gloves, then took the pistol from Ace's limp hand.

"This is how he goes out," Lacy said, holding the pistol. "Word's all over the street about Wednesday night. Niggers talking about Preacher like he came back from the dead. If we don't do something, they're going to be too strong to handle."

"I thought you said we were getting out of bopping," Sunglasses said. "We're going to be part of the—"

"That's right," Lacy cut him off. "And it's going to be just like I said. But you don't just sign up to be with an organization like Mr. Beaumont's. We have to prove in. Show our true colors. And this," he said, pointing to Ace's body, "this is what they told us we have to do."

1959 October 08 Thursday 22:24

"Sherman!" Holden Satterfield exclaimed. "Boy, am I glad to see you. I got a lot of new stuff in my logbook."

"Good," Sherman said, moving closer to where the woodsman stood in the darker-than-night shadows. "But that's not why I came out here, Holden."

"What do you mean, Sherman?"

"I wanted to talk to you about a job."

"A job? But I already got a job, Sherman. Working for you."

"This would be the same thing," the big detective said. "Working for me. But not doing this. Not anymore."

"I don't get you, Sherman."

"I've got some land, not too far from here. Twenty-two acres. It's just about all forest; I only cleared a little bit of it, for my house."

"But I don't drive a car, Sherman. And this forest, it's mine. I mean, it's where I live. You know. . . ."

"Yeah, I know where you live, Holden. Remember, you let me come and visit you there, once? But I was thinking, how would you like to live in a house? A real house. A little one, you could build yourself. In your own forest?"

"I couldn't do that, Sherman. If anybody found out—"

"It wouldn't matter," the big detective said. "Because it wouldn't be out here, it would be where I live. On *my* land. We could put up a dandy little house, you and me. It wouldn't be much, but it'd be a house, Holden. A real one."

"But what would I do? I mean, I have my job. . . ."

"You could watch the forest for me, Holden. And, in the daytime, you could be clearing the land, working on the house. I always wanted to breed dogs. Maybe we could—"

"I don't like those hounds, Sherman. They go after—"

"Not hunting dogs, Holden. Dobermans. Do you like them?"

"I . . . guess so."

"Sure you do!" Sherman Layne said, patting Holden's shoulder. "And you could take care of animals that get hurt, same way you do now, only it would be easier if you had a stove and a refrigerator, right?"

"I . . . I think I could. But, Sherman . . ."

"What?"

"How come things have to change?"

"Because we're friends, Holden. And I'm changing, so I thought you might like to come along with me."

"You're moving away, Sherman?"

"No," the big detective said. "I'm getting married."

1959 October 08 Thursday 22:49

"Uriah got shot," Kitty said. "But he didn't get hurt."

"I know."

"He wouldn't tell me how it happened. But I know, if you hadn't told me about the gun, he couldn't have done . . . whatever he did to protect himself, Harley."

"I wouldn't let anything happen to your family, Kitty."

"When I talked to Uriah, it was just for a few minutes. But he's different now. Like he aged a lifetime."

"Scared?"

"No. Not at all. It's like he's got a . . . purpose now. I could tell, from the way he was talking. He might even make up with my father. But you know what?" she said, sadly. "You saved his life, and he hates you."

"Me?"

"Not you yourself, Harley. All white people. That's what he was going on about. How the whole gang thing was something the white man tricked them into doing, and he wasn't going to be tricked anymore."

"Yeah."

"Locke City will never be the place for us, Harley."

"Never's a long time, baby."

"I know you have plans," Kitty said. "Big plans. And I know you're smart. You're so smart, Harley. I wish you'd go away with me."

"To college, huh?"

"Yes!"

"Give me another year, honey. One more year. If I can't . . . if we can't be together then, right here in Locke City, I'll come and be with you, Kitty, wherever you are. I swear."

1959 October 08 Thursday 23:16

"Compass. Procter speaking."

"If I get you something so hot it could turn this country upside down, could you get it into the paper?"

"Ah, you again. Yeah, sure. If it's newsworthy. I mean, *really* newsworthy, not just some gossip about a politician's wife, do we understand each other?"

"Yeah, that was just to— Look, this is a guaranteed blockbuster, a bigger story than the Rosenbergs. If I deliver, can you do the same?"

"Absolutely," Procter said.

"You're lying," the voice on the phone said. "You're not the boss of that place. Your editor would kill it in a minute."

"This isn't the only paper in the world," Procter said. "And there's magazines, too. More every day. I can—"

"You promise, you *swear,* that if what I hand over to you is genuine dynamite, and I have all the proof, you'll get it published somewhere? So people can see it?"

"That's what I live for," Procter said. "And if you did as much checking up on me as you seem to have, you already know that."

"I don't have much time. There isn't much time left. You're my last hope. The next time I call, I'll have everything for you."

1959 October 09 Friday 00:01

"I need my car," Dett said into the phone.

"Name a time," a man's voice replied. "You know what you got to bring, and where you got to bring it to."

1959 October 09 Friday 14:02

A decorous dark-blue Cadillac sedan pulled up to the guard-house. Seth emerged, empty-handed.

The Cadillac's front window slid down. The driver said, "I've got Mr. Dioguardi in the back. He's supposed to see—"

"You're expected," Seth said, half-saluting toward the back seat, noting the two men sitting there. "I'll get someone to come and walk you over, just be a minute."

Seth walked back into the guardhouse.

"Last time, he searched my car like I was bringing a bomb with me," Dioguardi said to the man seated next to him.

"Things are different now, right, boss?"

"They are so far," Dioguardi replied. "Hey, look. See that guy walking toward us? I remember him from the last time I was out here. He's a retard."

"Beaumont's got retards working for him?"

"Why not?" Dioguardi shrugged. "They got to be at least as smart as a dog. And probably just as loyal."

Seeing Luther approach, Seth stepped from the guardhouse and joined him alongside the Cadillac.

"Mr. Beaumont says you can all go in, if you want. Or just Mr. Dioguardi."

"You guys stay with the car," Dioguardi ordered.

"But, boss," the man next to him said, "I don't feel right letting you just walk in by yourself."

"It's the right play," Dioguardi said, self-possessed. "If he brought me out here to hit me, he could do it just as easy with you in the room. That's not Beaumont's style. Only thing I'm worried about is maybe someone putting something in the car, so it's better you stay with it."

Dioguardi got out, took the cashmere topcoat the other man in the back seat handed over, and slipped into it.

"Lead on," he said to Luther.

The slack-mouthed man walked off, Dioguardi in his wake.

"This isn't where I went the last time," Dioguardi said, as they approached the weathered wood outbuilding.

Luther opened the door without answering, and ushered Dioguardi inside.

"What is this, a garage?"

"Come on," Luther told him.

Dioguardi entered the meeting room. Beaumont wheeled himself over to the door, offering his hand. Dioguardi grasped it firmly, eager to test his strength against the man everyone said had once been the best arm-wrestler in the whole county. But Beaumont's grip wasn't a challenge.

"Thanks for coming," the man in the wheelchair said. "Sorry, we're in the middle of remodeling the whole place. . . ." His gesture took in the entire room. The sawhorse-supported desk was covered with a large sheet of white butcher paper, as were a side table and the broad wooden arms on three identical lounge chairs. "Take his coat, Luther."

Dioguardi did not hesitate, shrugging out of his cashmere overcoat as casually as if he were in a nightclub. *Wants to see if I'm packing,* he thought, not realizing that Luther had already registered his lack of a weapon.

"We're fixing the place up," Beaumont said, as he wheeled himself behind the makeshift desk. "When it's done, it's going to be connected to the main house. Like an extension. Only it's going to be just for me. My den, like. Will you have something to eat?" he said, pointing to the side table, heavily laden with a selection of cold cuts and breads. "Luther can make you any sandwich you want."

"That's a beautiful spread there," Dioguardi said, taking a seat. "But I had an early supper before I came out. Wouldn't mind a drink, though."

"Name your poison."

"I'm a scotch-rocks man."

"Luther," Beaumont said.

While Luther was preparing the drink, Dioguardi took out a cigarette. Luther stopped working on the drink and rushed over to Dioguardi's chair, a lighter in his hand. Dioguardi waved him off. "I got it, pal," he said.

Beaumont wheeled himself from behind the desk, until he was facing Dioguardi's chair. "I'll have one, too," he said to Luther, resting his hands on the flat arms of his wheelchair, palms-down. Dioguardi unconsciously imitated the gesture.

"I appreciate you coming all the way out here," Beaumont said, holding up his glass.

"Well, I admit, you got me curious," Dioguardi said, again unconsciously imitating his host's gesture. "I thought I was the one giving *you* the news. About me pulling up stakes. I meant that, by the way. Then you say 'partners,' and that kind of knocked me back on my pins. I thought you wanted this whole thing for yourself."

"If you reach for too much, you sometimes end up with nothing."

"I heard you were a blunt man, Beaumont."

"Fair enough," Beaumont said, smiling slightly. "I understand you made a deal with . . . some people. They want what I have . . . what I can do, anyway. And, me, I want you and me to stop warring over what's mine in the first place."

"Yeah. And so? I already said I was going to—"

"Oh, I think you're going, all right. I believe you. What I'm worried about is you coming back."

"I'm not—"

"Wait," Beaumont said, holding up his hand in a "stop" gesture. "Just let me finish. The way I have it doped out is like this: I can do what the politicians call 'deliver the district.' Only I can deliver a lot more than that. In a lot bigger area than you might think. That's what the people who came to you want from me. And they'll get it. In exchange, I'm supposed to have this whole territory for myself. Like I used to have, before you started making your moves."

Beaumont shifted position in his chair, paused for a second, then continued. "Okay, let's say the election's over. Before, I was gold. Now I'm a piece of Kleenex. They used me for what I was good for, and now they can throw me in the trash. If you decided to come back, they wouldn't stand in your way.

"Now, I know what you're going to say," Beaumont said, holding up one finger in a "pause" gesture. "Why should you come back? It'd be over a year that you'd be gone, and you'd be starting from scratch. But I'm thinking there might be one good reason you'd come back to Locke City. A very good reason."

"What would that be?" Dioguardi asked, his voice low and relaxed. He took a sip of his drink, every movement conveying that he was in no hurry.

"A good reason would be if we were partners," Beaumont said. "The future for men like us, it isn't in gang wars, it's in . . . cooperation. You use only your own people in your business; I use only mine. That's good in some ways. You know a man, you know his family, where he comes from, you can trust him, right? But it's also a limitation. If we don't learn to work together, we don't get the chance to grow."

"What kind of growth are you thinking of?" Dioguardi said, affecting mild interest.

"Drugs," Beaumont said, leaning forward, gripping the arms of his wheelchair, his iron eyes locked on Dioguardi's. "There's a fortune to be made. In the big cities, people are already making it. Locke City's like a . . . smaller example, that's all. I've got the network in place here. Men on the street, friends on the force, judges, politicians—everything. But what I don't have is product. It's your people who control that. You can get a steady, safe supply into the country. I want you and me to go into business, Sal."

"Starting when?" Dioguardi said. He expanded his chest and moved his shoulders in Beaumont's direction. He blinked, and his eyes snapped from bored to predatory.

"After this whole thing is over. It doesn't matter where you're going, you'll be someplace where you can put the whole thing together. At your end. And I'll be doing the same thing at mine."

"We don't do business with—"

"Yes, you do," Beaumont interrupted. "At some level, you *have* to, am I right? They sell drugs in the colored sections of every big city, don't they? I mean, it's coloreds themselves who are selling it. Come on."

"That's different," Dioguardi disclaimed. "We're not partners with niggers. It's like we're wholesalers and they're retailers, is all."

"Times are changing," Beaumont said. "You can be a spectator, or you can be a player. All I'm saying is, think about it. You don't have to give me an answer now."

Dioguardi sat back in his chair, tapping the fingers of his right hand on the armrest. "Tell me something," he said. "It doesn't matter anymore, I just want to know. Was it you who did Little Nicky? And Tony and Lorenzo?"

"Me?" Beaumont said. "I thought it was you."

"Me?"

"Yeah. Lorenzo Gagnatella was talking to the law. I thought you knew."

"I *still* don't know," Dioguardi said, his voice tightening. "How'd you find out something like that?"

"I told you, I've got a lot of friends on the force. You don't believe me, ask—"

"I know you got friends around here, Beaumont. A lot of friends."

"And I'd like you to be one of them," Beaumont said, finishing off his drink.

"You want me to go over it again?" Dett asked.

"I've got it," Harley said, trying to imitate the same utter absence of emotion exuded by the man next to him. *Freezing cold, but burn you bad if you touch it,* Harley thought. *Like that dry ice they use in freight cars.* His mind replayed his last meeting with Royal Beaumont: *You're going along because I want you to learn from this man, Harley. Learn what you're going to need to know—what I can't teach you myself, anymore. This guy, he's the best there is. But he's not one of us; he's a hired gun. After this is over, he's leaving. You, you're coming back.*

"You don't think there should be more of us?" Harley asked.

"What we're going to do, it's like an operation, in a hospital," Dett said. "Every man's got his job. Too many men, they just get in each other's way. And it's much easier for two guys to disappear than a whole mob."

"What if he pulls up in front?"

"From where we're going to be sitting, we can see whichever way he goes."

"But if he goes in the front, that's right on the street," Harley persisted. "People passing by . . ."

"So they'll tell the cops they saw two men," Dett said, unconcerned. "Once we pull those stockings over our faces, put the hats on our heads and the gloves on our hands, nobody'll even be able to tell if we're black or white, never mind describe us. This car was stolen from a parking lot—the owner won't even know it's missing for a couple of hours, yet. And the plates on it come right out of the junkyard—you cut them in half, then you solder a little seam up the back, make one plate out of two. Anyone grabs the number, all that'll do is confuse the cops more."

"But we don't have the letter yet."

"That's not our job. If it doesn't get here before they do, the whole thing's off."

"Give Jody a five-minute head-start and he'll beat them here by a half-hour. He's not good for much else, but he can drive better than a stock-car racer."

"We'll see soon enough," Dett said.

"Like to show you around, if you've got the time," Beaumont said. "You've got to walk out, anyway."

"Sure," Dioguardi replied.

Luther handed the mob boss his coat, draped a blanket over Beaumont's shoulders, and piloted the wheelchair back through the garage, Dioguardi following.

As they started to stroll the grounds, Cynthia entered the room where they had met. She was nude, wearing only a pair of white gloves and a surgical mask.

Cynthia stripped the butcher paper from the right arm of the chair Dioguardi had occupied, and carried it over to the desk. There she laid out a bottle of white paste, a small brush, and a pair of scissors. Seating herself, she trimmed the butcher paper, using a sheet of typing paper as a template. Then she carefully opened a manila folder, laying it flat on the desktop. *Quick, quick!* she commanded herself, fingers flying.

One by one, she pasted words cut from the *Locke City Compass* onto the butcher paper.

WE have the BOY
we Just WANT A faVOR
PUT ad IN the COMPASS *PERSONALS*
John Please CALL DIAnne
put IN A phone *number*
WE will CALL YOU
NO COPS or IT is *OVER*

She folded the paper neatly, and placed it inside a stamped envelope, already addressed with letters and numbers cut from the same newspaper. *Careful, now* . . . She sealed the envelope, using a dampened sponge. Then she reached for the telephone.

1959 October 09 Friday 16:59

A beige '57 Plymouth two-door sedan tore across the back roads behind the Beaumont estate in what looked like one continuous controlled slide. The driver was a young man with a bullet-shaped head and jug ears. His small mouth was exaggerated by pursed lips, as if he were getting ready to whistle. His hands were light and assured on the wheel, carving corners like a surgeon's scalpel.

The Plymouth fishtailed slightly as it merged with the highway. The driver picked up cover behind a highballing semi, checked his rearview mirror, slipped into the passing lane, spotted a clot of cars ahead, and fed the Plymouth more gas.

No tickets! played across the screen of his mind, as he smoothly took the exit marked LOCKE CITY, his eyes burning evangelically.

1959 October 09 Friday 17:11

"How'd it go, boss?" the man seated next to Dioguardi in the back seat asked.

"You know what, Carmine? I think he's all done."

"Beaumont? You've got to be kidding. He's been the man around here for—"

"He's not the same. Not the same at all. I braced him about the guys we lost. I was watching his eyes when I did it. I can tell when a man's lying to me. And he wasn't."

"You mean it wasn't his boys who—?"

"No. That's what he said, and I believed him. In fact, he said he thought *we* did that."

"What?"

"Yeah. Beaumont, he said that Lorenzo had been talking to the feds."

"That's a lot of—"

"Don't be so sure," Dioguardi said. "Because I'm not. You know what convinced me? He never even asked about that collector of his, Hacker."

"That's 'cause, the way we did it, he couldn't know if Hacker just took off with the loot. That's one body that's never going to be found, so he'll never know. Not for sure."

"Right. And that's why we did it that way, remember? If we left him in the street, like a message, there wouldn't have been any doubt. Now they can never know the truth, just guess at it. But there was something else, too, Carmine. He wants to go partners."

"Let us in?"

"Not that," Dioguardi said. "He wants to keep everything here for himself. But he wants to go into the dope business. And he wants us to be the suppliers."

"But if we're pulling out . . ."

"He thinks we're coming back. After the elections. He didn't say it out loud, but that's what he was thinking. So he figures, he makes a deal with us—for the dope, I mean—there's no reason for us to come back here, see? Not when we'd be making more by staying away."

"Yeah. I guess. But . . . I don't know, boss."

"I do," Dioguardi said, confidently. "Beaumont's a big fish in a little pond. And he knows, if we wanted to, we could put enough men together to pave him over like a fucking parking lot. He's just trying to survive. He can't blast us out, so he makes a deal for us to leave peaceful. And he can't *keep* us out, so he makes *another* deal, so we stay away. You see what I'm saying?"

"Yeah. I'm just not so—"

"You'll see, Carmine. A couple of years from now, we'll be making more money out of this burg than we ever could've by taking it over."

The beige Plymouth pulled to the curb. The driver exited, and started walking. When he spotted the stolen Dodge, he changed course, so that he was approaching it from the front.

"That's Jody!" Harley said. He reached his hand out the side window and waved a signal.

The driver climbed in behind Dett and Harley. He reached into his jacket, extracted an envelope, and handed it to Dett.

"You remembered," Harley said, approvingly, noting the driver's gloved hand.

"I remember everything," the driver said. His voice was high and thin, but as steady as his hands. "When you get out, I'll be right behind you. Whichever way you go, front or back, I'll be there."

"We don't need a getaway man," Harley said. "This car we're in, it can't be traced."

"Then leave it where it is," the driver said. "They won't be able to trace the one I've got, either. And if something goes wrong, they'll never catch it. I'll get you to the switch car in the garage, and then I'll take off. Let the cops chase me, they think they have a chance."

"We can handle it," Harley said.

"I'm in," the driver said, gripping the back of the front seat with both hands. "If you don't want me to drive you, I'll be the crash car."

The men in the front seat were silent, staring out the windshield.

"I'm bound to do it," the driver said. "I got to be in on this."

"Why?" Dett asked, coldly.

"He's Jody Hacker," Harley explained. "It was his brother Dioguardi's men killed."

"My big brother," the driver said. "I know some people say he just run off, with the money. They don't say it to me, but I know they say it, some of them. Mr. Beaumont, he never thought that of my brother, never. He told me my time would come. And this here is it."

"You drive," Dett said.

The dark blue Cadillac sedan turned the corner, picked up by three pairs of eyes.

"Going around back," Harley said. "They'll have to circle the block first."

The driver was already out the back door.

"He'll be there?" Dett asked.

"Jody? Bet your life."

"Let's go, then," Dett said. "Drive over and park as close to the front of the joint as you can, and we'll walk from there."

Harley started the car. "I can't see any empty space," he said, anxiously.

"Double-park," Dett told him.

Harley pulled up so they were partially blocking two other cars at the curb. He looked over at Dett. "Okay?"

"Yeah," Dett said. He reached into the satchel on the floor between his legs and threw a switch. "We've got five minutes."

The two men got out of the stolen car and walked to the corner. Harley carried a gym bag. Dett's gloved hands were empty. They turned the corner and started down the alley just as the Cadillac backed into the space always kept vacant for it. Dett's left hand went into his outside coat pocket, his right reached under his arm. He stepped into his private tunnel, and the world shifted to slow-motion.

The driver of the Cadillac got out, and reached for the handle to the back door. Dett drew his .45 with his left hand and shot him in the spine.

Harley raced toward the rear door of the restaurant.

Dett wrenched open the back door of the Cadillac and emptied both barrels of his sawed-off shotgun into the two men seated there. The explosion was deafening in the enclosed space.

Harley threw the restaurant door open and tossed the gym bag inside.

Dioguardi moaned. Dett shot him in the forehead with his .45. Harley was down on one knee, a pistol in his hand, covering the rear of the restaurant. Dett emptied his .45 into the two men in the back seat, shoved it back into his pocket, and holstered the shotgun, pulling his second pistol loose with his right hand.

Harley held his position, down on one knee, scanning the area, pistol up and ready.

Dett reached toward the blood-and-flesh omelet of what had been Dioguardi's torso. *Not the suit jacket—this was on him* before *he got hit.* His left hand quickly probed the lining of the dead man's cashmere overcoat. . . . *Clean!* Dett slipped the letter carefully into the inside pocket, then refolded the overcoat so it lay flat on the seat.

The Plymouth roared up, skidding the last few feet on the brakes. Harley jumped to his feet and ran toward the open rear door. Dett fired three more times as he backed toward the Plymouth. The second he was inside, Jody Hacker stomped the throttle.

As the Plymouth careened around the corner of the alley, the stolen car parked in front of the restaurant exploded.

1959 October 09 Friday 18:28

"Nobody saw a thing, right, Chet?"

"It's not what you're thinking, Sherman," the jowly cop said. "Nobody inside *could* have seen any of this," gesturing at the fleshy carnage inside the Cadillac. "The kitchen's a blast zone. Two dead, body parts all over the place. Looks like the place was bombed. Then you got that car that blew up right in front, too. Nobody was even thinking about back here in the alley."

"This one got to pull his piece," Sherman Layne said, pointing to the body next to Dioguardi, "but he never got off a shot. And Sally D., he wasn't even carrying."

"Had to be Beaumont," the jowly cop said. "He's the only one around here with this kind of muscle. I always thought he was going to get payback for Hacker. That's how those hillbillies are."

"Uh-huh," Sherman Layne grunted. He said nothing about the envelope he had taken from the inside pocket of Dioguardi's cashmere coat.

"It was a gang hit, all right," the jowly cop said, in a voice of respect. "A real massacre. Like they used to have in the old days. You think we should go out and talk to Beaumont?"

"Not just yet," Sherman said. "He'll have a cast-iron alibi, anyway. There's something I want to check out first."

1959 October 09 Friday 18:49

"Mr. Dett? He checked out this morning," Carl told the big detective. "Earlier than we expected."

"Did he leave a forwarding address?"

"Let me see. . . . Yes, it's right here: Star Route 2, Rogersville, Oregon."

Same as his driver's license, Sherman thought to himself. *And probably just as real.* "Have you rented his room yet?"

"Yes, sir. To a Mr.—"

"Never mind," the big detective said. "I'm sure you give the rooms a thorough cleaning every time a guest checks out. Before you rent them again, I mean?"

"Well, certainly, Detective. This is the Claremont, after all."

As the two men spoke, another man entered the lobby. A drab, anonymous man, with a prominent harelip-repair scar. He took in the scene at a glance, turned on his heel, and went back out.

1959 October 09 Friday 19:11

"That Buick was returned a couple of days ago," the car-rental clerk told Sherman Layne.

"Mind if I take a look at it?"

"Soon as it comes back, Detective."

"Somebody rented it?"

"Half an hour after the guy who had it dropped it off. It was so early, we got two days on it for one. Pretty lucky, huh?"

1959 October 09 Friday 23:13

Why was Dioguardi writing to a man like Ernest Hoffman? Sherman held the envelope carefully, his hands encased in surgical gloves. And what's with the cutout letters? Looks like a damn ransom note.

Sherman Layne sat for several minutes, watching his options spin like a roulette wheel. Finally, he took a deep breath, reached into his pocket, took out his penknife, and carefully slit open the envelope.

1959 October 10 Saturday 10:10

"It had to be Beaumont, Sean," Shalare said. "Nobody else had the cause. Or the balls."

"But why?"

"That's a puzzler. It could be that he wanted us to know that he's not going to play."

"That makes no sense," the bulky man said, shaking his head. "Beaumont's not just a bad actor, he's a slick article, too. If he's dealing with the other side on the votes thing, he'd want to be saving that for a surprise, not putting up a bloody billboard, wouldn't he?"

"No. No, he wouldn't. Any chance this was some of Dioguardi's own people?"

"A palace coup?"

"No, not his *local* people. The Mafia boys."

"That's not their style, either. Why slaughter so many when they could just ask Dioguardi to come in for a sit-down, and plant him where he landed? All this attention, it's bad for business. Even those people are smart enough to know that dead meat brings flies."

"What do we do, then?"

"Beaumont's the shooter, Mickey. But that doesn't mean he won't still come along with us on the big thing. See what you can find out. In the meantime, I'm going to send a man to you, just in case."

1959 October 10 Saturday 10:13

"Yes, I know, Mr. Hoffman isn't going to come to the phone for some hick-town cop," Sherman said, not a trace of sarcasm in his voice. "But you tell him it's about his grandson, see if he'll talk to me."

1959 October 10 Saturday 10:19

"Do you think it will work? All that we did?"

"It's too late to worry about it, Cyn. It's done now."

"And that man, he's gone?"

"Harley said he dropped him off, and he just walked away."

"But you know where to reach him. Like you did before."

"What does it matter, honey? Our dice are already tumbling. All we can do is wait to see what we rolled."

1959 October 10 Saturday 11:26

"Could I come and see you? Tonight, when you get off work?"

"I wish you would," Tussy said. "I miss you."

1959 October 10 Saturday 17:49

Sherman Layne drove for four and a half hours, arriving at the Hoffman mansion a few minutes before his six o'clock appointment.

"This is Mr. Cross," the old man said, nodding his head in the direction of a nondescript man who stood to Hoffman's left. "He handles my personal security. I assume you don't mind if he sits in on our meeting."

"It's your meeting, sir," Sherman said, politely.

"May I see the letter?" Cross asked.

"Yes. But please don't touch it," Sherman said, taking a slim cardboard box out of his briefcase. "You understand."

Cross took the box from Sherman without speaking. He opened it carefully, and read the contents without changing expression.

"It's a kidnap note," he said to Hoffman. "Whoever wrote it wasn't going to send it until they already had the baby."

"How much were they demanding?" Hoffman asked.

"It says, 'We just want a favor.' "

"What kind of . . . ?" Hoffman turned his gaze to Sherman Layne. "You're certain this is . . . was Dioguardi's work?"

"It was on his body, sir," Sherman Layne said. "But I wasn't re-lying on that alone. We've got Dioguardi's prints on file. We didn't find them on the envelope—it was absolutely clean—or on the cut-out letters themselves. But the paper it was written on—looks like it came from a butcher shop, so it could have been sitting around in his restaurant—it's got three separate partials. Not enough to con-vict him in court, maybe. But good enough for me. Sal Dioguardi wrote that note. Or he handled it, anyway."

"The letter was addressed to me?" the old man said, his eyes laser-focused under heavy, untrimmed brows.

"Yes, sir."

"And the envelope, when you found it, it was sealed?"

"Yes, sir."

"And you opened it . . . ?" the old man said, something undefin-able in his voice.

"I had to make a judgment call," Sherman Layne said, calmly. "I wanted to make sure I was doing right by you, Mr. Hoffman. Which is why I called you privately. My chief doesn't even know. But this is a murder investigation. I had to look before I acted. And now I'm glad I did."

"Do you have any suspects? In the Dioguardi homicide, I mean."

"Suspects, sure. I can almost guarantee you that the Dioguardi killing was the work of Royal Beaumont. They've been feuding for a long time. Over territory. Beaumont's territory, Locke City. Dio-guardi was trying to move in. A while back, one of Beaumont's men disappeared. A man named Hacker. Vanished without a trace. Then one of Dioguardi's collectors gets himself clubbed on the head and left for dead. After that, two more of his men are gunned down in the street.

"Beaumont's whole crew are mountain men, Mr. Hoffman. They take a feud to the grave. So, whether it was business or revenge, I couldn't tell you. But it was Beaumont, you can take that one to the bank."

"What's your rank in the department, Detective?" Hoffman asked.

"You just said it, sir. Detective. Detective First Grade, actually. But that's not a rank, all by itself. I draw a sergeant's pay, if that's what you're asking."

"And the chief . . . ?"

"Jessup. George Jessup."

"Yes. Would I be wrong in surmising that he and Mr. Beaumont are good friends?"

"No, sir."

"All right, Detective. You did me a real service this day. Mr. Cross will show you out."

1959 October 10 Saturday 18:03

The man with the repaired harelip approached the front desk of the hotel.

"May I help you, sir?" Carl asked.

"No. I can help you. A good friend of yours wanted you to have this," the man said, holding up an attaché case of black, hand-tooled leather. "A gift."

"It's beautiful," Carl said. "But I don't know anyone who would want to give me such a—"

"Look inside," the man said. "When you're alone. Don't do it here."

1959 October 11 Sunday 00:13

"Walker, you're all dressed up. And I'm . . ." Tussy made a vague gesture toward her outfit, a lumberjack's shirt over a pair of jeans. She was barefoot, face freshly scrubbed. "We're not going out at this hour, are we?"

"No. I'm going away."

"When will you be—?"

"I won't be back, Tussy. Not unless . . . Look, I have to tell you something."

"What?"

"I have to tell you my story," Dett said. "You're the woman I'm supposed to tell it to."

"You're scaring me, Walker."

"You don't have to be scared of me, Tussy. You're the only person on earth who never has to be."

"You're really . . . going away?"

"Yes."

"This story you want to tell me—is it that you're married, Walker?"

"I don't have anyone," he said, very softly. "And I never will. Could I tell you? Please?"

1959 October 11 Sunday 00:28

"I'm not a real-estate man," Dett said. He was seated on the couch, Tussy a cautious distance from him on the chair. "I think you knew that."

"I didn't at first," Tussy said. "Now I know you must be some kind of a . . . criminal, Walker. But I don't care. You can always—"

"Let me just tell you, please," Dett said. "I . . . I waited a long time for this, and I need to get it right. The truth. Truth as pure as you. Let me just . . . talk, all right? When I'm done, you'll know everything. Please?"

"Go ahead, then," Tussy said, setting her jaw. She adjusted the lumberjack shirt tightly around her, sitting with her knees together, back straight.

"I was a wild kid," Dett began. "Always in trouble, for one thing or another. Nothing big, but plenty of it. Mostly because I had a foul temper. When I turned seventeen, I went to prison, for robbing a store. That's where I learned how to fight. Not like I had before, in a temper. This was the cold way.

"When I got out, I was twenty-one years old, and the war was on. I went in the army. Not to be a hero, or a patriot, or anything. Just to get away from everything I . . . didn't have. They were taking anybody then.

"I served in the Pacific." Tussy's eyes started to flood. "That wasn't it," Dett said, sharply. "I'm sorry, Tussy. I didn't mean to yell at you. But you need to understand—what happened, it didn't have anything to do with the war. It was just me, what I did, later. Okay?"

Tussy nodded, lips pressed tightly together.

"When I got out, I was almost twenty-six, and I didn't know how to do anything. But that's no excuse, either. I could have gone to school. To college, even. On the GI Bill. I could have gotten a good job, bought a house. . . . I could have been a regular person."

Tussy opened her mouth to interrupt, but reached for a cigarette instead.

"I just . . . drifted," Dett said. "But wherever I went, I was always in the same place. I'd work for a while—there was plenty of jobs: oil fields, timber mills, cotton crops—then I'd just sit around and do nothing. Have a few drinks, get into a fight, spend a couple of nights in jail. Three months on the county farm, once."

Dett paused, lit a cigarette of his own. "Then I killed a man," he said. "I didn't mean to. I'm not saying it was an accident, but I wasn't thinking about killing him. It was just another fight. If he'd been a white man, my whole life would have been different."

Tussy squirmed in her seat, as if awaiting a sign from Dett to speak.

"They took me down to the jail," Dett said. "And that's when it started. A couple of men came to see me. Government men. I say it was two men, but it could have been one; they were so much alike I couldn't tell where one started and the other left off.

"They told me I might get off on self-defense, this being Mississippi and all. But I might not, especially with my record. I might spend a long time down at Parchman for what I did. They said everyone was watching now. They meant the whole world. It was right after that boy was killed for whistling at a white woman. They said the law might have to make an example of me. I was scared.

"Then they said there was a way I could make it right. They could fix things so I wouldn't have to go to prison, fix it so nobody would even be mad about it. And what they wanted in exchange, they just wanted me to join the Klan."

Dett took a deep drag of his cigarette, closed his eyes for a split second, then went on. "See, I was a natural, Tussy. Anybody checking me out, they'd find I was in prison before. The Klan wouldn't care about that, the government men told me. What they'd care about was that I went to prison by myself. I never told who else was in on that robbery with me. So it was like a good mark on my record. And being in the army, overseas, that was a good thing, too. It showed I could . . . do stuff, they said.

"But the best thing, that was me killing that man. They said the Klan was mostly loudmouths. Brave when they were burning a cross, but just bullies, hiding behind sheets. You know, scared to fight a man fair. But me, I had done that. 'You killed a nigger,' one of them said. 'In hand-to-hand combat. For the Klan, that's a better medal than any you could get from Uncle Sam.'

"I would be like a federal agent, they said. I'd have to use my eyes and ears, and make reports to them. They said the Klan was a danger to America. A subversive organization, they called it. I would be like a spy, for the government. When I found out the names of the people who were doing the lynchings and burnings and bombings, I'd tell the FBI—that's what they said they were, the FBI—and they'd move in and clean things up. Because it was for damn sure the local cops were never going to.

"They said I might have to commit crimes, just to prove I was a good Klansman, but that would be okay because I was working undercover. I'd get a full pardon when I was done, for everything."

Dett stubbed out his cigarette. "I'm not sure why I did it," he said. "Not even now. I could say I wanted to do something good. For

America, like they said. I could say I felt guilty about killing that man. I could say I didn't want to go to prison. I could even say I wanted the money—they paid me, just like a salary—but that would just be . . . saying things. Because I really don't know.

"My trial only lasted one day. A bunch of colored people testified that they saw the whole thing and the other guy had pulled his knife first. I don't know if that was true—it all happened so fast—but I know not one of them had been out there in that parking lot. So they were all lying.

"I was found not guilty, and nobody was mad at me, not even the dead man's own mother. I know that because she said so, right in court. She said her son would get crazy-wild when he was drunk, and that he had been drinking all that day it happened. That was a lie, too. He wasn't drunk when we fought. Everything was all lies. I never even had to say anything.

"It was that same day, right after it got dark, when the night riders came to where I was staying and took me. The government men were right. The Klan thought I was the greatest man in the world for what I had done."

Tussy's green eyes seared into him. *Finish it,* he ordered himself. *Get it done.*

"The first time I went riding with them, it was a few nights later. We burned out a family. I don't know what the man who lived there was supposed to have done. They said he was some kind of agitator.

"I called the number the government men had given me, and I told them everything. Who was there, what they did. They said I was doing a good job, but they were after bigger fish."

Tussy opened her mouth, caught Dett's eye, and reached for another cigarette without speaking.

"They were all scared then," Dett said. "Not the colored people. I mean, I guess they always were, but I wasn't among them, so I couldn't say. But the Klan, the people in it, *they* were scared. Of . . . the future, I guess. You could feel it coming. It was all in the air. Things were going to change.

"The way one of them explained it to me, it used to be, if you were a colored man who wanted to have a chance, you went north. Lots of them did that. But now the strongest ones weren't leaving. They were staying. If they got the vote—I don't mean *got* the vote; they already *had* the vote; I mean, if they got to actually vote, cast a ballot—they could be running things in twenty years, that's what he said.

"Everywhere you looked, you could see it. The way it was told to me, there was a wall between whites and coloreds for a good reason. Like how you have to keep gamecocks away from each other. If that wall came down, we wouldn't be shaking hands with what was on the other side, we'd be fighting it to the death. Segregation was good for the coloreds, that's what they all said. It protected them, kept them safe. It was just the outsiders, the people from up north, who stirred everything up.

"And the Jews were behind everything. You couldn't see them, but they were there. They didn't care a damn about farming—they needed more and more people to work in their factories. That's what started it all. The Civil War, I'm talking about. It wasn't to free the slaves; it was because the Northerners needed people to work in their factories."

Tussy arched her eyebrows, tilted her head a fraction.

"Did I believe that myself?" Dett answered her unspoken question. "Maybe. It sounded like it made sense, kind of. But I didn't really pay attention, because I was just there to do a job. But if you're thinking, Did I ever argue with them?, no. I don't know if that was because I was working undercover, or because I believed what they said. I didn't think about it, not then."

Dett put another cigarette in his mouth, lit it mechanically.

"It was just past ninety days," he said. "I crossed off each day on my little calendar, just like you do in the county jail. I got to know who every single one of them was. I don't mean just by face; I knew their names and what they did for a living, even where most of them stayed. I told all of that to the government men. I would just call them and talk, sometimes for a couple of hours. They would ask me questions, but they never told me what to do, exactly. They would just say I was doing good work, and to keep it up."

Dett suddenly ground out his cigarette and stood up, startling Tussy.

"I'm sorry," he said. "I didn't mean to . . . I was just . . ." He quickly sat down again.

"On the ninety-second day, they killed a man," Dett said, struggling with the words, but determined to go on. "Dragged him out of the shack where he was staying, took him out to a field, and whipped him. I think that was all it was supposed to be, but I . . . I just don't know. One of them felt his neck, and he said, 'This nigger is dead, boys.' That's when they got the idea—to string him up over a tree limb, like a lynching.

"In the morning, the word shot around town like a fire spreading. The sheriff went out to the field, and his men cut that colored man down.

"The head man called a meeting for that night. He said we'd have to lay low for a while, until things died down. Some of the other men argued about that. They said we had the niggers on the run now, so we should keep going, but the head man won out.

"I thought I was done then. I told the government men everything. I mean, I was right there. I even . . . I helped them do it, Tussy. I could say I didn't know they were going to kill the man, and that would be true. But I can't say what I would have done if I *had* known, so it doesn't mean anything.

"The man on the phone said they had to have my story in person. I drove all the way over to Jackson to see them. There were a lot of men in the room they took me to. I showed them where it happened—they had a map of the area that was so big it covered the whole wall—and they had me put different-colored pins all over, everyplace something had happened. The last one, the killing, it got the only red pin.

"Then they made me go over what they called a 'bracket.' The twelve hours just before it happened, and the twelve hours after. They wanted to know how many people, how many cars, who spoke first, who made the decision to string the man up after he was dead—everything.

"It took so long that we stopped and had a meal. Sandwiches and coffee they had brought in.

"The more I talked, the better I felt, Tussy. Like I stuck a needle in an infection, and the pus was coming out. The more I told them, it was like the tighter I was squeezing, to get out every last drop, and be clean again."

"Walker . . ."

"I have to say it all," he said, inexorable.

She nodded, reached for still another cigarette. As she did, Fireball strolled into the living room and regarded her appraisingly for a moment before curling up at her feet.

"It was late at night when we finally finished," Dett said. "And that's when it happened."

Dett closed his eyes, concentrated on his breathing.

Tussy watched, the cigarette smoldering in her hand.

"They told me I wasn't done," Dett said. His voice was thin, as if short on oxygen. "What I had given them was a good start, but it wasn't enough. They had information that the most committed— that was the exact word they used—the most committed members were coming from all over, for one big splash. Alabama, Louisiana, Texas . . . everywhere. Not just the Klan, either. All kinds of groups. They were going to be making a statement. Do something so big that nobody would even *think* about trying to register the coloreds to vote, ever again.

"It was going to be a bomb, they said. A bomb big enough to blow up a whole city block. But that was all they knew. They needed me to find out when it was going to be done.

"I was . . . upset. I told them that wasn't the deal we made. I thought all the people who had killed that colored man would have to answer for it. That would be like a bomb, too. Only a bomb for good, like the one we dropped on Japan.

"But the government men, you know what they said? They said, first of all, the man who died, it was an accident. I'd even said so myself, that they hadn't started out to kill him, so what kind of witness would *I* be? Maybe a few men would go to prison, for a couple of years or so, but that wouldn't do anything but make them heroes. 'Just like you were,' one of them said, pointing his finger at me like a gun.

"So I went back to work. I did everything they said I was supposed to do. That's funny, huh? You probably don't know who I mean by 'they,' do you, Tussy? Do I mean the government men, or the Klan? I was just thinking, even as I said it, I don't know myself. Because I did what they *both* wanted me to do."

Dett clasped his hands in front of him, took a deep breath, and looked into Tussy's eyes for a long moment. She stared back, green eyes unblinking.

"I did terrible things, Tussy," he said. "Not because I lost my temper, not because I was angry. Not even because I was scared, anymore. I did them in cold blood. I knew, when it was all over, I could never come back. I didn't think about what would happen then. I guess I had a . . . fantasy, you could call it, about going to work for the government myself, in some other town. You know, being a spy. But, most of the time, I didn't think about it at all. I just . . . did things.

"One night, three of them came to where I was staying. Parnell James, William Lee Manderville, and Zeke Pritchard. I remember their names like they're engraved on my heart. Like someone took a chisel to the stone. They said it was time to ride, and I didn't ask any questions.

"When I saw the car they had—it was a station wagon, and I knew it wasn't any of theirs—I knew. Something was going to happen. Something terrible.

"We all had guns. In the back of the wagon, there were chains. Heavy chains, like you'd use to tow a tractor out of the mud. Zeke was driving. I was next to him in the front seat. He said there was this nigger, Lewis, I don't know if that was his first or his last name, and he was stirring things up *bad*. Going around with some white boys. Strangers, not from around there. They were night-riding, just like we had been. Visiting the coloreds in their homes. Telling them they all had to register to vote. Signing them up.

"This Lewis, he was a big man, Zeke said. Not big in size, but in power. The coloreds were all getting ready to follow him. They, the other men in the car that night, they had their orders. It was time.

"We rode way out into the country. Lewis was staying in this sharecropper's shack, on land that wasn't being worked anymore.

"He was a squatter, they said. Didn't even have the right to be on the land. 'We have to sneak up on him,' Zeke said. 'Lewis is a real bad nigger, not the kind to just go along and take what's coming to him, like most of them.' He had a gun, and he'd use it.

"We got to where he was staying. There was no light on in the cabin. We came at it from the sides. I was the first. Because I knew all about sneaking up in the dark, from the army, is what Zeke told me.

"When Lewis woke up, I was standing over him, with a shotgun aimed right at his face. We chained him up and put him in the back of the wagon. He didn't fight—it wouldn't have done him any good—but he didn't cry or carry on, either, the way some of the others had done.

"Zeke drove us out to a spot they had picked out. They made him walk to a tree, and Parnell took out a rope. Zeke asked Lewis if he had anything to say, and that's when I knew. That's when I knew for sure."

"They were going to murder him?" Tussy blurted out.

"That's one thing I knew," Dett said, his voice just above a whisper. "But I knew something else, too. I knew it as sure as I had ever known anything in my life. When it was over, when I told the government men about what happened to Lewis, it *still* wouldn't be the end. They'd just send me back. To do more.

"Lewis might have been scared, but you couldn't see it in his face. He looked . . . not even angry . . . more like he was looking down on all of us. Like we were dirt. 'You can't stop the train from coming,' is what he said. And I knew what he meant, even if the others didn't. I remember thinking, *There's five people, standing out in this field, in the middle of the night. But there's only one man.*

"The moon was shining. Cold light, making us all into ghosts. I had a pistol in my belt. My old army .45. I could feel it against my stomach, pushing at me.

" 'You got the sickle, Parnell?' Zeke said. Then I knew what they were going to do . . . after they hung him. The shotgun in my hand came up, like it had its own mind. I cut Zeke down. Parnell and William Lee just stood there. Their mouths were open, but nothing came out. I pulled my .45 and shot them both. At that distance, I couldn't miss.

"Then it was just me and Lewis. I had nothing left. I couldn't even talk. Like killing those men had taken all I had, and I was done.

" 'Get these chains off me,' Lewis said. I felt like I was moving underwater, so slow and heavy, but I did it.

" 'You can't never go back now,' he said. 'Me, neither. They'll never find me where I'm going. I'm just another nigger, I can disappear. But you, they know you.'

"He walked over to the bodies of the three men, went through their pockets like rolling a drunk. 'Got almost sixty dollars here,' he said. 'You got anything?' I told him I had about forty on me. I thought he would want that, too, but he just said, 'Good. We got a little time, not much. Give me a ride to the crossroads; I'll be all right from there. They probably won't even start looking until morning, when this trash don't come home. Got a few hours. They going to expect you to go north, man. But you can't do that. You going down to Louisiana. To my auntie's place. It ain't got no address, but I'm going to tell you how to get there. Tante Verity, she take care of you until you ready to make your move.'

"I was still . . . not in shock, but stunned, like. Whatever he said, I just nodded 'okay.' We got in the station wagon; I drove him to the crossroads, and I never saw him again."

"Did you go to his aunt's?" Tussy said.

"I didn't know what else *to* do. I just kept driving and driving. I was scared to be in that station wagon, but I was scared to steal another car, too. It was still dark when I got close to where I was supposed to go. I buried the car in the swamp. Just opened all the windows, put it in neutral, dropped a heavy stone on the gas pedal, reached inside, and threw the lever into drive. It disappeared; the swamp swallowed it. Then I started to walk.

"It took a long time. I didn't have anything to eat. The bugs were fierce, and I was in a panic over everything that moved out there. Like being back overseas. All I had was the landmarks Lewis had given me. But they were good ones.

"Even once it got light out, the swamp was dark. I finally found the house. It was right where Lewis said it would be, and it had the bottle tree outside."

"What's a bottle tree?" Tussy said, bending forward to stroke Fireball's head.

"It's just a regular tree, with all kinds of bottles attached to the branches. Like fruit. When there's a breeze, you can hear it tinkle. I'd never seen anything like it."

Tussy started to speak, then clamped her lips together.

"Tante Verity was an old woman," Dett said. "Real old, like a hundred, maybe. She was just sitting on her porch, watching me come out of the swamp. I came up to her real slow, so I wouldn't frighten her. But when I got close, I could see that nothing would ever frighten her. She acted like she was expecting me.

"I told her what happened. From the very beginning, like I just told you. She didn't say a word, just sat there, rocking in her chair. But I knew she heard me.

"I remember telling her about dropping Lewis at the crossroads, and then I must have passed out. When I came to, I was inside her house, lying in some kind of hammock, with netting over me. The old woman gave me something to drink. It was in a mug, but thick, like stew. I remember it was very hot, burned going down, and then I passed out again."

Dett got to his feet, rotated his neck, giving off an audible crack. Seeing the expression on Tussy's face, he returned to the couch.

"I don't know how long I stayed with Tante Verity—that's what she told me to call her, too—but every day, I got stronger. And every day, she taught me things."

"What kind of things?"

"Like roots you can grind up, to keep the inside of your body clean. About the things in the swamp, how you can live among them if you know how to make peace. But, mostly, she taught me what I had to do.

" 'Two trains coming, son,' she said to me. 'Headed for the junction. You can't stop either one. But you can slow the dark one down. You can put a log across the tracks, make Satan late enough so that the righteous train gets by clean.' "

"What does that mean?" Tussy demanded, her voice caught between anger and dread.

"It means I kill people," Dett said, dead-voiced. "You can say they're bad people, but that's not why I have to do it. Those three men out in that field that night, they were bad men. And whoever sent them there, to do what they meant to do, they're worse. But the worst of all are the people who sent *me* there."

"The FBI?"

"Not even them, Tussy. Not even them. I don't think I'll ever know who makes things the way they are. And it doesn't matter. My job is to roll that log across the tracks in time. It doesn't matter who hires me, because they're all guilty or they're all being used by those who are. It's like being surrounded. Wherever you shoot, you hit the enemy."

"You came here, to Locke City, to—?"

"Beaumont hired me," Dett said. "He wanted something done about Dioguardi. And I did that."

"*You* were the one?"

"Yes. And I left things set up so that there may be more. A lot more. What I do is like throwing a rock into a pool. The splash doesn't matter, only the circles it makes."

"But Mr. Beaumont isn't a—"

"Yes he is, Tussy," Dett said. "He's just smarter than other men like him. He knows you do better being nice to people than stomping all over them. He owns this town, top to bottom. And what he owns, he can deliver. He brought me in here to make sure he could keep his power. But I never really work for any of them, even though I take their money."

"Walker—"

"That's not my name," Dett said. "I don't have a name, anymore. Just one I use. Even this face, it's different from the one I started with. There's people who can do that. There's people who can do just about anything, if you pay them."

"You only . . . kill white people? Because of what—"

"No," Dett said, making a harsh sound in his throat. "I kill the people I get paid to kill. You think it's only whites that run gangs?"

"But if they're all criminals . . ." Tussy said, desperately searching.

"I'm not a vigilante," Dett said. "I'm not out doing justice. I'm just trying to slow that train down. I was given seven years."

"I don't understand."

"When I left, Tante Verity told me my time started in that field, when I killed those three men. And it would run for seven years. By then, the first train would be through the crossroads, no matter what. If I'm not already dead, I can start walking my own road, that's what she said. I'll be clean then."

"That's not for another—"

"About four years," Dett said.

"It's too . . . horrible," Tussy said, sobbing.

Dett sat with his fists clenched, unable to look away.

1959 October 11 Sunday 02:21

"Why did you tell me all this, Walker?" Tussy asked, an hour later.

"I had to. Tante Verity told me I could never have a friend, not for seven years. I could never be close to anyone. But she promised I would find a pure woman. And when I did, I could tell her."

"But how could you possibly—?"

"She said I'd know. And she was right. The second I saw you, I knew."

"I can't . . . It's like it's too big to even *think* about, what you said. That's really you, Walker? A man who goes around killing people?"

"I have to do it," Dett said. "I just have to. I did my best to explain, but I know how it sounds. Like I'm insane. Chasing ghosts. Trying to slow down some train. I know. But every word I told you is the truth, Tussy."

"I . . ."

"You know it's true," Dett said, relentlessly. "You know *I'm* true, true for you, or you never would have told me what you did. About your . . . about your life."

"But . . . what's going to happen, Walker?"

"I don't know."

"You're just going to disappear? And then do another . . . ?"

"Yes. Until the time has passed. Or until I get killed."

"You sound like it doesn't matter to you at all."

"It can't matter, not until the seven years has passed."

"What are you saying?" she said, struggling with tears.

"I'll come back then, Tussy. If I'm alive, I'll come back."

"For me?"

"If you would have me."

"How can you even—? I . . ."

"I'll just call. On the phone. If you hear my voice, and hang up, I'll have your answer."

"Walker . . ."

"I'm gone, Tussy. If you ever see me again, I won't be Walker Dett. I'll be . . . I'll be clean. I thought of just . . . telling you a story. About some secret mission or something. Hoping that you'd wait for me. But if you're going to have the truth of me when I come back, you had to have the truth of what I am now. What I was before that, too."

"I can't . . ."

"I know," Dett said. He got to his feet and walked out into the night.

1959 October 11 Sunday 09:30

"Yes. I'll get him," Cynthia said.

She handed the phone to Beaumont, mouthing, "It's him," as she did so.

Beaumont picked up the receiver, a determined look on his face.

"This is Royal Beaumont," he said.

1959 October 11 Sunday 13:21

"I thought you said he was going along with everything."

"That's what he said," Lymon answered Shalare. "And I still think he is."

"You didn't know he was going to hit Dioguardi?"

"I don't know *who* knew that. Sammy didn't, that's for sure. And him and me and Faron, we're the senior men."

"But it's that young one, Harley, that you said Beaumont had picked out to be next in line, not any of you, isn't that right? Isn't that why you came to us in the first place, Lymon?"

"Yeah. That's right. Harley's just a kid, maybe twenty-five. I don't see why Roy would—"

"Never mind that now. Give me something I can use, Lymon. If Beaumont did it—and I can't see anyone else—why would he make such a move?"

"For Hacker."

"Hacker?"

"One of our guys. A collector. He disappeared a while back, and Roy always said it was Dioguardi's work."

"Yeah," Shalare mused. "He's that kind of man, is he?"

"That's one of the things that kept us together, all these years. We're not a gang, we're more like a . . . family, maybe. And Roy, he's the father."

"And you, Lymon, you're his brother, then?"

"And my name should be Cain, that's what you're saying?" Lymon snarled, his voice thick with fury. "You fucking *swore* there was to be no blood. I came to you—"

"You came to me to betray your brother," Shalare said, pronouncing judgment. "And now it's time for you to fulfill your contract. I want the exact layout of the—"

Lymon lunged for Shalare, an unsheathed hunting knife in his right hand. Shalare took the first thrust on his left forearm and rolled to the floor as he lashed out with his boot. Lymon sidestepped the kick, got in one of his own to the ribs, raised his knife, screamed, "You won't make dirt of me, you—" And then Brian O'Sullivan had him from behind.

1959 October 11 Sunday 16:22

Mickey Shalare's white Chrysler slowed at the guardhouse. Seth strolled to the lowered window, shotgun in hand. When he saw Brian O'Sullivan behind the wheel, his face opened in a smile of greeting. A man in the back seat shot Seth in the chest, the silenced pistol inaudible past twenty yards.

As the Chrysler sped forward, four more vehicles followed. Armed men spilled out, shooting.

Return fire from the house sent Shalare's men running for cover. Two didn't make it. Brian O'Sullivan leaped from behind the Chrysler and ran to one of the fallen men. Udell cut him down with a single shot to the chest, worked the bolt on his deer rifle, and put another round into the man he had wounded. From his perch on the second floor, Udell calmly scanned the scene, then began firing methodically at the scattered cars, hunting for gas tanks.

Faron slithered around a corner of the stone house, dropped to one knee, and aimed his rifle at a clump of three men crouched behind one of the cars Udell was firing at. The men bolted for a safer spot. Faron dropped the first two; the third made it.

An armored car suddenly roared up to the front door. The small-arms fire from inside the house bounced harmlessly off its reinforced steel plating. A small, runty man with three fingers missing from his right hand jumped out of the driver's seat and ran back toward Shalare's men, his body hunched over. "Down!" he screamed.

The truck mushroomed. The entire front of the stone house crumbled, replaced by a wall of fire.

As Shalare's men charged, Luther walked through the flames, a pistol in each hand, no expression on his slack-mouthed face. The first three men who saw him died.

A shot tore the sleeve of Luther's gray flannel suit. A pistol dropped from his useless left hand.

"They're after Roy!" Faron shouted to Luther. "Go back and cover him."

Luther turned his back on the gunfight and ran through the house. When he got to Beaumont's office, he yelled, "They're all around!"

"Come on, Beau," Cynthia said, calmly. "We have to get to the car."

"No!" Beaumont said, as Cynthia reached for his wheelchair. "There's no time to push this goddamned thing out the long way, and it won't fit through the escape hatch. Go out the back way, like we planned."

"We can carry you—"

"Not a chance. Luther's only got one arm. Now, get going!"

"Not without you," Cynthia said, grimly.

Beaumont turned his iron eyes on his childhood friend. Luther's beloved gray flannel suit was dark with blood; one arm dangled at his side, useless.

"Stay with her, Luther," he ordered. "No matter what, understand?"

"Yes, Roy," the slack-mouthed man said.

"Beau! Come on!" Cynthia pleaded.

"Get out!"

"No!" she cried.

"Yes, honey," Beaumont said. He took a revolver from his desk drawer. "I love you, Cyn," he said, stuck the pistol into his mouth, and pulled the trigger. The wall behind him turned red.

Cynthia stumbled toward her fallen love.

"Roy said!" Luther yelled. He grabbed Cynthia by the hand and pulled her toward the escape door.

1959 October 11 Sunday 22:12

The field phone sounded in the warehouse.

"Team One," the man behind the binoculars said.

"Subject RV fifty-six minutes. Behind the abandoned building at 303 Drexel. Copy?"

"Roger."

1959 October 11 Sunday 23:06

"We're not done," Harley said. "Shalare knocked off the roof, but he can't touch the foundation, like Roy always said."

"What's our move?" Sammy asked, his question passing the torch as no ceremony could have.

"For now, we stay low and we wait. We have to see if Shalare already got what he wants. If he just wanted Roy, because of that whole election thing, well, he got that. So he may lay back for a while. But it doesn't matter. Tomorrow or ten years, he'll never take what's ours."

"That Irish fuck should have finished us when he had the chance," Udell swore. "Now he's going to have to deal with some dangerous damn hillbillies."

"Mountain men," Harley told him, his voice pulsating with the strength of command. "We're mountain men."

1959 October 11 Sunday 23:08

"Sixty yards," the spotter said, peering through his scope, then glancing at a photo in his right hand. "But that's not our man."

"It's not time yet," the sniper said, glancing at the luminous dial of his watch.

Mack Dressler came around the corner of the abandoned building, walking toward the figure waiting in the darkness.

"Yes?" the sniper said.

"Confirming . . . Yes."

"There's two, then."

"We only got orders on—"

"The man said 'RV,' right? 'Rendezvous,' that's a meet. More than one."

As the shadows of the two figures merged, the sniper's rifle cracked. Mack Dressler dropped. The other man immediately dove for cover, but a second shot caught him between the shoulder blades.

Procter reached for his reporter's pad, *Have to write . . .* headlining through his mind. Then the sniper's next shot spiked his last story.

1959 October 11 Sunday 23:29

"Where are you going at this time of night, Carl?"

"I thought you were asleep, Mother."

"I suppose I was," she said from the darkness of her bedroom. "I can't imagine what would have awakened me—you didn't make a sound."

"Go back to sleep, Mother."

"But you haven't told me where you're—"

"I'm going to work," Carl said. "There's something I have to do."

1959 October 11 Sunday 23:31

"This is our time," Rufus said, urgently. "White men killing each other like it's a war zone out there."

"Our time to do what?" Darryl asked. "Lay in the cut?"

"No, brothers," Rufus said, addressing everyone in the room. "Our time to cut the cord."

"What's that mean, Omar?"

"The guns, K-man," Rufus said. "We got another shipment coming. The biggest one yet. Those crackers we've been buying from? They're the only ones who can connect us to the guns we've been sending out to all the units."

"Gonna kill white men, now's the time," Moses said, casting his vote. "Couple more bodies in this town won't even be noticed, the way things been going."

"That's right," Rufus said. "And I got just the man for the job. Don't I, Silk?"

1959 October 11 Sunday 23:47

"It's the Mercedes again," the spotter said.

"Huh!" the rifleman answered. "You think the other one went in the back way, like before?"

"Let's go see."

1959 October 11 Sunday 23:48

"I did *not* order it," Wainwright said into the phone. "I did not authorize it. I did not sanction it. I did not *know* about it."

"Two men were hit," a carefully calm voice said. "Do you think it's possible the target was the other man, not ours?"

"It could be. The other man was one James Hammond Procter. He was a reporter for the local paper."

"Procter? Do we have a file on him?"

"Yes, sir."

"And?"

"It's possible that our man was meeting him for the purpose of . . . transmitting information."

"But we don't know this for sure?"

"No, sir. By the time we . . . The local police were on the scene very quickly. Whatever was on the person of either man is in their possession now."

"Do we have someone we can speak to there?"

"I'll take care of it," Wainwright said.

1959 October 11 Sunday 23:51

Karl maneuvered his Mercedes behind the building, a flashlight extended in one gloved hand. *There!* He stopped the car, climbed out, and walked over to a padlocked back door. A thin slice of white showed between his lips. He prowled the back of the building with his flashlight until he found a window along the side.

Karl returned to his car, drove just beneath the window, then climbed lithely onto the roof of the Mercedes. The window glass yielded to his gloved fist.

Inside the building, Karl made his way to the front, found the pulley, and levered the garage door open. Moving quickly, he trotted around to the back, reclaimed his car, and drove it through the opening. Then he pulled the door closed behind him.

Breathing hard, Karl removed his topcoat. Underneath, he was clad in an immaculate brown uniform, with red epaulets and a red stripe down the pants. His jackboots were black mirrors. Around his waist was a heavy leather belt, connected to a matching shoulder strap worn across his chest. The uniform shirt had two armbands, red, with a black swastika in a white circle on each. Karl reached inside his Mercedes and withdrew a uniform cap and a cardboard folder.

He placed the cap on his head and checked his image in the mirror. The sight calmed him, regulating his breathing. He held out one tremorless hand. *Hard and true.*

Karl gently opened the folder and removed the contents. He carefully arranged the photographs and copies of official documents on the hood of his Mercedes, fussing until the proof, the indisputable proof, that his Führer was a half-Jewish, race-mixing fraud was perfectly aligned.

From the inside pocket of his uniform tunic, Karl took a single sheet of his personal stationery. The words "Blood and Honor" were written in a strong, assured hand.

Karl examined his display with a critical eye. Finally satisfied, he unsnapped the flap of his holster and took out a virginal black Luger.

1959 October 11 Sunday 23:58

"Hoffman's not happy, Mickey," the bulky man said.

"I know how to fix that, Sean."

"Yes? Well, tell us, then."

"It wasn't Beaumont who took out Dioguardi," Shalare said. "It was us, wasn't it?"

"Aye," the bulky man said. "That should mend our fences, right enough . . . if he buys it. But why did we do it, Mickey?"

"Beaumont was playing a double game," Shalare said, speaking slowly, as if working out a complex problem. "Planning to cross us on the election. Remember, we had his own man, Lymon, working for us. And that part, we can prove. Lymon was an insider. He told us Beaumont was in cahoots with Dioguardi. They were going the other way. It was them or us."

"Dioguardi's people, we already talked to them, they're not a problem," the bulky man said. "But Beaumont . . . he may be gone, but there's plenty of his men still around, Mickey."

"You forget, Sean. I had the pleasure of dealing with Mr. Royal Beaumont my ownself. The man was a leader—a rock for the others to cleave to. Without him, they'll just scatter back to the hills they came from."

"I hope so, with all my heart," the bulky man said. "Because we still have a job to do here."

1959 October 12 Monday 00:06

"That was a shot," the rifleman said.

"You sure?"

"If there's one sound I know, it's that."

"Fuck! This is a sterile zone. We can't have any police around. We'll have to wait for one car to leave, then go in and get the body."

Another shot rang out, clearer than the first.

"I don't think anyone's coming out of there," the rifleman said. "Time for us to break camp."

1959 October 12 Monday 21:22

"Where you at now?" a harsh voice hissed through a long-distance line.

"What difference does it make?"

"Right. You ever been to Omaha?"

"No."

"Doesn't matter," the voice whispered. "It's the same everywhere."

"I know," the man called Walker Dett said.

ABOUT THE AUTHOR

Andrew Vachss has been a federal investigator in sexually transmitted diseases, a social services caseworker, and a labor organizer, and has directed a maximum-security prison for youthful offenders. Now a lawyer in private practice, he represents children and youths exclusively. He is the author of numerous novels, including the Burke series, two collections of short stories, and a wide variety of other material including song lyrics, graphic novels, and a "children's book for adults." His books have been translated into twenty languages and his work has appeared in *Parade, Antaeus, Esquire, Playboy,* the *New York Times,* and numerous other forums. A native New Yorker, he now divides his time between the city of his birth and the Pacific Northwest.

The dedicated Web site for Vachss and his work is www.vachss.com.

ABOUT THE TYPE

The text of this book was set in a typeface called Times New
Roman, designed by Stanley Morison for *The Times* (London), and
introduced by that newspaper in 1932.

Among typographers and designers of the twentieth century,
Stanley Morison was a strong forming influence, as typographical
adviser to the Monotype Corporation of London, as a director of
two distinguished English publishing houses, and as a writer of
sensibility, erudition, and keen practical sense.

In 1930 Morison wrote: "Type design moves at the pace of the
most conservative reader. The good type-designer therefore realizes
that, for a new fount to be successful, it has to be so good that only
very few recognize its novelty. If readers do not notice the consum-
mate reticence and rare discipline of a new type, it is probably a
good letter." It is now generally recognized that in the creation of
Times Roman, Morison successfully met the qualifications of his
theoretical doctrine.

Composed by Creative Graphics,
Allentown, Pennsylvania
Printed and bound by Berryville Graphics,
Berryville, Virginia
Designed by Virginia Tan